The Eagle and the Dove

Abul's hands cupped Sarita's face. "Will you take off your robe?"

The question shocked her. He stepped closer again and with calm deliberation unfastened the first of the pearls at the neck of her robe.

"What are you doing?" She spoke for the first time.

Abul hid his pleasure and simply raised an eyebrow. "Unbuttoning you."

"You would force me, then?"

"No. What enjoyment would there be in that for either of us? Besides," he added, continuing with his work, "it will not be necessary."

Other Books in
THE AVON ROMANCE *Series*

CONQUEROR'S KISS *by Hannah Howell*
DIAMONDS AND DREAMS *by Rebecca Paisley*
LOVE ME WITH FURY *by Cara Miles*
ROGUE'S MISTRESS *by Eugenia Riley*
STORM DANCERS *by Allison Hayes*
TIGER DANCE *by Jillian Hunter*
WILD CARD BRIDE *by Joy Tucker*

Coming Soon

LORD OF DESIRE *by Nicole Jordan*
PIRATE IN MY ARMS *by Danelle Harmon*

Avon Books are available at special quantity discounts for bulk purchases for sales promotions, premiums, fund raising or educational use. Special books, or book excerpts, can also be created to fit specific needs.

For details write or telephone the office of the Director of Special Markets, Avon Books, Dept. FP, 1350 Avenue of the Americas, New York, New York 10019, 1-800-238-0658.

The Eagle and the Dove

JANE FEATHER

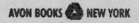

AVON BOOKS ◆ NEW YORK

If you purchased this book without a cover, you should be aware that this book is stolen property. It was reported as "unsold and destroyed" to the publisher, and neither the author nor the publisher has received any payment for this "stripped book."

THE EAGLE AND THE DOVE is an original publication of Avon Books. This work has never before appeared in book form. This work is a novel. Any similarity to actual persons or events is purely coincidental.

AVON BOOKS
A division of
The Hearst Corporation
1350 Avenue of the Americas
New York, New York 10019

Copyright © 1991 by Jane Feather
Published by arrangement with the author
Library of Congress Catalog Card Number: 91-92074
ISBN: 0-380-76168-8

All rights reserved, which includes the right to reproduce this book or portions thereof in any form whatsoever except as provided by the U.S. Copyright Law. For information address Writers House Inc., 21 West 26th Street, New York, New York 10010.

First Avon Books Printing: December 1991

AVON TRADEMARK REG. U.S. PAT. OFF. AND IN OTHER COUNTRIES, MARCA REGISTRADA, HECHO EN U.S.A.

Printed in the U.S.A.

RA   10 9 8 7 6 5 4 3 2 1

Chapter 1

Late fifteenth century
Moorish-held Granada

It was midafternoon. Snow iced the mountains, blinding white against the harsh blue summer sky where the great copper ball of the sun hung, its heat clawing at the earth.

The girl slipped out of the encampment, her bare feet soundless on the parched grass and scrub of the olive grove. There was no movement, no sign of life. The tribe was all stretched in siesta, sleeping through the heat; even the birds were silent. The dogs opened an eye at her passing but, recognizing her, didn't bother to raise their heads. She didn't breathe easily, however, until she was through the grove and out on the blinding, shimmering white dirt track that wound its way up to the Sierra Nevada behind her and down to the distant sea ahead of her. She stood on the track, drawing the searing air into her lungs, feeling the violent beat of the sun on her bare head. The air was filled with the scent of wild thyme.

A flicker of red showed across the track, from behind a cluster of rocks. He was there.

Heedless of the broiling heat, Sarita broke into a scrambling run up the rock-strewn slope. Her bare soles were like leather, and she hardly felt the scrape of rock or the prickle of thorns in the scrub. Her hair

1

hung unbound down her back, the sun setting aflame bright fires in the unruly mass of ruddy curls. She had kilted her dress, freeing her stride for the climb, and her legs, strong and sun-browned, covered the ground with easy speed.

"Sandro! Ah, you were able to come." Laughing, she leaped behind the outcrop of rock and into the arms of the young man who was waiting, smiling. A pony tethered to a thornbush hung its head in limp patience. Two mules, wine kegs slung across their saddlecloths, cropped the scrub.

"Tariq will not expect me back for an hour," Sandro said. "He will assume I kept siesta in the village. Only mad dogs would go out in such heat!"

"And we are mad dogs," Sarita said, taking his hand and pulling him down into the slight shadow thrown by the rocks. "Mad to court such danger, but no one will see us here." She raised her arms to him in hungry welcome.

Kneeling astride her, he took her face in his hands and kissed her. Her mouth opened beneath his, her tongue dancing, and her breasts pressed warm and firm against his red tunic. "No one saw you leave?" He drew back for a minute, his fingers going to the lacing of her bodice.

"No . . . no, I am sure not. My mother was snoring when I left the wagon." She laughed, exultant, excited, yet frightened . . . by the intensity of her feelings, by the immediacy of their danger, by the absolutely forbidden nature of this meeting.

Sandro slipped the loosened bodice off her shoulders and bent his head to her breasts. Sarita moaned softly, arching her body against his mouth as his tongue teased her nipples, his teeth lightly grazed the tight, hardening buds.

"I want you," he whispered, his breath damp and warm on her heated skin. "Oh, Sarita, I want you so much I can hardly contain myself."

She responded only with her body, drawing him tightly against her, pushing up his tunic, sliding beneath his shirt, her hands caressing, stroking, pinching with sudden urgency as her own need spiraled.

A dog barked: sharp, staccato sounds of warning in the motionless air. Their movements stilled; breathlessly they drew apart. The sound was coming from the olive grove. Probably the dog had simply caught an unfamiliar scent, but the damage was done. The encampment would be alerted, the peace of siesta broken.

Sarita sat up, pulled up her bodice; her eyes, the color of seaweed, were still liquid with the desire of a minute earlier, and her hands trembled as she fumbled with the laces. "You go back first," she said, whispering, although there was no one close enough to hear them. "If you make much of reporting on your errand to Tariq and the other men, you will hold their attention, and perhaps no one will notice that I am missing. I'll come into the camp from the rear, as if I have had private need."

Sandro stood up slowly. He looked down at her, his face twisted with frustration. "What can we do? I don't understand why Tariq forbids our marriage."

Sarita shook her head. "Neither do I. But while he does, you know what we risk by meeting in this way."

Somberly, Sandro turned to untether the pony. Tariq's word was law in the tribe of Raphael on all matters, both political and domestic. Heredity gave him the right to his leadership of the kinship network; his enormous strength and fighting skills ensured that the right could not be wrested from him. Marriage between two members of the tribe was both a political and a domestic issue, and it was for Tariq to approve or forbid. This union, for some untold reason, he had forbidden. Sandro could challenge the edict, but to do so he must challenge Tariq himself. He knew he could not do so successfully. He was no physical match for their leader, and twenty seemed very young to die.

Sarita jumped to her feet. "One last kiss," she demanded urgently, reaching her arms around his neck, standing on tiptoe, pressing herself against his length.

The young man groaned in his need. "I love you so!" He bit her bottom lip with a desperation to match her own, and Sarita tasted the salt of her own blood. It should have checked her urgent passion, but it simply augmented it, and it was Sandro who finally tore himself away from her. "Stop! Holy Mother, Sarita, *stop.*"

They stood for a second fighting for control, both awash with the despairing sense of unfulfilled desire and the love they must conceal. Then Sarita licked her finger and reached up to wipe a smear of her blood from his mouth. "Go," she said.

Sandro went without another word, leading the heat-sodden pony and the laden mules down the hillside before mounting and riding through the olive grove and into the encampment as if nothing had occurred to break his progress from the city of Granada, where he had been negotiating the purchase of Malaga wine for the tribal encampment.

Sarita remained behind the rock outcrop for a few more minutes. Her lip stung, and she wondered how noticeable it would be. Very little evaded her mother's seemingly lethargic scrutiny, and even less that of Tariq, these days. But a cut lip could be easily explained.

Judging that Sandro would now be in the encampment and involved in the ritual greeting and reporting, she came out from behind the rock and began the descent to the dirt track. It was slower going down, perhaps because she had no excitement as spur. This time, she was conscious of sharp stones and thorns against the soles of her feet.

Just as she reached the track, a cavalcade of horsemen rounded the bend, coming up from the coast road. The horses were beautifully caparisoned, harnesses glinting silver and gold in the sunlight. Their riders were richly dressed in the embroidered caftans and soft Cordovan leather of the Morisco-Spaniards.

Sarita's clan of traveling entertainers, craftsmen, and artisans had crossed the frontier from Castile into Granada two weeks ago. It was Sarita's first visit to the kingdom of the Moors, although as individuals they were not an unfamiliar sight. There was free passage between Spain and Granada, and a superficially amiable sharing of frontiers; members of the tall, gold-skinned, commanding race were often to be seen on the streets of Spanish towns and riding the highways.

There was something particularly striking about this group, however, that kept her standing by the side of the track, waiting for them to pass. They were riding upward into the mountains, toward Granada and the great glowing red palace of the Alhambra. Ten of them on glossy black steeds, curved knives at their belts, jeweled collars and belts, silk tarbooshes beneath embroidered scarves.

One man rode slightly ahead of his companions. He drew in his horse as he came abreast of Sarita, and the others followed suit. Sarita found herself subjected to a silent, intense scrutiny.

The caliph, Muley Abul Hassan, sat his horse easily, the reins loose on the animal's neck. He didn't know what it was about the pedestrian that had given him pause, but he was accustomed to following instinct and now indulged his curiosity. It was an indulgence that whetted rather than satisfied. The girl had a fragility to her frame belied by some emanation of strength. Two hands would span her waist, and her breasts beneath the laced bodice were as small and firm as nuts, her hips a slight rounding of the gay orange dress kilted about her calves. She was dressed with the somewhat tattered carelessness of the peasant, yet she was neither ill-nourished nor self-effacing, exhibiting none of the characteristics of the poverty-stricken, downtrodden peasantry. Her feet were planted squarely upon the ground, her chin slightly lifted.

There was a wildness to her, the caliph thought, a sense of something untamed. That was where the strength came from. Her eyes, as green and lustrous as dark, wet emeralds, met his gaze unfearingly. Her mouth was full but firm, the bottom lip slightly swollen. The bridge of a small, straight nose was lightly dusted with freckles, the cream and ivory of her cheeks blushed with the sun. As he stared, she tossed her head as if rejecting his gaze, and the rich burnished tangle swirled like fire around her shoulders. Muley Abul Hassan had never seen a woman quite like this one.

"How are you called?" he asked in Spanish.

Sarita did not reply. She was fascinated by the man, as much by his attitude as by his looks. His eyes were as black and sharp as an eagle's, deep-set beneath black arched brows; his skin was a deep gold, tinted with olive. His mouth was incisive under a neatly clipped mustache. Black hair curled from beneath the tarboosh and scarf. He held himself with an unconscious power, the arrogance of one who never has need to question who or what he is. A man of Tariq's stamp, she thought, yet with some essential difference, one she could not identify.

He repeated his question, and she snapped out of her strange trance. Shaking her head abruptly, she sprang out in front of his horse, across the narrow dirt track, and disappeared into the silvery depths of the olive grove.

The caliph watched her go. "Discover what you can," he said in Arabic over his shoulder and nudged his horse into motion.

Sarita was shaken by that strange, almost silent encounter. The man had in some way reached out to her, had somehow touched her. So absorbed was she in her thoughts that she forgot she had intended to approach the encampment from the rear and instead broke through the olive trees into the clearing from the direction of the road.

The camp was orderly, wagons and tents in a circle, cooking fires damped down, horses grazing on the outskirts, the guarding wolf hounds lolling. At night they would be alert, pacing the perimeter of the camp, on the watch for predators, man or beast. Women were moving slowly about their domestic tasks, still lethargic after siesta. They wouldn't begin to make preparations for the evening meal until the sun went down and were enjoying this relative respite from the work round, talking in small groups, nursing infants, sewing in the shade of wagons or olive trees. Small children scampered between wagons and tents, threading their way through the knots of adults, shrieking, laughing, fighting. No one took any notice of them. Their elder siblings, also granted respite from the tasks that fell to their hands, hung around in gossiping clusters or in conspicuous pairs. The pairs were closely if unobtrusively monitored by the women.

Sarita stepped into the clearing and felt suddenly exposed, standing alone at the edge of this gregarious scene. The men were gathered outside Tariq's wagon. Sandro was talking. There was laughter, as if he were telling an amusing story. He probably was, Sarita thought. He was known as a good raconteur in a group where the ability to entertain was much prized. He would be doing his best to divert observation and attention until she had been able to merge into the scene, but as she moved forward, Tariq turned, almost as if he had sensed her sudden appearance. Leaving his group, he came toward her, his pace slow and measured. A hush fell over the encampment, a hush of expectation.

Sarita stood still as he approached her. Tariq towered over her. The men of the tribe of Raphael were in general tall, broad, and prided themselves on their physical strength and fitness, but even by these standards Tariq was a giant of a man. His swarthy skin was blackened by the Mediterranean sun, his eyes a hard blue, his luxuriant red-gold beard a pointed contrast to the thinness of the mouth it framed. He was a dangerous man, but he did his work well—was an effective and respected leader—and Sarita knew that the first was necessary to achieve the second.

"Where have you been?" he asked, standing in front of her, feet planted wide, hands resting lightly on his hips.

Frustration, disappointment, and the disturbing encounter on the road all contributed to Sarita's response. Her chin lifted, and she met his hard blue stare with a flash of anger. "I'm well past marriageable age, Tariq. Surely I may be allowed to walk where I choose."

A year ago, such a response would have earned her the back of his hand, the swift, automatic clout that kept the youngsters in their rightful place, but things had changed in the past months. These days, Tariq rarely took offense at what she said, although she was aware that he paid closer attention to her than he did to any of the others of her generation. The extra notice she put down to her mother's recent widowhood. It was customary for the protection and guardianship of the leader to be extended to widows and their children. The tolerance she had initially attributed to her advancing years. But daily observation proved that maturity, marriage, even maternity didn't protect a woman from a man's hand or fist raised in anger against her.

Now Tariq remained silent, a frown in his eyes as he contemplated her challenging stance, the annoyance in her voice and stare. It should anger him, but it didn't. It merely increased his attraction.

Sarita, waiting in some trepidation for his response, became aware of the silent watchfulness of the camp around them. Not many people were within earshot, but there was a sense of suspended animation, as if everyone were waiting for something dramatic to occur. She had a sudden foreboding, as if something unpleasant was in store and everyone knew it but herself.

Surprisingly, Tariq merely touched her lip with an unusually gentle fingertip. "How did you do that?"

A little tremor went through her, but she answered

with some of her earlier boldness. "I tripped on a stone and bit my lip as I fell."

He continued to frown, then said abruptly, "Go to your mother. She's been looking for you. There is something she has to say to you." He turned on his heel and went back to the group of men. The camp seemed to draw breath in unison, resuming its activities.

Sarita tried to shake off the feeling of foreboding. She looked across at Sandro, but he had his back to her, and she knew he was deliberately avoiding catching her eye in case they should give anything away. She made her way across the encampment to her mother's wagon, mentally bracing herself for the storm. Tariq had as good as told her that her mother was angry at her disappearance, and Lucia had a fearsome temper when roused. Usually, though, she was sanguine and indolent, preferring peaceful coexistence to the more energetic emotions.

The wagon was small, but its possessors considered themselves much better off than those whose only shelter was a tent. In the wagon, they slept well clear of the earth on solid wood. The wooden sides were relatively draught-proof; the canvas roof kept out the rain. There was room for a small brazier on chilly winter nights, a rod on which they could hang their sparse wardrobe, shelves and hooks for domestic possessions. Sarita's father, Estaban, had been as proud of his family's comfortable living quarters as he had been of his skill as a carpenter and wheelwright. He had considered himself a cut above those in the tribe who earned their living as casual artisans or public entertainers—acrobats and the like. Wherever they stopped for a few weeks, he would set up his booth in the nearest marketplace, soliciting commissions from rich and poor alike, and generally doing a roaring trade.

In his lifetime a curtain had been hung down the middle of the wagon, separating Sarita's sleeping pallet from that of her parents. It was only token privacy, and Sarita, like all her peers, had grown early into the knowledge of the true congress between man and woman. Since Estaban's death, though, she and Lucia shared the larger sleeping pallet and everything else in generally amicable companionship.

As she climbed into the wagon this afternoon, however, Sarita was apprehensive. "Mother? Tariq said you wanted me."

"Ah, there you are! Wherever have you been?" Lucia had her back to the wagon entrance but turned as Sarita spoke. She was certainly agitated, but she didn't strike Sarita as angry. She was more excited than anything. A cascade of rich material, crimson, emerald, and turquoise, tumbled from her hands. "I have been looking everywhere for you. Why did you not keep siesta?"

"I had a pain in my stomach," Sarita improvised. "Something I ate, I expect." She wondered why her mother seemed so nervous. Her color was high, her hair escaping from her kerchief as if she had put it up in haste after siesta. Sarita ducked through the entrance into the wagon. "What is that material?" Then she recognized it. It was her mother's wedding dress.

Lucia suddenly flung her arms around her daughter with an exultant laugh. "Oh, I am overwhelmed, Sarita. Such news. Your father would have been so proud—"

"About what, Mother?" The foreboding was now a hard, sharp knot.

"Can't you guess?" Lucia seized her hands. "My darling child, it is Tariq. He came to me at the end of siesta. Surely you must have sensed how he favored you . . . although, to be sure, I didn't see it myself, really. I just thought he was taking extra notice because we were without a man's protection . . . but no, you are to marry him, Sarita. You are to be the wife of the leader—"

"No!" Sarita interrupted with a cry of mingled dismay and fury. "How can you talk so? You know how it is between Sandro and me. How can you talk—"

Lucia slapped her face, her expression one of fear and horror. "Do not ever mention Sandro in that way again! Are you mad? Tariq has spoken for you. The wedding will be in three days' time. Everyone knows of it now. The preparations will begin tomorrow—"

"No!" Sarita interrupted again, beside herself with the panic-stricken sense of an unstoppable nightmare. "You cannot consent to this—I will not consent—"

"You fool!" Lucia shook her shoulders. "Listen to me. Tariq has no need of my consent. He is the leader and he has spoken for you. You will go to him tonight to mark the bethrothal."

Sarita forced herself to be still, to think. While it was true that no marriage could technically take place without the consent of both parties, in practice it was unthinkable that she should refuse Tariq as husband. She would be excommunicated, banished from the tribe and its supports, from the intricate networks that protected and gave identity. She would be a raceless, homeless, friendless vagabond cast upon a world that gave short shrift to those who belonged nowhere. Prostitution or death were her only alternatives. Faced with such a choice, what girl would refuse the honor of becoming the leader's bride? Would refuse the honor of the leader's bed, traditionally to be sampled at betrothal as confirmation of intent by both parties? She thought of those moments of passion with Sandro; snatched moments, so often interrupted. But the need to be together, to love together, was the driving force of her life—of Sandro's life. How could she pretend such love didn't exist? How could she deny that all-consuming desire for which they had already dared so much?

Slowly she shook her head. It couldn't be denied. Tariq was a dangerous man, but he was not evil. He had shown some softness toward her in recent months; perhaps he would listen to her. But even as she thought this, it came to her why he had refused her marriage to Sandro. He had wanted her for him-

self, even six months ago, when Sandro had gone to
him in the blithe expectation of success and been refused so curtly and without explanation.

Was she to tolerate this? Meekly accept her fate
in Tariq's bed this night, and stand by as Sandro
married someone else? No, it was impossible!

Impetuously, she ducked back through the entrance and leaped to the ground, hearing her mother's imperative voice calling her back. She ran across
the clearing to where Tariq and the men were still
gathered, sitting down now, leather tankards of Malaga in hand as they sampled the fruits of Sandro's
expedition.

She flew into the circle. "Tariq, please, I must talk
with you. You cannot do this."

Slowly he rose to his feet, taking in the wildness in
her eyes, the strain in her slight frame. Her hair
swirled unkempt around her shoulders, adding to her
distraught air. "I cannot?" he said. "What are you
saying, Sarita?"

"You cannot marry me," she said. "Please, Tariq,
I love Sandro. I cannot marry you."

Tariq's blue eyes went as dark as the deepest ocean.
"Cease this foolishness now," he said, "and it will
be as if it had never been spoken." He gestured to
the audience, and she knew even in her distress that
he was being magnanimous, was willing to ignore
that she was humiliating him in front of the other
men, in front of the entire camp, she realized as people began to approach across the clearing, drawn by
the emanating tension, by the certainty of some impending disaster.

Sandro's pallor was ghastly. He had heard nothing
of the betrothal until this moment and now stood up
also, unable to speak even as Sarita proceeded to destroy them both.

"It is not foolishness," she said. "Only let me explain, Tariq—"

"There is nothing to explain," he interrupted in
harsh anger. "You have said all there is to say." He

turned to Sandro. "You have been with this woman."
There was no questioning in his voice, and his eyes
glittered with an almost feral fury.

Sandro found his voice. "I love her," he said. "We
will go from here, accept exile from the tribe."

"*No, you will not.*" Tariq took a step back, all expression wiped from his face. He held his arm straight
out, two rigid fingers stabbing at the younger man.
"You have challenged me, Alessandro. When you
defied my edict you challenged the leader of the tribe
of Raphael and you will make good that challenge.
The woman and the tribe belong to the winner."

"*No.*" Sarita's cry of horror fell into the sudden
silence. "You will kill him."

Tariq turned to look at her, his face still a mask
from which all emotion had been banished. "Or he
will kill me."

Lucia's noisy sobs could be heard in the deathly
hush that greeted the words. Sarita struggled with
her horror, her panic, the same desperate sense of
being in an unstoppable nightmare. She looked at
Sandro and saw that despite his pallor he was quite
still, his face set in resolute lines. He had no choice—
honor was being forced upon him. He had offered to
accept for both of them dishonor in exile, and the
offer had been refused. Now he would die in honor.
But he would die. She had seen it before, knew its
inevitability, and on one deep tribal level she, like
Sandro, accepted the code and its exercise.

The men began to move backward, making a rough
circle around Tariq and Sandro. Tariq pulled off his
tunic and tossed it to the ground. He rolled up the
sleeves of his shirt. The muscles in his arms were like
small hills.

Sandro prepared himself similarly. He was younger
by some ten years, strong in his own right, but without the muscular solidity that came from those extra
years of toil and battle.

Sarita had entered a cold void where nothing
seemed to reach her. She was there in the clearing in

the olive grove in the simmering heat of late afternoon, but she was not there. She was drifting on some cloud, some cool, rainy cloud where none of this was happening. She saw their knives, the plain steel glittering in a shaft of sunlight. She watched them move, circling each other, coming together in their deadly dance.

It was over so quickly it was almost impossible to believe it had happened. Tariq exacted vengeance and confirmed his leadership, quickly and cleanly. He was not interested in a cruel prolongation of the inevitable or in providing a spectacle. When it was over he stepped back. "He died with honor. We will bury him tonight."

The circle parted as he walked to where Sarita stood, her eyes closed as they had been throughout the brief horror. But as he reached her, her eyes opened, and they were as cold as a green glacier. "I will never marry you," she said, softly articulating every word. "Never, Tariq. You have Sandro's blood upon your hands for nothing." Then she turned and walked away. No one made any attempt to prevent her as she moved through them, proud and unbowed, seeming to be insulated from all around her.

Tariq knew he should go after her and assert his mastery over her as publicly as he had asserted it over her lover, but he found he could not. She *would* marry him, of course. She *would* come to his bed that night, if he demanded it. But the bright gilt of certainty was suddenly tarnished. And it couldn't possibly be so, not when he had so powerfully demonstrated the invincible power of his leadership.

He swung round on the still noisily sobbing Lucia, his voice harshly commanding. "You will send your daughter to me tonight." Then he strode from the circle toward his own wagon.

The man hidden in the shadows of the olive grove had missed nothing. He had heard little of what was said, but gestures and events had told their own tale

as loudly as any town crier. There was little more information to be gleaned by further spying. Silently,
he slipped from the grove, back to the track and his
waiting horse. He rode upward, toward the rose-red
bulk of the Alhambra, ablaze against the snowcapped
mountains under the last rays of the dying sun.

Chapter 2

"Will you take a tisane, my lady?" The waiting woman approached the sultana Aicha
with some hesitation. The wife of Muley Abul Hassan
had been in uncertain temper for some time, since
before the caliph had left on his journey to Almería,
and her reactions were unpredictable.

Aicha did not immediately reply. She leaned forward into the basin of the massive fountain in the
Court of the Lions, holding her fingers into the falling
water. The water was cool and clear, and the sound
of it filled the court, an oasis in the still heat of the
afternoon.

"Where is my son?" She spoke finally, letting her
wet hand fall upon the head of one of the twelve lions
on whose back the basin rested.

"With his tutor, my lady." The woman did not add
that the caliph had decreed that his son's lessons must
continue until sundown. Aicha knew that perfectly
well, just as she knew that her husband was attempting to lessen her maternal influence over the growing
boy, the caliph's heir.

Aicha moved restlessly down one of the paths radiating from the fountain. The sound of water accompanied her as it flowed through a delicate channel in
the center of the path. The air was heavy with the
scent of red and white oleanders massed in luxuriant
brilliance between the paths, noisy with the humming of worker bees among the flowers. A swallow

16

dived into the court, then soared upward over the pillars, up into the deep blue ether above the palace roofs. But she was aware of none of this delicate beauty as she sought the shade of the arcade.

Abul should be returning soon, maybe even this afternoon. Would he call her to his bed when he returned? It had been many weeks since she had received the summons, not since she had angrily refused him the night after he had told her he was removing Boabdil from her primary care. She had raged at him, then wept and pleaded, saying the child was too young to be given over to the management of tutors, that he still needed his mother. Finally, Abul had coldly told her that he didn't approve of her care, that she spoiled and overprotected the child and did the boy no service by it. In anger, she had withheld herself from him. Abul was not a man to insist when a woman was unwilling, and she had hoped that by continuing to punish him, she would persuade him to change his mind. It had had the opposite effect. Once having been refused, he no longer asked for her.

He had summoned others, though, and Aicha had had to pretend a lofty indifference when one or other of his concubines was regularly preferred to the wife.

"Will you take a tisane, my lady?" the waiting woman ventured again.

"At sundown," Aicha said with a snap. "I will take a tisane with Boabdil when he is released from his tutor. Leave me now."

The woman departed immediately, her slippered feet soundless on the rich mosaic as she went into the palace.

Aicha paced the colonnade. She had miscalculated, taken her husband's gentleness too much for granted, overstretched his easy tolerance. She had assumed he was not like other men, but she had been mistaken. Abul would not permit a woman the upper hand, although he stood on little ceremony and was always considerate. If he did not return prepared to forgive, she must swallow her pride and beg for his forgiveness. She lost status through his neglect, and with that loss went the loss of authority. But more importantly . . . much more importantly, it threatened her plans for her future: the future she had been planning for so many years—the future she would have through Boabdil.

Abruptly, she went through an arched doorway into the cool tiled hall where another fountain played gently in the center. Women moved about the hall, their silken caftans as brightly mingled as a field of butterflies. They gossiped in low-voiced clusters, played dice, sipped sherbet, nibbled little cakes, placed delicate stitches in rich fabrics against the sound of soft music coming from the gallery above the hall.

Aicha walked among them, her progress acknowledged by slightly bowed heads, a polite cessation of talk. She was still the caliph's wife. In her own apartments she found as always the peace and seclusion in which she could think most productively. She went up a narrow flight of stairs to the mirador, a belvedere whose arched windows looked over the garden and out over the mountains. The sweetness of the cool mountain air filled the chamber from the windows on all sides, and as she reclined on an ottoman beneath them, she could let her mind expand to absorb the majestic vista, imagine herself an eagle, soaring over the white peaks. The light breeze fluttered her skirt, lifted the gauzy scarf covering her midnight-black hair, and a mood of optimism crept over her, replacing her previous apprehension. She and Abul would make love here when he returned, laved by the mountain breeze, soothed by the exquisite beauty of the balcony chamber.

Then the tranquility was shattered by the strident call of the bell from the alcazaba. The sentries in the watchtowers were announcing an arrival. Aicha stood up swiftly. Her windows didn't look toward the granite edifice of the fortress, but she could recognize the rhythm of the bell. Niether stranger nor foe approached. The caliph was returning. Her heart beat fast. Should he find her waiting to greet him with the grand council and senior members of the household in the antechamber adjoining the ambassador's salon? Should she go to the Court of the Alberca to greet him as he rode in? Or should she stay here and hope he would come to her as he used to do? No, nothing was ever gained by passivity.

The official antechamber seemed the best place, as it suggested she was neither overeager nor lagging back, simply appropriately respectful. She rang a handbell, but one of her waiting women was already in the doorway, bearing a jug of hot scented water. While Aicha bathed her face and hands, the woman brushed and rebraided her hair, repinning the scarf to fall gracefully from the top of her head. Aicha drew the scarf over the lower half of her face as she hastened from the privacy of the women's sanctum, around the Myrtle Court, and into the caliph's official apartments.

Muley Abul Hassan dismounted in the Court of the Alberca. The white marble paving stones threw back the sunlight with a dazzling glare, and out of habit he averted his eyes to the immense fishpond in the center of the court. The expanse of water brought instant relief from the glare. A gigantic goldfish lay still beneath the surface as if mesmerized by the heat, and Abul paused to breathe in the rich fragrance of roses from the massed bushes bordering the fishpond. His attendants were accustomed to the caliph's leisured enjoyment of his home whenever he returned after an absence of more than a day or so, and they adapted their pace to his as he walked slowly around the pond. But they were aware of an unusual quality to his present preoccupation, a degree of intensity not usually aroused simply by the beauties of the palace.

This air of preoccupation was also noticed by those waiting to greet him in the salon as he entered with his entourage. Those who had reports to present decided to wait for a more propitious moment and contented themselves with making the ritual reverence. The caliph acknowledged them individually, although absently, until his eye fell upon his wife, standing modestly to one side, flanked by two waiting women. She bowed her head as his gaze met hers.

It was unlike Aicha to make public submission, Abul reflected, acknowledging her reverence with a small bow of his own. He hadn't thought much about her during the days of his absence, but he realized now that that absence had done nothing to soften his annoyance. She was a very beautiful woman, but she had a shrew's tongue and a certain deviousness that was beginning to trouble him. She had a talent for intrigue, for manipulation, that he had taken little notice of until recently, when his cadi had obliquely hinted that the sultana might have had a hand in the discrediting of one of his council.

Abul had pretended to ignore his magistrate's hints, but he had made some discreet inquiries of his own, had probed Aicha so subtly that she had no idea she had been questioned, and he had drawn his own conclusions. His wife had quarreled with the wife of the discredited council member, and she had plotted her revenge. Abul had not suspected intrigue and had taken the issues as they were presented to him. The incident had given him a distaste for his wife, one that her actions over their son had increased. Now as he looked at her, he realized nothing had happened to alter that distaste, and her evident attempt to make peace was not going to affect it.

However, he could not let that thought show in public. He greeted her with soft courtesy.

"Will you eat later with me and our son?" Aicha asked, smiling with her kohl-lined eyes over the scarf. She had hesitated to mention Boabdil but then decided it would only be natural to do so if they were to behave as if their quarrel had not taken place.

Abul frowned as he looked down at his wife. He saw the carefully dark-rimmed brown eyes; the artificially thin arched line of her eyebrows in the broad, smooth forehead; wisps of her hair, black as night. The eye of memory showed him her body beneath the richly embroidered caftan, lushly curved, golden-fleshed, still firm despite Aicha's predilection for sweetmeats and honeyed sherbets.

Green eyes and vivid hair, a slight, wiry body in a tattered orange dress, bare feet and sun-browned legs replaced the image. Indeed, they had hardly left his internal vision since she had run from him into the olive grove earlier that afternoon. He had no wish to eat with his wife and son. He wanted to hear what Yusuf had discovered about the girl. Was she for sale? It was the only issue that held his attention.

"No," he said. "Not today. I have pressing matters to attend to. I will speak with our son's tutor, however." He offered her another small bow and turned back to the waiting reception.

Aicha's hands were suddenly clammy, and she felt the first stirrings of real fear. She was still out of favor. The caliph was not obliged to keep a wife whom he no longer favored. But Abul would not repudiate her. He could not. Not over such a trivial issue. She would go to him tonight. If he sent for one of the other women, Aicha would take her place. And if he sent for no one, she would go on her own initiative. There were many tricks she knew for arousing a man's interest, and once it was aroused, she knew how to maintain it.

She left the salon with her women, returning to the reassuring serenity of her own chamber to plan the seduction of her husband.

Abul completed the rituals of return, still preoccupied, then went to the baths. The keepers of the baths could be relied upon not to disturb him with idle chatter, just as his courtiers knew instinctively not to accompany him on this occasion. This was not simply a bath for cleansing purposes. Abul needed the time and the conducive atmosphere for meditation.

He lay for a long time in the hot perfumed water in

the hall of immersion. Once, a long time ago, he had become obsessed with a woman, one of his father's young concubines. He had been little more than a boy himself, and when his father had discovered his secret, he had laughingly placed the girl at his son's disposal. The obsession hadn't lasted beyond the first three nights. Since then, Abul had rarely felt more than a fleeting attraction for a woman. It had been a little different with Aicha—she was his wife, she was beautiful, she was skilled at love. They had a partnership, and he had counted himself blessed that she pleased him in all the important ways . . . until he had discovered that one needed to be pleased by a woman in more than the flesh. Knowledge of her sordid intrigues now prevented him from desiring her as a woman.

He pulled himself out of the hot water and plunged into the marble tank of cold water beside it. The icy immersion took his breath away but cleared his head and made his skin tingle. Could he really have become obsessed after one brief roadside encounter when not a word had been spoken? It made no sense.

An attendant began to rub him down vigorously with thick Turkish toweling, abrading his skin. He stretched, still frowning as the rubbing continued. Maybe it made no sense, but it had happened nevertheless. He wanted her. And he would pay anything to have her.

He went into the steamy heat of the next room, stretching out on a marble slab as the attendant fed the brazier. The searing steam cut through his lungs, brought the sweat flowing on his skin. He closed his eyes, feeling the impurities in his body pour from him. Maybe she could not be bought. No, everyone had a price . . . not necessarily money, but there was always something. And if he couldn't buy her, then . . . then there were other ways.

Abul moved lethargically to the hall of repose and handed his body over to the oiled hands of the attendant. The girl was presumably Spanish, although she

had not answered him when he had asked her name
in that language. But it hadn't seemed to him that her
failure to answer had been rooted in incomprehension. Then she had leaped away from him like some
dainty forest animal. He closed his eyes.

"My lord . . . my lord Abul."

The whispered summons brought him out of his
voluptuous trance. The man he had left to trace the
girl stood by the cushioned bed.

"What did you discover?" Abul was instantly
awake and alert, both body and mind refreshed.

The man told him what he had seen and what he
had inferred.

"One killed another over her?" Abul said slowly,
struggling for comprehension. Why would a man kill
another over a woman? But different peoples had different laws, different rites. It was not for him to question the customs of others. And perhaps a man *could*
kill another over this woman. Suddenly it didn't seem
such an outlandish thought. But the man who had
done the killing would not willingly yield his prize.
So what now?

He swung off the bed. "We make a sortie, Yusuf.
I would see this encampment and these people for
myself. Just the two of us. There's no need for a war
party, and I would go in stealth."

The attendant brought him a robe, and he went
back to his own apartments, suddenly famished. But
the baths did that to a man. Despite his eagerness to
be off, he ate in a leisurely manner in the privacy of
his own salon, refusing all entertainment but the gentle plucking of a harpist.

Those who served him could not guess by the caliph's bearing that a fever of excitement ran through
his blood. He felt as if he were about to go into battle,
that strange comingling of fear and exultation, of certainty of success and sudden doubt. And he prepared
himself as if for battle, concentrating on the body's
relaxation and satisfaction in order to clear and calm
the mind.

Yusuf was waiting for him in the outer court, mounted on a fast Arabian stallion. A groom held the reins of the second horse, as fast and as sleek as Yusuf's. Abul nodded his approval of this choice of mount. These were not war-horses; they were bred for speed and stamina, not for brute strength.

The two men carried knives, but no other weapons. Their destination lay not far from the palace and the city of Granada, and the caliph's garrison regularly swept the roads clean of brigands. It was also a clear, moon-washed night, and as they rode through the wide horseshoe arches of the Gate of Justice, the dirt track glimmered whitely ahead, snaking down the hill.

In her own apartments Aicha prepared herself to go to her husband's bed.

"You are certain, Nafissa, that the caliph has sent for no one tonight?" She let her head fall beneath the rhythmic brush strokes of her handmaid.

"Quite certain, my lady." Nafissa began to thread fragrant mimosa through her mistress's hair, the delicate pale yellow of the blossoms standing out against the blue-black tresses.

Aicha's hand drifted over the jeweled jars of perfumes on the table before her, trying to decide which would most suit her mood and purpose. Musk or gardenia was too heavy. If Abul himself were eager, then such scents would match his ready passion, but if she must seduce and arouse, then something more delicate, less obvious, was required. Something to complement the mimosa, she decided, selecting one of the jars and lifting the lid. The delicate, flowery scent of lilies of the valley filled the air as she smoothed the fragrant oil onto her temples, behind her ears, at the pulse points of throat and wrists. She slipped the robe off her shoulders and anointed her breasts before carefully darkening her nipples with rouge.

Nafissa brought her the night-robe of white gauze and

the heavy brocade robe to cover her on her journey to the caliph's apartments.

"Go and discover if my lord has gone to his chamber, Nafissa. He might still be dining with his companions."

Alone, Aicha lay back on the ottoman beneath the windows as she had done that afternoon. The night breeze wafted the scents from the garden below, mingling with those of her body and flower-strewn hair. She turned her head to look through the low window at the dark huddle of the mountains, their peaks glinting white under the moon glow. It was a night for love. A night for turning love to one's own advantage.

Nafissa returned within a few minutes, and Aicha knew from her face that something was wrong.

"The caliph, my lady, has gone from the palace," the handmaid said, standing nervously by the doorway. She knew from experience how the bringer of bad tidings could suffer at the hands of the sultana.

"Gone?" Aicha rose, graceful yet impatient. "What do you mean gone? Gone where?"

"I know not, my lady." Nafissa wrung her hands. "He and Yusuf, my lady, took horse and left some ten minutes ago, after the caliph had finished eating."

"Just the two of them?" Aicha began to pace the chamber, her pleasure in the beauty of the night destroyed. Abul had only just returned from a long and arduous journey. What would take him out again so soon, at night and with only one companion?

"I believe so, my lady."

"Then he will return soon." Still frowning, Aicha continued to pace. She could go to his apartments and wait for him. But Abul was jealous of his privacy. He could well be displeased at her presence in his absence. No, she would simply wait until his return.

"Leave me." She waved Nafissa from the room and then resumed her position on the couch by the window. Her hands drifted slowly, sensuously, over her body as she allowed the magic of the night to embrace her, her imagination to follow the paths of arousal.

"You know that you must go to Tariq." Lucia knelt beside the pallet where Sarita lay unmoving, as she had done throughout the hours since Sandro's death. The girl gave no sign of having heard her mother. "If you do not go, the other men will come and fetch you," Lucia said, tentatively touching her daughter's shoulder. This motionless silence alarmed Lucia more than anything else could have done. It was so unlike Sarita. She had expected anger, tears, grief, but she hadn't realized how far matters had gone between Sarita and Sandro, and for that she was to blame. Tariq would hold her responsible. Had he suspected it, he would have stopped it long before so much damage could have been done. But it was up to Lucia to know how matters stood with her daughter and to report such as was necessary to Tariq. Now she was afraid for herself, and she knew that if she didn't ensure that her daughter obeyed the leader tonight, she would stand doubly accused. She also knew that it would go hard with Sarita if she didn't comply willingly. Tariq would not easily endure another humiliation.

"Drink a little of this." She held a cup of wine toward Sarita. "It will calm you, give you strength."

With sudden violence, Sarita swept the cup to the floor. Red wine splattered, and the tin cup clattered and bounced.

Lucia lost her temper. "I wash my hands of you! You're an ungrateful, deceitful little fool! You have no choice but to go to Tariq tonight. If you choose to suffer unnecessarily, then that is for you to decide. I shall tell him you are unwilling and I can do nothing with you."

Sarita sat up on her pallet. She was very pale, but life had returned to her eyes. "I have no choice if I remain with the tribe," she said clearly. "Help me to leave here, Mother."

Lucia stared at her, uncomprehending. There was no possibility of her daughter's existing outside the kinship network of the clan. "That's madness, Sarita. Where would you go? How would you live?"

"I'll take my chances," Sarita replied with the stubbornness her mother recognized. "Anything will be better than Tariq."

"One man is surely better than hundreds," her mother said bitterly. "You know that is the only life available to you."

"I would rather have hundreds than the one who has Sandro's blood on his hands," Sarita said with her mother's bitterness. "Help me."

"You will recover from Sandro," Lucia said uncertainly. "A first love, child. We all recover from first love."

Sarita shook her head. "Even if that were true, it is hardly the point. You expect me to be bedded with the man who murdered the man I loved. I will kill myself first."

Despairingly, Lucia heard the conviction and the determination in her daughter's voice. "But you must have known how it would be," she said. "You knew what would happen when you and Sandro defied Tariq. Even if Tariq had not spoken for you himself, once he had discovered the truth, he would have taken Sandro's defiance as a challenge for leadership."

Sarita nodded. "Yes, I know." How could one explain the blind, driving power of a love that counted such risks as naught? How to explain that they had lived only for each stolen moment, each breathless second of shared passion?

"Help me to leave here," she repeated, kneeling on her pallet, her sea-green eyes filled with urgent appeal. "Go to him and say that I will come, but not until the fires have been covered. Tell him that I am distressed, that I cannot bear to show my face when the camp is still awake."

"And when he discovers that I have deceived him . . ." Lucia let the sentence hang.

"You must tell him that I have asked to be alone—that I asked you to come and prepare me in two hours' time. Stay outside with the other women. Let it seem that you are angry with me, but that you have no doubts as to my compliance. Indeed, how should you? When you come to the wagon in two hours, then you will find me gone. They will believe that you knew nothing." Despite this plan, Sarita knew she was asking her mother to take a considerable risk. She knew as well as Lucia that Tariq would hold Lucia accountable for the debacle with Sandro. Sarita's disappearance from her mother's care would be even harder to explain.

Lucia was bewildered. The rites and laws of tribal life were bred so deep in her she couldn't begin to understand how her daughter would prefer to face what could only be a short and savage future rather than accept her destiny within the clan. But there had always been something out of the ordinary about Sarita, some sense that she held herself a little apart. And she was a grown woman now. Lucia had the unshakable conviction that if she refused to help her daughter, Sarita would still try to leave the camp before Tariq sent for her. But without her mother's help, she could not gain sufficient time to be clear away before the hunt began. If Lucia did not help her now, then she would by default have betrayed her.

"I will help you," she said finally. "I will help you because I would not expose you to the consequences of failure, not because I believe you are right to do this."

Sarita stood up and embraced her mother. She still had shed no tears for Sandro, but she wept now for her mother. "I have loved you," she said.

Lucia smiled and stroked her shoulder. "Yes, I know. As I have loved you. You will leave me now with neither husband nor child. I shall not know my grandchildren. I don't understand why you cannot stay, but I know that you cannot. Therefore, go with my blessing. Take what coin we have." Then she put her daughter from her and left the wagon.

Sarita stood there for a minute, recognizing the full extent of her mother's renunciation. In a tribal community, she would grow old with none of her own immediate kin to support and comfort her. She would be cared for, but she would have no useful place, no clear identifying function. A woman without family. And if Tariq chose to make life unpleasant for her, then he could do so.

And if Tariq chose to come after the runaway, then she would find it hard to hide from him. The thought galvanized her. The sooner she was away, the longer start she would have. She would make her way to Granada. The city was big enough to swallow one woman until the hunt had died down.

With feverish haste, she wrapped what few useful possessions she had in a kerchief. Their small currency store was kept in a leather pouch beneath the pallet. Theft was unheard of within the tribe, but one still took precautions against strangers. Sarita tipped out the contents. There were two ecus d'or. Those she wouldn't take. They represented what little wealth her mother had received from Estaban. But there were twelve silver pennies, a Venetian ducat, and two florins. She took only the pennies, having the feeling that too much coin could be worse than too little. It could invite robbery and worse. Her best chance for safety was to mingle inconspicuously in the poorer streets of the town and look as if she belonged. Drawing attention to herself in this kingdom would be the first step to the slave market.

She couldn't risk leaving the wagon from the front; there were people everywhere. The afternoon's drama and the knowledge of its continuance tonight had created an atmosphere of surreptitious excitement. Everyone was restless, the usual tranquil order of the evening disturbed. So she crept to the rear and gently unloosened one of the backboards. Once, as a child,

she had escaped surveillance this way when she'd
wanted to go dawn hunting with the boys. She'd been
even smaller then and she'd not tried it since, the
consequences not encouraging a repetition.

The board came loose easily enough, however, giving a space she reckoned would be wide enough for
her to slide through sideways. She tossed her bundle
to the ground. It fell with a soft thud. She stopped
and listened. The sounds of camp life continued behind her, and she couldn't hear or sense another
presence close by. There was a short, open space between the back of the wagon and the first line of olive
trees. The moon was too bright.

Sucking in her stomach, Sarita edged sideways into
the gap. It could be done. She stretched her left leg
straight out and slid the rest of herself after it. Her
dress tore on a splinter, rough wood scraped the back
of her thigh, pressed against her breasts, but she was
through, crouching on the ground, hugging what little shadow was thrown by the wagon.

Hardly breathing, she listened again. The sounds
from the camp continued without pause. The brightness of the moon worked in her favor as well as
against her. She could at least see that the coast was
clear. Gathering up her bundle, she took a deep,
steadying breath, then plunged, crouching low, across
what seemed like an interminable acreage of bril-
liantly illuminated space. And then she was in the
grove. Panting, breathless, she leaned against an olive tree, hardly daring to believe there were no alerting
shouts behind her. But there was nothing; only the in-
cessant scraping of cicadas, and somewhere, a blackbird
pretending it was a nightingale.

Once her heart had slowed, she began to make her
way through the grove, circling the encampment.
There was music, someone strumming a guitar,
laughter, the smells of cooking. All that was familiar
she was leaving behind. She felt an instant of panic.
Then for the first time since it had happened, she allowed herself to see Sandro, as he had been that af-

ternoon behind the rocks, and as he had been later on, so still in death.

She broke through the trees and onto the road. The city lay downhill, and she turned toward it, wanting to run but knowing that she was not yet pursued and there was no need to waste her strength.

Muley Abul Hassan could not at first credit such coincidence. He and Yusuf were still some few hundred yards from the entrance to the olive grove when the slight figure in its unmistakable bright orange dress slipped onto the track into the moonlight.

Yusuf pointed silently and Abul nodded. Then he put his horse to the gallop, simply following the spur of impulse.

Sarita heard the pounding of hooves behind her. Her first thought was that it was Tariq. Somehow, he had discovered her gone . . . hadn't believed her mother . . . hadn't been prepared to wait for the two hours. She began to run. She ran without looking behind her. Then in sudden, fatalistic despair, she stopped. She could not outrun him. She turned, as motionless as the rabbit petrified by the fox.

The horse was not Tariq's. That was her only thought before the animal plunged to a rearing halt beside her. The rider swung sideways, downward. She was caught beneath the arms. Her bundle fell, scattered across the track, the silver pennies winking in the moonlight. She seemed to fly upward before landing with a solid thump in front of her captor, before the scream in her throat could be released.

Abul held her firmly across the saddle, one arm behind her shoulders, the other across her waist, one hand gripping the reins. He was aware only of exultation, of the feel of her body. Her bones were so tiny. He looked down into her face. Her eyes were filled with outrage. They were that same dark, wet emerald he remembered, and they contained no fear. Her mouth opened, and again without thought he put his hand over it, forestalling the alerting scream.

Her teeth bit deep into his palm. He drew breath on a swift inhalation of pain but kept his hand where it was. Her teeth sank deeper, and he increased the pressure slightly. He wasn't hurting her, but it was as uncomfortable for her as it was for him.

"If you promise not to scream, I will take my hand away," he said softly in Spanish.

Thoughts tumbled in her head. If she screamed, the encampment would hear. Did she want to be rescued by what she had determined to escape, even if it could only be escaped through death? Whatever this was, it wasn't what she had left. She remembered him, this man with the bright black eyes, the smile on his lips, the hand over her mouth. What did he want of her? She could taste the salt of his skin. With no clear thought, she released her teeth.

Abul whistled soundlessly in relief, removing his throbbing hand and shaking it. His hold had relaxed, and Sarita instantly took advantage, twisting and pummeling as she fought to slide down from the horse, still standing on the track.

Abul pulled his cloak from his shoulders and swung it over her, capturing her flailing limbs in its folds, twisting it securely around her until she lay as tightly wrapped as a babe in swaddling bands.

"Be still, *paloma mía*," he said gently, stroking her cheek. "You will hurt yourself, and I would not have that happen." He was smiling at her, amused by her struggles yet not mocking. "I came to buy you," he said. "But only a fool would pay for the dove that flies into his hands." He chuckled softly and turned his horse up the hill.

Sarita lay still. The tight folds of his cloak were curiously comforting, the inability to fight strangely soothing. She could do nothing. But she was achieving her goal. She was not in the least frightened. Her abductor gave no excuse for feeling threatened. She could be angry at the abduction, but for the moment it rather suited her own plans. No one would look for her, wherever she was being taken.

Yusuf picked up her scattered bundle, including the silver shower of coins, and followed the caliph and his guest up the hill.

Sarita entered the palace of the Alhambra. Her eyes widened as they passed beneath the outstretched hand of the Gate of Justice, its five open fingers representing the five precepts of Koranic law. She still had said nothing. There seemed to be nothing to say.

Chapter 3

"**Y**usuf and the lord Abul have returned, my lady."

Aicha came out of the dreamy trance that had occupied her since Abul's departure. She turned to look at Nafissa, standing in the archway. "Good. Help me to rearrange my hair." She rose gracefully from the ottoman. "Has the lord Abul gone to his apartments yet?"

Nafissa stepped aside as her mistress moved past her, down the staircase to the sleeping chamber beneath the mirador. "I do not believe so, my lady."

Aicha paused on the bottom step. "Whatever do you mean, girl, you do not believe so?"

Nafissa swallowed uncomfortably. "I heard that he has gone to one of the perimeter towers, my lady. And Yusuf went immediately to have speech with the vizier. It is not known what about, but he has been closeted with him this last quarter hour."

Aicha frowned as she sat on a low-cushioned stool before her crystal mirror. "Put fresh mimosa in my hair. Why would my lord go to one of the towers?"

Nafissa drew out the drooping flowers from the sultana's hair, keeping her eyes watchfully on the face in the mirror. "It is said he had someone with him, someone he carried before him on his palfrey."

Aicha made no immediate response. She had no idea how or where Nafissa acquired her information, but the handmaid always knew everything that went on in the palace. It made her an invaluable attendant.

"This person," Aicha said finally, "is man or woman?" She watched Nafissa's busy fingers rethreading her hair with the fresh yellow blossoms . . . she must put on more perfume too . . . "Well?" she demanded when the girl remained silent.

"I do not know for sure, my lady, but those who saw say that the person was enwrapped in my lord's cloak and was easily carried by him into the tower."

"Woman or child, then," Aicha mused, chewing irritably on her lower lip. Had Abul acquired a captive during his absence, some dependent of an important family to be held for ransom; as hostage, perhaps; or given to him in gift or payment? Such transactions were hardly unusual in a world where competition and the threat of combat were the primary tools of diplomacy and negotiation, one where alliances and fidelity must be bought or compelled. Muley Abul Hassan was in general a merciful captor, charitable in victory, but he manipulated his world in the manner of the times and would not balk at taking into slavery for tribute or vengeance a highborn child or woman from the family of an adversary.

Abruptly, Aicha decided that her plan of seduction must be postponed. If Abul was preoccupied with politics, he would be an unwilling partner, and she would be a fool to increase her present disadvantages. And if it was a woman he had acquired for his own purposes, then he would presumably be occupied with her during the night. She tore the mimosa from her hair with rough petulance, tossing it to the floor, where it seemed to lose its delicate freshness immediately, the color fading against the rich turquoise mosaic of the tiles.

"Help me to bed; then discover what there is to know of this captive. You will bring me a full report when you wake me in the morning." Standing, she threw off the heavy brocade robe, letting it fall to the floor with the discarded mimosa. Nafissa ran to pull back the silken coverlet on the bed set into an alcove facing the windows, but when she bent to pick up the wrap and the flowers, her mistress curtly dismissed her.

Alone with her frustration, Aicha lay in the moon-washed room. Her body, carefully aroused during the earlier hours when she had prepared herself for a night with Abul, was not now to be satisfied, but the physical disappointment was as nothing compared to her chagrin at the thwarting of her plan and the very real anxiety, now akin to fear, that she was in danger of losing all influence with her husband. Tomorrow, she *must* get his attention, after she had discovered the identity of the captive in the tower. Only by knowing everything of significance that went on in the palace could Aicha keep ahead of events. And only by keeping ahead could she ensure her dominant position.

As they had ridden through the courts of the Alhambra, Sarita had wriggled upright so that she was sitting straight, although still held firmly and still swaddled in her captor's cloak. They had stopped in the first large court, and her captor had had a short exchange with his companion, who had dismounted and disappeared into one of the buildings. Two turbaned footmen had then joined them, trotting beside the horse as they moved on again.

The sound of water was everywhere, fountains splashing, streams running softly in marble channels. The mingled scents of myrtle, oleander, mimosa, roses, and orange blossom were so luxuriant that Sarita had trouble identifying the separate components in the general fragrance. Lamplight poured in golden rivers from the arched porticos, and torches swung in iron sconces beneath the colonnades, illuminating the buildings and gardens they passed with a soft glow, in muted contrast to the brilliant clarity of the stars in the velvet black canopy of the sky, their white light glittering on the snowcapped mountain peaks.

Sarita had the strangest sensation of inhabiting some enchanted world. The reality of her mother's wagon and the tribal fires of the encampment became smudged in her mind, as if she had taken some potion to distort the hard edges of the corporeal world. The dreadful events of the afternoon had lost some of their vividness. They seemed to bear no relation to her being held by a strange man on a strange horse, riding through fairyland, and if this was real, then perhaps that had not been. She knew that such thoughts were fanciful, of course; the pain of Sandro's death was like a boil beneath the skin of her mind, waiting to erupt, but for the moment she was content to drift on a charmed sea and let events take their course. She had certainly contrived a most thorough escape from Tariq.

They turned onto a cypress-lined path, leaving the main cluster of the palace buildings behind them. Again their way was lit by pitch torches, and she could see ahead the looming height of the perimeter wall. One of the two footmen spurted forward to open a small gate into a trellised garden, at the end of which stood a tower set into the outer wall of the palace compound. It seemed they had reached the end of the present journey. Did a tower signify a prison? Prisons were not usually found in pretty gardens. They were forbidding buildings, but there seemed nothing forbidding about this one. Before she could decide how she should react, her captor had swung deftly to the ground, still holding her cradled in his arm. Sarita knew she was small, but there was something a little dismaying about the ease with which he accomplished the maneuver. It certainly didn't offer much hope for a successful bid for freedom, had she been contemplating it.

The footman opened a door and she was carried into the tower, where she was set carefully on her feet. This was most definitely not a prison. She was in a small hall, more like an inner courtyard than a room. The walls of fragile fretwork were exquisitely decorated in lapis lazuli and delicate artwork; an alabaster fountain surrounded by flowers and fragrant shrubs played softly in the middle of the room; slender marble pillars supported a filigreed colonnade.

The cloak slipped from her shoulders as she gazed in delight. Nothing in her experience had prepared her for such man-made beauty. The grandeurs of nature—majestic vistas, vivid rioting color of flowers and trees—all these were familiar to her, taken-for-granted aspects of life for one who lived upon the road. But Sarita had had no great acquaintance with interiors. Occasionally she had stayed in an inn. She had been inside shops and churches, the latter often richly decorated, but she could never have imagined anything like this. It was more beautiful than any church, and even in her delight, she felt a flicker of disapproval that anyone should have the arrogance to beautify a simple abode as if it were the house of God. But then she remembered that these were infidels. She opened her mouth to ask, "What place is this?" and then closed it again. The initial decision not to speak had not been conscious, but she felt somehow safer in her silence, as if, without words, she would not be placing any permanent construction on what was happening to her.

Abul watched her face closely. He read her pleasure in her widened eyes, in her parted lips, and he waited for her to speak. When she closed her lips firmly on whatever she had been about to say, he sighed internally, but comforted himself with the reflection that at least she wasn't mute. She clearly had the power of speech.

"This is where you will live," he said, deciding to talk to her as if she were responding verbally. "Come up to the gallery." He gestured toward a staircase.

Sarita looked up and saw an upper gallery running around the inner court. The vaulted cedar roof of the court rose to the summit of the tower, it seemed, and glimmering moonlight came through arched windows at the rear of the gallery.

He had said she was to live in this place. For a minute Sarita was too taken aback by this blithely assured statement to move. Her instinct was to stay where she was, to refuse to cooperate in any way with her abductor, thus indicating her refusal to accept his assumptions. But he hadn't waited to see if she would obey him; instead he was already halfway up the stairs. Besides, what harm would it do to see what was up there? Curiosity won with only a skirmish, and she followed him upward to find herself in what was clearly a galleried sleeping chamber surrounding the courtyard below. The walls of the pillared gallery were hung with Damascus silk. A richly cushioned silk-hung divan stood in a recess in the outer wall between two deep window embrasures. There was a crystal mirror on a low marble table. She had never seen such a mirror before; the only reflection of herself she had ever seen had been in a sheet of beaten copper. Her hand ran over the silk covering of the ottoman in front of the table. She thought of her straw pallet in the wagon, the coarse sheet and thin blanket she had in the winter. That or this: one or the other was fantasy.

"How are you called?" Abul asked her for the third time that day. Sarita made no answer. Instead she walked to the window. Below her was a dark ravine, and across the ravine stood the massed shadows of a group of roofs, the mountains rising behind them. She wanted to ask him about the buildings, but again she stubbornly kept silent.

"I am called Muley Abul Hassan," Abul persevered. "I am caliph of Granada, and this is my palace: the palace of the Alhambra. But I imagine you are aware of that?" he suggested. The suggestion fell on stony ground.

He felt a spurt of impatience. He was receiving no sense that the girl was in the least cowed by her abduction. Her silence was much more in the nature of a challenge, and he was powerfully aware again of that untamed quality emanating from her, despite the slightness and fragility of her frame. She had been running away, he remembered. Not a cautious act.

She would not have run far unmolested on the night-time roads of his kingdom, and it was a safe assumption that the hands that caught her would have been much less appreciative than his own. Even had she managed to reach the city, there would have been no security there for a lone and unprotected woman, and an unbeliever into the bargain. No, not a cautious act; one of desperation, perhaps?

Coming up behind her, he caught her shoulder and obliged her to turn toward him. She glared her annoyance from those eyes the color of seaweed, but set her lips tight. He touched her lower lip with the tip of his finger where he had earlier noticed the slight swelling, then deliberately rolled her lip forward, revealing the faint redness of the cut just inside.

One man had killed another over this woman that afternoon. ''Passion's bite?'' he guessed softly, watching her eyes. Shocked acknowledgment was followed by a flash of anger, then a deep grief. ''Ah,'' he said as softly. ''I begin to understand.'' The violent death of a lover could be a powerful spur to a desperate flight.

Furious rejection of this statement chased all else from her wonderfully expressive eyes, and he knew how close she was to speaking out her resentment and scorn. He found suddenly that he wanted to hear her voice more than anything, even raised in anger. But with a supreme effort of will she kept her fury within. On impulse, he bent and laid his mouth gently over hers, touching the sore spot with the tip of his tongue.

Sarita felt the shock of the touch rip through her, from the top of her head to her suddenly curled toes. She was aware of outrage, of violation, yet of something else too; something quite contradictory, some strange sweetness coming from the man who held her so lightly. With a muffled gasp, she backed away from him until she was leaning against the gallery, her hand over her mouth as if she would protect it from further caressing assaults.

There was a sound from below, the soft opening

and closing of the door. She looked down into the court. Two women had entered, dressed in plain dark robes, scarves over their heads. Looking up, they saw her in the gallery, the tall figure of the caliph behind her, and swiftly they moved to the stairs, coming into the gallery in a soft-footed rustling whisper of their robes. They bowed before Abul, letting the scarves fall away from their faces as they did so.

He responded to the reverence with a careless gesture. Sarita examined the new arrivals curiously. They were both young, she judged, not much older than herself. One of them was rather plain, her face badly pockmarked, but her homeliness was redeemed by a sweet expression and gentle dark eyes. The other had a pointed face and sharp features, and merry, intelligent eyes that met Sarita's scrutiny with her own brand of interest. Sarita was instantly drawn to her, as sometimes happens when two people meet for the first time and recognize the potential for a deep and lasting friendship.

"How are you called?" Abul asked them in Spanish.

"Zulema, my lord," the plain one answered.

"Kadiga, lord Abul," replied the other, glancing sideways at Sarita.

"You are familiar with the Spanish tongue?"

"A little," they replied modestly.

Abul nodded. He had instructed Yusuf to consult with the vizier and summon the two most fluent Spanish speakers among the younger female palace servants to attend his mysterious captive. It seemed Yusuf and the vizier had done their work well. These two were young, and if they lacked linguistic subtlety, they would find other ways of communicating.

"Prepare the bath," he said before turning back to the ever-silent Sarita. He smiled and touched her cheek where a streak of dirt stood out against the dusting of freckles and the sun's bloom. "You are in sore need of attention, *querida*. Tomorrow I will instruct you in the use of the baths, but for tonight your women will attend you in the court below.''

Before the full import of his statement, not to mention the soft endearment, had struck her, he had disappeared down the stairs. She hung over the gallery and stared in some disbelief. A round wooden bathtub had appeared from which steam curled upward. The two women were moving around purposefully, sprinkling something in the water, laying out thick towels. They stopped and stood still when their lord appeared from the stairs. He spoke to them in Arabic.

"Yusuf will come for her in an hour.''

Fortunately for Sarita's peace of mind, she couldn't understand the short sentence and saw only the two women bow again as the caliph left the pretty little court.

"Lady, will you come down?'' Kadiga called up to Sarita, still hanging over the gallery. "Your bath is prepared.''

"I do not want a bath,'' Sarita declared, descending to the courtyard. "And even if I did, I am quite capable of giving myself one.''

"Oh, but you will enjoy a bath, my lady,'' Zulema said, coaxing, her smile sweet as she came over to Sarita. "You must have been long upon the road to have become so dirty.''

Sarita glanced down at her bare feet. They were certainly grubby, and there was dirt beneath her fingernails where she had pried loose the backboard of the wagon . . . had it only been this evening? She was aware suddenly of fatigue, a rare sensation, but this she sensed came from the day's emotional strains as much as from the physical trials she had endured. A most enticing fragrance curled with the steam from the tub, and the prospect of a bath became appealing. She moved to unlace her bodice, but Kadiga was quicker, and before she was fully aware of how it had happened, the two had stripped her of the orange dress and her shift beneath. She wore nothing else; she never did in the summer.

"No, leave my clothes," she protested with a note of panic as they seemed about to discard the only things she possessed to connect her with the person she had been before Muley Abul Hassan had scooped her off the road.

Kadiga held up her dress and shift, looking doubtful. "They are in need of washing, lady, and the seam is torn." She indicated a rent at the back. It must have happened when she had snagged herself on a splinter from the wagon, Sarita thought, snatching the garments from the other girl's hands.

"Then I will wash them. And do not call me 'lady.' My name is Sarita." She laid her clothes carefully on a table.

"But we are your waiting women," Zulema said in her soft voice. "Will you step in the bath?"

"I shall not be here very long," Sarita declared firmly, stepping into the deep water. "And if you must pretend to wait upon me while I am here, I insist you call me by my name." She slipped down with a little whimper of pleasure as the hot scented water came up to her neck.

Zulema bent over her, pouring water over her hair. Sarita closed her eyes under the unaccustomed luxury of having her hair washed for her. All her life she'd been bathing in streams and rivers, using the coarse soap her mother made from rendered animal fat. In winter, they made do with an occasional pan of water heated on the brazier. The wonderful luxury of this bath served to increase her sense of unreality, and she wondered vaguely where she would have been by now if Muley Abul Hassan had not been on the road in search of her . . . in some filthy lodging in the stews of Granada probably, or hiding in a doorway . . .

"Why do you say you will not be here long?" Kadiga asked. She lifted Sarita's feet, then exclaimed with a thrill of horror at their condition. "Allah! But look at your poor feet!"

"What's the matter with them?" Alarmed, Sarita struggled up against the back of the tub and peered at her feet, held in both hands by Kadiga. They looked perfectly normal to her.

"But they are so hard," Kadiga said. "Look, Zulema, only feel. They are like wooden boards."

"There's nothing the matter with them!" Indignantly, Sarita jerked her legs back into the water with a splash.

"We must rub the skin with oil and pumice," Zulema said. "It will no doubt take many days to restore the softness—"

"I am not going to be here several days," Sarita interrupted with some acerbity. "And I like my feet just as they are. How will I be able to walk if they are soft?"

"You do not wear shoes?" Kadiga stared. "It is not a Christian habit to wear shoes?"

Sarita thought of the merchants and the ladies she had come across in the towns on the tribe's travels when she had been selling the gloves her mother made out of kidskin. She shrugged. "Some do, if they live in houses in towns. But we who live on the road do not need them, except in winter, when there is frost or snow upon the ground. Then I wear clogs."

Her two attendants were looking at her as if she were some barbarian from the outlands. It occurred to Sarita, as she looked around her exquisite surroundings, that from their perspective such a viewpoint was probably justified. But how to explain the freedom of the road to birds who had only lived in a gilded cage? She decided not to bother. She would not be here long enough to form a true friendship with these women, so there was no need to explain herself.

Zulema had finished with her hair and was now soaping her arms and neck while Kadiga worked on her feet and legs. It felt very strange to Sarita, but she didn't know quite how to stop them, and anyway, it was not unpleasant in her present otherworldly trance. Without thought, she knelt up in the tub when Zulema asked her to, and then squealed in furious protest, slapping away her hands as they moved onto the most intimate territory.

"Don't touch me!" she exclaimed when Zulema sprang back, an expression of hurt bewilderment on her face.

"But why not?" the woman asked. "We are your attendants."

Sarita stared at her for a minute, then grabbed the soap from Zulema's hands and grimly washed herself while the young women stood watching in the same confusion. "Christians do not touch each other there, whatever infidels might do," Sarita said, standing up. "Pass me the towel."

"Not even men and women?" Kadiga demanded as she began to dry her. "What a strange race you must be." She chuckled impishly, and Zulema allowed herself a giggle.

Sarita flushed. "It's different between men and women."

"Well, of course!" Kadiga exclaimed, throwing up her hands, and the two Moorish women collapsed with laughter.

Sarita felt a bubble of answering laughter in her throat. They were making fun of her strange prudishness, but they were also sharing the kind of secretive laughter she was accustomed to sharing with her girlfriends of the tribe. A chuckle escaped her, and then they were all three laughing, and she ceased to notice as they dried her with an objective thoroughness before anointing her skin with a perfumed oil.

After all this cleansing and perfuming, reassuming her worse-for-wear shift and orange dress seemed somewhat inappropriate, and she was not in the least surprised when Kadiga produced an emerald silk robe, richly embroidered with flowers and peacocks. It fastened down the front with little loops of material over pearl-colored buttons. Only they were not pearl-colored, Sarita realized. Each one was a perfect, pink-tinged, translucent jewel. Again that sense of unreality flooded her. What was she doing here?

After the previous comments about her feet, she didn't balk at the slippers, although their pointed toes seemed ludicrously exaggerated and she couldn't imagine how she would walk in them. But then she was only going to bed, up in that gallery in that wonderful cushioned embrasure. In the morning, when she had slept off this trance, she would be able to face what had happened and decide what to do about it.

"Do you wish to eat before you go to lord Abul?"

The question from Kadiga brought her back to reality with a jarring thud.

"Go where?"

"To lord Abul. Yusuf will come for you in half an hour. We must brush your hair, but if you wish to eat first, there is fruit and pastries." Zulema moved to a table set beneath one of the marble columns, where a bowl of dates and figs sat beside a dish of savory pastries. "There is honeyed sherbet, or orange flower water if you prefer."

An unpleasant tremor started up in the pit of her stomach, and Sarita felt suddenly queasy, all sleepiness vanished. Yet why was she taken by surprise? For what other purpose had she been brought here? His attitude, the kiss, should have made it clear, but in her dreamy drifting she had lost touch with reality.

She had just been prepared for the bed of the lord Abul as assuredly as in the other life her mother would have prepared her for Tariq's bed. But she could not take issue with these women as to the plans made for her this night. Only with the man who had made them could she discuss them.

"Yes, I am hungry," she said, her voice amazingly calm as she realized that indeed she was hungry, ravenous in fact, having eaten nothing since midday. And she would need her strength to deal with whatever awaited her at the hands of the caliph of the Alhambra.

Chapter 4

⌒◯◯⌒

The two women rubbed her hair with a towel and brushed it while she ate: delicious flaky pastry cases filled with lamb and rice and pine nuts. She would have liked a tankard of the rough red wine that had always accompanied her meals hitherto, but it seemed she must make do with the innocuous, though pleasant-tasting, sherbet. Her hair sprang out damply in extravagant curls under the careful brush strokes, the bright color glowing under the light of the oil lamps. She nibbled a date and had the absurd image of herself being groomed and fattened for the sacrificial altar. It was not a sacrifice she had any intention of supplying.

That was a bold thought. How could she be so sure when she had no idea what choices were available to her? She had fled one sacrificial altar already today. She was not going to be able to run from this one . . . not tonight, at least. She would need to find a more subtle way of avoiding it. Absently, her finger went to her mouth, to the spot he had kissed, and she felt again that strange emanation of sweetness in the air around her. This was not a man to fear. And then with a blinding sorrow came the vivid recollection of how the blemish had occurred: the wild passion of that moment, the desperation of their love—a desperation that had led to Sandro's death. Maybe she did not fear Muley Abul Hassan, but she would fight to her own death to keep him from taking what had be-

47

longed to her lover. She threw back her head in an unconscious gesture of purpose and defiance.

Kadiga ceased her brushing, asking with a puzzled frown, "It is enough? It is not quite dry yet."

"Enough?" In the intensity of her reverie, Sarita had ceased to be aware of her attendants or of the rhythmic brush strokes, and she now shook her head briskly. In the light of her determination, these preparations were pointless. "Yes, it is quite enough."

"Then if you have finished eating, I will prepare your face." Zulema came forward, and Sarita saw that she carried a tray on which were a variety of little jars and brushes. She dipped a slender pointed stick in a pot of kohl.

"No!" Sarita cried, horrified as she realized what the other woman was about to do. She jumped off the ottoman. "I will not have that . . . that whore's paint on my face!"

"But, lady, it is customary." Again that note of hurt bewilderment was in Zulema's voice. She stood there holding the stick of kohl. "You must darken your eyes to be pleasing."

"I am no whore," Sarita spat. "I do not need to please any man."

There was a stunned silence in the court: a silence filled by the soft plash of the fountain, the faint sputter as one of the lamps fueled with perfumed oil caught a breeze from the upstairs windows.

"You have been given to the lord Abul against your will?" Kadiga finally ventured.

"No, no, not *given*—" Sarita began.

"Sold, then?" put in Zulema.

Sarita shook her head. "No, neither sold nor given. I belong to no one." They looked blankly at her, and she tried again. "I was leaving my tribe because . . . oh, because I had to . . . and your lord Abul, who had seen me earlier in the afternoon, decided . . ." She paused. They were still looking at her as if struggling for comprehension. "Your lord Abul decided he wanted me," she said baldly. "So he took me." Did

he always simply take what he wanted? she wondered. He certainly had the air of a man to whom
nothing was gainsaid. It had been one of the first
things she had noticed about him.

The two women nodded with expressions of relief
as all became clear. "You are the caliph's captive. You
belong to him."

"No!" Sarita exclaimed in frustration. "That is not
in the least the case. I may be a captive, but I do not
belong to the caliph. I belong only to myself."

She saw that she had lost them again, but before
she could begin a more elaborate explanation, there
was an imperative bang at the door.

"It is Yusuf," Kadiga said. "He has come for you."
She drew her scarf across her face. Zulema did the
same before hastening to open the door. The man
who had accompanied the caliph that evening stepped
into the court. He didn't acknowledge the two women
who had moved to one side, but laid a bundle on a
bench beside the door.

It was her own, Sarita recognized. She remembered
dropping it when the caliph had swept her up, and
she had assumed it was lost forever. Now, with a
joyful exclamation, she hurried over to examine it.
Everything was there: the wooden combs for her hair,
the silver bracelet her father had given her on her
twelfth birthday, the lace mantilla that had belonged
to her grandmother, her clean shift, wooden clogs for
the winter roads, and best of all, the twelve silver
pennies. Everything that established her in her own familiar world was there. The present fairyland receded
properly for the first time since she had entered it, and
she felt a resurgence of her real self.

The man called Yusuf said something to her in Arabic. She shook her head, indicating incomprehension, and saw his face darken. He spoke again,
harshly, and she realized he had thought she was refusing to do whatever it was he wanted.

Kadiga spoke rapidly in Arabic, explaining that Sarita didn't speak that language. The man's face cleared.

"You are to go with him," Kadiga said in Spanish. "But he doesn't like it that you do not cover your face. It is not modest and God-fearing for a woman to show her face in the company of a man not of her family . . . except for the lord Abul, of course," she added. "That is different. He is our supreme lord, and we are all of his family."

For answer, Sarita looked directly at Yusuf, meeting his eyes. She smiled and said politely in her own language, "I am ready to go with you. But I am not of your people and I do not hide my face."

Kadiga translated rapidly and Yusuf shrugged, as if the matter no longer interested him. He turned back to the door, gesturing that Sarita should accompany him. A boy stood outside the door holding a lantern. The extra light seemed unnecessary to Sarita as she followed Yusuf through the garden and down the cypress-lined path with its torches still flaring in their sconces. The entire Alhambra was lit up like the market square during Shrovetide revels, and people were scurrying about their business as if it were broad daylight.

Yusuf turned into an arcade surrounding a court with a long rectangular pool in its center. Lilies floated on the water, and light and music spilled from the arched doorways they passed. Sarita paused to peer through one of these archways, but her companion barked something at her. She couldn't understand the words, but the tone was sufficiently peremptory for the meaning to be clear. As a point of principle, however, she lingered for a few more seconds. There were men in the hall within, lounging on ottomans and divans, some deep in conversation, some engaged over chessboards, the sounds of lute and lyre providing a delicate accompaniment to their entertainment. No women, though. But then in the tribe such a male gathering would have excluded womenfolk also. They would have been sitting around campfires, not disporting themselves among silks and frescoes and fountains; someone would have been playing a guitar; a few voices would have contributed a song, instead of the professional musicians here in the gallery. But in essence the scene was familiar to her.

Yusuf seized her arm. She pulled it free, making an elaborate play of brushing at her sleeve where his hand had been; then she turned from the hall, gesturing airily that they should continue on their way. The look on his face was daunting, and she held her breath for a minute, trusting that some umbrella of protection came to her from the interest of Muley Abul Hassan. Apparently her trust was not misplaced, for Yusuf swung abruptly on his heel and strode ahead of her along the portico.

At the end, they turned within an archway into a quiet, lamplit hall where two men—guards of some sort, she judged by their uniform robes and the curved scimitars at their belts—stood on either side of a doorway at the far end. It seemed they had entered some sanctum, and the sounds of the palace faded behind them.

Yusuf approached the door, knocked softly, waited, then opened the door and waved Sarita into the caliph's presence.

Abul believed in the virtues of variety when it came to love partners, and although for the sake of domestic politics he had until their falling-out ensured that his wife was clearly his favorite, he regularly summoned other women from the seraglio. His four concubines were all free women, the beautiful daughters of the great Morisco-Spanish families, given to him to cement alliances or to buy friendship. They posed no threat to Aicha and seemed content enough to inhabit the seraglio in the Alhambra, coming willingly to their lord's bed when summoned and engaging in sometimes intense competition as to who might please him the most. He was aware of the competition and amused by it and was not averse to stirring the waters now and again by summoning one woman several nights in a row. But in truth, none of them pleased him more than another. They had all borne him children, which gave them status and permanency. Maternity made a woman special in the seraglio, while it separated her from her lord, who throughout her pregnancy left her to the sole attentions of the other women and on the production of a healthy child gifted her with clothes and jewels. These gifts were again a source of fierce comparison and competition.

In addition to these secondary wives, Abul had on occasion bought a female slave who had caught his fancy, or taken into captivity a particular woman as part of the spoils of battle. These women had not the legal status of his concubines and, once they no longer pleased him, became ordinary members of the palace household. They were assured of the caliph's protection throughout their lifetime, but beyond that he troubled little about them once he had tired of them. Women had but two tasks: to minister to their lord's pleasure and to be fruitful if he desired it of them. He did not breed children on the bodies of his slaves, and they were free to marry once they had left his bed. Abul considered himself a considerate master.

Now, as he waited out the hour before Yusuf would bring the girl to him, he was aware of an unusually high degree of anticipation. He enjoyed lovemaking, enjoyed the women who shared his bed, but he couldn't remember when he was last excited by one of them, when he had last felt this burgeoning lust for one particular body. But the moment he had seen her on the road that afternoon, barefoot, her hair a tangled cloud around the small face, a wildness to the green eyes as if some fire had been kindled and inadequately doused, he had wanted her. He hadn't questioned his wanting, and since he was not in the habit of failing to acquire what he wanted, he had simply set out to do just that. She was neither concubine nor slave nor captive justifiably acquired during hostilities. He had plucked her from her world to gratify an immoderate obsession that had hit him like a bolt from the blue . . . but he had not yet won her.

No, he had not yet won her. And therein lay the core of his rapidly mounting excitement, he decided. Judging by what he had seen so far, she would not prove an easy conquest. A woman who refused to speak even when words of outrage bubbled to her lips was a formidable challenge. Abul had the unmistakable impression that his new acquisition was a woman of some spirit. Only such a one would for whatever reason deliberately leave the protection of her kin to brave the dangers of a strange land whose inhabitants were not well disposed to her race and would certainly consider a lone woman fair game. And she was a woman who had had a lover, of that he was convinced. No timorous maid, this, but one who had known the joys of love and passion, one over whom men had fought to the death.

He did not yet know exactly what had happened in the encampment that afternoon, but he guessed that her lover had been killed and she had run from whatever consequences she was now to face. How deep ran her feelings for that man? He had seen the grief in her eyes earlier. If she was going to hold herself loyal to a memory, then he would have an added obstacle to overcome. She came from a monogamous people, of course, and they tended to be absurdly simple-minded about relations between men and women. Or was it that they complicated such relations unnecessarily? Either way, the thesis struck Abul as nonsensical and certainly a potential hindrance to his present aim.

Women had not hitherto presented him with any obstacles. They came when he sent for them, offered him only soft words and obedience, and did everything they knew to please him. He found he was deeply relishing the prospect of the challenge this nameless girl represented.

As she stepped into the room, he saw immediately that he had been right. There would be no subdued yielding to fate. She stood unmoving just within the doorway, her head up and her eyes meeting his unwaveringly across the room. He was unprepared for the effect she had upon him, dressed in the traditional caftan of his own people. It wasn't a garment worn by women with fiery hair springing to their shoulders in still damp curls; green-eyed women who stared a man down with lifted chin and feet planted squarely upon the ground. The bare-legged, tattered waif had disappeared, but the woman in her place still carried that sense of something untamed, and his blood rushed with sudden speed in his veins, the pulse in his throat beating with an almost painful rapidity under a thrill of arousal he hadn't felt since his youth.

"How are you called?" It was the fourth time of asking.

Sarita again made no answer, but her chin lifted a fraction higher, and Abul drew breath sharply. He stepped toward her, holding his hand out invitingly, in the manner one might use to coax a creature of the wild to one's hearth.

"If you will not tell me your name, then I must give you one of my own." He smiled as he reached her.

Sarita found she was holding her breath. He had shed the embroidered tunic, the leather britches, the studded belt and leather boots of the horseman, and wore a plain dark burnous. His head was now uncovered, and the thick black hair curled luxuriantly around his ears, waved off his broad forehead. His teeth gleamed white in the olive-gold of his complexion as his smile broadened. Never before had she been so aware of masculine power. She had never thought of power when she was with Sandro. Theirs was an equal love and passion, and they had both been powerless in its pursuit. Tariq had power, and she had felt it on many occasions, but it was the power of the leader, the power of his authority she had felt, not of his masculinity. Tonight she would have felt that male power, though. And it would have been of a different order from that exhibited by this man. She knew that absolutely. She knew that Tariq would have taken and used her body, would have exacted some vengeance upon her body for the humiliation she had caused him, and for the virginity she had given to another. Muley Abul Hassan's power did not emanate from the advantages of brute strength. But if not that . . . from where? From what inner well?

Slowly she let out her breath, keeping her eyes on his, throwing the same mute defiance in the face of his smile, his hands now lightly cupping her face.

"Zoraya," he said. "It means Morning Star. You shall be my morning star until you decide to resume your own identity." His hands left her face, and he stepped back as if to look at her properly. "Will you take off the robe, Zoraya?"

The question shocked her, although it should not have. But it seemed to have come too quickly, without any preliminary discussion of what she was doing here, as if his assumptions were hers and could not be otherwise. She shook her head, wishing that she had moved further into the room when she had first entered. Her back was to the door, the caliph was in front of her, and there seemed no room for maneuver.

He stepped closer again and with calm deliberation unfastened the first of the pearls at the neck of the robe. She tried to push his hands away, but he continued to the next one as if she hadn't moved.

"What are you doing?" She spoke to him for the first time, and her voice sounded strange to her, as if it were thick and creaky with disuse.

Abul hid his pleasure and simply raised an eyebrow as if at a silly question. "Unbuttoning you," he said, sliding the third button free of its loop.

"You would force me, then?" She held herself rigid, aware that she could do nothing to stop this if he was determined.

She saw that for some reason her question had startled him; a shadow of displeasure appeared in his black eyes. "No. What enjoyment would there be in that for either of us? Besides," he added, continuing with his work, "it will not be necessary." The button at her navel came undone as he said this.

Sarita could feel the warm night air on the inner swell of her breasts, now partially revealed. Why would it not be necessary? What kind of statement was that? But even through her shocked confusion she sensed what he meant, and an inkling of its truth shivered in her belly. She tried again to push his hands away, this time with a flurry of desperation, as if she would banish with his hands that suspicion of her body's potential for betrayal.

"If you do not intend to force me, why are you doing this?"

"Because I wish to look upon your body." It was said calmly, as if he were stating an obvious truth. And she realized that for him it *was* an obvious truth, as obvious as his belief in his right to do it. He had wanted her, so he had taken her, and while he would not hurt her, he would do with her as he pleased because he always did as he pleased. There was no one to gainsay the caliph of Granada in the palace of the Alhambra.

Except perhaps a Spanish girl with the open road in her blood.

The thought brought her renewed strength, drove the moment of weakness into the shadows. She stood immobile as he slipped the opened robe off her shoulders, and she tried to transport herself out of this lamp-lit room of cushioned silk and painted walls, back to the encampment with the rough grass beneath her feet and the sun in her face and the scent of wild thyme and marjoram mingling with the rich smells of roasting meat turning on spits over the cooking fires.

She had never been naked for a man before. There had been neither place nor opportunity for such luxury with Sandro; they had learned each other's bodies with their hands, not their eyes. Now she closed her eyes on a wash of vulnerability that she would not, must not, let this man see. He could look upon her body, but she would not let him look into her soul.

"How did you scratch yourself?" Abul asked, his voice little more than a rustling whisper in the quiet room. He touched the angry red mark across her right breast and then turned her to touch its twin across the back of her left thigh.

The splinters as she'd squeezed through the space in the backboards, she remembered as her stomach lurched at his touch and her knees seemed to lose their sinew. The light brush of his fingers had created an effulgent warmth on her skin, so that she could almost believe her skin was glowing and he would see the radiance in the room's dim light.

"You must be more careful," he said as if she had answered his question and they were having a dialogue. "Your skin is too delicate to misuse in this way."

"I do not live in a gilded cage," she said, finding her voice and her asperity at one and the same moment. "The women of my tribe endure more than scratches when they are about their work."

"Well, it will not happen again," Abul said. "And these will soon heal." He took her hands and drew her further into the room, observing, "We do not have to stand by the door all night. Sit there." He gestured to an ottoman and, when she didn't immediately take it, pushed her down quite gently. "You would like a glass of wine." It was a statement, not a question.

Sarita had been drinking wine and small beer since she was twelve. There really wasn't any alternative. Water often seemed to cause sickness and was drunk sparingly. There was milk, but the main supply was kept for the children. She accepted the goblet of Malaga with visible relief and for a minute forgot her nakedness with the familiar reassurance of a drink that anchored her to her self and her place in the world.

Abul took a sip from his own goblet and stretched out on a divan opposite her. "Must I call you Zoraya, or will you tell me your name . . . now that you have found your tongue?''

The softness of the silk cushions beneath her caressed her skin and made her vibrantly aware of her nakedness again. A light breeze lifted a curtain at a window, and she felt its stroking touch across her breasts. Her nipples hardened, and she knew it was not just from the coolness of the breeze. She was becoming aroused by her own nakedness in this golden bower and in front of this man.

"I wish to put on my robe," she said, standing up.

"There is no need. If you're cold, I will close the shutters."

"I wish to put it on," she said stubbornly. "Why should I be naked when you are not?"

She realized her mistake immediately. Muley Abul Hassan simply stood and pulled his burnous over his head. Beneath, he was as naked as she. She wanted to avert her eyes but found she couldn't. His body was lean and golden, tautly muscled, with not an ounce of spare flesh. She thought of Tariq, the muscles like small hills in his arms, rippling rivers across his shoulders as he had fought with Sandro that afternoon. There was no such overt display here, but she had the impression that the body was as rock-hard, as much an efficient machine as Tariq's, as powerfully strong as any she had seen. Her eyes drifted inadvertently downward, and she felt a warm flush suffusing her cheeks. The caliph was powerfully aroused. She sat down again abruptly.

"Come now, my morning star," he said, having no difficulty reading her blush and finding himself much amused by it. "What did you expect? You are no maid, you have told me as much. You must know what effect such beauty will have on a man."

"I am called Sarita," she said, trying to sink into the cushions of the ottoman, hugging her arms tightly across her breasts. Telling him her name was an attempt to reassert her sense of self, not a capitulation, but she was too disconcerted to care if he realized it.

"Sarita," he said slowly, as if trying the syllables on his tongue. "It seems we make progress, Sarita."

"Toward what, my lord caliph?" She was relieved to hear a healthy snap in the question despite her present disadvantaged position.

"I have told you my name. Can you not use it?"

She regarded him through narrowed eyes. "It is something of a mouthful, my lord caliph."

He laughed and came over to her as she shrank deeper into the cushions. " 'Abul' is no mouthful. It is how I am called."

"I wish to put on my robe and return to the tower." She turned her head away from the still powerfully aroused body, the evidence of that arousal now at eye level. "And tomorrow I will leave here."

"We will discuss tomorrow when tomorrow comes," he said, and there was a new note in his voice, a hint of steel that she hadn't heard before, yet it didn't surprise her. It seemed inevitably a part of the natural unspoken arrogance of the man, the unquestioned and unquestionable power of him. "Let us make ourselves more comfortable." Bending, he took her hands and drew her unresisting to her feet. She seemed to have lost all power of resistance. He led her through a curtained archway into a sleeping chamber where a wide divan stood in a pillared recess. He gestured that she should take her place on it.

"I will not get into your bed," she heard herself say, her voice shaking slightly. "You said you would not force me."

"I am not going to," he said quietly. "But we will be more comfortable sleeping in the bed than elsewhere."

"But I wish to go to my own bed in the tower." Her voice sounded plaintive, like a small child pleading for a reprieve.

"We will sleep in this bed," he said, firmly denying the reprieve. He pulled back the coverlet. "You need have no fear."

She had no choice but to trust him. And if he proved untrustworthy, still she had no choice. Sarita kicked off her slippers and crept beneath the coverlet, drawing it up to her chin. She watched as he moved around the room extinguishing the oil lamps, except for one that he brought over to the divan and placed on a low table, so that the bed and its occupant were bathed in a soft puddle of light, an oasis of light in the darkened room.

"I cannot sleep with the lamp burning," Sarita said, trying to sound firmly matter-of-fact, as if she were accustomed to sleeping beside a man in silken feather-bedded depths, the air delicate with perfumed oil and orange blossom.

"We aren't going to sleep just yet." Abul gently pried her fingers loose from the coverlet and drew it away from her body. "I wish to discover what gives you pleasure." He came down on the divan beside her, and Sarita shivered as if he had just pronounced a Draconian sentence. But it was not Muley Abul Hassan she feared; she feared only herself. She feared only that her body would betray Sandro's memory.

He drew a hand down her length in a slow, sweeping caress from the hollow of her shoulder to the soft flare of her hip; and where his hand touched, that same effulgent warmth spread across her skin. His eyes were bent upon her body as if he would imprint every curve and hollow on his mind, and his absolute concentration was more unnerving than anything she could have imagined. He placed a cupped hand over her breast; the hand seemed very large as her breast disappeared into the palm, and the warmth of his skin, the slight pressure of his palm, lifted her nipple.

He looked into her eyes then as he felt the movement of her breast in his hand. "There is nothing to fear," he said, seeing panic flickering in her emerald eyes. "There is only pleasure." Still covering one breast, he bent his head to the other, lifting the nipple with a grazing tongue so she shivered and cried out a muted protest.

Abul drew back. He knew the response she was denying, but he had promised he would not force her. "Perhaps we are trying to run before we can walk," he said. "No, don't do that." He stopped her from covering her breasts with her arms. "They are so pretty. So perfectly formed, round and firm." He moved his hand again in another long, lazy caress, this time from hip to ankle. "Such pretty feet, too." He lifted one foot and then gave a little gasp of shock. "What *have* you done to them?"

Dangerous passion scuttled abruptly into the shadows. "I do not wear shoes," Sarita said, since an explanation was clearly required. "And I do not see what business it is of yours."

Abul began to laugh. "How absurd that you should mar such perfection in this way. We will start to work upon them in the baths in the morning."

Sarita jerked her feet away from him, drawing her knees up and planting the soles flat on the bed. "In the morning I am leaving this place."

Abul made no verbal response. Instead, with a tiny smile, he moved his forefinger down the length of her drawn-up thigh from the hollow of her knee to the delicate fold where her thighs met her buttocks. Sarita, realizing too late how her indignant protection of her feet had exposed her, slammed her legs flat on the bed, and he laughed.

"I have a feeling that you enjoy a little combat with your loving," he said. "It can be most powerfully arousing."

Sarita stared at him. Did she? Or rather, would she? There had never been time for games with Sandro, and there had been enough danger in the forbidden act itself without creating playful scenarios. But Abul's words had sent a jolt into the pit of her stomach, and a seeping warmth spread through her loins.

"Well," he continued coolly, "we shall discover that one day soon. Perhaps not tonight."

"Please," she said. "Please, no more. Let me go back to the tower."

For answer, he dipped a finger in the shell of her navel and then brought his mouth to hers. His kiss was gentle as he ran the tip of his tongue over her lips, probing the corners of her mouth, tasting her sweetness. She found she was holding her breath, that the sensation was delicious: the warm pliancy of his lips, the darting probes of his tongue. Her mouth opened and his tongue was on hers, then as quickly withdrawn in a teasing, tantalizing play that forced her to move her mouth to recapture his tongue, drawing it deep within.

Leaving her mouth, he placed his lips against the fast-beating pulse at her throat, before raising each wrist in turn to press a kiss against the matching pulse. Sarita stirred on the divan, her mind cut loose, so that she felt as if she were floating somewhere above, looking down on herself on the divan, seeing the whiteness of her body on the white sheet, the lean golden body moving across hers. She felt her thighs part under the pressure of his hands, and her loins leaped beneath the delicate touch of a fingertip.

And then her mind rejoined her body with an anguished jolt. The image of Sandro as he had been that afternoon filled her internal vision, and she fought the rising sensations . . . fought them before they were beyond fighting. She held herself as rigid as steel on the bed, her arms tight at her sides, her fists clenched, eyes closed in the agony of the battle she fought with her willful body. A trail of salt trickled from beneath her eyelids down her cheeks.

Abul knew that he could win if he continued, but he also knew it would be a hollow victory. He could not bear her tears, the desperation of her struggle to contain her body. He sat up. "It's all right, *querida*. There will be no more." He smudged the salt tears from her cheeks with his finger, feeling her shudder as the rigidity subsided. Her eyelids fluttered open, showing him the drowned emerald pools beneath. "You see that I keep my promise," he said, although he could not hide the edge of frustration, of disappointment, in his voice. "I suspect I am mad to do so. And even madder to go on doing so. But you will give yourself to the pleasure in the end, Sarita."

She was utterly drained, her limbs like molten wax, and she had no strength to protest the statement or even to understand that he meant this gentle yet diabolical persuasion was going to continue. She tried to sit up.

"I want to go back to my own bed. I must sleep."

He pushed her down again. "You shall sleep, but it is too late now to make your way back to the tower." He drew the coverlet over her. "Mad though I am, I wish to lie beside you, so I will endure for the rest of the night."

She looked up at him, the startled expression in her eyes reflecting the startling thought. "Are you in pain?"

He gave a short laugh. "What do you think, *cara*? Of course I am. I could send you back to the tower and summon some other woman, but I am deranged enough to wish to spend the night beside you. Try not to touch me." He bent and extinguished the lamp, then slipped into the bed beside her.

Sarita lay still, staring into the darkness above. She had shared a bed with her mother but never with a man, never with quite such a large, warm, naked mass so close to her. Her body ached, and she too was conscious of a void that should have been filled, of a path of sensation abruptly diverted. If it was bad for her, how much worse must it be for Abul?

The sacrifice he had made had the strangest effect on her. It reassured her, soothed her mind and her body, and with a little sigh, she turned onto her side and slept.

Chapter 5

$\sim\!\infty$

Abul awoke before the first cockcrow and was for
a disoriented moment surprised by the presence
of another body in his bed. Occasionally, Aicha would
spend all night with him, but it was a privilege rarely
extended to his other women. He turned his head
drowsily on the pillow, and a wisp of red hair tickled
his nose. Memory returned, some of it uncomfortable. He propped himself on one elbow and looked
down at the sleeping countenance beside him. His
eye ran along the length of the small mound of her
body beneath the coverlet.

She looked far too insubstantial to have caused him
so much grief, he reflected with a wry grin. But he
should have been warned by that mouth, which even
in sleep had a decisive set to it; and her chin, although far from square, was decidedly firm. Her nose
wrinkled as she snuffled in her sleep, and he had
great difficulty resisting the urge to kiss it. With an
outflinging of her arms, she turned onto her side, facing away from him, presenting him with a rounded
shoulder, the tip of a pointed shoulder blade.

Slowly and carefully, he drew down the coverlet
and lay, still elbow-propped, dreamily surveying the
back thus presented. Her knees were slightly bent and
the curve of her bottom was entrancing. His loins
stirred, and he knew that this time he would have to
do something about it if he wasn't to spend the day
in priapic torment.

He touched her shoulder. "Wake up, Sarita." His voice was brisk. When she didn't respond, he tapped her bottom. "Wake up, Morning Star. It's time you went to your own bed."

She rolled onto her back, her eyes wide and staring, although it was clear she was still more than half asleep. Then her gaze focused on his face, and he saw recognition and memory flood back.

"Up," he instructed again, springing from the bed. "One of the guards will escort you back to the tower."

Sarita sat up, blinking in bewilderment. This briskness was quite new. Last night she had begged to go back to the tower and he had insisted she stay, so why now was he all but throwing her from the room? He had picked up her robe and was bringing it back to her, and her eyes involuntarily took in the condition of his body. She blushed deeply and seized the robe as he tossed it on the bed, shrugging into it, sliding to the floor as her fingers fumbled with the loops and buttons.

"Ready?" His tone was still brisk. She nodded, moving to the door. "Your slippers," he reminded her. "We do not go barefoot in the Alhambra."

For a moment, rebellion flickered across her face; then she pushed her feet into the curly-toed slippers. She had no intention of being in the Alhambra by sundown today, so there was little point in provoking skirmishes.

Abul opened the door and spoke in rapid Arabic to the two men outside. One of them went off immediately, on some errand, Sarita assumed; the other indicated that she should follow him. She looked over her shoulder at Abul, who was unconcernedly naked in the doorway. She felt the need for some ceremony of farewell, something to make sense of being thrust from his presence in indecent haste, but he wasn't looking at her and abruptly turned and went back into the room.

The guard stopped and said something to her that

again she didn't understand, but she assumed he was impatient at her dallying and set off after him. What must he think of her? That was a silly question. What would anyone think of a woman who had spent all night in a man's bed? What Sarita did not understand was that the guard thought nothing of her at all. She was simply a woman who belonged to the caliph. No more and no less than that.

In the gray light of dawn, the journey she had made the previous night under starlight and in torchlight was very different. She had a sense of the reality of the Alhambra, that it was no longer an enchanted land but a place of bricks and mortar, earth and stone, a place that needed constant tending in order to maintain its fairy-tale qualities. There were fewer people about, only servants sweeping and washing down the marble-paved courtyards and porticos, tending the flower beds, but the dawn scents were as heady as those in the nighttime, and the omnipresent sound of water was as soothing. Swallows dived into the courts and soared over the red rooftops, now glowing as they caught the rays of the rising sun.

Sarita looked up to the Sierra Nevada: nature's majesty ringing man's attempt at competition. She watched and shivered as the first eastern peak turned crimson. This place, however beautiful, was indeed a gilded cage. True beauty lay beyond the perimeter walls with the fresh breath of freedom and the hard earth beneath her feet. Disdainfully, she curled her shod toes against the marble paving of the court where she stood. Her escort stopped and called again. Shrugging, she followed him onto the cypress-lined path leading to her tower.

Kadiga and Zulema were in the court when she entered and greeted her cheerfully. All traces of the previous night's bath and supper had vanished, and the room had a fresh washed look about it.

"Have you been here all night?" Sarita asked, wondering where they had slept.

"Oh, no," Zulema said with her easy smile. "We

have just come to attend you." She regarded Sarita closely. "Will you be going to bed for a few hours?"

Sarita opened her mouth to express her surprise at such a question. Why on earth would she want to go back to bed at dawn, when the day was just beginning? And then she understood. A tinge of pink blossomed on her cheekbones. They probably assumed she had spent an energetic night in the caliph's bed. She could hardly tell them she had passed a dreamless, undisturbed night in as sound a sleep as she was accustomed to having.

"No," she said. "I wish to go for a walk."

"A walk?" Kadiga looked surprised. "You will break your fast first, though . . . and there is this." She extended a small cup to Sarita, who took it and peered at the contents, wrinkling her nose at the strong aromatic smell coming from the small quantity of viscous liquid.

"What is this?"

"It will ensure that a child will not lodge in your womb," Kadiga said matter-of-factly. "Unless, of course, you should wish it?" She shrugged carelessly, as if the question were of no great significance, and turned to a table where dishes of food were laid out. She unwrapped a napkin from a basket of flat bread, and the warm, steamy aroma of fresh baking filled the room.

Sarita was for a moment at a loss. Again, she could hardly tell them that such a precaution was unnecessary. They wouldn't believe her; indeed, why should they? She stared into the cup. She knew such potions existed. She had overheard her mother and some of the other women discussing it after the death in childbed of one of their number. But the women had been vehement in their disapproval of such things. Babies came or they didn't; they brought happiness or sorrow, life or death. They were a woman's lot, and it was not for women to interfere with that lot.

"Does it really work?"

"Oh, yes," Kadiga said, surprised at the innocence

of the question. "All the women of the palace use it if they do not wish to conceive."

"It's said even the lady Aicha uses it," Zulema put in. "Will you choose which robe you will wear today?" She gestured to a mass of colored silk draped over an ottoman.

"Who is the lady Aicha?" Sarita took the cup and turned her back on the two women. Deftly she tipped the contents into the soil at the base of a sweet-smelling shrub beside the fountain. Hopefully the potion wouldn't kill it.

"Why, the sultana, of course," Zulema told her. "The lord Abul's wife."

A wife. Of course he would have a wife. Why was she so astounded? She knew something of the customs of his people; strange, barbaric customs they were, for the most part. Despite this knowledge, she had to fight a surge of anger that she knew was irrational.

"Why would his wife not wish to conceive?" Her voice sounded stiff, and she put the empty cup on a table and went over to the pile of material on the ottoman, trying to appear insouciant as she sifted through it.

"Oh, it is said she wishes no rival for Boabdil," Kadiga said. Zulema made a softly protesting sound, and Kaliga shrugged. "Oh, there is no one to hear, Zulema, but the three of us."

"But if the lady Aicha were to hear you speak thus, she would have you flogged."

Kadiga shrugged again. "You know as well as I that Boabdil is everything to her. She could never endure to have another child because of what it would take from her son."

"The child is the caliph's son?" Sarita pushed the massed garments to the floor and sat abruptly on the ottoman. "How old is he?"

"He is ten." Kadiga passed her the basket of bread. It was warm and buttery, and Sarita found herself taking a piece without conscious thought.

"There is just the one child?"

"Oh, no." Zulema laughed. "His secondary wives have given the caliph children. He has three sons and two daughters."

Sarita was holding the flat bread halfway to her mouth. Butter dripped down her wrist, and absently she licked it off. "How many other wives?"

"Four."

Muley Abul Hassan had five wives and five children, and wanted to add Sarita to the list. No, not to the list of wives. There's been no mention of wifedom, just pleasure sharing. He'd talked of buying her, she remembered, hearing his soft laugh as he'd held her on his horse and told her that only a fool would pay for the dove that flew into his hand. A wave of anger broke over her again, and she had to breathe deeply to bring it under control.

"I am going for a walk." She stood up and went to the door.

"Oh, but you must change your clothes and finish eating. Will you have some jasmine tea? There is yogurt and honey . . ." Zulema followed her, chattering distressfully like a disturbed starling.

"I wish only to be alone." She stepped outside into the tower garden. Kadiga and Zulema stepped behind her. "Alone!" she said, swinging round on them. Impatiently, she pulled off her slippers and tossed them to the ground behind her. "I am going for a walk on my own."

"Very well," Kadiga said, laying a restraining hand on Zulema's arm. They stood watching until Sarita had gone beyond the garden and turned onto the path continuing around the perimeter wall, away from the palace. Then they set off after her, keeping a discreet distance.

Sarita walked fast, reassured by the feel of the ground beneath her feet, the fresh morning air cooling her heated temples and soothing the tumbling thoughts within. She had allowed herself to be brought to this place as a means of escaping Tariq . . .

a purely temporary measure of expediency. Now it seemed as if she had volunteered for a place in the caliph's seraglio. She had not thought of the consequences of her initial compliance because of that overwhelming sense she had had from their first silent meeting that she had nothing to fear from Muley Abul Hassan. But she had been thinking only of the obvious dangers to life, limb, virtue. He had shown no inclination to threaten any of those things . . . he posed no threat even to the latter. That threat was within herself, unleashed by him, certainly, but there was no violation.

He could not hold her against her will. Yet even as Sarita told herself this, she knew it to be untrue. He could; but would he?

The path had taken a steeply uphill turn, and her steps slowed. Pausing, she turned to look behind her, down the path to the gardens and buildings spread out below. Zulema and Kadiga stopped when she did and stood on the path some hundred yards away, clearly waiting for her to make another move. They looked uncomfortable and confused, very much as if they were unused to taking morning walks around the ramparts of the palace enclosure. Had they been given instructions to accompany her everywhere? It was time to force the issue with her gently yet alarmingly persuasive captor.

She walked back down the path to where the two women stood. "We'll go back now, if you wish."

"It's if *you* wish," Zulema said in her sweet way. "But I am sure you must wish to change your clothes and perhaps have some jasmine tea. It's most refreshing in the morning."

Sarita smiled slightly at the other woman's clear relief that the morning was about to assume normal and expected paths again, but she said nothing, merely walked ahead of them past gardens and towers until she reached her own.

* * *

Aicha carefully licked honey off her fingers before reaching for another little cake from the plate of sweetmeats beside her on the divan. She was addicted to the honey and almond delicacies.

"You are certain the lord Abul kept this Christian woman in his bed throughout the night?"

"Yes, lady." Nafissa poured scented water into a crystal finger bowl and approached the bed. "The guard returned her to the tower at dawn. Zulema and Kadiga were there to attend her." She placed the finger bowl on the bed and proffered a linen towel.

"But where did she come from?" Absently, Aicha dipped her sticky fingers into the bowl, swirling the rose petals on the surface.

"It is not known, my lady." Nafissa confessed ignorance reluctantly. "Only Yusuf was with the lord Abul, and Yusuf—"

"Yusuf has a mouth like a trap," Aicha broke in with a hint of impatience. She pushed aside the coverlet, heedless of the water slopping from the bowl onto the divan. "I will get dressed and send for these women. She may have talked with them."

"I understand that the lord Abul sent for the girl Fatima, the one he bought in the bazaar at Marrakesh," Nafissa said with a sly look as she mopped up the water with the towel.

Aicha turned slowly from her dresser. "When?"

"After the Christian woman had left him," the handmaid said, still apparently busy with the mess on the cushions. "Fatima was with him for an hour. She left his apartments but twenty minutes ago."

Aicha moved to the window. "If he was displeased with the other woman, why would he keep her until dawn?"

It was not a question Nafissa felt qualified to answer. She picked up the empty plate. "Shall I bring you more stuffed dates, my lady?"

"No." Aicha stood gazing out of the window and waved a hand over her shoulder dismissively. "I will have a jasmine infusion. Then send at once for Zulema and Kadiga . . . no, perhaps not." She turned back to the room, a sharp glint in her dark eyes. "I shall visit my husband. Do you talk with those women. There is no need for me to seem interested beyond the ordinary in this new arrival. Find out what happened with the lord Abul. They will have attended to her afterward and will know whether she shared pleasure with my husband last night . . . Oh, and talk also with Fatima. You may discover what it was my husband wanted of her . . . the degree of his need," she added. "Now bring me water to wash. I will wear the caftan of gold tissue with the belt of amber studs."

She said no more while Nafissa helped her dress, brushed her hair, and secured it with ivory combs beneath a scarf of the same gold tissue as the caftan. It was Abul's habit to keep to his apartments until the sun was well risen. He broke his fast alone and prepared himself for the day, discussing with his vizier and his cadi what administrative matters required his attention. She had always found him receptive when she had visited him at this time with some matter of domestic moment to impart. Today, she would present him with an unimpeachable reason for visiting him. It would not be a comfortable audience for her, but a wise woman knew when to bow to necessity.

She prepared her face with care, outlining her eyes with kohl, touching her cheekbones and lips with rouge. But there was nothing seductive about her this morning as there would have been if she had been able to carry out her plan of the previous evening. It was important that she appear pleasing and dignified, graceful and modest in her approach. If all went well, maybe she would have the opportunity to bring up this puzzling new arrival.

She left her apartments and made her way through the internal halls to the caliph's private domain. Servants stepped aside, pausing in their sweeping and polishing, as she passed. She hesitated on the threshold of the anteroom, where a small group of Abul's personal retinue waited to be summoned to his presence. Aicha, holding her scarf across the lower part of her face, stepped up to the guard at the door.

"Will you inquire if my lord Abul can spare a few moments for his wife?" Her voice was low, but nonetheless assured. There would have to be a very good reason for the guard to deny her access.

Abul looked up from the parchment he was reading when the door opened to admit the guard. His face showed no expression as the man told him that the sultana was outside and requesting an audience. "Show the lady Aicha within," he said, rolling the parchment and laying it on the table beside him. He had been feeling relaxed and good-humored after his session with Fatima and had been contemplating with amusement and pleasurable anticipation his next attack on the citadel of Sarita, but some of this good humor faded as his wife entered the chamber.

She let the scarf fall from her face and bowed, smiling. "I give you good day, Abul."

He returned her smile with a semblance of warmth. "Good day, Aicha." She was looking very beautiful, he observed. But there was something beneath the beauty, a brittle quality, that he was not used to seeing. He studied her closely and thought she seemed nervous. Her hands moved in the folds of her gown, and her eyes slipped away from his.

"It has been long since we had speech alone," she said, her smile suddenly forced. "I am afraid I have offended you."

Abul stood up. "You must *know* that you have," he said gravely.

"I was foolish," she said, her voice low and rushed. "I had no right to question your judgment about our son. Can you not find it in your heart to forgive me?" Her soul screamed denial of her statement even as she made it. No one, only she, Boabdil's mother, had the right to order the child's life, but in the interests of the greater good, she must appear to bow to her husband's decrees.

"I have forgiven you," he said. It was the truth. Her petulant and ill-advised refusal of her body had caused him no more than transitory annoyance. He had punished her for it, but his present loss of desire for her had other causes, causes that could not be eradicated, since they were firmly rooted in the person he now perceived her to be.

Aicha came close to him, laying her hand on his arm. "I have missed you, my husband. I have not known how to ask for your forgiveness." She kept her eyes down, hiding her resentment at being obliged to make this mortifying speech. But Abul was not fooled. He knew his wife too well to believe that anything less than desperation had driven her to this pass.

"We will not speak of it again," he said lightly. "Did you have other business with me this morning?"

Aicha ground her teeth in frustration. She knew she had achieved nothing more than a surface smoothing of matters between them, but if he had forgiven her, then what was continuing to cause her husband's present disaffection?

"No," she said in the same soft tone. "I came only to see if I could make matters right between us. I thank you for your generosity and your forgiveness, my husband. I will not take up any more of your time." She glided to the door, then paused, still with her back to him. "Is there anything you wish me to do for the woman you brought into the palace last evening? Should she be accommodated within the seraglio?"

Abul allowed a small smile to touch his lips. So this was really what it was all about. It didn't surprise him. Aicha kept herself well informed of all events in the Alhambra and was presumably devoured by curiosity over this one.

"You are always so thoughtful and conscientious, Aicha," he said gravely. "But there is no need to concern yourself over the woman. She is Spanish and

would not be at home within the women's apartments."

Aicha waited for a few seconds, hoping to hear
more, but Abul said nothing. She controlled her disappointment. "As you wish, my lord. You will inform me if I should give order for any further
arrangements."

"I will indeed," he replied with the same solem-
nity, well aware of her annoyance and frustration.
"Thank you."

Aicha left with her gliding footfall, drawing her scarf
across her face as she passed the men in the antechamber. There was no indication in her demeanor of
the furious turmoil in her head. She had achieved
nothing during the interview but her own mortification. She had no sense that she was returned to her
husband's favor, and she had gleaned no impressions, let alone information, about the mysterious occupant of the perimeter tower. And no enlightenment
of the most curious fact of all: why, if Abul had acquired a new woman, one who spent all night in his
bed, had he had need of Fatima this morning?

But maybe Nafissa would have some answers by
now. She would at least have discovered from Fatima
the extent of the caliph's need.

Abul stepped through the arched door of his chamber into the portico of the Myrtle Court. A pair of
green finches trilled at him from a cage swinging from
a hook in the roof of the colonnade. He whistled at
them, and they regarded him with beady eyes, heads
tilted to one side. That earlier smile played over
Abul's lips. Aicha had been so transparent. He wondered if she had heard of Fatima's visit. Probably.
The entire seraglio would be in a ferment of speculation by now. His smile faded. He was going to have
to make some move indicating his wife's reinstate-
ment, even if it meant calling her to his bed once or
twice in the next few days. It was his responsibility
to ensure peace and harmony in the palace, and erod-

ing Aicha's authority with the women would do little
to achieve that.

Suddenly impatient, he turned back to his chamber. The sooner he dealt with the waiting courtiers
and the day's business, the sooner he could resume
the siege of his determined captive, and let his wives
make of it what they wished. It would certainly en-
liven the ordinary routine of the seraglio. He rang the
handbell that would summon his waiting vizier from
the antechamber.

It was midmorning before Yusuf knocked at the
door to Sarita's tower. Kadiga opened it.

"I am come to escort the woman to the baths," he
announced, standing in the doorway, arms folded.
"She is to come immediately."

Sarita had spent the time since her return from her
walk examining her new wardrobe. Zulema and Kadiga had told her the caliph himself had given order
the previous evening that she be provided with this
wealth of jeweled and brocaded garments, and they
had entered enthusiastically into the examination. For
Sarita, it had been a game. She had never possessed
more than two dresses at a time, one for summer and
one for winter: plain, serviceable garments that would
survive bareback riding as well as scrambling across
rocks and marching on the highways and byways.
The caliph's choices had no utilitarian qualities whatsoever, as far as she could see. The silks were of the
finest, the embroidery the most delicate, and the lav-
ish sprinkling of jewels would have taken her breath
away if she could have taken any of it seriously. They
were definitely clothes for languid drifting in fairyland. But there was another quality to them which
she found more disturbing. When she wore them,
they clung delicately to the swell of her breasts, swung
gracefully around her hips, and the material, while
far from transparent, yielded a very definite sense of
the flesh beneath. There was, Sarita decided, something more than faintly immodest about them, and it

struck her that they had been designed by men with men's pleasure in mind. In view of what she had already discovered about life in the Alhambra, it seemed a reasonable supposition.

She had insisted on mending and washing her orange dress, despite Kadiga's vigorous protestations, and it now hung reassuringly to dry in front of one of the windows of the gallery. When it was dry, she would be ready to leave this place.

She ignored Yusuf's arrival at first, for she couldn't understand a word he said anyway; but she couldn't ignore Kadiga's translation.

"He has come to take you to the lord Abul in the baths."

Here was the opportunity to force the issue. Sarita selected an apricot from the bowl on the table. She took a leisurely bite. "I will remain here, Kadiga. Tell Yusuf that he must tell the caliph that I have no wish to attend him in the baths or anywhere."

Zulema gave a little whimper, and Kadiga came slowly across the court. Her eyes were alight with intelligent speculation, her pointed features seeming more finely drawn than usual. "You do not know what you are saying, Sarita."

"Oh, but I do." Sarita spat the apricot stone into the palm of her hand and tossed it aside. "If the lord Abul wants me, then he must come for me himself."

"But we cannot tell Yusuf that." Zulema had her hand over her mouth as she shot anxious looks at the still figure standing in the doorway.

Yusuf spoke in his sharp, abrupt manner, turning to leave the court. Clearly he expected her to follow, Sarita thought, like an obedient puppy. She selected another apricot.

Kadiga spoke swiftly and at some length. Sarita had no idea what she said, but the effect on Yusuf was not reassuring despite the woman's obviously conciliatory tone. His face darkened, and he stepped back into the court, harshly interrupting Kadiga.

"He says you must go with him," Kadiga said with

a helpless shrug. "I told him you were feeling unwell, but he still says you are to accompany him."

"Then tell him the truth," Sarita said. "Tell him that I *will* not go with him."

"You are mad," Kadiga whispered, but a gleam of admiration showed in her eyes. "Why will you not go?"

"Because I do not belong to your lord Abul. Because I am not obliged to obey him. Because I am a captive held against my will," Sarita explained succinctly.

Zulema stepped across to Yusuf, drawing her scarf across her face. She spoke hurriedly, her voice soft and sweet and pleading.

Yusuf stared at the Spanish woman, who still sat on the ottoman, calmly eating apricots with her face brazenly exposed, just as if he weren't there. He found himself at a loss. Lord Abul had told him to escort the woman to the baths. He had not told him to bring her or to fetch her. Had the caliph used such words, Yusuf would have had no hesitation about picking up his recalcitrant charge and carrying her off. But he hadn't been told to do that, and he knew that this woman had an unusually powerful effect on his lord. He couldn't imagine where it came from, himself. She struck him as too small and uncontrolled to be attractive, with that extravagantly curly red hair and those turbulent green eyes. But it was not for him to question the caliph's flights and fancies.

Zulema was suggesting that the woman was reluctant to leave the shelter of the tower in the daylight because she was frightened and uncomfortable in a strange place. Yusuf looked searchingly at the girl, still calmly eating apricots. She didn't look in the least frightened or uncomfortable to him, but Zulema's explanation gave him a face-saving way of avoiding confrontation. On his return, he would have different instructions from the caliph.

The door closed with a snap on his departure, and Kadiga gave a gurgle of laughter. "I have never seen

Yusuf at a disadvantage before," she said, helping herself to an apricot. "But you were wonderful, Zulema." She went into a peal of laughter.

Zulema's smile was rather more restrained, but Sarita was developing the impression that the softer of the two was no less humorous than her friend. "I don't think he believed me," Zulema said, and then began to laugh also.

"But what did you say to him?" Sarita demanded, laughing although she didn't yet know why, simply because their laughter was so infectious.

Zulema told her. "It would have been more convincing if you hadn't been spitting out apricot stones as if you hadn't a care in the world," she said. Then she sobered abruptly. "But what will happen now?"

Sarita shrugged with a nonchalance she was not entirely sure of feeling. "We'll wait and see. But I expect your lord Abul will come here as I requested."

Kadiga grinned. "That was a strangely worded request. But why would you refuse to go to the caliph? You passed the night with him."

Yes, thought Sarita, but not the night you might imagine. Again she couldn't think how to explain the truth, so she just shook her head and said, "I am not here of my own free will. I wish to leave, and the lord Abul must arrange it."

Abul was waiting in the Court of the Cypresses outside the baths. His administrative tasks completed, he was relaxing in the sun, listening to the play of fountains and contemplating a leisurely progression through the halls of the baths, introducing his resolute and intriguing guest to their sensual and spiritual delights, delights that would hopefully further wear down her resistance. He had little difficulty hearing the truth behind the diplomatic explanation for Yusuf's empty-handed arrival. A frown touched his eyes, replacing the languid anticipation of pleasure. It could become tiresome if she threw down the gauntlet over the smallest matters.

"Do you wish me to bring the woman, my lord?"
Yusuf sounded eager to do so.

Abul shook his head. There would be no satisfaction in a victory won through brute strength. He
would play the hand as it had been dealt him. "I will
go to her myself."

Without apparent haste, he strolled through the
courts of the palace, taking the trouble to acknowledge the obeisance of those he passed. Outside the
walls of his home, there was turmoil, conflict, constant upheaval. There were rival factions among the
Morisco-Spanish families in Granada, the roads were
plagued with brigands, and the Spanish pressed ever
closer to the border of Castile, their eyes as always
set upon the prize of Granada, the last remaining
Morisco-Spanish kingdom in Spain. Abul knew that
for Ferdinand of Aragon and Isabella of Castile, their
lands now united by their marriage, the completion
of the reconquest of Spain after nearly eight hundred
years of Moorish domination had taken on holy significance. He knew he had to fight constantly to hold
on to his kingdom, and not always with sword and
lance; mentally, he must be alert to the slightest
threat, the hint of a move against him, the merest
whisper of an alliance between one of the rival families in Granada and the Spaniards. He could be
ousted, he knew, only by such an alliance: a combi-
nation of treachery within and armed power without.

When he left the Alhambra on his journeys of diplomacy, of outright battle, of trading and bribery, he
lived and breathed the turmoil and the danger, drawing satisfaction from the knife-edge, as he had been
born and bred to do. But within the walls of the Alhambra palace, his home, he wanted only tranquility,
harmonious relationships, beauty and symmetry to
soothe and gladden all the senses. He worked as hard
to achieve this as he did to secure his kingdom, but
the methods were different. Gentleness, courtesy,
consideration—these were the tools by which Muley

Abul Hassan created harmony within the walls of his home.

It struck him, as he opened the wicket gate to the garden of the tower, that with Sarita he had introduced an unharmonious facet into the serenity of the palace compound. Her refusal to fit into his scheme of things created a discordant note. Paradoxically, he was enjoying the challenge she presented, but in keeping with the physical perfection of their surroundings and his own emphasis on peace and order, he determined to use only the most sensuous means of persuasion to bring her within the embrace of the Alhambra and all that would follow from that embrace.

He entered the tower without an alerting knock and thus surprised the three young women in the midst of their laughter. As the caliph entered, however, Kadiga and Zulema leaped to their feet, instantly sobered, although amusement still lingered in their eyes.

Abul had the unmistakable sense of having intruded. It was not an unusual sensation. When he visited the seraglio unexpectedly, he always felt as if he had disturbed some very private world. It didn't trouble him; the private world of women was all they had within the dominating sphere of their menfolk, and they were entitled to it.

Sarita remained reclining on the ottoman and made no overt acknowledgment of his presence. As he watched, she selected an apricot from a bowl on the table beside her and slowly bit into it. The insolent sensuality of the gesture lifted the hairs on the back of his neck.

"Leave," he said to the attendants. They scurried past him as he stepped aside. He closed the door quietly. "So it seems you are reluctant to venture outside the tower in the light of day," he observed, crossing the court toward her. He stretched out on an ottoman facing her and raised his eyebrows slightly at the plethora of apricot stones scattered across the table and the floor. "You do like apricots, don't you?"

Sarita was no longer sure that she did. She seemed to have consumed a vast quantity, and the one she now held had been taken purely for effect. She discarded it half eaten on the table. "I wish to leave this place now." It seemed best to come straight to the point.

Abul pursed his lips. "That color suits you."

Taken aback, Sarita looked down at her robe of apple-green silk. The color did suit her; the glass had told her so as eloquently as had Kadiga and Zulema. It set off her hair and did rather nice things to her eyes. Whatever she might think of this style of garment, her vanity was not beyond gratification. However, she was not about to show it.

"It is a ridiculous garment," she declared roundly.

"Oh? In what way?" He seemed politely interested.

"Well, one cannot do anything in it except lie around eating apricots," she said.

"And why should you wish to do anything else?"

Sarita swung herself off the ottoman with a vigor that belied her complaint. The rich material was caught beneath her breasts with a girdle of twisted silk and fell straight to the floor, skimming her hips. Abul smiled appreciatively.

"I do not like to lie around," she said, impatient at this diversion. "Perhaps you didn't hear me. I said I wish to leave here."

"Very well," Abul said, as if there had never been any question about it. "I will return you under escort to your people. They are still encamped in the olive grove. You will be back with them within the hour." He watched her through narrowed eyes. It was a calculated risk he took, but he was counting on the desperation that had already driven her from the tribe's protection.

The color in her cheeks ebbed. Her hands twisted. "No, I cannot do that. You don't understand."

"I understand that you ran from them yesterday. But if you do not wish to remain here, then I can only assume that you wish to return to them."

"No, I do not wish to return."

He heard the tiny tremor in her voice. His own voice was all sweet reason. "But there is nothing else for you to do, Sarita. I know the dangers in my land. You would be taken from the open road by the first brigand band and sold to the first slave trader they came across . . . after they had amused themselves with you, of course," he added, making a steeple of his fingers.

"I will take my chances," she said fiercely. "I knew the risks yesterday. They have not changed."

He shook his head. "But they have changed. You have come under my protection—no, let me finish," he said as her mouth opened on a surge of indignant protestation. "I am the caliph of this land. All who travel in it do so with my permission and under my writ. Only thus can I keep order within my frontiers. If I turn you loose to roam the highways alone, some offense will be committed against your person, and since you are under my protection, that offense will therefore be committed against me. I would have to punish the perpetrator. You see my difficulty." He smiled, tapping his fingertips together.

There was a certain diabolical logic to it, if you looked at it in a certain way, but Sarita had no intention of using those eyes. "Your reasoning is specious," she declared. "An offense has already been committed against my person . . . by *you*."

"How have I hurt you?"

"You abducted me. You cannot deny that."

He shook his head. "I removed you . . . a lone and unprotected woman . . . from the dangers of the open road."

Sarita felt as if she were wading through quicksand. The grounds for complaint slipped and slithered beneath her, yet she knew they were just. "You

are holding me against my will," she said finally. That
at least was unarguable.

But again Abul shook his head. "No. I have said I
will return you to your people. I have said simply that
I will not permit you to leave here with no protection."

Sarita turned from him. Leaning her elbows on the
marble basin of the fountain, she stared down into
the cool, clear surface, rippling beneath the constant
plash of the descending stream. She was remembering a woman of the tribe who had run away from her
husband with a man from another clan. The husband
had hunted her down, killed the lover as Tariq had
killed Sandro. The woman's screams and the crack of
his lash had rung out from the woods around the
camp for hours, it had seemed. Sarita remembered
how nauseated she had felt, how she had tried to
drown out the sounds, but the camp had been hor-
ribly silent, as if they were all participating in the
man's vengeance. He had tethered the woman to the
wheel of his wagon with a cord around her ankle.
There had been enough play in the cord to permit her
to perform her domestic duties. Sarita could see her
now, stumbling between wagon and hearth, lifting
the excess cord to carry it so it wouldn't chafe too
much when she had to go farther afield. And no one
had any compassion for her. It was tribal justice. It
had been many weeks before her husband had freed
her. But she had been a broken woman then, silent,
walking with her shoulders hunched, cringing at the
slightest unexpected movement.

"I cannot go back," Sarita said.

Abul stood up. Coming up behind her, he laid his
hand on her back between her shoulder blades. Her
body leaped beneath the touch, her skin rippling
through the thin silk. "Did you run from the man
who killed your lover?"

Shocked, she straightened and turned to face him.
"How could you know that?"

"Yusuf saw the killing," he said. "I had sent him

to discover what he could about you after I saw you on the road in the afternoon.''

"Tariq had forbidden our marriage. We didn't know why." She spoke over his shoulder, aware of how close he was to her, feeling the warmth from his body, wanting suddenly to be held. She forced herself to continue speaking as if such a wanting did not exist. "It was because he wished to marry me himself. When I refused . . ." She stopped. He knew the rest.

Abul put his arms around her, drawing her against his chest. "You cared deeply for this man?" Her tears wetting his tunic were answer enough. He stroked her hair, frowning. She had all the headstrong commitments of youth informed by the mores of her people, and could not yet see that there were many different kinds of relationship between men and women; that enjoying pleasure with one was not necessarily a betrayal of another.

He felt her trust, though, as she wept in his arms. So long as she trusted him, he could teach her to see things his way, to yield to the pleasure she had denied them both with such fierce despair last night. But he must do it lightly, tapping the rich currents of her sensuality to keep her on the brink of arousal, but without seeming to threaten the integrity she had taken upon herself. It would put a considerable strain on his own powers of self-control, Abul recognized wryly, but it could be done, and her eventual capitulation would be all the sweeter.

"No more weeping," he said, holding her away from him. Her tear-drenched eyes were like drowned seaweed. He slipped a hand to the nape of her neck and bent her head over the fountain, splashing her face with the cool water. "I am going to teach you the delights of the baths. You will learn to relax and allow both grief and pleasure to be a part of you."

Sarita shook her head free of his restraining hand and wiped her wet face with her palm. "There is no need to drown me."

Tears and the recounting of tragedy had not cowed her, he realized with satisfaction. The recuperative powers of the young were always to be relied upon. "Did your women not bring you towels? You're dripping all over your robe."

Sarita wiped her face dry on a square of linen that smelled of sunshine. She sniffed vigorously. They were the first tears she had shed for Sandro, and in their wake had come a resurgence of energy. Muley Abul Hassan was not going to give her free passage from the Alhambra. He had made that perfectly clear, and she was under no illusion that she would be able to change his mind. Therefore, she must contrive her own escape. To do that, she must persuade him that she accepted his edict: if she would not go back to the tribe, then she must remain here. He had promised he would force nothing upon her but his company, and she would yield to that until her opportunity came.

In truth, she had no objection to his company, quite the opposite. But that didn't alter the fact that she was his prisoner, she reminded herself hastily.

"I had a bath last night," she said. "I do not need another."

Abul chuckled. "This is not a bath solely for cleansing purposes, as you will see. It is to refresh the spirit as much as the body. Come."

He walked to the door, and Sarita, after a moment's hesitation, followed. What was there to lose?

Chapter 6

Abul paused at the garden gate, waiting for Sarita
to come up with him. "Do you have questions
about the Alhambra?"

"Many," she said frankly. "But what is the place
across the ravine?" She gestured behind them to the
cluster of roofs showing above the deeply wooded
mountainside.

"The Generalife." He turned onto the cypress-lined
path, taking her elbow in a light clasp. "A place of
gardens and miradors, terraces and porticos. A place
of repose and of beauty. We will go there in a day or
so."

Sarita kept pace with him, finding his clasp of her
elbow strangely reassuring. She was not accustomed
to men adapting their pace to that of their womenfolk, who were generally expected to trot along in the
rear, keeping up as best they might. Either that, or
they strolled in their own groups at their own pace,
deep in their own discussions. Walking so compan-
ionably with a man was a novel experience, and she
was not to know that it was as novel for Abul to walk
arm in arm with a woman. But he felt the need to
offer her some protection, some sense of belonging in
a place that must be alien to her.

He talked easily about the palace, telling her of the
great aqueducts that brought water from the mountains and circulated it through the palace, feeding its
streams and fountains and ponds. He pointed out the

great edifice of the alcazaba that she had seen from
the road to the city of Granada, and told her that an
army of forty thousand men could be garrisoned
within the fortress.

"Are there that many now?" It seemed incongru-
ous to Sarita to talk of soldiers and fortresses amid
the exquisite beauties of the palace, yet it was true
that the palace was contained within the fortress and
not the other way around.

"No." Abul turned into a garden of massed flower
beds. The air felt pleasantly damp, as if it had just
been watered, and Sarita realized that the ground beneath her feet was damp. The warmth of the midmorning sun falling on the freshly watered earth set
up a rich loamy scent to mingle with that of the flowers. "No," Abul repeated. "Not at the moment.
There is no need for such a garrison. I could call in
that many if there were need . . . if, for instance, your
Spanish monarchs decided to attack." He looked
down at her, his expression unusually grave. "Such
an event is not unlikely."

"But why would they?" Sarita had no knowledge
of politics, or of the wider world outside the clan's
journeyings. She knew of and feared brigands, slave
traders, the Inquisition, dishonest merchants, any
who might impinge directly upon her life. But the
dreams and territorial aspirations of their most Catholic Majesties, Ferdinand and Isabella of Spain, were
unknown to her.

"Because many centuries ago my people conquered
this land," Abul told her. "The Spaniards have been
slowly winning it back, kingdom by kingdom, for the
last two hundred years." He stopped and looked
around him, waving an all-encompassing hand.
"Only Granada remains to us now."

"And you would keep it so?" She had heard the
intensity in his voice, seen the shadow in his black
eyes as he glanced down at her.

"But of course. I would keep it for my son, as it
was kept for me."

This was another topic, one she had intended to bring up when he gave her an opening. "You did not tell me you had a son . . . or a wife, for that matter."

Abul took her elbow again and began to steer her across the garden toward a marble portico at the rear. The intensity had left his face and voice as he put aside the affairs of the world outside the Alhambra. "My wives and my children are no concern of yours, *hija mía*. Any more than you are any concern of theirs."

"But they are," she protested. "And do not tell me no one wonders who I am or what I am doing here."

He laughed. "They know what you are doing here, Sarita. Or at least," he added with a crooked smile, "they know what I had hoped you would be doing here."

Sarita said nothing for a second, since this had already been made abundantly clear to her by Zulema and Kadiga, who could see only one possible reason for her arrival and continued presence in the caliph's palace.

They stepped through the portico and into a cool hall where the light was a soft, diffused green, instantly restful.

"But your wives and children do concern me." Sarita returned to the attack. "I do not understand how you could think—"

"It is our way," he interrupted with a touch of asperity.

"But it is not *our* way. My people do not—"

A hand went over her mouth, and she found herself staring into the bright black eyes of her companion bent upon her with something less than tolerance. "Sarita, this is not a place for contentious subjects. It is a place where the mind and the body may meet in mutual refreshment, where you will have only quiet thoughts and speak only soft words. That is *our* custom. I see no reason why you should find it difficult to comply. Do you?"

Not when it was put like that. Sarita shook her head vigorously, and the hand left her mouth. It went instead to cup her chin. A thumb ran lightly over her lips before he bent his head and laid his now smiling mouth over hers, and it was as it had been the previous night: that same delicious sensation, that same desire to make of a casual salute something deeper and more committed. Involuntarily, her lips parted in encouragement, her tongue darting to touch and taste the corners of his mouth.

His hand dropped from her chin, leaving a cool space on her skin. And with the cool space came the knowledge that there was no compulsion. His holding her had offered a pretense of such, and in the safety of that assumption she had allowed herself to respond. Now any response she made was entirely her own.

She stepped back from him, saw the flash of regret in his eyes, and ruefully recognized its match in the flutter of loss in her belly. But such reactions were impermissible, and she turned from him, looking around the cool green hall where they stood.

"It is as if we are belowground," she commented casually, her voice sounding miraculously steady. "There is no sense of the heat outside."

"No; it was designed for that effect." Abul spoke as casually as she, and again she felt reassured. He would keep his promise in more than just the letter. "We will go within, to the hall of immersion."

He moved ahead of her, deeper into the palace, through marble-pillared halls and little chambers like grottoes where fountains played amid luxuriant shrubbery. Everywhere was the same greenish light, the same freshness of the air, the same omnipresent sense of water. It seemed as if they were penetrating deeper into the side of a mountain—an exquisitely decorated mountain where the walls were encrusted with beautiful tiles, the floors of white marble or elaborate mosaic.

They met no one until they came to the central hall, where two sunken marble tanks stood amid pillars and fountains. There were two women waiting in this room. They wore simple white robes with muslin scarves on their heads, but their faces were uncovered; they stepped forward, bowing to the caliph and his companion.

"Leila and Zayda are the keepers of the baths," Abul said. "They understand the need for the tranquility that leads to true repose."

Sarita wasn't quite sure how to respond, since her bathing hitherto had had no such elements. It had also belatedly occurred to her that since one could not bathe fully clothed, she and Muley Abul Hassan were going to be naked again in each other's company. She remembered with uneasy clarity the unbidden arousal that had crept over her when she had been unclothed in front of him the previous evening, even before he had touched her. But there was a different atmosphere in this hall. Perhaps it came from the presence of the two women, for whom such nakedness was presumably all part of the working day. Zayda was already assisting Abul with his clothes in the most matter-of-fact fashion. If Sarita could cultivate the same attitude, or at least appear to do so, perhaps she would be able to keep unwelcome sensations at bay.

She became aware that Leila was standing waiting to help her undress. "I can manage, thank you," Sarita said, unfastening the girdle of her robe.

"Leila speaks no Spanish," Abul said, raising one foot so that his attendant could pull off his boot. "Let her do what she expects to do. You are here to learn the pleasure of the baths. Don't impose your own expectations and experiences on something that bears no relation to either."

Sarita had never come across people who spoke like Abul, with such assured wisdom on such abstract issues. She wondered what kind of life he had led, what training and education he had received that had given him this complexity and authority. Were all his people like this? Did they all have the time and the inclination for abstruse reflection?

Covertly she watched as the woman removed his tunic and britches. His physique was that of a warrior. There was nothing soft about this man for all that he spoke on occasion as if only the pleasures of the mind and senses were important.

Her robe slipped to the tiles at her feet while she was absorbed in these thoughts, and she found herself naked without conscious awareness. Her attendant caught up the mass of bright curls and pinned them into a knot on the top of Sarita's head, then smilingly gestured toward the sunken bath into which Abul was now stepping. They were to get in together, it seemed. But the space was quite large, and again she felt that there was something about the presence of the two women, not to mention Abul's insouciance, that made it all seem quite ordinary and natural.

Sarita stepped daintily into the hot perfumed water of the bath. She sank down on a bench cut into the marble side of the tank, stretching out her feet. Her toes touched Abul's, and she withdrew her feet with an impulsive jerk. He chuckled and chased her foot with his own, but his eyes were closed even while he was playing, and she sensed his relaxation. Insidiously, she felt a delicious lassitude creep up on her as the water lapped against her neck, and she let her head fall back against the edge of the bath. In the tempered light of the hall she felt as if she were looking up through water, seeing images wave, break apart, coalesce under the gently moving surface. She wondered if there were something in the air or maybe in the perfumed water that created this sense of inhabiting a world of images, rather than one of concrete reality. But then she had had that sensation several times since Abul had brought her to this place.

She became aware that her fellow bather was standing up. Slyly, she let her gaze from half-closed eyes run up his body. The inspection was a mistake: her nipples grew erect; prickles of excitement tightened her skin. She closed her eyes fully, but not before she had noticed to her chagrin that Abul's body had evinced no signs of arousal. Was it just the baths, or had he ceased to find her body desirable?

His voice broke into the seclusion she was trying to create behind her closed eyes. She felt his hand on her shoulder beneath the water. "Come," he was saying. "It is time to move on."

She opened her eyes and found herself looking up into his smiling face bending over hers. "Move on to what?"

"The next bath."

"Why isn't one enough?" Grumbling, she hauled herself out of the water and watched as Abul plunged into the second sunken bath. He drew in his breath on a sharp cry as he sank beneath the surface, then rose up with the same rapidity, leaping out, his teeth chattering. Zayda came forward with a thick towel and began rubbing his skin vigorously.

Puzzled, Sarita dipped a toe in the second bath and leaped backward with a shriek. "It's colder than a mountain lake!"

"Of course." Abul laughed at her. "It's to stimulate the blood."

"My blood has no need of stimulation," she said firmly. "I like the other bath."

"Oh, don't be such a coward." Still laughing, Abul moved away from the attendant's ministering hands and came toward Sarita. She backed away from him. "Come on," he said, coaxing. "It only takes a minute, and it feels wonderful when you get out."

She shook her head. "No, I am perfectly happy with the other—oh, no, Abul, you cannot!" She squealed as he reached for her, pulling her hard against the cold, fresh length of his body. "No—no, you cannot throw me in."

"Of course I won't," he said, picking her up nevertheless. "Such violence would not be consonant with the peace and harmony of the baths." He stepped with her to the edge. "However, I trust you realize what you are subjecting *me* to with a double immersion.'' But there was a chuckle in his voice as he stepped off the edge and plunged them both deep into the icy water.

Sarita couldn't scream, the cold took her breath away, and she clung to Abul's neck like a limpet, her body rigid in his arms as he resurfaced, shaking water off himself with all the vigor of a wet dog.

He set her on her feet where she stood hunched and shivering, her eyes glazed with shock. ''Don't fight it, Sarita,'' he instructed. ''Relax your body.'' When she looked blankly at him, still a rigid huddle, he took the towel from the waiting Leila and flung it around Sarita and began to dry her with a rough friction that set her skin atingle. Her eyes focused again, and she uncurled herself as the bitter cold gave way to the tingling warmth and a wonderful sense of energy and refreshment surged through her, replacing the earlier lassitude created by the hot water, and every bit as delicious.

''That's better,'' Abul said. ''Now tell me it wasn't worth it.'' He handed Sarita's towel back to Leila, and Zayda began swiftly to dry him again.

''It was brutal,'' Sarita declared. ''There was nothing peaceful or harmonious about it.''

''That's because you fought the sensation.'' He was speaking quite earnestly as he raised his arms for Zayda's toweling. ''The lack of serenity was within yourself.''

''You really do take this bathing seriously,'' she said wonderingly.

''Have you only just realized that?'' Abul shook his head in faint reproof. ''I thought I made that perfectly clear.''

''You did, but I still didn't understand. It's rather outside my realm of experience.'' She shrugged at this truth. ''My people don't do things just for the sake of them . . . or . . . or to create harmony with their minds and their bodies.''

''Ours is an ancient civilization,'' Abul said. ''We

have learned values that your world has not yet come to recognize."

"Perhaps we have different values," she ventured, for some reason stung by this implicit criticism.

Abul shook his head, a vestige of contempt curling his lip. "Not what we would call values."

"Well, we do not believe a man should be allowed to have as many wives as he wishes," she snapped. "We believe a man should be true to one woman as she should be true to him. That is a value."

Disconcertingly, Abul laughed. "That is not a value. That is a denial of the infinite variety of relationships possible between men and women. Variety does not exclude loyalty or commitment."

Sarita flushed. "Since we have finished this bath, I would like to return to the tower."

"Oh, but it is not finished, *cara*. On the contrary, we have barely started." He took her face between his hands. "I said there must be no disharmony. Have you forgotten?"

"But it did not come from me in the beginning," she retorted. "I did not criticize your people the way you criticized mine."

"It was no criticism, simply a statement of fact." His hands slipped to cup the curve of her shoulders. The surface skin of his palms was cold, yet she could feel the warmth of the blood pulsing beneath, just as she could feel it beneath her own cooled flesh. His body was very close to her, so close that if she breathed deeply, her lifting bosom would graze his chest. She wanted to step back, turn her head, do something—anything—but found she was rendered as immobile as Lot's wife.

"Cry truce," he said softly. "I will draw no more unfavorable comparisons."

"No more cold water, either?" It was not a bad attempt at a playful response under the circumstances, but her voice sounded slightly thick.

He shook his head and released her shoulders. "A

little more, but this time I promise you will welcome it. Follow me."

She followed him across the hall of immersion, through an archway, and then into a small enclosed room where the searing heat scorched her lungs and set the sweat flowing on her skin almost before she had stepped inside. "What is this?" She stared as Leila bent to feed the brazier in the corner of the room. Zayda laid fresh towels on marble slabs set within arched recesses at the sides. Both women then left the mist-wreathed chamber.

"Here we bathe in steam," he said, stretching out on his belly on one of the towel-covered slabs. "Lie down and keep very still."

Gingerly, she imitated him. It was hard to breathe, and a deep enervation seemed to reduce her to a mere formless, sinewless puddle of sweat. "Is this supposed to be pleasant?" she inquired breathlessly of her silent companion.

Abul turned his head indolently to regard her. "It is if you keep very still and don't talk. Let your body do its own work."

"But I can't breathe properly."

He sighed, stretched out a hand, and lifted a small handbell. "Go with Leila, then."

"But are you not coming too?" She sat up slowly as the attendant came in. Her head spun for a second.

"I am accustomed to it. My tolerance is much greater. Leila will bring you back if you wish it when she has cooled you off."

Sarita couldn't imagine wishing to return to this steamy inferno. She followed Leila into a chamber next door, and this time the icy water the attendant poured over her sweat-slick skin as she stood in a small sunken well felt astoundingly wonderful. She turned under the stream, offered her body for the slightly abrasive pads Leila used to rub her down, and purred with contentment. She was still twirling and purring for the patient Leila when Abul came through from the steam room.

She looked so like an utterly contented cat as she arched her spine and threw back her neck in the extremity of bliss that he was hard pressed to keep his laughter to himself. Amusement was only a part of his response, however, as he watched the gyrations of that lean, sinuous, exquisitely formed little body, and he welcomed Zayda's jugs of cold water with more enthusiasm than the natural progression of the baths might seem to warrant.

"You will grow more used to the heat with practice," he observed, turning his back on the entrancing sight of her.

Sarita was about to tell him that she wouldn't have the opportunity to become used to it, then remembered she was supposed to give the impression that she had accepted his edict and was no longer planning a precipitate departure. She mumbled vaguely.

Leila, having patted the surplus moisture from her skin, was gesturing invitingly toward an archway leading into another hall. Sarita followed and then stopped with a cry of delight.

The most entrancing music filled the hall, a gentle plucking of lute and lyre, the delicate purity of a flute. She couldn't at first see where it was coming from. There were four marble columns in the center of the hall, and perfectly matched arches built into the walls on all four sides. The walls were inlaid with tiles, penciled with lapis lazuli and gold leaf. Leila was indicating that she should lie upon a cushioned divan, but she hesitated, still searching for the source of the music.

"What is this place?" Her voice was not above a whisper. An ordinary pitch would have seemed sacrilege.

"The Hall of Repose." Abul spoke behind her. His voice was soft, though not a whisper.

"Where is the music coming from?"

"From the gallery. The musicians are up there." He pointed upward, and she saw the four galleries of the upper story.

There were people up there . . . men . . . and she was standing quite naked. Her arms flew to cover her breasts.

"There is no need. They are blind. The women of the seraglio use the baths frequently, and they must not be seen by any man but myself. But that is no reason why they should be deprived of music."

Her arms dropped and she gazed at him in horror. He looked puzzled for a minute, then gave a short laugh. "Foolish!" he said. "I did not say they were blinded. They are blind because they were born that way."

Sarita bit her lip, guilty as charged. For one dreadful moment she had thought these people capable of such a barbarism. She did not understand them or their ways, and with the inexcusable arrogance of ignorance, she had drawn an appalling conclusion.

"I am sorry," she whispered, staring at the tiles at her feet. "I don't know why I would think such a thing."

Abul tucked an errant curl back into the knot on top of her bent head, saying mildly, "You will learn. I understand that we are strange to you."

"But I am not strange to you." She knew that to be true. "My people are not strange to you."

"No," he agreed, "but then, I have traveled many places and done many things. I know much that you do not." He smiled down at her. She looked so crestfallen, the physical euphoria of a minute ago vanished. "Oh, dear, this is not achieving what I had hoped it would, Sarita. I can feel you jangling like an ill-hung bell. Let Leila ease you now." He pushed her gently toward the couch. "We must address such issues in a different environment."

Sarita was still too discomfited to respond and obediently lay on her front on the cushions, aware of Abul stretching beside her on the couch's twin. She watched as Leila held a small pan over a candle, shaking it gently. The strains of music floated down, and the air became filled with a delicate perfume. Her embarrassment faded as her body relaxed again.

Leila tipped the contents of the pan into the palm of her hand. Rubbing her palms together, she turned to Sarita's prone body and began to massage the warmed, perfumed oil into her spine. Sarita's eyes closed involuntarily, all tension now dissipated. Maybe there *was* some justification for treating the rituals of the baths as something almost sacrosanct. Maybe she could become accustomed . . .

"Allah!" Leila's soft-voiced exclamation was no less filled with horror for its lack of volume. She had come upon Sarita's feet.

Abul said something lazily in Arabic.

Tutting, Leila turned to a table on which reposed a variety of instruments and more oil.

"What were you saying?" Sarita opened one eye. "I did not understand."

"You will," Abul murmured.

She did the minute Leila, her composure seriously fractured, lifted her feet with a distressed murmur. Sarita felt something scraping against the leathern soles and with an indignant exclamation pulled her feet away. Why would these people not leave them the way they were? Surely they must understand that they served as shoes? But they didn't understand; she'd had ample opportunity to realize that.

"My feet are my own," she announced with great clarity. "I do not wish you to touch them. Would you translate that please, my lord caliph?"

"No," Abul said definitively. "It is uncivilized to mar your beauty in that hideous way. Besides, there is not the slightest need for it anymore."

Oh, but there is. Sarita bit her tongue but pulled her feet again free of the woman's grasp. She made as if to turn over and then subsided with a gasp as Abul, in one swift movement, swung himself off his couch and straddled her, sitting lightly on her bottom.

The feel of his flesh pressed with such an intimate weight against her own shocked her into rigid im-

mobility as she buried her face in the pillow. She felt
Leila resume work on her feet as if nothing out of the
ordinary was happening. But then perhaps the caliph
made a habit of sitting naked on naked women to
keep them still. In this place, when it came to the
caliph and women, anything seemed ordinary.

"Such a small creature is very easy to restrain."
Abul's laughing tones came from above as he moved
his fingers strongly into her neck and shoulders so
that, despite her shock, she could feel herself relaxing
again. "Are you going to lie still for Leila, or shall I
stay where I am?"

"Keep still," Sarita mumbled into the pillow.

"I didn't catch that," he said politely, bending
closer to her ear. "Speak a little louder."

"*I said I'll keep still*," she declared on a rushed
exhalation.

"Pity," Abul said, swinging off her. "I was enjoying
the feel of you."

Sarita slumped into the cushions. "You aren't playing fair."

"I never promised to play fair, only that I wouldn't
force you," he returned, sprawling again on his own
divan. "You know perfectly well that I intend to use
every opportunity for persuasion that I can create."
He turned his head sideways, regarding her with a
mischievous gleam. "And that, my obstinate guest,
includes sharing the long hours of the night."

Another night like the last? No, it wasn't to be
borne. "I shall refuse to come to you," she said with
a bravado she recognized as only form. "You cannot
compel me into your bed."

"You confuse *cannot* with *will not*," he said rather
thoughtfully. "In this place, I can compel anything,
but I don't see the need. I shall simply come to you."

And you won't find me, Sarita thought with the fierce
resolution that seemed all she had left with which to
combat the insidious persuasiveness of her present
situation.

Leila was drawing something down her back,

something with an edge to it. "What is she doing?" Sarita tried to crane over her shoulder.

"Pulling the dirt from your body," Abul said. "It comes away with the oil."

"I cannot possibly be dirty," Sarita exclaimed. "Not after all those baths."

Abul chuckled. "Ordinary water cannot purify in the same way. The steam releases the impurities; the oil and the strigil remove them."

How was it possible to be so amazingly ignorant about something as basic as cleanliness? Sarita wondered. Or perhaps she meant, how was it possible to be so amazingly fussy, to invest such a basic matter with so much science and importance? She could imagine how the men of her tribe would mock, would regard such nicety as effete, some sign of weakness. But there was nothing weak or effete about Muley Abul Hassan.

"Turn over," Abul said, his voice drowsy as he rolled onto his back. "Leila wants to do the rest of you."

Sarita complied, glancing sideways at her companion. His eyes were closed, his body perfectly at rest as Zayda applied oil and the strigil. How could he be so apparently unmoved by the proximity of her nakedness? He must still desire her; why else would he promise to carry his battle of persuasion to the next inexorable stage? It was a mortifying truth that she was not similarly unmoved by his body. Indeed, the urge to run her hand over the golden length of him, to feel the muscular swell beneath the skin, to linger in the concave well of his belly, to move her fingers downward . . .

She suppressed a soft moan as her nipples burned, her body shifting uneasily on the cushions, and closed her eyes tightly on an embarrassed prayer that Leila had noticed nothing. It occurred to her that she was responding exactly as Abul wished, that this was all part of a devious purpose. He knew from last night that she was far from impervious to him. In these

sensuous, perfumed halls devoted to the body's pleasure, where nakedness was so natural, how could one
help but be aroused, or at least abidingly aware of
one's body and its sensations? The artful persuasion
was all around her, she realized. It was not to be resumed; it had never ceased. Only in escape lay salvation . . .

Escape from what? What was salvation? She woke
in languor with these questions buzzing gently in her
head. Her eye fell on the deserted couch beside her,
and she was conscious of a deep disappointment.
"Where is the lord Abul?" She spoke without volition into the silence, forgetting that she had no verbal
means of communicating with the keepers of the
baths.

"He is with his son. He always spends this hour of
the day with him."

The soft voice was a woman's, one she had not
heard before. It came from behind her head. Sarita
sat up and turned sideways. The woman who stood
there was very beautiful: midnight-dark hair caught
up beneath a scarf of silver tissue; dark eyes delicately
outlined with kohl; skin the color of the golden bloom
on apricots; a tall, luscious body that made Sarita
think of an orchard in full harvest. "Who are you?"
But somehow she knew.

"The lady Aicha, sultana to the caliph." The
woman inclined her head slightly. "And how are you
called, Christian?"

"Sarita of the tribe of Raphael," Sarita said, for
some reason giving her full identity, as if she were
undergoing a formal interrogation. She looked around
for something to cover herself with, feeling suddenly
vulnerable in her nakedness in front of this woman
whose rich, bejeweled, flowing robes bespoke authority and considerable status.

"Ring the bell. Leila will come to you," the woman
said. "They left you to sleep."

Sarita saw the handbell on the table beside the divan. She rang it, filled with a sharp annoyance that

Abul should have left her alone, exposed in her sleep, for any within the Alhambra to come upon.

"How is it that you come to be here?" Aicha covertly examined the woman as she slipped off the divan. What could Abul see in her? She was tiny, unformed . . . no, ill-formed . . . with those breasts like small lemons and the barest flare to her hips. Childlike. But as Aicha watched, she realized that there was nothing childlike about the woman's body. It was perfectly mature, perfectly formed, perfectly proportioned. Her waist was minute, and Aicha could see the beginnings of the rolls of flesh at her own waist, the lumping of her hips, the incipient sag of her breasts. She felt heavy and cumbersome beside this small-boned, slender creature. Perhaps Abul had also noticed the signs of overindulgence. She must give up the cakes and the sherbets, Aicha resolved uneasily.

"I am your husband's prisoner," Sarita replied, seeing no point in prevarication. Besides, she hardly wanted to give the caliph's wife the impression that she was willingly engaged in a liaison with her husband. She turned with relief toward Leila, who came hurrying in with a robe over her arm.

"You are bought or captive?" The sultana seemed to find nothing strange in Sarita's reply.

"The latter, it would seem." She covered herself with the robe and felt instantly more comfortable.

"For what reason?"

Sarita shrugged. "Your husband's whim."

Aicha frowned. The woman sounded as if she resented her present position. But no woman could resent the caliph's favor, and she knew her husband well enough to know that he would not force himself upon a woman. At least, she thought she knew he wouldn't. But then, Aicha doubted he had ever met a woman unwilling to accept his favor and protection. The women of her own race would not consider they had such a choice, even if they were so blind as to be impervious to Abul's most potent charms. Could he have met such a woman in this diminutive creature with that unruly tangle of flaming hair and those dauntingly direct green eyes? Kadiga and Zulema had confirmed only that the woman had not returned to her tower until dawn, but Fatima had told Nafissa of Abul's dawn urgency. Incredible though it seemed, maybe here lay the explanation.

"You are unwilling to lie with my husband?"

Sarita heard the surprise behind the sultana's question. She had been about to respond with a vigorous affirmative, but the words wouldn't come. It was not as simple as that, was it? Not a simple matter of being unwilling to share bodies with Muley Abul Hassan. Because she knew that on the most primitive level, she was not unwilling . . . was desirous, even. Not that she was about to confess that to Abul's wife, even if, as seemed likely, the lady Aicha would not be disconcerted by such a confession. A woman who already shared her husband with at least four others would probably accept another without rancor. But there *was* an invincible reason why she was resisting Abul.

"Who would not be unwilling?" she said finally. "Scooped up off the road and brought without consent to some . . . some . . ." She gestured around her, feeling for words to describe this extraordinary place. "Some fantastical place; as if one had no other life, no family, no personal attachments, no past, no future but what was to be imposed upon one."

Aicha nodded her head slowly. "You are not of our people," she said. "Our women accept such impositions. The women of the tribe of Raphael do not?"

Sarita sucked in her bottom lip, considering. Men made the decisions in the tribe of Raphael, and it was a rare woman who would challenge those decisions and a rare man who would accept the challenge. But women were nevertheless essential to the network, to the organization. They had their place and their function, and no man would ever interfere in those spheres where women ruled supreme. Unlike this place, where she had the unmistakable impression that women had no sphere, no function except that directly dependent upon a man's whim and pleasure.

"Our women have some measure of power over their lives. But not sufficient, it is true."

Aicha spoke the thought as it came to her. "And you do not accept these limits."

Sarita shook her head. That was after all why she was in her present predicament. "No."

It was unlike Abul to make such a mistake, Aicha reflected. Or to persist in a mistake, she amended. And it would seem that he was persisting in this one. Why else would he have brought the girl to the baths after what must have been a most unsatisfactory night? The first stirrings of unease disturbed her previous pragmatic acceptance of this new woman in the Alhambra. Could she hold a deeper attraction for Abul than the merely physical? Therein would lie a threat to the sultana from another woman. And only therein.

"Perhaps I can talk to him," she said. "I have some influence with him and can perhaps persuade him to release you."

Sarita wondered whether she really wanted the sultana's intercession. But to refuse would be ungracious, and the woman was looking at her, smiling pleasantly, complicitly almost; but the smile didn't reach her eyes. A flicker of disquietude touched Sarita's mind, but she dismissed it. The sultana was only offering to help, had evinced no hostility, had shown only smiles and friendship. She understood the rules of this place as Sarita did not. It would be foolish to spurn her offer.

"Thank you," she said. "I would be most grateful for your help."

"I will walk with you back to the tower." Aicha turned to the doorway. "You must tell me about yourself. It's not often our seclusion is enlivened by a stranger from such a different world.''

Sarita didn't see the calculating glint in the sultana's eyes as she walked beside her out of the baths and into the brass-taloned glare of early afternoon.

Chapter 7

"You are not concentrating, Boabdil." Abul spoke mildly, disguising his exasperation as the boy made the same mistake in the same calculation for the third time. The boy's tutor pulled nervously on his long beard and tried again to explain the mathematical principle.

Boabdil stared sullenly at the slate in front of him. He didn't understand what Ahmed Eben was telling him, and he didn't particularly want to understand. He would be caliph one day, and then none of this would matter. His father didn't spend his days on mathematical calculations, or examining globes, or studying the Koran, so what was the point of having learned about all those things in the first place? The caliph went to war with his curved scimitar, and he ruled the kingdom of Granada from the Hall of the Ambassadors, and everyone did what he said, even the vizier.

He looked from beneath his eyelashes to the figure sitting with such contained stillness opposite him. His father was looking grave, but he always did these days. Boabdil hated this hour of the day. It was always a relief when the caliph was gone from the Alhambra on some business and Boabdil was spared the daily progress examination. He wasn't good at his lessons, even when he tried, and he knew this displeased his father. His mother understood, though. She had always told him not to worry about doing those things that didn't come easily to him, because when he was a grown man and caliph, there would be other people to do the things he didn't want to do or wasn't good at doing. And she'd always be there, even when he was caliph, to make sure things happened the way they were supposed to happen. When he'd lived with his mother and the other children in the women's apartments, everything had been easy and comfortable. The children had always done what he'd told them because he was the caliph's first son, and their tutors had never made him work at something he didn't like. And when they wanted to go and play in the gardens or the stables instead of doing lessons, he had only to ask his mother.

Now, every minute of his day was set aside for some task or activity. There were only men around him, and he missed the perfumed, rustling, pillowy warmth of the seraglio. He missed cuddling in his mother's arms while she fed him stuffed dates and sugared almonds and preserved oranges. Tears welled suddenly behind his eyes, and he sniffed. His father would be angry if he cried and would tell him he wasn't a baby any longer. His mother always wiped his tears and kissed him. A tear rolled down the side of his nose. Hastily, he wiped it away, looking apprehensively at his father.

Abul saw the tear, but he was more concerned by his son's clearly apprehensive look. There was no reason for the boy to be afraid of him, but he did seem to be. Abul tried to control his impatience with what sometimes seemed the child's deliberate stupidity, his babyishness, and the whining complaints when things didn't go the way Boabdil wanted them to. He didn't always succeed and was sometimes betrayed into an irritated snap, but he had never said or done anything to justify his son's apparent fear of him.

Except that he had removed him from his mother.

That in itself was perfectly normal and should have caused no difficulties. The boy was now too old to live in the seraglio, and it was time he learned to live

as the men of the Alhambra lived. But Abul knew that
the bond between Aicha and her son was of a peculiar
nature. Its intensity disturbed him, but he also knew
that he had made no attempt to lessen it before it was
too late. He had let matters in the seraglio go their
own way, casually assuming that when the time came
to remove Boabdil, he would be able to correct any
damage Aicha's excessive indulgence would have
caused. But it wasn't as easy as that. The maternal
influence hadn't lessened, even though Abul had re-
stricted the time the two could spend together. And
he knew that Boabdil hated him for those restrictions,
just as he feared him, because he saw only unkind-
ness where in fact there was the deepest concern and
the father's caring need to prepare his son for the
world that awaited him.

On impulse, he leaned over and lightly brushed the
tear from the boy's face. "Don't weep, Boabdil. It's
too lovely a day for mathematics. You shall have the
rest of the afternoon free."

The boy's face lit up, instantly reassuring Abul,
who began to think he had been fanciful, seeing hostility and fear in those now shining dark eyes. Boabdil
mumbled his gratitude and leaped for the door.

His father called him back. "Where are you going?"

"To my mother."

Regretfully, Abul shook his head. "No, not until
sundown, Boabdil; you know that."

The boy's eyes were turned slowly upon him, and
they held angry frustration and that same fear and
animosity. Abul tried to smile, as if he didn't see the
look. He spoke invitingly. "Let us spend the afternoon together. Would you like to go hawking? Or
ride in the mountains? Perhaps fishing?"

Boabdil shook his head and sat down again at the
table, idly scribbling with his stylus on the waxed
slate.

Abul felt his own anger rise with his hurt at his
son's rejection. Such an unexpected offer from his
own father used to throw him into transports of dizzy

delight, and he remembered each and every one of those father/son excursions, undertaken in the spirit of truancy with such wicked relish. Was it too late to build such a relationship with Boabdil? Even as he asked himself the question, he knew with a leaden heart that it was. He stood up abruptly.

"Very well, if you don't wish to have a holiday, then I can only commend your studiousness. I will leave you to your lessons. You would do well to apply yourself to those calculations with Ahmed this afternoon. I will not expect you to repeat your errors tomorrow." He left the room.

Boabdil stared through his tears at the slate and the impossible figures. His mother had told him that his father was being cruel when he separated her from her child. She'd told him that his father was a harsh man who mustn't be angered or he might become even more cruel. The caliph had been only a peripheral figure in his life until Boabdil had been taken from the seraglio and installed in his own apartments with tutors and attendants. Then his father had become a very real presence. Everything that happened to him happened at his father's ordering. His father was there every day, examining him, talking with his caretakers, making decisions about him. Decisions that made his life tedious and uncomfortable and kept him from his mother . . . Maybe his father would go off on one of his journeys and not come back.

A prickle of guilt ran up the back of his neck at the wickedness of the thought. But if his father did go away, then he, Boabdil, would be caliph, and there'd be no one to say he could spend only two hours a day with his mother.

Ahmed Eben was talking about the figures on his slate again, and with a sniff Boabdil tried to concentrate. He mustn't get it wrong tomorrow. He'd already angered his father.

Abul stalked through the early afternoon peace of the palace, his customary serenity, the slight air of amusement with which he viewed his domestic world, destroyed by that encounter with his son. He was hurt, but he was also angry, and his anger was with Aicha. It seemed she undermined him at every turn, filling Boabdil's head with fears and mistrust whenever they were together. The only way to stop her would be to remove the boy altogether from his mother's sphere, and Abul shrank from imposing such a decisive separation. It certainly wouldn't improve his relations with his son. But why would Aicha encourage the boy to regard his father with such fear and animosity? Surely they must both realize that no one would benefit—not Aicha, nor Boabdil, nor Abul—from such a mangled relationship. Or was it simply Aicha's twisted need for power? Through her son, she would have a power that transcended the seraglio; a power that could eventually go further than managing to engineer for her own reasons the discrediting of an important councillor.

It was a most unpleasant train of thought, leading to an even more unpleasant conclusion. If Aicha was an enemy in his camp, and could be so proved, then she would have to be removed. It boded ill for harmony both within the Alhambra and without, where her father, the powerful emir of the Mocarabes, crouched, ever watchful over his daughter's and thus his family's interests.

It was in no great good humor that Abul went into the Mexuar. It was one of the two days of the week when he, or in his absence his cadi, administered public justice in this hall, and he was aware that his present lack of equilibrium would do no good service to his clarity of thought and therefore to those he judged. He walked through the hall and into the small mosque at the rear. The place of private prayer looked over the lush river valley, the prayer niche pointing to the east. Abul stood in contemplation of the inscription above the niche: *Be not among the negligent. Come and pray.*

He allowed the peace of the place to enter his soul, the sense of wholeness to return to him, the sense of being at one with his surroundings and with his God. He must find a way of giving this to Boabdil. Without this sense of certainty at one's core, a man could achieve nothing. He owed his son one thing: the ability to face the world as a whole man, not a disparate and dismayed tangle of emotions and needs. Without that certainty of completion, a man had no authority, no power, none of the sense of himself that ensured he could rule justly, his wisdom trusted by those whom he ruled.

He could hear the movements from the hall behind him, indicating the arrival of the council, the cadi, the plaintiffs, and the defendants for the afternoon's session. Renewed and at peace, Muley Abul Hassan returned to the work of his kingdom.

Sarita and the sultana reached the tower after a slow and pleasant stroll. Sarita's unease dissipated under the older woman's charm and friendliness. She found herself telling Aicha something of life in the tribe, but she stopped short of the events that had brought her to the Alhambra. Sandro was still too private a grief to be discussed in this easy female fashion, but she opened under the friendly questioning, the obvious interest, the aura of female companionship to which she was so accustomed.

She was aware of a quietness in the palace and assumed it was siesta. The dawn housekeeping was long over, the gardens tended, the day's main business finished until the cool of the evening when things would start up again. From the alcazaba came the regular sounding of the bells from the watchtowers, but it was a sound signifying ordinary routine, informing the inhabitants that all was well, that they could take their ease through the heat of the afternoon without worry.

"Do you not keep siesta?" They had reached the wicket gate of Sarita's tower garden.

Aicha smiled. "But of course. Until sundown, when my son is returned to me."

"Returned to you from where?" Sarita looked her puzzlement.

"Why, from his father." Aicha shrugged with apparent carelessness, but Sarita sensed the edge beneath the surface. "His father has taken him from me. And now I may be with him for but two hours a day."

"But that's dreadful!" exclaimed Sarita. "Why would he take a child from his mother?"

"He wishes the child to show allegiance only to him," Aicha told her. "He is jealous of any influence I may have."

Sarita frowned, wondering why she felt something was not quite right. Aicha was smiling bravely, telling her that that was the way with men—they didn't fully understand the depth of a mother's love for her child, the wrenching pain of a separation for both mother and child. Abul saw only the need to educate his son as his heir, but the child was so young, so tender, so vulnerable. Aicha was so afraid that his father was expecting so much more of him than could reasonably be expected of such a baby. She was so afraid that the methods Abul used were harsh . . .

And then she stopped. "But I mustn't trouble you with my private concerns, Sarita. They are between my husband and myself."

"Yes," Sarita said slowly. "Yes, I think they are." She couldn't reconcile the Abul she knew, the gently humorous, quietly wise, although compellingly persuasive man, with a man who would mistreat a child. Yet she had felt his power, his absolute assumptions about who and what he was, about the authority he held and the right he had to use it. The first time she had met him, she had recognized him as a man of Tariq's stamp, but she had sensed a great difference between the two men. She knew what that difference was now. It was the gentleness in Abul, the sense that his authority and power were intrinsic and did not have to be fought for. They would never leave him. Such a man surely would not exercise that power and authority indiscriminately over a child.

She turned to Aicha, her hand outstretched in farewell. "Thank you for bearing me company, lady."

Aicha heard the dismissal in the polite tones, and she heard the questioning of her statements. Had she made a mistake? She had thought if the woman was not content to be in her husband's power, she would make an easy ally with potentially useful access to Abul's thoughts and plans. A slight distortion of a truth that would be guaranteed to enrage any woman with a heart worthy of womankind should draw her into Aicha's net. But the woman sounded as if she didn't want to hear any more, almost that she wasn't sure that she believed what she had heard.

Aicha swallowed the acid surge of resentment. She still wanted this woman as an ally. She wasn't sure quite why, but only that it might be potentially useful. And if Abul desired her, and she remained unwilling, then she could be very useful. So she smiled. "Thank you for listening to me. I wouldn't wish you to think ill of my husband. He has only done what all men do in his position when their heirs reach a certain age, but . . ." She touched a finger to her eyes. "But he has not properly understood the closeness of my relationship with Boabdil. He was a sickly child, you see."

"I see," Sarita said gravely. She knew how close the women of her tribe grew to their children, but the children were never removed from their mothers' sphere of influence. Sons simply gravitated to the men as they grew older and their interests and pursuits took them in that direction. Boabdil's separation did sound forced, even if Aicha was exaggerating.

"I will talk to the lord Abul about you, if you still wish it," Aicha was saying. "Do you wish to return to your tribe?"

"No," Sarita said frankly. "Your husband has said he will not stand in my way if that is what I wish, but

he will not permit me to leave his protection unless I
return to my people."

Aicha felt the ground shift beneath her feet. So her
husband had offered to return the woman, but had
presented her with an unacceptable alternative.
Something very much out of the ordinary was going
on here, and she would need time to dig and delve
and come upon the truth.

"I go to keep siesta," she said, still smiling. "We
will meet again soon."

"Yes, indeed. I bid you farewell." Sarita stood and
watched the woman turn the corner of the cypress
path before she went into the cool, fountain-soothed
peace of her tower.

Her nap in the Hall of Repose had left her with no
desire to sleep through the afternoon. Zulema and
Kadiga were presumably keeping siesta themselves,
since the tower was deserted. Sarita paced restlessly,
moving from the court to the upper gallery. The windows at the rear looked out over the ravine to the
Generalife and the mountain peaks behind; at the
front they faced within the compound, looking across
the trellised garden and over to the main buildings
and gardens of the palace.

She stood at a front window, staring across the garden, absently shaking out her orange dress, noting
that it was now quite dry. A sleepy air lay over the
Alhambra, as sleepy as the atmosphere had been in
the encampment yesterday afternoon, when she had
slipped out to keep her tryst with Sandro. Sorrow
stabbed, a shank of iron in her heart. But now she
felt also a sense of finality. Sandro was dead. That
whole period of her life was over. She must take the
experiences within herself, part of the river of experience, and move on down that river, enriched by the
loves and hatreds of the past, by the good and the
bad.

And then it came to her. What was to stop her
from simply walking out of this place in the quiet of
afternoon? There were no locks on her doors, no

guards, no watchdogs. She had her bundle, her own clothes. No one had taken any notice of her when she had walked around before; why would they this time? They had seen her with the caliph and with his sultana, clearly on friendly, easy terms, clearly no prisoner.

It was such a simple thought, brilliant in its simplicity. Sarita stripped off the caftan and with a sigh of relief put on her shift and dress, feeling instantly returned to herself. Fortunately the overly sensitive people of this place hadn't had time to do too much damage to her feet, but if she stayed around much longer, she'd have soles like butter. She kicked off the detestable slippers with their silly toes and rolled her feet around, feeling the shape of the ground, regaining her true sense of balance.

She found her bundle where Yusuf had placed it the previous evening. Everything was there. Her hair was still pinned on top of her head from the baths. She let it down and pulled a comb roughly through the unruly curls. It was fairly perfunctory grooming since the springy mass resisted all ordinary attempts at tidying, but it made her feel better. Then, after one last look around the exquisitely gilded cage, she went out into the hot afternoon.

Where was Abul? The question was an unwelcome one. She had been doing her best to put all thoughts of her captor out of mind. For some reason, it didn't feel right to walk away without a word of farewell, yet she knew such niceties were absurd. If she paused to say farewell, she would have no reason for the salutation: she wouldn't be going anywhere. On such a resolute determination, she left the garden and began to walk toward the palace, hoping she would remember the way through the maze of courts to the great outer court and that strange gate with its open hand and splayed fingers. She'd been on horseback when she'd made the reverse journey, and the light had been dimmer, softer. Everything looked quite different, somnolent under the sun's glare, but there was bound to be some indication as to the way out of this fairyland.

There were few people about, and those there were barely glanced in her direction, until she found herself in a court full of soldiers in pronged round helmets like steel skullcaps. The alcazaba rose behind her, and Sarita realized that the fortress of the Alhambra obviously didn't keep siesta. Here she was noticed. The men stared at the slight, bareheaded figure in the bright orange dress, and some of them looked away. Others spat on the ground with a gesture of disgust. Sarita began to feel very uncomfortable. Were women not permitted in this part of the palace? Was it because she was different from their own women . . . because she was unveiled?

Whatever it was, her discomfort increased with each step she took, and she had to fight the urge to run across the court to the horseshoe gates she could now see standing open at the rear. She felt like some wanton, brazenly exposing herself in an exclusively male setting. Blushing, she walked steadily, head lowered, through the armored throng.

She had reached the gate when it happened. Suddenly, her feet left the ground and she was crushed against a massive chest encased in a leather jerkin. A stream of Arabic, violently imperative, competed with her terrified screams. Blindly, Sarita struggled, but she was like a fly in the hand of a giant . . . and the giant had turned with her and was carrying her back across the court, through the now grinning soldiers. She kicked out, trying to find purchase with her bare toes against his shins, pushing with her hands against his chest. The man gave out a short, sharp exclamation, and Sarita felt herself being moved, as if she were a doll, lifted and slung around his neck. He gripped her ankles with one hand at his shoulder and her wrists with his other, so that she dangled limply like a hunter's kill. There was nothing she could do in this position to change anything. She had no power of movement. Her head was hanging against his chest, bumping with each step, and she could hear her own heart thudding in her ears. She opened her mouth on another scream of protest, but the man carrying her like so much dead meat didn't falter in his purposeful stride as he bore her back through the courts and colonnades.

He was clearly in no doubt as to his destination. The thought calmed her, stilling the violent thudding of her heart. She was not being carried off to provide sport for a garrison of hungrily lusting Moorish soldiers, but back into the palace. As her fear died, a ferocious rage took its place, blinding her mind to all clear thought.

They were crossing a small courtyard where robed men, either turbaned or with silk scarves over their tarbooshes, stood in groups. Sarita had the feeling they were in some kind of antechamber. Her anger superseded even the dreadful embarrassment she felt as the men all stared at the soldier and his burden. Then he had elbowed his way through half-open double doors, and they were in a hall filled with people.

Abul did not at first notice the interruption. He was concentrating on the arguments of a citizen of Granada who was vociferously defending himself against his neighbor's accusation that he had sullied the water cistern with the refuse from his tanning yard.

A buzz in the generally attentive silence of the Mexuar brought Abul's head around from the two principals. A member of his garrison walked to the center of the hall, between the four marble pillars that supported the cupola. Abul took in the man's burden and wondered distantly why he was surprised. Of course, he didn't expect anyone to disobey him, because no one ever did. It hadn't occurred to him that the Christian girl would simply ignore his edict. But he should have recognized the possibility, from what he knew of her already.

The soldier unslung Sarita, dumping her unceremoniously on the marble floor at his feet. She was on

her own feet without thought. Her hand slashed
through the air, smashing against his cheekbone with
a resounding crack as she brought one bare foot up
in a vigorous kick against his shins. There was, it
seemed, a collective indrawing of breath, and then
the soldier moved.

Sarita's head was caught in the crook of his elbow.
His eyes, black and fierce, stared with implacable fury
into her own. At her throat was the curved blade of
his scimitar. She was staring her own death in the
face. The blade pricked her throat, and black dots
danced in front of her eyes; her chest tightened and
she struggled for breath.

Then the caliph's voice rang out in that breathless
instant of silence. It was a harsh command. She saw
the soldier's eyes shift even as his arm gripped her
neck with a convulsive jerk. Then the command was
repeated, a fraction higher, a fraction louder. The soldier's eyes shifted again, and his grip loosened. The
knife point moved, and she was dropped to the floor.
This time she made no attempt to get up. Her heart
was beating so hard she thought she was going to be
sick, and her body was bathed in the sweat of pure
terror. The marble was cool beneath her cheek, and
she struggled to keep the whimpers in her throat from
bursting from her lips.

Abul was still speaking. She could hear his voice in
the mist-wreathed air over her head as she pressed
herself to the cool marble. She could make no sense
of the words, but his tone remained harsh and commanding. He was giving a string of orders, it seemed.
But why would he say nothing to her? Why would
he not come and raise her from the floor? Touch her
cheek in the way he did? Smile at her with that gentle
amusement . . .

What was she doing, thinking like that? What was
she doing, lying here like a broken reed? Sarita lifted
her head . . . She got no further. The soldier bent
over her, scooped her off the floor, and slung her

across his shoulders again. Turning, he walked out of the hall.

Sarita knew now she was not going to be harmed. Abul had spoken, had prevented the soldier from reacting according to instinct, had reminded him of his duty and obeisance. But Abul had done nothing to reduce the ignominy of her present position. In fact, he had probably ordered its continuance. Nevertheless, she had learned her lesson well and lay limp and quiescent across the soldier's back as he strode through the palace, turned onto the cypress path, and marched through the wicket gate of her own tower garden. At the door of the tower, he set her on her feet and pushed her within, still treating her as if she were inanimate, Sarita recognized vaguely. The door snapped shut behind her, and she heard a new sound—that of a key turning in the lock.

Now she really was a prisoner. Or was it simply that her prisoner status had been made manifest? Either way, it made no difference to the present situation.

Her legs were trembling, her knees buttery. She sat down abruptly on an ottoman beside the fountain. After such a manhandling, she felt bruised, battered, as if she'd been viciously beaten, yet she doubted there were any marks on her skin. The bruises were to her pride and sense of personal integrity. For the moment, she was defeated.

Chapter 8

No one approached the tower as the afternoon drew to its close. Sarita sat huddled over her knees for a long time, seeing the soldier's eyes, her death contained within their dark depths, feeling again the knife point pricking her throat. But eventually her spine ceased its shuddering and her customary equilibrium reasserted itself. She hadn't had her throat cut. Abul had prevented that. But he'd done nothing else to improve her condition. Quite the opposite.

Sarita went up to the gallery. The light was fading fast beyond the windows, the first star a faint point in the darkening sky. She became aware for the first time of hunger. She hadn't eaten since that morning, and then only a piece of buttered flat bread and a cup of jasmine tea. There were no apricots left in the bowl; in fact, there was nothing edible in the entire tower. Water aplenty from the fountain, but the staff of life was dismayingly absent. And where were Kadiga and Zulema? For supposed attendants, they were being remarkably negligent.

It grew darker. She knew there were oil lamps in the tower; they'd been lit, the scent of the perfumed oil filling the air, last night when she'd bathed and eaten lamb pastries. Her mouth watered. She set out on an exploration in search of flint and tinder, and came up empty-handed. Her stomach complained loudly. It grew yet darker. The stars were bright now

121

against the night sky. She could see the glitter on the snowcapped peaks of the Sierra Nevada. The air had cooled, and from the front windows of the gallery the deafening cacophony of cicadas filled her ears, and the rich scents of the garden rose heady and luxuriant as she leaned out. But a grumbling belly couldn't be satisfied with the fragrance of mimosa and oleander and roses.

Craning out of the window, Sarita could see the flickering lights of the palace. She could almost smell the suppers being eaten in the well-lit courts and galleries, could hear the musicians with lute and lyre and flute entertaining the diners.

This was ridiculous. She leaned farther out of the window, trying to gauge if there were footholds in the outside wall. But the stone was as smooth as glass. Anyway, what good would it do her? A simple walk to freedom through the palace was impossible. If she'd learned anything this afternoon, she'd learned that.

She retreated to the moon-washed gallery. The rear windows offered only the steep fall to the ravine, a fall into now pitchy black. She was hungrier than she could ever remember being. If she could find some light, it would improve matters. But a renewed search for a tinderbox came up as empty as the last. The court was darker than the gallery, the starlight from the upstairs windows shining less effectively among the columns below.

Bed seemed the only sensible option. The only possible option to pacing hungry and increasingly exasperated around her dark prison. But she wasn't tired. She was hungry. She wanted a cup of wine. And she wanted to do battle. More than anything, Sarita wanted to do battle with Muley Abul Hassan.

Flinging herself down on the cushioned, silk-hung divan in the gallery, she let her mind loose on all the offenses committed by the caliph. They were legion, beginning of course from the moment of her abduction. And they were all exacerbated by the insidious persuasion. Not that persuasion seemed his present tactic. Imprisonment and starvation were not the tactics of the gentle persuader. Apparently she had met the other side of the caliph of Granada: the authoritarian side he had told her existed, but that he felt no need to bring into play. Clearly, he now felt that need.

When she heard the door open downstairs, she didn't move. It seemed to have come after such a lengthy period that it no longer mattered. She lay still on the divan, hearing the footsteps on the stairs. She recognized the footsteps. Muley Abul Hassan had entered her darkened prison. She lay still, waiting.

"Why do you have no light?" He spoke from the head of the staircase, his voice as calm and unruffled as if this afternoon hadn't happened.

"There in no tinderbox." She remained on the divan, staring up at the high ceiling.

"Did you look in the cedar chest below?"

Sarita let her silence provide the negative, and he turned and went back to the court. Steel and flint scraped in the quiet, and a soft glow rose to the gallery, offering faint illumination.

"Come down, Sarita. There are some things we have to talk about." His voice from below was still unruffled, but Sarita fancied it had a rather forceful undertow. She turned onto her side with a thump.

There was a minute or two of silence while she waited with a tingle of curiosity to see what he would do next.

"Sarita, do not put me to the trouble of fetching you."

She reassessed the forcefulness beneath the calm tone. She had every intention of talking with him at some length and with some force of her own, having first made a silent statement of her annoyance. However, if noncooperation was going to invite further manhandling, it was not a viable option. She wanted nothing that would increase her present disadvantages.

Sliding off the bed, she went to the stairs and made

her way down to the now well-lit court. Abul was leaning against one of the pillars, his arms folded. He was wearing the britches, tunic, and leather boots of his working day, a sheathed knife in the broad belt at his hip.

"I am hungry," Sarita announced without preamble as she stepped into the court. It was intended as an accusation, but Abul failed to respond accordingly.

"Good," he said. "That was my intention. Contemplating one's foolishness on an empty belly tends to be salutary."

Sarita's eyes narrowed as her temper rose. "Oh," she said. "So it's foolish, is it, to wish to escape imprisonment? I consider it to be a perfectly reasonable aim."

"It was foolish to imagine you could leave here without my permission," Abul responded. "However, I wasn't referring to that piece of idiocy."

"Now, you just listen to me, my lord caliph." Her voice shook with anger. "I have been hauled around like a sack of flour by some savage. I very nearly had my throat cut. I have been starved and imprisoned in the dark for hours, and I have had as much as I can tolerate. I will not stand here listening to your pontificating on the subject of foolishness . . . or on any other subject, for that matter." She spun on her heel, intending to go back up to the gallery, where she could regain her composure in solitude. But Abul moved swiftly away from the pillar, catching her arm.

"No, you *will* listen to me, Sarita. For your own safety."

"No! Let go of me!" Her anger now burst its banks, and she twisted violently in his hold, beside herself with rage and a despairing frustration at her own powerlessness to alter anything, either the fact or the terms of her present situation. Abul hung on to her, and she whirled suddenly toward him, bringing her knee up in a vicious jab to his groin.

Either he was expecting it, or his reflexes were remarkably swift, for he swung his body sideways, catching her knee in a jarring thud against his thigh.

"*Fiera!*" There was anger now in his voice, and his black eyes flared. "Have you learned nothing this afternoon?"

"Oh, yes, I've learned the true nature of this fairyland of yours." She bent to rub her knee, bruised against the muscled hardness of his thigh. Tears filled her eyes, but she didn't know whether they were of pain or rage. "It's all beauty on the surface and sheer barbarism beneath. You can prate all you wish about the true harmony of the body and mind, and the importance of repose, and the superior values of your culture, but you're all savages beneath . . . even if you are very clean," she muttered sotto voce.

Abul's anger died as swiftly as it had arisen, to be replaced with a reluctant amusement. He rubbed his thigh ruefully, trying not to think how he'd be feeling if her knee had met its intended target with such force. "Are you telling me that you, a mere and rather small woman, could have attacked with impunity a man of your tribe the way you attacked my soldier this afternoon?"

Sarita hesitated. Her rage seemed to have dissipated in the aftermath of that tussle. "Not with impunity," she said finally. "No . . . but I wouldn't have had my throat cut," she added, glaring at him. "And I wouldn't have been carted around like a dead deer, either."

"As far as the men here are concerned, Sarita, you are first a woman and second an unbeliever. Women do as they're told and keep to their own place, and for a man who believes in the One God, the fact that you are also an unbeliever renders you basically worthless and certainly not warranting consideration, most particularly not when you attack a man and a believer. If you were a woman of our people, you would know how to behave and would not put yourself in danger of incurring a man's wrath."

"I'm not to resent being carted around like a dead

deer, then?'' She began to pace the court, rubbing her crossed forearms as if she were cold.

"No, first because you're a woman, and second because you were defying my ruling," he said, as if he were reiterating some axiom. "My rule is absolute in this kingdom, Sarita. All who travel through it or do business here do so under my writ. For your own safety, you must understand these things. I may not always be there to protect you."

"Oh, yes, and shutting me up in the dark with no food for hours is how you protect me? Forgive me for not expressing my gratitude for that protection earlier. I expect it was because I didn't fully understand that I needed to be protected by my abductor from the consequences of his abduction."

"How eloquent you are," Abul murmured. "Hunger must sharpen your wits as well as your tongue."

Sarita picked up a cushion and hurled it at him. He ducked, laughing, and she followed with a rain of cushions, grabbing them at random from the ottomans and divans scattered around the court. Abul dodged them, still laughing, until her hand fell upon something more serious. A small onyx box curved through the air, sailed past his ear, and crashed to the marble floor.

Abul stood still, the laughter fading from his eyes. "This ceases to be amusing," he said.

"I never believed it was," she said coldly, although a little flutter of apprehension made its appearance in the pit of her stomach. "The humor was all on your side. Just as the offenses are all on your side."

He shook his head. "No. You chose to remain here rather than return to your people. You are not held against your will. And it is most definitely discourteous for a guest to throw dangerous objects at her host." He began to walk toward her.

Sarita began to walk backward. "That is a spurious argument, and you know it. I don't wish for either of those alternatives. I will go back into Castile. At least

there I'll be treated like a Christian woman and not
. . . not . . .''

"Like a dead deer," he supplied, coming closer.
"Believe it or not, *hija mía*, but your safety and well-being have become amazingly important to me in the
last day. I am not letting you loose, not just for myself, although I won't deny that's a major imperative,
but for your own safety."

"*I* will take responsibility for my safety," she cried,
backing away, not sure that she liked the look in his
eye, for all that he sounded quite patient and equable.

"Not under my writ," he said. "Are we going to
continue this curious mode of progression indefinitely? Or are you going to stand still?"

"Stand still for what?" She had reached the staircase.

"For whatever penalty the caliph rules as appropriate for throwing dangerous objects at him. We'll
forget that earlier attempt to cause me considerable
impairment. I'll excuse that and the cushions on the
grounds of aggravation, but not the box."

Sarita turned and fled up the stairs. Abul followed
her without increasing his speed, yet he seemed to
arrive in the gallery with dismaying rapidity. She
danced backward, leaping over an ottoman, relaxing
as she realized that her escape route was always clear
in this circular space. Abul kept coming. And again
he was moving fast, although he didn't seem to be.
It occurred to Sarita that it was probably because his
legs were so long and he could cover a considerable
distance in a few strides, whereas she had to keep
running to maintain the same pace. A silken rug
slipped beneath her feet and she tripped, grabbing
wildly at the balcony rail. Imperceptibly, Abul slowed,
giving her time to right herself, and she realized that
it was all a game. Or at least she thought it was. Her
pursuer still looked convincingly stern. She scampered around the far corner of the gallery, aware that
her breath was coming fast, although she was not out

of breath from running. She stood still, watching him, her eyes shining.

Abul made a sudden lunge for her and she shrieked, hurling herself around the other side of the gallery toward the stairs. What happened next occurred so fast she couldn't at first believe it. Abul reversed himself in midair, it appeared, and arrived facing her at the staircase as she reached it.

She made to retreat, but he tapped her shoulder lightly. "Caught you," he said.

She shrugged, nibbled her bottom lip, and smiled a little nervously. "So it would seem."

He stood looking down at her for what felt like an eternity. But Sarita couldn't see what he could see: her hair tossed around her face, her cheeks slightly flushed, her eyes a-sparkle, her lips parted. Abul was lost anew. Ever since he had first seen her, he had felt this insuperable tug, as if she were some lodestone for all the energies, the urges, the love he had within him that had not yet found an object. She didn't feel that for him, he knew. But he also had the absolute conviction, the *trust*, that what he felt for her would by definition have to be returned eventually. It was too powerful an emotion, too sharing an emotion, to fail to be reciprocated.

And he knew she was stirred by him. She was stirred now; he could feel the excitement radiating from her skin almost, could see the deep currents of arousal in the great green pools of her eyes. He had only two strings to his bow: the knowledge that he could create that unbidden arousal, and the power to keep her with him until she yielded to the yearning of her body. He believed she would not do that until mind and body were in accord, when her heart had healed, when she accepted how she felt and the rightness of it. Until then, he could only continue his gentle persuasion.

"I was right," he said. "You do find a tussle adds sauce to the loving."

Sarita felt the blush warming her cheeks as his

words struck an undeniable chord, but she came back strongly. ''I don't know where you see the loving. I'm aware of nothing but coercion, anger, and hunger!''

''Oh, yes, anger,'' he said thoughtfully. ''I was forgetting what brought us to this pretty pass. You look so desirable I forgot about the box for the moment.''

The time for running was clearly over, so she stood her ground, meeting his eye with her usual unspoken challenge.

Abul caught her face between his hands, letting his fingers run through the cloud of curls springing off her forehead. A slightly quizzical smile quirked his lips, and she knew what he was going to do, just as she knew she wanted him to do it.

He had the most beautiful mouth, she thought the instant before he covered her mouth with his and coherent thought ceased to be possible.

It was a hard, assertive kiss, far from the gentle assaults she had come to expect, and it set up a deep, responsive throb in her belly. Hungrily, she opened her lips for his probing tongue. He raided her mouth, plundered, held her breathlessly in thrall to the invasion, then withdrew, looking down at her, his hands still gripping her face, a warm, firm clasp that began to feel as if it were an extension of her skin.

''Sufficient punishment?'' he asked softly, running a thumb over her kiss-reddened, parted lips. Her skin was flushed, her eyes unfocused. ''Perhaps not,'' he said when she made no response to his teasing question. ''After all, it was only your poor aim that saved me from a fractured skull.'' He brought his mouth to hers again.

Sarita felt like a boat slipping its anchor. She seemed to be losing touch with the solid world, where she knew who and what she was and what she wanted and the values and beliefs that lay behind those wants; now she was cast adrift on a chaotic sea of feelings in which her mind and spirit were as much involved as her body. She didn't want this, yet she did. She didn't believe it was right, yet she couldn't believe something this powerful was wrong.

His touch moved from her face to her breast, and she moaned softly against his mouth, her lower body shifting closer to him of its own volition, so that she could feel the heat of him through the thin orange dress, could feel the hardness as his body rose in its own wanting. His hand moved to caress the slight swell of her hip, to smooth over her bottom, pressing her closer to him, and the last anchor rope snapped.

Abul reveled in the feel of her, the smallness, the fragility that was belied by the strength of her mounting arousal, the rapid swell of a passion to match his own. It would be easy now, with no break in the spiraling need, to move with her to the divan. She would come to him, be with him, because she was as much at the mercy of her body's passion as he was.

And then he knew that he could not. That it wouldn't work. Oh, the moment would work; it couldn't fail to do so. But she wasn't yet truly willing, not in her self. And if he took advantage of her now, it would rebound. She would be angry, with him and with herself, because she still had so much unreconciled emotion within her, and they would be left with the sour aftertaste of guilt and regret.

He put his hands at her waist as he raised his head, and gently lifted her away from him. Shock sparked in the seaweed depths of her eyes at this abrupt cessation, and a quiver of loss shook her frame to match the wrenching ache in his own body at such a harsh interruption of stimulus.

Sarita placed her fingers on her swollen lips; her eyes were still focused on the world she had been inhabiting. Why had he stopped? He must have known she had no defenses against him anymore. She stared at him, uncomprehending. His face had an unusual pallor beneath the golden tinge, his mouth was drawn tight, and a muscle twitched in his cheek. Abul had not found that self-abnegation easy.

He drew in a deep breath, steadying himself before

he spoke. "That's not the way it should be. I don't want you taken by surprise."

Sarita took her own deep breath. "Why not? You keep me prisoner for one reason, as I understand it. Why hold back when you were so close to achieving your object?"

Abul shook his head. "You understand perfectly well, so don't play any more games. I've had enough for one evening."

"*You've* had enough?" Anger flared again, a welcome diversion even if it was only the other side of passion's coin. "How do you think I feel?"

"Hungry . . . or so you've been telling me," he said dryly. "Kadiga and Zulema will attend you while you change out of those clothes, and then we will sup together."

"These are *my* clothes," Sarita said. "I see no reason to wear the robes of the harem."

Abul looked at her, a thoughtful glimmer in his eye. "But you do want your supper?"

"What has that to do with it?" Her eyes told him that she too had had enough of games.

Abul laughed and retreated. "Nothing at all. But you cannot wish to wear the same clothes you have worn all day. They are working clothes. Why are you reluctant now to put on something suitable only for lying around and eating apricots? We will sup and listen to music. You have no need of working clothes." He didn't wait for a capitulation, but left her immediately, knowing that she would be better left alone, to make her own decision, to see the sense of his statement, and to deal in her own way with the dislocation of the past minutes.

The door of the tower clicked shut, and Sarita listened for the turning of the key. She didn't hear it. She ran down the stairs and tried the door. It opened at a touch. So he was that sure of the impossibility of escape! Frowning, she closed the door again and went to sit on an ottoman beside the soothing murmurs of the fountain. She'd been locked in all afternoon simply for punitive reasons, then. Abul was not afraid she would succeed in leaving the Alhambra without his permission.

With this knowledge came the absolute determination to prove him wrong. She had ceased to care about where she would go or what she would do, or even whether she really wished to leave anymore. She was conscious only of the need to make her own statement, of the need to prove that she could not be held by a spurious, imposed contract. It now had nothing to do with whether she would choose to stay if the choice was truly given to her. The choice had not been given, and without that choice, there was no possibility of a furtherance of this strange relationship. She must and would deny the magnetism of the man, the fact that he drew her as the moon draws the tide. She must and would deny the fact that she liked him, trusted him, was amused by him, was warmed by him . . .

She must and would deny all these things because the caliph was making no attempt to understand her point of view. He was blithely imposing the norms and rites of his own people upon her, and he must understand that she would not accept that. She neither could nor would sink into the sedentary, seductive ways of the Alhambra's seraglio, dependent upon the favor of the caliph, with no function but to please him. She came from an active people, accustomed to shaping their world, to working hard and playing as hard. Women had a place and a status of their own, based on their functions within the network, and those functions were vital. Oh, it was certainly true that men were the powerful ones, but they yielded to women in the areas where women's skills and wisdom were acknowledged superior. Here, it seemed to Sarita, women existed only within the shadow of men, and if they attempted to step outside that shadow, a man was entitled to take what corrective measures he pleased. Muley Abul Hassan believed that; it was in his blood, bred in his bone, and not all the gentleness, humor, warmth, and trustworthiness in his character could erase the consequences of that fundamental belief.

So she was going to leave this place. And her next attempt would succeed.

Kadiga and Zulema came in just as she had reached this firm, yet uneasily melancholy, resolution.

"I think you must be moon-touched, Sarita," Kadiga declared without preamble, hurrying across to her. "Everyone is talking of how you disrupted the caliph and his cadi in the Mexuar during the hours of justice."

"I do not know how you could dare to do such a thing," Zulema said, shaking her head, tutting gently.

"I think you have the story a little confused," Sarita said. "*I* did not disturb the caliph through any decision of my own. I was dumped in front of him by some . . . some species of wild boar in the guise of a man."

"But of course the men would take you to the caliph if you were doing something you shouldn't," Zulema said in her sweetly reasonable voice.

"I was not doing something I shouldn't." Sarita wondered if it was worth trying to explain. It would require a massive program of reeducation.

"But you must have been." Kadiga was picking up scattered cushions. "However did these come to be on the floor?"

"Because I threw them," Sarita said, getting up from the ottoman. "At your caliph, if you must know."

There was a moment's stunned silence, then Kadiga gave a little choking sound, suspiciously like a giggle. "You did not, Sarita. You could not."

"I could and I did." She went to the staircase. "And if someone doesn't bring me some food very soon, I am really going to lose my temper."

There was a brittle edge to her voice that brought both of her attendants to her side. "Supper will come shortly," Zulema soothed. "Let us go up to the gallery and change your robe."

"I can eat perfectly well in this." But she said it purely as a form protest, having reached the stage where she would have eaten naked if that was the only way she was going to sit before a plate of food.

"What were you doing that made the man take you to the caliph?" Kadiga inquired, her eyes alight with curiosity as they reached the gallery.

"I was trying to walk out of this place." Sarita thumped down on the divan and began absently to massage her toes. It was generally a soothing exercise, but since it did nothing to satisfy her empty belly, it had little power this time to lessen her irritability.

"*Why?*" The two spoke the one-word question in unison.

"You are so fortunate to have the caliph's favor," Zulema went on.

"Yes, and to live in this fashion," Kadiga put in with a hint of envy. "You are housed in such luxury, with these beautiful clothes and jewels. You have nothing to do . . ." She looked ruefully at her own work-reddened hands.

"The life of a whore," Sarita said succinctly. "I would rather be a washerwoman." The incomprehension on their faces was beyond breaching, she realized, and gave up, lying back on the divan with a sigh of defeat.

"Well, what robe will you wear?" Kadiga moved to an embrasure where now hung the robes they had all been examining that morning with such interest.

"I couldn't care less."

"There should be one of ivory silk, embroidered with topaz," said a deep voice.

Sarita sat up abruptly, and the two other women turned with a gasp to the head of the stairs, where stood Abul. His soft-footed arrival was explained by the simple slippers he wore beneath the loose folds of a burnous.

"How do you know?" Sarita asked.

"Because the choices were mine," he said, coming over to the divan. "I picked them very carefully with your coloring in mind. Tonight, I would like to see you in ivory with topaz." Taking her hands, he drew her to her feet. "It should make a startling contrast with your hair." He ran his hands lightly through her curls in a gesture that was rapidly becoming familiar, before taking her place on the divan. "Hurry now. I had thought to find you dressed and ready for your supper."

Zulema's busy fingers were already unlacing the bodice of the orange dress. Sounds came from the court below, the soft plucking of a harp accompanying the wonderful chinking of china, a tinkle of glass, and the most succulent aromas drifted upward. Sarita lost all interest in argument and stood compliant while her dress and shift were removed. She wondered if she was becoming accustomed to being in Abul's company in nothing but her skin, or whether it was just that she was so tired and hungry that she was unmoved by the knowledge of those black eyes roaming over her body as she stood waiting for Kadiga to bring the ivory robe. But when he reached out a seemingly indolent hand and stroked her flank, her body leaped at the touch, her skin rippling beneath his hand as if she were a caressed cat.

She turned on him, saw his eyes amused, desirous, smiling at her. "You're not playing fair," she said tightly, as she had done in the baths.

"I never promised to do so," he replied, as he had done before.

Sarita remembered uncomfortably that they were not alone. Kadiga was looking frankly fascinated by the exchange, Zulema puzzled. "Hand me that robe," Sarita snapped, holding out her hand for the garment hanging over Kadiga's arm. "It's cold."

Abul rose from the divan with a soft laugh. "I will await you in the court, *querida*."

Sarita joined him within a couple of minutes, having rejected all her attendants' efforts to brush her hair or put slippers on her feet. She was far too hungry for such niceties and came running down the stairs, holding up the hem of the ivory silk, her mouth watering. She was only peripherally aware of the harpist beside the fountain, the sweet melody filling the air.

"What is it that smells so good?" She came over to the low table that had been placed between two ottomans. Abul was stretched out on one of them, his head resting on an elbow-propped palm.

"Come and see," he said, gesturing to the couch opposite. "I will pour you wine."

Sarita decided that lying down to eat was hardly a Christian habit and sat down instead, facing the table. She watched Abul pour wine from the jug into delicate crystal goblets. In other circumstances, she would have paused long enough to admire the rare and precious crystal, but tonight she simply drank deeply of what she judged to be a rather special Rioja. Her eyes met Abul's over the goblet, and she saw that he was laughing.

She found Zulema at her elbow, proffering a bowl of rose-scented water, and impatiently followed Abul's example, dipping her fingers in the water, drying her hands on the linen towel draped over the woman's arm.

"Better?" Abul said. He tore off a chicken leg from the golden-brown roasted bird sitting in the middle of the table. "Try this." He placed the drumstick on Sarita's plate.

Sarita tried very hard to eat daintily, but until she had satisfied the growling monster within, she found it impossible to pick slowly and eat savoringly from the array of dishes on the table. In addition to the chicken, which tasted of lemon and garlic and spices, there were cubes of lamb, stewed with honey and tossed with whole almonds, and there was a curious substance like steamed flour that would have been bland except that it had boiled raisins and pine kernels in it; there was flat bread and yellow butter and

white goat's cheese; and yogurt with honey; and a
great platter of cakes and sweetmeats.

They ate with their fingers, but frequently Zulema
and Kadiga presented the towels and finger bowls.
Again it struck Sarita that the passion for cleanliness
among these people was somewhat overdone. Her
own people ate with knives and fingers around the
campfires, using bread for trenchers, passing the
leather flagons of wine from one to another. She was
accustomed to licking the grease off her fingers, wiping her mouth with the back of her hand, sharing
knives and flagons. But she noticed how particular
Abul was, how he took relatively small mouthfuls,
kept his hands clean, ate slowly; and once her initial
hunger had been satisfied, she found herself emulat-
ing him because she felt uncomfortable otherwise. Yet
another example, she thought, of the delicate surface
of this fairyland, a surface that concealed a base far
from delicate, if her experiences of the afternoon were
anything to go by.

Abul maintained a considerate silence while his
companion satisfied her hunger. The harpist continued to play, and an insidious relaxation crept over
Sarita, dispelling the emotional stresses and strains of
the day. She found she couldn't keep hold of her anger, which did surprise her since she believed herself
so ill-used as to justify continual fury until the ills
were redressed.

Kadiga and Zulema discreetly left when the table
was sufficiently depleted to indicate that their presence was no longer required. Sarita swung her legs
up on the divan, since Abul looked so very comfortable in that position, and took another sip of her wine
with a little sigh of contentment.

"Happy?"

The question took her by surprise, as much because
she realized that somehow she was. "No," she said.
"Have you ever heard of a happy prisoner?"

Abul shook his head slightly, not in response to her

question, but in resigned reproof. "The constant re-iteration of that complaint, Sarita, grows tedious."

"My apologies, my lord caliph, but I fear you will continue to hear it for as long as I am held in this way."

He closed his eyes. "Listen to the music."

Sarita's hand moved surreptitiously to the cushion behind her head. She pulled it out and held it on her lap, tapping her fingers against it with calculated insouciance.

Abul turned his head, regarding her with narrowed eyes. "You *do* like the spice of provocation, don't you?"

"The provocation is on your side, not on mine. It isn't as if I've thrown it."

"Well, do so, if you wish. I've no objections to the consequences in the least."

Sarita looked away from Abul, evincing a fascination with the harpist to hide her laughter. She lay watching the musician for a minute or two, remembering the morning. "Is he blind also?"

"Not as far as I know."

"Why do you not let your son spend time with his mother?" It was the wrong way to introduce the subject of Aicha, but too late to retract.

The silence crackled, all languor vanished, yet Abul did not appear to move. "Where did you hear that I did not?"

This was dangerous ground. It shouldn't have been, but somehow she knew it was. The danger pricked the air like so many dagger tips. How to contain the damage?

Sarita stretched languidly. "Oh, it was just something your wife said this morning. She came upon me in the baths." Rolling onto her side, she faced him, allowing a petulant note to enter her voice. "You had left me all alone, asleep and exposed to anyone who might have chosen to enter. Or have you forgotten?"

"You were in the care of the keepers of the baths,"

Abul said, but she could hear the faintest hint of hesitation.

Abul silently blamed himself for his lack of foresight. He should have known that once her curiosity was aroused, Aicha would set out to satisfy it. And how better to do so than face-to-face with the object of that curiosity? But what had been said between them? If they had discussed Boabdil, then they had presumably covered considerable ground. He would have given much to avoid a meeting between Aicha and Sarita at this juncture, particularly one he hadn't prepared for. There was no knowing to what devious use Aicha might decide to put the new arrival. His wife was too expert a schemer, Sarita too unversed in the political and domestic machinations in which the women of the Alhambra excelled and delighted. In fact, he rather thought his Christian import didn't believe that the women of the Alhambra had any sphere of influence at all. She would discover the truth, eventually, but he would prefer that discovery to happen once he had stormed the citadel and was certain of her allegiance.

"Nevertheless, it was not comfortable to wake alone in a strange place, with no friendly face and rather confused recollections of how one arrived there," Sarita was saying. "Your wife was kind enough to escort me back to this tower. We talked a little on the way."

"And you talked of Boabdil?"

"Among other things."

"What did you tell Aicha of yourself?"

Sarita thought. "Of myself . . . very little. Of the people of my tribe, rather more."

"Of how you came to be here?"

"The barest bones."

So she was not innocently incautious. But had Aicha influenced her . . . tainted the trust he knew Sarita had in him?

"What did Aicha tell you of Boabdil?" He made his

voice mildly curious. "She has a great love for the child."

"So do most mothers."

"I wasn't decrying the power of maternal affection," he said mildly. "Far from it."

Sarita paused. She had responded with unthinking belligerence, springing from what Aicha had told her of the father with the son and the sense she had had a minute before of the unseen danger inherent in this topic. It seemed time to ease the subject to a close.

"She said little." Sarita sipped her wine, closed her eyes, pretending to be absorbed in the music.

"But she did say I prevented her from spending time with Boabdil."

Why was Abul persisting in this? Sarita looked for a palliative response. "Yes, but she also said that was the way of your people. It was just that such a separation was hard for a mother to bear."

And for such a son. But he kept that sad thought to himself. He bore his own responsibility for the difficulty Boabdil was having with the *rite de passage.* However, he felt the need to explain himself, although why he should, Abul didn't know. He was hardly answerable to this diminutive, hot-tempered creature of the olive grove.

"Boabdil is my heir," he said, as mildly as before. "He has reached the age when he must learn to live with men. He has things to learn that will enable him to govern wisely, to fight well, to behave with wisdom, that he cannot learn among women."

"But there are things women can teach: matters of wisdom also. A child must learn those things as well."

"Among your people, maybe." Abul sat up, swinging his legs off the ottoman, suddenly irritated by a viewpoint so far removed from the realities of the situation. Sarita knew nothing about it, and she was sounding uncomfortably like Aicha, who seemed to have done her work well. He spoke curtly, definitively. "But among ours, a boy must grow to manhood in the values of his father. He must learn to eschew women's weakness and embrace the sword and scale of authority.''

There was no possible response. Muley Abul Hassan was simply stating the facts as he believed them and making it very clear that he would entertain no opposing opinion. Sarita felt a gut-deep surge of fellow feeling with the sultana, a feeling that transcended her earlier unease . . . unease amounting almost to disbelief in Aicha's description of her husband's attitude toward his son. Aicha knew her husband a great deal better than Sarita knew the caliph, and it must be assumed she spoke with authority.

''Come.'' Abul leaned down and took her hands, pulling her to her feet.

That morning in the baths he had promised that the long hours of the night would be spent in his very own brand of gentle persuasion. Surely in the present chilly atmosphere he could not be so insensitive as to propose such a thing, she thought. But then, perhaps he could be. He didn't think like she did.

''No,'' she said.

''No, what?'' He looked puzzled.

''I am not coming to bed.''

So that was what she was thinking? Well, for the moment he'd lost interest in the sensual coaxing of his intransigent guest. He had enough obstacles to overcome in that area without finding her ranged against him on an issue that was no business of hers. Besides, it was time to deal with Aicha. He had let matters slip far enough.

He gestured to the harpist and the man rose immediately, bowed, gathered his instrument, and left the tower in a swishing of robes and soft pad of sandaled feet.

Sarita stood still, meeting Abul's steady gaze with her own. She looked so fiercely determined, as if prepared to do battle to the death to hold him off, that he decided with a touch of grim amusement to exercise a little vengeance.

"You are looking tired," he said, as if they were having an ordinary conversation. "It is time you were in bed, after such a day."

"No," she stated, wondering for how long one could rely on statements to ensure events.

Abul smiled, pinched her nose as if she were a small child making a token protest, and lifted her in his arms. "*You* are going to bed, Sarita. I didn't say I was coming with you."

Before she could absorb what he had said, he had carried her upstairs. He set her on her feet by the divan. "I'll leave you to put yourself to bed. After my earlier self-restraint, I don't think I have the energy for further trials of endurance. Sleep well." He dropped a kiss on the nose he had pinched and left her.

Sarita stood there, frozen with surprise and indignation. He had neatly turned the tables, making her feel like a presumptuous fool. But at the same time, the knowledge that she was at last alone, through choice, filled her with an indescribable relief. She unbuttoned the ivory robe, pushed it away from her body, and went to a rear window. The cool air of the nighttime mountains bathed her skin. The dark ravine below offered not menace but the possibility of salvation. The star-glitter on the snowcapped mountains drew her soul out of captivity, out to the open road.

Her eyes dropped downward again. It would have to be the ravine. No one would suspect such an escape route. She could follow the valley to the city walls, parallel to the road. How to get down, though? Her gaze roamed around the gallery, around the richness of Damascus silk, the plethora of luxury. Somewhere in this tower an inventive mind would find the wherewithal for escape.

But not tonight. Tonight was for recuperation.

With a murmur of thankfulness, Sarita slipped beneath the silken coverlets of the divan. She stretched, glorying in the space, the absolute sense of privacy.

Privacy was a rarely experienced luxury. There was birdsong from outside her windows: the song of freedom.

Sarita slept.

Chapter 9

Abul strolled back to the palace, allowing the peace of the evening to clear his mind and soothe a vexation that arose not because Sarita didn't understand the necessities of life in the Alhambra, or even that she presumed to align herself against him on such a vital issue, but because, aligned against him, she placed herself firmly beside Aicha, whether she intended it or not.

It was a thoroughly disagreeable thought on a purely personal level. It piqued his pride, Abul realized with astonishment. Women did not pique a man's pride. Aicha had no such power, but it seemed as if the little Christian did.

His step slowed and he almost turned back to the tower, fired by the sudden urge to overpower Sarita and her pride and her obstinacy in the way he knew he could. But it would be a sham victory and would besides do nothing about his problems with Aicha.

He continued on his way. He was certain Sarita had not told him everything of her discussion with Aicha. She had implied that Aicha blamed the system rather than himself for her separation from her son, but Abul knew that Aicha did not think that, and he found it hard to believe she had convincingly pretended otherwise. So what had been said? Had Aicha started with her subtle venom, found that it didn't work on Sarita, so had changed her tune, playing the grieving but bravely resigned wife and mother? The latter approach would certainly work better with Sarita, Abul was convinced. He didn't think she would easily believe ill of him . . . or was he deceiving himself? What did he know of her? Apart from the fact that she delighted him, sent rivers of sunshine through his blood even when she was at her most infuriating, filled his mind when he wasn't with her . . . She had become, in other words, his most powerful obsession. Apart from that, he knew nothing of her.

It was a sobering recognition, made even more so by the intuition that it was not an obsession that would soon pass. But for tonight, he must try to put her out of his mind. He was going to reinstate Aicha publicly, as he had decided to do that morning. He would have little chance of circumventing her cunning if he continued to ostracize her, and he couldn't run the risk of her going behind his back with Sarita as she was so clearly doing with Boabdil. If, as he suspected, she had already begun the process with Sarita, although for what ends he couldn't yet guess, he must keep a step ahead.

Tonight he would, superficially at least, return matters between them to their pre-quarrel amity, and he would make absolutely certain from now on that nothing happened between Aicha and Sarita of which he was unaware. He could see no way of forbidding their meetings that wouldn't give rise to awkward speculation and put Aicha on her guard, so he must orchestrate those meetings himself.

He crossed the Court of the Lions and entered a marble-paved hall where musicians were playing. He paused to watch the delicate, sinuous motions of two veiled dancing girls. The men in the hall were relaxing, their voices low in deference to the music. Moonlight filtered down from the cupola, blending with the soft glow of oil lamps. Abul glanced up to the balcony over a small inner porch. It communicated with the women's apartments, and he wondered if any of them were watching the entertainment from behind the latticed jalousies.

He crossed to the stairs in the porch and went up to the balcony. As he expected, the balcony was deserted. Anyone who had witnessed his arrival below would have hastened to alert the seraglio to his impending appearance. As he stepped through the arched entrance to the main parlor of the seraglio, he was immediately greeted with a welcoming chorus of soft voices as the women came forward in a silken rustle, clearly ready for him. Aicha was not one of their number.

They poured him sherbet, offered stuffed dates, chattered of their doings, but no questions were asked of the caliph. His business was his own to divulge or not as he felt appropriate. He spent a few private minutes with each of them, asking about their health, their happiness, the health and happiness of their children. It was a routine visit. The vizier kept him informed of any changes or problems within the seraglio, so he knew who had had a tooth pulled the previous week, whose child had fallen off its pony, who had quarrelled with whom, and was able to weave his way through the delicate domestic politics of this feminine domain without awkwardness.

Aicha continued to be conspicuous by her absence, but Abul was content to give her the opportunity for a gracious belated appearance that would demonstrate her status as sultana. She was probably harrying her handmaid over the all-vital business of her dress and hair, jewels and perfume.

His supposition was quite correct. When Aicha had been told of Abul's approach, she had left the parlor and gone immediately to her own apartments, summoning Nafissa. This morning, he had said he had forgiven her, so maybe this visit would be a public demonstration of that fact. But she couldn't appear eager and placatory in front of the other women; that would imply she had reason to be anxious for his forgiveness. She must make a dignified entrance after he had spent time with the others, thus indicating that she had a special place in his attentions and was not to be grouped with the rest, but she would be dressed to seduce, as she had planned last night. And maybe he would stay with her . . .

"No, not the pearls, you idiot girl! Not with this robe." She slapped Nafissa's hand as the girl attempted to fasten a rope of opalescent pearls at her throat.

Nafissa moved out of reach and maintained a prudent silence. The sultana always wore the pearls with the crimson robe.

"Rubies," Aicha demanded. "Quickly, girl. There is no time to waste."

The rubies against the crimson were a declaration. Nafissa was obliged to acknowledge the fact as she fastened the clasp. However, she reflected sourly, the sultana might have informed her that she wished to make such a declaration this evening.

She proffered the tray with the kohl and rouge, watching as Aicha prepared her face. Her hair she wore unbound, a blue-black river pouring down her back, startling against the crimson. A mist of perfume hung around the sultana, a rich and heady fragrance that spoke of love, a fragrance that the caliph would not misinterpret.

"There, that will do." Aicha rose to her feet, smoothing down the soft folds of her caftan. It clung to the luscious swell of her breasts, hinted at the hollow of her waist, snugly delineated the curve of her hips. Aicha nodded in satisfaction. Then, annoyingly, the image of the Christian girl rose in her mind's eye. She saw again that perfectly proportioned daintiness. The girl's robe, cut like Aicha's, had clung and curved, but it hinted at more hollows, offered newripened fruit rather than a full harvest.

Since when had Abul's concubines troubled her? She took herself vigorously to task. This woman would come and go like the others. She was no wife, could not be a wife. Christians could not be wives, and most particularly when they brought no gifts or payments with them. This one seemed singularly devoid of all external inducements, brought to the Alhambra in the night, a member of one of the tribes who wandered the peninsula, close-knit, frequently inbred, artisans and entertainers. The newcomer had nothing to offer Abul but the transitory pleasures of her body. He would tire of her soon enough, and then she would take her place in the household like all the others. In the kitchens or the laundry, if Aicha had any say in the matter, and she saw no reason why she shouldn't have.

"Have fresh mimosa placed in the mirador," she instructed Nafissa. "Bring jasmine tea, as my lord Abul enjoys the infusion, and . . ." She had been about to say "almond cakes" but swallowed the demand. She had forsworn sweetmeats. "Make sure the lamps are filled and then leave."

Nafissa bowed the sultana from the chamber, reflecting slightly maliciously that it was to be hoped the lord Abul decided to honor the sultana's bed after all this anticipation. The lady Aicha wouldn't be fit to approach for days if she suffered a further snub from her husband.

Aicha was not permitting herself to consider such an outcome as she entered the parlor. She stood for a moment in the doorway, taking in the scene. The women were clustered around Abul's divan, bright as butterflies in their embroidered silks, heads nodding, voices skipping as they competed for the attention of the man who informed their existence.

Abul sensed Aicha's presence. It was a waft on the air. Of perfume? Of purpose? He turned his head and smiled at her as she stood in the doorway. The smile cost him an effort, but he was a consummate diplomat and well able to dissemble when the occasion demanded.

Hiding her relief at the clearly inviting smile, Aicha swept across the room in a graceful swirl of silk. "My lord Abul, you honor us."

"Not at all," he said, rising from the divan. The other women discreetly moved into the background, but their eyes were all sharp observance. "I am always refreshed in such company." Taking her hand, he bent and lightly kissed her cheek. The mingled scents of perfume, powder, and rouge assailed him, and he found himself longing for the straightforward freshness of a woman's skin, the unalloyed smell of new-washed hair.

But that woman was denied him this night. This one was his obligation and his purpose. "I would be private with you," he said.

Aicha's cheeks pinkened with pleasure and relief. "The mirador is pleasant on such a night, my lord," she murmured. "The breezes are sweet and the air cool." She laid a hand lightly on his arm, smiling her own invitation, and against his will he was stirred. For eleven years they had been man and wife, and she had never failed to please him between the sheets. There was no reason to resist with his mind the ease his body craved and the contact common sense told him was necessary for the greater good.

They left the parlor, the women's whispers surging in their wake. The sultana's apartments were left exactly as she had ordered, lamps lit, wicks trimmed, the scent of mimosa mingling with the perfumed oil of the lamps. But Aicha didn't linger in the bedchamber. She went instead to the stairs leading to the mirador. Here, yesterday, she had prepared herself for a night of passion with her husband and had been disappointed. Tonight she was determined not to be.

Abul followed, losing himself in the magic of the night, the aura of sensuality Aicha conveyed. He needed to be ministered to, his wishes paramount, his demands anticipated. It would make a refreshing change from coaxing and teasing his resistant guest, from answering provocation with its like, from holding back in extremis because the woman didn't yet understand that each loving had its own integrity and need be in no wise shadowed by past lovings, or by the possibility of future ones.

In the mirador, Aicha moved to help him with his

burnous. "No," he said. "I would watch you, Aicha."

He reclined on the cushions beneath the window, watching his wife as she slowly removed her clothes. There was skill and artistry in her disrobing, and he felt the slow mounting of desire as those golden curves were revealed and she stood, naked but for the rubies at her neck and ears, before him.

He reached for her, and she came down to the cushions with him, her hands moving now with the same skill to undress him. She caressed him, brought him throbbingly alive, set his nerve endings atingle, filled his head with the red mist of desire, and he gave himself to the hands and lips and tongue that she knew so well how to use.

Aicha felt the slow burn of triumph as Abul surrendered to her. She had always known that this was the way to heal all breaches, to reaffirm her ascendancy. No one could do for him what she could. She had known that she had made a grave error in imagining that depriving him of her skills would be a bargaining counter. She knew better now, knew she must use what she had to hold him, to bind him to her, to keep her secure in his trust and confidence, because only thus would her and Boabdil's entwined future follow the course she had set. She bent her head, grazing the hard shaft of his passion with her teeth before drawing him into her mouth, placing her tongue where her teeth had been.

Abul moaned in the extremity of his pleasure, gloried in the climactic explosion, and Aicha moved slowly up his body, smiling to herself as she felt his total dissolution. Her own lack of fulfillment was of no importance. She had allowed herself no hint of arousal tonight, and Abul had made no attempt to include her in his own pleasure. But that was as it should be sometimes. The important thing was that he had come to her apartments, that everyone knew he had done so, and if she could contrive to keep him here until the morning, then her triumph would be complete.

She lay down beside him as he slept the sleep of satiation.

Abul woke abruptly and with a dreadful sense of unease. For a minute he lay staring out into the darkness, at the star-glittered mountains heaped in the distance. And for a minute he didn't know where he was or how he had come to be here. Then he felt Aicha's body, soft . . . too soft . . . beside him. He smelled the residue of her perfume, and his nose wrinkled. Suddenly it was disagreeable, or maybe it was because it had been on her skin too long.

Self-disgust washed over him. Not because of what had happened, but because he had enjoyed it. He no longer desired Aicha as a woman. He had used her tonight for political reasons, but he had been pleasured by her, nevertheless.

He imagined Sarita, sleeping alone in the tower between crisp sheets, her skin fresh, her hair massed in unruly curls around her face. He remembered how she had been the previous night—a naked tumble of limbs beside him, sleeping the sleep of an exhausted innocent.

He leaped from the cushioned divan as if he had been stung. The air was cool on his heated skin, but its freshness could do nothing to cleanse him of his disgust.

Aicha appeared to be sleeping heavily and did not stir as he slipped on his robe and slippers. He looked down at her in the moonlight for a minute, then trod softly from the room in search of the cleansing seclusion of his own apartments.

Aicha kept her eyes closed, her breathing even, until she heard his soft pad on the stairs to the bedchamber below. Her first instinct when he'd left the divan had been to entice him back with pleas and sensual promise, but self-protective wisdom kept her still. There had been something disquieting about the haste of his departure, almost as if something was driving him from her. And if Abul refused her pleas, was unseduced by her promise, then she would lose face. It was better to let him go and not know whether a word or a gesture from her would have kept him at her side until dawn. But her disappointment was great and her anxiety now unalleviated. Somehow, matters were still not right between them, for all that Abul had publicly returned her to favor and allowed himself to be pleasured by her. But what was still wrong? How had she erred?

The image of the Christian Sarita rose again. What had she to do with Abul's abrupt departure? Was he leaving his wife's bed in such haste to go immediately to his new mistress? Was the other one more skilled than Aicha? She might have the advantage of novelty, but Aicha couldn't believe she would have greater skill, would know as his wife did exactly how to please the caliph. But then she remembered that so far the woman was resisting Abul. She had even attempted to escape. Aicha had heard of the fiasco in the Mexuar and how angered Abul had been. But was he also intrigued?

Aicha threw off the thin silk coverlet and stood up, going restlessly to the window. The palace slept, all but the sentries in the alcazaba and the watchmen doing the rounds of the ramparts. Aicha looked out toward the ramparts and the shadowy shapes of the towers. Why did Abul keep the Spaniard separate? If he was taking her into his seraglio, then her rightful place was in the women's apartments with the rest of them, under the authority of the sultana. And if he was simply intending to enjoy her as a slave or captive, once she had capitulated, then why was she housed and attended with the ceremony and status he would accord a highborn concubine? He had said it was because she was Spanish, but that was no reason to accord her special treatment. Most of the women of the seraglio were familiar with the Spanish tongue to some extent.

No, there were mysteries here, and mysteries were intrinsically threatening, particularly when they had a bearing on the female domestic structure of the Alhambra. That was the sultana's province. It came under her authority, and that authority could be eroded by secrets which the sultana didn't share.

She would seriously cultivate the Christian, beginning this coming morning. She would contrive a meeting, play on her feminine sympathies, try to draw her within the circle of the seraglio. It shouldn't take long to gain her confidence, to discover what motivated Abul in his continued pursuit. Then maybe she would be able to discover whether the girl was the root of the problem. If so, she could be easily removed as long as Aicha had access to her. She had seemed open enough yesterday, unsuspicious, although clearly deeply resentful of her present position.

Fertile soil, Aicha decided, making her way down to the chamber below. And there were many possible approaches to sow the soil aright. Once she had made an ally of the newcomer, she would pose no threat.

Decision-making always reassured Aicha, restored her sense of purpose and control. Perhaps she had been overly disturbed by Abul's leaving her bed so abruptly. How often had he remained beside her all night? Hardly ever. He liked his privacy; she knew that perfectly well. Probably he had left in such haste so as not to disturb her. And if that wasn't the case, then she'd soon discover what was and correct it.

Thus resolved, Aicha went back to bed to sleep the disfiguring shadows from beneath her eyes.

Sarita awoke with a sense of purpose to match the sultana's, her decision of the previous evening etched as clear-cut in her mind as when she had made it. It infused her with the possibility of power: the power to change her situation. Only now did she realize how the belief in her inability to effect a change in her position had crept up upon her since her abduction,

each failure gradually sapping her will. And no failure had been more potent than that of yesterday's so
blindly stupid plan. How could she have imagined
that she could simply walk out of this place?

Energetically, she swung herself off the divan. The
snowy mountain peaks were faintly tinged with
salmon, and she knew that within twenty minutes
they would blaze crimson. Dawn was her favorite
time of day. She always woke before cockcrow, as if
some internal timepiece alerted her the instant before
the sun's first finger touched the eastern skyline.

Dropping onto a cushion on the floor of one of the
little balconies at a long, arched window, she rested
her elbows on the rail and looked out over the ravine,
watching the day begin. The River Darro danced, a
narrow, spritely thread at the base of the ravine below her. How to get down? Her reflective pleasure in
the sun's rise was interrupted with the question that
had really brought her to the window.

The tower was set into the ramparts. The wall of
the ramparts clung to the steep side of the mountain.
But the steepness was not insurmountable. Once at
the base of the wall, she could scramble down, with
the aid of the bushes and scrub as handholds. She'd
done such things many times, knew how to avoid the
thorns, where to watch for nature's traps for the un-
heeding foot. Once in the valley, she would simply
follow the course of the river into the city. She would
meet none but goatherds and peasants, and they
would have little interest in molesting one whose
dress and manner would offer neither prize nor
threat. Her coloring would advertise her race, but
Sarita didn't think she would be bothered by country
folk. In the city, it would be different. Townsfolk were
dangerous. She would cross that bridge when she
reached it. For the moment, her pressing concern was
to contrive a way out of this window, to the base of
the wall.

Jumping was out of the question. There were no

handholds and footholds. She needed a rope of some sort.

She turned away from the first scarlet flush on the peaks to look within. Her eye roamed the gallery. Silk was a strong material. Silk in this tower was plentiful: hangings, rugs, coverlets, and, above all, the luxurious wardrobe with which Abul had so considerately supplied her. She began to wander the tower intently, assessing which items could best serve her purpose. At the end of her reconnaissance, she had decided that a rope of sufficient length and strength could be fashioned. It might not be long enough for her to step to the ground, but a small drop would pose no difficulty. How to fasten it? But, of course, the balcony rail was of iron. It would be simple enough to tie the makeshift rope to the rail and slither hand over hand down the length until it was safe for her to drop. Of course, there would be no way of retrieving the rope. It would remain to advertise her escape route, but with luck, if she timed it right, she'd be well away and hidden in the shadows before any pursuit could start.

How to time it? Absently, Sarita wandered down to the court. The remains of last night's supper still stood on the low table. Abul had presumably given the order that she not be disturbed. She took a fig from the bowl, sipped from her wineglass, broke a little bread. It was dry and crumbly, but she didn't notice, eating simply to make up for the night's abstinence and prepare for the long morning's work.

The palace slept throughout the heat of the day. She'd seen that yesterday. Or at least, she amended, most of the palace did. The garrison did not, and neither, it seemed, did Muley Abul Hassan, who went about a caliph's business regardless of the sun's zenith. No, siesta was not a good moment for clandestine activities. She dismissed the hours between one and four and turned her mind to the night.

Last night she could possibly have effected an escape. Alone in the tower, unwatched . . . But last night Abul had left her to sleep alone because they had quarreled. *Had* they quarreled? That seemed too large a word for what had happened. They had disagreed. But over something that obviously cut very close to the bone for Abul: trouble with his wife and son. He had promised she would spend the long hours of darkness in his bed—or he in hers—but last night he had changed his mind. Maybe she could use the same tactics again, but this time deliberately, to keep him from sharing her bed.

She took an orange from the bowl, peeling it thoughtfully. Straightforward fighting with him wouldn't send him away. It had the opposite effect, as she'd discovered yesterday. It had had the same effect on her, but Sarita chose not to dwell on that truth. So, although the idea of deliberately wounding him was repugnant, she would have to employ a more underhand method to produce the desired result.

She went back upstairs, anxious to begin this day. She put on her orange dress, aware that by wearing it she was reiterating her protest against her captivity, and aware that the protest alone would do nothing to convince the caliph of her desperate need for freedom . . . freedom, or the power to order her own life? Which was it? Sarita paused, her fingers fumbling over the lacing at her bodice.

It didn't matter which it was. In essence, they were one and the same. What mattered was that she should make her own decision to leave this place and put that decision into effect. And Muley Abul Hassan must never be in any doubt that she did not accept the arbitrary self-interest that lay behind her present captivity . . . whatever yearnings her treacherous body might evince.

The door below opened. She stood very still, listening, unwilling to look over the gallery rail and declare herself wide awake and fully dressed until she knew who was down there. The sounds were those of people clearing away, the voices muted as if in deference to a sleeper. She crept to the rail and peered down.

Three women were busily removing the debris of last night. The door stood open to the garden.

Zulema and Kadiga appeared in the open door before she could draw back. "Ah, you are awake already, Sarita." Kadiga greeted her gaily, coming up the stairs. "Do you wish to walk again this morning? We could take the path to the Generalife, if you wish it."

Sarita remembered the puzzlement and unease these two had evinced over her desire to walk yesterday morning. Something had changed since then.

"Yes, I should like that," she said. "I have broken my fast already. But there is no need for you to accompany me." A slight note of challenge was in her voice as she watched for their reaction.

"But surely you do not wish to walk alone," Kadiga said, bending to pick up the discarded ivory robe of the previous evening. Her voice sounded perfectly natural.

"Besides, you might miss the path," put in Zulema, beginning to straighten the divan.

"If you wish to join me, then I shall be happy to have your company." Sarita yielded without further comment. In truth, she was not averse to their society. Tribal life was essentially gregarious, and she was accustomed to the companionship of her peers.

The two women exchanged a look of relief, a look that Sarita failed to notice as she brushed her hair before the crystal mirror. But then, Sarita was not to know that her attendants were under instructions from the sultana, instructions that required Sarita's unwitting cooperation.

The three went out into the freshness of early morning. It was the time of day when energies were at their highest, when the air felt light and dust-free, the sun a friendly presence, not yet grown to its full hostile ferocity; the time of day when much could be accomplished. The sounds of the palace at work were carried on the air: the chip of hammer on stone, the ring of the anvil, the clip of pruning shears from the trellised gardens.

Sarita strode out, her bare feet covering the ground at a pace too rapid for her slippered and robed companions.

"Please, Sarita, slow down," Zulema begged. "Why must we run?"

"If we were as immodestly dressed as you, we might keep up," Kadiga declared a touch acerbically, using her headscarf to wipe her brow.

Sarita paused, turning on the path to look at them. Their robes clung to their ankles, unlike her own dress, which flowed free around her calves. Their pointed-toe slippers dragged in the dust. The scarves they wore must be very hot. Unconsciously, she ran her hands through her own unbound hair, feeling the breeze lift her curls, cool her scalp.

"Do not come if you do not wish it," she said. "You are right. You are not dressed for the kind of walking I like to do. Although," she added with a grin, "I deny the charge of immodesty."

"We will keep up," Kadiga said doggedly, mindful of her instructions and the waiting sultana. If Sarita was left to her own devices, there was no way to be certain she would take the direction that would bring her into the sultana's path.

Kadiga started upward again, linking her arm with Sarita's. "If we take the left fork at the top of the hill, we will come to the gate of the Generalife."

Sarita slowed her pace, prepared to compromise, and began to ask them about themselves, about their position in the Alhambra, about others like them, about all the women in the Alhambra. It was a monumental subject, and her companions were not very enlightening, since they had never considered the facts themselves and so failed to ascertain what particular aspects of their situation Sarita might find of special interest.

Sounds of voices reached them from around a corner of the path. One of them was unmistakably a child's, high-pitched and excited. The other Sarita recognized almost immediately as the lady Aicha's. They rounded the corner and saw Aicha, a young boy, and a bearded, venerable-appearing gentleman in a turban and black robes.

"Why, Sarita, what a happy coincidence." The sultana turned as they approached. "The second happy coincidence." She took the child's hand and drew him forward. "I happened to meet my son out with his tutor when I was taking my own walk. Greet the lady Sarita, Boabdil."

The child stared at Sarita, and to her surprise she read hostility in his dark eyes. But he bowed his head slightly and murmured something in Arabic.

"The lady Sarita speaks only Spanish," Aicha said, patting his head. "You can greet her in Spanish, can you not?"

Boabdil shook his head and turned his back on Sarita.

"You must not be discourteous," Ahmed Eben said, sharply remonstrative. Boabdil hurled himself at his mother, and Aicha bent to enfold him.

"Do not scold him so harshly, Ahmed Eben," she said, caressing the child's cheek. "He is young."

"Your pardon, lady, but not too young to practice good manners," the tutor said. "We should continue on our way." He looked uneasily down the path, trying not to say outright that this meeting, while purely coincidental, mustn't be prolonged. It was against the lord Abul's dictate.

Sarita had not followed the words of the conversation, but the meaning was fairly clear. The clinging child, his overt rudeness, the overly protective mother, the remonstrating tutor were all too obvious.

"Who is she?" Boabdil suddenly asked in perfect Spanish, raising his head from his mother's skirts. He shot Sarita another look of pure distaste. "Is she one of my father's wives?"

"Not exactly, *caro*," Aicha said gently. "She is new to the Alhambra."

"When I am caliph, I shall send all my father's wives away," Boabdil announced, still in Spanish. "And then we shall be here alone, won't we, my mother?"

"You must not speak like that," Aicha chided, but Sarita heard no conviction in her voice.

Abul's son was clearly an ill-behaved, spoiled brat, Sarita decided, somewhat shocked, as she wondered why Aicha couldn't see it. But then, fond mothers frequently failed to see their children's shortcomings, and presumably when time together was so limited, Aicha wouldn't wish to disrupt it with unpleasantness. Deciding to continue with her walk, she looked around for Kadiga and Zulema. They were nowhere to be seen.

"Your attendants returned to the tower," Aicha said blandly, seeing Sarita's surprise. "They would know that their presence would not be required when you and I are together."

"Oh," said Sarita, at a loss.

"Lady," Ahmed Eben was saying on a note of urgency, "we must continue on our way. In an hour, Boabdil must be in the stable for his riding lesson."

"But I do not want my riding lesson!" exclaimed Boabdil. "It is a horrid horse, Mamma. Too big, and he bites."

"Nonsense." The unmistakable voice of Muley Abul Hassan preceded by an instant his appearance through a screen of rhododendron bushes at the side of the path. "Sultan is as gentle as a lamb. He is bigger than your pony, I grant you, but it is time you learned to ride a man's horse." He stepped onto the path. "How fortuitous that we should all contrive to meet in the same spot when there are so many acres in which to walk." His voice was cold and angry, making Sarita feel uneasily at fault, though she couldn't imagine how she could be.

"Good morning, my lord caliph," she said.

He glanced toward her, saying unsmilingly, "I give you good day, Sarita," before turning back to his wife. "I was unaware you liked to take the morning air, Aicha."

She met his coldness with a soft smile, as if she heard only gentleness in his voice, and her own voice was honeyed with sensual memory. "I was filled with such joy when I awoke this morning, my lord Abul, that I couldn't remain within doors."

"The lady Aicha came upon us, my lord, just as we had reached this place," the tutor put in, his nervousness apparent. "Boabdil and I were taking our nature walk. We were examining the wildflowers."

"Commendable," Abul said in the same cold tone. "I suggest you continue on your way, Ahmed."

"Why can't my mother stay with us?" With an impassioned whine, Boabdil flung himself at his mother again, clinging to her waist. "I want to walk with my mother. It's not fair that I cannot . . . I want to . . . I want to . . ." His voice rose with each repetition.

Whining must be the least attractive childhood feature, Sarita thought dispassionately. Whiners in the tumbling pack of children in the tribe received short shrift from their peers as well as their elders. Well, it was none of her business how the boy's parents handled him, although it seemed to her that no one could be doing things too well, judging by his general lack of appeal. Deciding that she had no place in this scene, and particularly in view of Abul's lackluster greeting, she moved away, intending to go back and take another fork in the path.

"Sarita, wait for me on the stone bench where the path divides. We will walk together." Abul spoke peremptorily over his shoulder.

Sarita stopped and turned back to him, her eyes flashing green fire. "I have no desire to walk further, my lord caliph. I am returning to my prison." Despite her irritation, she was hard put not to laugh aloud at the sheer surprise on Abul's face. No one spoke in such tones to the caliph of Granada. Aicha gasped and for a moment forgot her son's continued pleas.

Abul was momentarily at a loss for words, and the

astonishing thought crossed his mind that women had suddenly become most troublesome.

While he stood thus silenced, Sarita moved swiftly away from the group, almost running back down the path, her hair swirling out behind her, her bare feet and strong brown legs seeming at one with the ground they covered. He was reminded again of some dainty forest creature, bounding away from him into the brush, unbroken by restraints, untouched by a domesticating hand.

He let her go, aware that a failed attempt to call her back would leave him at considerable disadvantage in front of his wife and son, who was still whimpering.

"Oh, be quiet, Boabdil," he snapped. "You are far too old to cry like some infant. Take him away, Ahmed Eben."

The tutor touched the child's shoulder, but Boabdil kicked backward at him and clung tighter to Aicha's waist. Abul took a step forward with a furious exclamation, and hastily Aicha loosened the child's grip.

"Go with Ahmed, Boabdil," she said, stroking his hair, wiping his tears with the edge of her scarf. "Oh, do not weep so, darling. Soon it will be sundown, and we will be together again. Then you can tell me everything you've been doing."

Only a deaf man would fail to hear the message under the cajoling tones, Abul thought . . . the underlying message of conspiracy against the bad man. But at the moment, he could openly accuse Aicha of nothing. It was not impossible for the meeting to have been accidental, and on the surface she was behaving exactly as he would wish, sending the child on his way with cheerful promises of their next meeting. But how to circumvent that underlying message? And was it purely coincidence that Sarita had met up with Aicha and Boabdil? What conclusions had Sarita drawn from that nasty little scene? It certainly hadn't put *him* in a particularly good light, if she chose to accept the surface and not look beneath it. And after last night, he had a fair idea where her sympathies would lie.

"I have asked you many times not to undermine what I am trying to achieve with our son," he said when he and Aicha stood alone on the path. "Encouraging him to cling to you in that way can only do him a disservice. He has to learn to be more self-sufficient, to do things he doesn't like or isn't good at."

Aicha lowered her eyes, the gesture as much to hide her true feelings as to imply submission. She must present Abul with the appearance of agreement. If she did not, there was no knowing what further restrictions he would place upon her. "I know you are right, Abul," she said softly, "but it is so hard. He is still such a baby."

"And he will remain so if you encourage him." Abul looked closely at her. He didn't believe the act, but he couldn't challenge it. "When he is less dependent on you, then you may spend as much time with him as he will be able to spare from his duties and education."

"Yes, I understand." Aicha offered him a smile. "Last night, my lord Abul, brought me such a mixture of joy and pain. Such pain to think of all the nights my foolishness has deprived us both of the joy." She touched his sleeve, careful to leave the invitation and plea for a repetition unspoken, except in her eyes, words, and gestures. She knew she had angered him again by this meeting with Boabdil, but she also knew he couldn't be certain that she had contrived it. She must be extra careful next time, but she had wanted the Spanish woman to see the child, to see the child's need of his mother, so that she could play on the sympathy Sarita *must* feel for so cruelly separated a pair. She must surely feel distaste for a man who would do such a thing, and distaste combined with resistance would make her a powerful ally.

Aicha's mouth was smiling up at him, showing him the full set of white teeth of which she was so justly proud. Few women of the sultana's age could boast such a feature. Their smiles offered gaps and blackened stumps as often as not. But her eyes were not smiling, Abul noted. They were all calculation. Beautiful though they were on the surface, there was no depth to them, only a cold flat plane. Why had he not noticed that before? Probably because he had never troubled to look. It was a dismaying thought. He hadn't bothered because she was simply his wife . . . a woman.

A chill of premonition lifted the hairs on the nape of his neck and brought goose bumps prickling along his arms. Would he pay for such arrogant negligence? Pay in some incalculable way?

It was an absurd thought, some distemper brought about by the irritations of the morning. He turned from her with a dismissive gesture and strode back toward Sarita's tower.

Aicha stood still, her hands pressed to her lips, until the cold fury at that abrupt dismissal had abated. He had treated her with such disdain, contemptuously ignored her soft words and sensual memories. And for the first time, the previously inconceivable took concrete shape.

If Abul repudiated her as his wife, then her son would cease to be his heir, and that would be the end of all her plans. Through Boabdil, *she* would eventually rule Granada. She would bind the child so completely to her that he would be unable to make a decision unless he consulted her first. In a few years, when he was grown, she would find the means to remove Muley Abul Hassan. Poison was the simplest, most efficient method, and she was well versed in its use. It would happen as long as she stayed close to Abul, receiving his trust and confidence: that trust and confidence she was trying so hard to regain. But if Abul found some other woman to set up in her place, then . . . then her careful training of her son would be in vain, her glorious plans so much chaff on the wind.

Slowly, she brought herself under control, allowed the fear and the fury to die. If a threat lay in the Spanish woman, then she would remove that threat permanently. But first, as she had already resolved, she must gain her confidence. So far Abul had not put any difficulties in the way of their meeting. Discretion would ensure that he didn't do so.

Aicha walked back to the seraglio, debating her next move.

Abul stepped through the open door to Sarita's tower into a whirlwind of housekeeping. Women were sweeping, straightening cushions, filling jugs with flowers. They stopped and lowered their eyes as he walked past them.

He went to the stairs, considered calling her, then decided on a direct approach. He went up to the gallery.

Sarita was alone, standing on the small balcony of one of the rear windows, her back to the room. Her body was rigid with a concentration that for a moment distracted him. What was she so intent upon, looking out over the ravine to the mountains?

"Sarita?"

She whirled. "Oh, it's you, my lord caliph. And what do you want of me?"

His irritation faded as the familiar game began. "You know perfectly well what I want of you." He approached, smiling, holding out his hands.

She sidestepped. "You seem to forget, my lord caliph, that the tower is filled with women. Or perhaps you consider them to be of no account and can therefore behave as if the place was empty."

Thoughtfully, he nodded. "You could be right. But I see no one up here. Will you not bid me good morning in a more friendly fashion?"

"I see no reason to do so. You accorded me little civility earlier when I greeted you."

Abul frowned and pulled at his chin. Then he sighed and abandoned the game in favor of honest revelation. "I was sadly out of temper, Sarita. My son was not behaving in a mannerly fashion, and I felt his mother was encouraging him." He shrugged, hopefully putting an end to the conversation. "I ask your pardon if I seemed brusque and discourteous. May we begin the day afresh?"

"Why does your son behave in such a fashion?" For a moment, Sarita forgot the tensions inherent in this subject and asked the question with a natural interest. "Why would Aicha encourage him to do so?"

Abul felt a resurgence of irritation, but he forced himself to speak quietly. "I tried to explain last night that Boabdil's mother doesn't understand the need for her son, my heir, to develop the skills and wisdom for his future as caliph. I am obliged to force the issue."

"But surely it would be better for Boabdil if he didn't feel that you and his mother were fighting over him." She spoke the logical truth as she saw it, genuinely concerned, forgetting her earlier decision to use this subject as a wedge between them.

Abul's face closed. "You do not understand the ways of our people. I have no wish to be in conflict with Aicha, and indeed I am not. It is not possible for a man to be in conflict with a woman."

"Is it not?" murmured Sarita. "And are we not in conflict, my lord caliph?"

He laughed suddenly. "No, indeed we are not. We simply play a game that will come to its conclusion soon enough."

That was what he thought; that was all he considered the matter of her freedom: a game of conflict. Well, he was about to discover unplayful conflict with a woman. Sarita spoke with great deliberation, choosing the harshest words she could.

"I think you will find that a mother's love for her son carries much more weight with the child than a father's dominance. You are building a child's hatred, my lord caliph, not his strength and maturity. I suggest you examine your motives and tactics a little more carefully."

Abul stood stunned. She faced him calmly, her eyes

quiet but direct. And then she laughed, softly insolent, and turned her back on him, to look again out of the window at the ravine that would ensure her freedom.

He left her. To let loose his anger as he longed to do would be undignified. Men did not lose control with women, but to his dismay and discomfiture, Muley Abul Hassan could imagine doing so with *this* woman. So he left her in haste and silence, conscious of a sense of defeat but for the moment unable to think of a way of snatching victory out of that defeat.

Chapter 10

Zulema and Kadiga were stepping through the wicket gate as Abul emerged from the tower into the garden. They both faltered at the caliph's forbidding expression and hastily bowed as he passed.

Abul barely acknowledged them at first; then, struck by a thought, he paused. "Why did you not accompany the lady Sarita on her walk this morning?"

"Oh, we did, my lord Abul," Zulema said in hasty defense. "To lead her to the lady Aicha—" She broke off with a funny little sigh as Kadiga trod on her foot. Blushing fiercely, she struggled on. "We . . . we met up with the sultana, my lord, and our presence was not wanted."

Abul's earlier frown deepened as he regarded them both in silence. Neither of them moved, since they hadn't been dismissed; both stood staring at the ground.

"You were instructed to bring the lady Sarita to the sultana, Zulema?" he clarified finally, putting his question to the woman he judged the more guileless.

Kadiga raised her head with betraying speed, her anxiety to speak clear in her eyes, but he ignored her, fixing his gaze on Zulema, who blushed and looked in appeal to her friend. But Kadiga was forbidden by custom to speak when she had not been addressed.

"Come, Zulema, it is a simple enough question,"

Abul said impatiently. "Did the lady Aicha wish to meet with Sarita this morning?"

"Yes, my lord." Zulema yielded with another nervous sigh. "She said she would be walking on the top path to the Generalife and wished us to direct Sarita to her."

"That wasn't so hard, was it?" Abul said, now nodding pleasantly. "A simple answer to a simple question. There is no harm in either." With that, he continued on his way.

"How could I not tell him?" Zulema whispered, biting her lip. "And why was he not to know?"

Kadiga shrugged. "Some plot. You know the lady Aicha as well as I do."

"She will be very angry if she discovers we have told the lord Abul." Zulema shivered, tears starting in her gentle eyes at the prospect of the sultana's wrath. She was a most unforgiving lady.

"Somehow," Kadiga said thoughtfully, looking toward the wicket gate swinging in the wake of the caliph's departure, "somehow I do not think she will discover it. I feel that it's a piece of information the lord Abul will keep to himself."

Something very puzzling was afoot, Kadiga was certain, but that was not unusual in the closed courts of the Alhambra. There was always some intrigue somewhere. On the surface there seemed no reason why the sultana and the caliph's newest woman shouldn't spend time together. There would be no rivalry between them; such a thing would be absurd. The lady Aicha was supreme in the seraglio, and only her husband could take that away from her. So why had the sultana instructed them to ensure that everyone, including Sarita, believed the meeting to be an accident? And why had the caliph found the information of interest?

Kadiga shrugged again. The answer was impossible to divine at this stage, but perhaps if she kept her eyes and ears open, the pieces would eventually form a pattern. It was always wise to keep one's wits about one in this world.

"Let us go within, Zulema, and see how Sarita wishes to spend the hours until the caliph summons her again."

"She will probably wish to walk again," Zulema said, a touch glumly. "And the sun is getting high."

Kadiga laughed. "Let's see if we can persuade her to sit with us in the court and play chess instead."

But they found Sarita in an abstracted mood, willing enough to sit with the chess pieces in the cool quiet of the inner court, but clearly her mind was elsewhere. The two women made no comment, however, keeping up a soothing flow of chatter that covered Sarita's silence.

As Abul went about the day's business, no one would guess from his demeanor the questions and speculations roiling within him. He listened to the reports of his envoys to the various courts of the other leading families in Granada; he read the report from his spy at the Spanish court across the border in Cordova; he listened to the reports of his spies sent to patrol the roads and towns of Castile; he listened to his vizier, to his cadi, to the chief officer of the alcazaba. He listened, questioned, absorbed, and made judgments, stated opinions, as if he were not struggling to control his anger and bewilderment at the unknown. Never had he been challenged in the way Sarita had just challenged him; never had he been attacked on his most private ground by anyone, let alone a woman.

But as the morning wore on, his customary equilibrium reasserted itself. Wasn't it, after all, Sarita's potential to do all of those things that had first fascinated him and then drawn him to her so powerfully? It was that unique quality she had, that sense of the untamed, the uncompromising, that was the moon to his tide.

Aicha was the problem, not Sarita. Aicha was setting something in motion, and it was for Abul to discover what and why. And it was for Abul to ensure where Sarita's loyalties lay.

"My lord, the ambassador of the Aziz wishes to know if he may take your opinion back to his emir." The softly imperative voice of the vizier interrupted his musing, and he returned his attention to issues much less interesting.

"You may tell the lord Aziz that I approve the marriage of his daughter with the family of Hayzari. The alliance will strengthen all the families of Granada." Rising, he smiled, inclined his head in formal acknowledgment of the assembled court, and left the hall, his one thought now to repair fences with Sarita. She would not again transgress the boundaries of his family privacy, he was convinced, as long as he saw to it that the subject did not come up. And he had a treat in mind that should heal all breaches and ensure her amnesia on the subject of Aicha and Boabdil and parental conflict.

His vizier received the caliph's instructions impassively, saying only, "You expect to return by sundown, my lord? The deputation from Haroun Kalim has requested an audience at the supper hour."

"Yes, I will be back by then. Have the escort gathered in the court of the alcazaba within the half hour." Abul set off for Sarita's tower with a spring in his step, filled with pleasant anticipation at the prospect of giving pleasure. He had put aside his earlier defeat at Sarita's hands, discounting the harshness of her tongue as simply understandable reaction to his own curtness. She came from a different background, one where it was probably customary to return brusqueness with its like, even between men and women. He could accept that, just so long as they steered clear of those aspects of his private life that didn't concern her and concerned him so dearly.

Sarita was wondering if she had succeeded in driving Abul away for the rest of the day and hopefully the night, when he stepped into the cool dimness of the court. Immediately, she developed an inordinate interest in the chessboard, seeming to debate her next move with the utmost concentration.

Kadiga and Zulema had risen from their cushions at the caliph's arrival, and both tried to catch Sarita's attention, since it didn't occur to either of them that she could be deliberately ignoring the lord Abul. Presumably, she was so absorbed she had failed to notice him.

Abul, however, was under no such misapprehension. Amusement and annoyance warred. He stood in front of the board, his shadow, thrown by a ray of sunlight from the upstairs windows, falling across the squares. Sarita finally looked up.

"My lord caliph," she said coolly. "For some reason, I wasn't expecting you."

"Now, that was foolish of you," he returned, amusement winning over annoyance as he looked down at the small face, dominated by those great green eyes, surrounded by the extravagant cloud of fiery curls. Her chin lifted in unconscious response to his scrutiny as she tossed her head.

"You interrupt our play, my lord caliph."

"I do wish you'd drop this tiresome nomenclature," he observed, bending over the board and moving the white queen to king four. "That seems the best move in the circumstances."

Sarita folded her hands in her lap. "To what do I owe this dubious pleasure, my lord caliph?"

"Absurd creature!" Abul burst into laughter. "This display of cold dignity isn't convincing, *hija mía*. We both know you'd rather use your knee and your fists to express annoyance." Leaning over the board, he caught her lifted chin with his thumb. "Stop this nonsense now, and come for a ride with me into the mountains."

Her response was everything he had hoped it would be. She sprang to her feet, knocking over the board in her enthusiasm. "A ride? You really mean it? Out of here, on a horse?"

He laughed with pleasure at her delight. "Yes, I really mean it. I know how you dislike lying around eating apricots all day. If it's activity you crave, then you shall have it."

"Oh, I should like it of all things," she said, forgetting the need to quarrel with him, forgetting even her plan of escape at the prospect of riding free and clear of the walls of the Alhambra, up in her beloved mountains where the breezes blew cool and fresh, and the scents of wildflowers and herbs filled the air. Then her face fell ludicrously as a ridiculous obstacle struck her. "But I cannot ride. I have no drawers." She had left the simple linen garment in her mother's wagon. She only wore it for riding and in her hasty flight hadn't thought to pack it.

"You will find such things among the clothes upstairs," Abul said, chuckling at her dismayed expression. "I have anticipated your every need. There are leather hose and a tunic for riding."

Sarita frowned. "But then I must wear the clothes of your people." She had absolutely determined that during the few hours she would remain in this place, she would not again don the garments of the seraglio.

Abul raised a quizzical eyebrow. "I believe you have but three options: you must forgo the expedition, or wear the clothes of my people, or ride . . ." He paused, as if searching for the most appropriate term. "Or ride . . . uh . . . unprotected." He tapped out the options on his fingers. "Is the principle worth the discomfort and indelicacy of the latter, I wonder?"

A smothered choke came from behind him. Kadiga and Zulema covered their mouths with their scarves, trying to hide their giggles lest they seem disrespectful. The caliph, however, appeared unperturbed by the stifled disturbance. He stood, hands resting lightly on his hips, feet apart, watching the variety of expressions chasing one another across Sarita's mobile countenance: obstinacy, disappointment, mortification, resignation.

She bit her lip as her own ready humor finally surfaced. Without a word, she turned to the stairs.

"We will help you," Kadiga said hastily, moving behind her.

Sarita didn't trouble to discourage them. It would achieve nothing, and besides, she was becoming accustomed to their attentions.

Abul, sensing that he had won a significant victory, decided not to push matters further and remained where he was, idly picking up the chess pieces and setting them up again on the board.

Sarita surveyed herself in the mirror, clad in the skin-tight leather hose that fastened at her waist. They were amazingly comfortable, the material the softest doeskin, and they would be most practical for riding, with no extraneous folds to flap and impede movement. But she still couldn't help feeling they were vaguely indecent. However, they would be covered by the tunic that Kadiga was holding out for her. It was as richly embroidered as any of the garments in the wardrobe the caliph had chosen for her, the only difference being that the sides were split to the waist, and the cut was so generous that the splits would not be apparent to anyone but the wearer.

She was about to take the garment from Kadiga when it occurred to her that there was no reason she shouldn't wear her orange dress over the hose. She wore it over her own drawers when riding, so why not over these leather leggings?

"No, pass me my own dress, please," she said, with a quiver of satisfaction that she was going to be able to pull one small triumph out of the caliph's victory. She could not possibly have forgone the treat he offered, not after two days and two nights of incarceration in his gilded cage, but being obliged to wear the clothes of the gilded cage would have detracted from her pleasure. This way, she could still make her implicit statement that she did not accept her captivity, yet still enjoy the ride in comfort.

Kadiga and Zulema looked as if they would protest

her decision, but she gave them a fierce stare that produced a shrug from Kadiga and a placatory smile from Zulema, who silently proffered a pair of soft leather slippers that Sarita did not reject.

Dressed, she ran back down the stairs. "Let us go, my lord caliph."

Abul looked up from the board. A pained expression flitted across his dark eyes as he took in her dress. It came and went very swiftly, but Sarita saw it and felt that quiver of triumph again. "On one condition," Abul said.

"Oh?" Sarita's eyebrows lifted as she prepared for battle. "And what is that, my lord caliph?"

"That you stop calling me 'my lord caliph' in that nonsensical fashion," he returned with a hint of a snap. "It grows tedious."

Sarita put her head on one side, frowning slightly as if considering some request. Then she gave him a brisk nod. "As you wish, Abul. Shall we go?" She gestured to the door.

Abul began to feel as if his ordered world was tilting sideways and he was on the verge of plunging into some maelstrom of confused and unruly events, with emotions to match. One minute his desire for her threatened to overwhelm him, and the next he wanted nothing more than to wring her pretty little neck. She looked so smug at the moment, well aware that she had circumvented him, well aware that she was infuriating him, and perfectly prepared to continue doing so. And beneath that awareness was the other current, that rich, tangible current of arousal that was inextricable partner to her combative edge. He could feel it in himself as he knew it flowed in her. The recognition suddenly brought a smile to his eyes. It was a dangerous game she played. Abul didn't believe she yet fully realized how dangerous. But he was more than happy to play it with her.

"By all means," he said affably, placing a hand on the curve of her hip. "Do you find the hose comfortable?"

Sarita stepped away from his hand. "Practical, my lor—practical, Abul. I must thank you for your foresight."

"Not at all," he returned politely, letting his hand rest again on her hip. "Do they fit well?" His palm moved over her shape beneath the orange dress. "Not too tight, I trust. Or too loose . . . You are very small."

"They are a perfect fit. I thank you." Sarita jumped forward. His hand seemed to be burning her flesh, reminding her of the clear delineation of her body under the leather. She almost ran for the garden, and Abul, satisfied that he had moved ahead in the game, followed.

They walked in silence to the court of the alcazaba, Sarita racking her brains to come up with a topic that would give her the ascendancy again, Abul content to rest on his laurels.

The court of the alcazaba was a very different place this morning from yesterday when she had been so rudely stopped in her tracks. In the caliph's company, she received no sidelong glances, disgusted or lusting, no sense that she was in some way wantonly inviting such attentions. A small party of men, armed with scimitars, sat their horses by the Gate of Justice. Two laden mules, in the charge of a robed and turbaned driver mounted on a sturdy pony, waited just beyond the gate. But Sarita's attention was immediately drawn to two riderless horses held by a groom. One of them was a great black animal with powerful sloping shoulders and flaring nostrils, the other a dainty, high-stepping, dappled gray palfrey. Both were richly caparisoned with embroidered saddlecloths and silver harnesses.

"Are they for us, Abul?" All note of confrontation was gone from her voice, and her eyes raised to his face sparkled with excited anticipation.

He nodded. "Which one do you prefer?"

That made her laugh. "Your legs would scrape the ground if you rode the palfrey."

"And you would be no more visible than a pimple atop Sohrab," he responded.

"Oh, what an unpleasant comparison," Sarita protested. "I am not in the least like a pimple."

"Well, you do have a tendency to become red and irritating, with a certain capacity for breaking forth," he observed, chuckling. "But . . ." he added, forestalling the swift tirade forming on her tongue by placing his finger lightly on her mouth. "I withdraw the image. If I put you atop Sohrab, you would be no more visible than a rosebud in such a place."

"Shameless cozener." She gasped, pushing his hand from her mouth. "I will not be so beguiled, my lord caliph."

"Your what?" he demanded in severe tones, although his eyes danced.

"My nothing," she said. "A slip of the tongue, Abul."

"Try not to make it again," he requested pleasantly, moving toward the horses. "I trust the palfrey is good-tempered." He addressed the groom as he ran his hand over the horse's neck.

Sarita listened to the groom's fervent assurances as she made her own study of the horse. She'd been scrambling onto the backs of mules and ponies since she could walk, driving them as they pulled wagons or hauled loads. She rode them if there was a spare mount when the tribe was on the move, but never had she ridden such a magnificent specimen, or indeed ridden simply for pleasure.

"I am accustomed to riding bareback," she said rather doubtfully, examining the embossed leather saddle, the carved silver stirrups.

"Mules or ponies, maybe," Abul responded. "This animal needs saddle and stirrups if you're to control him. Are you ready to go up?"

Sarita nodded, took the reins in one hand, and lifted her foot to the stirrup.

Abul brushed aside the groom as the man moved to assist her and instead himself took the leg she bent in preparation and tossed her upward. "Ali will adjust the stirrups for you."

He swung effortlessly onto Sohrab and sat waiting while the groom compensated for Sarita's diminutive length. She settled into the saddle with a sigh of contentment, feeling suddenly empowered by the animal's strength beneath her, by the height from which she now looked down upon the strange world that had contained her for a lifetime, it sometimes seemed . . . and for a split second, it seemed at other times.

Abul moved his horse toward the gate, and she followed, conscious again of the power of her mount. He moved with a fluidity that hinted at reined speed and made all the other animals she had ridden seem as if they belonged to a different species.

As they rode out of the Alhambra and onto the track leading down to the olive grove and the city, the mounted soldiers fell in behind them, the mule driver and his charges keeping the rear.

"Why the escort?" Sarita inquired.

"The roads are dangerous," Abul replied. "I have told you that many times."

She nodded. "So they're not here to prevent my putting spur to this speedy animal and taking flight?" Her tone was dulcet as she gave him a sideways glance.

"Not at all," Abul returned airily. "I need no help to prevent such a thing. Sohrab is three times as fast as your mount."

She appeared to have lost that round, but then the day was so beautiful, the horizon limitless, the great brass ball of the sun a blinding glare in the vast blue cavern of the sky, that she lost all interest in thinking up further provocation.

Abul turned his mount upward into the mountains, to Sarita's relief. The olive grove next to her tribe's camp was too close to the track for comfort if they were to ride past it. But they went upward, escort and mules following, to where the eagles soared and the breeze was cool and the subtle scent of wild herbs crushed beneath the horses' hooves filled Sarita with a bone-deep joy. It made the heavy fragrances of the Alhambra, the roses and oleanders, myrtle and hibiscus, seem overstated, overluxuriant in their cultivated profusion.

Abul did not disturb her happy reverie. He sensed the pleasure radiating from her and for the first time felt a certain unease about the plan he was following with such single-minded determination. Perhaps such a creature of the groves and mountain pastures, one who had known no life but that of the open road, could not be shaped to the mold of the Alhambra.

No, he did not believe that. Anyone could be shaped to the mold. The question really was whether she could be happily shaped.

"How far do we go?"

She interrupted his musing, and he shook the unusual doubts from his mind. He looked up at the sun, judging that they had been riding for about an hour. "How far do you wish to go?"

"Oh, forever, as far as possible, up where the golden eagles nest," she said almost dreamily.

"Are you not hungry?" he asked, smiling.

Sarita frowned as the inconvenient practicality made its presence felt. She was, as it happened, very hungry. "Yes. It must be near the dinner hour, but I do not wish to go back yet. Are you very hungry?" She almost pleaded for a negative reply.

"Famished," Abul said cheerfully. He turned to look back at the escorting soldiers and called something in Arabic, receiving an instant and voluble response. "Let us try over there," he said, pointing toward an outcrop of rock off the narrow snaking path. "There may be some shade, and I believe I hear water."

Sarita listened with educated ears. There was indeed the gentle rushing sound of a mountain stream. "We cannot eat water," she objected, following him as he walked his horse carefully across the rock-strewn scrub.

"The horses will be thirsty, though."

She thought she heard a laugh in his voice, which seemed strange, since his observation had been something in the nature of a reproof for her thoughtlessness.

The stream ran behind the rocky outcrop, a silver trickle over flat stones, opening to a deep, naturally dammed pool, then spilling onward down the mountain in a rushing flow. A clump of scrawny olive trees threw thin shadows. More shade was created by the taller, misshapen pile of rocks.

"This should do nicely," Abul said, dismounting. One of the escort came forward to take the reins of his horse. "Down you get." He reached up and lifted Sarita off her palfrey. His hands were warm around her waist, and she felt his breath on her cheek as he held her longer than necessary before setting her on her feet. The soldier took her horse and led the two to the pool for water.

Sarita sat down on a flat rock and watched in wide-eyed astonishment as the mule driver began to unload his beasts. Some of the escort went to help, and an extraordinary assortment of objects materialized on the ground. There were big cushions, a silk carpet, a canopy supported on poles that they drove into the ground. Suddenly, a small pavilion had been created beside the stream, and Abul drew her up from her rock and led her over to the shady, cushioned, carpeted space.

"How clever!" Sarita exclaimed, sinking onto a cushion. "Are we to have dinner outside?"

"I thought you might like to do something familiar," he said, seating himself beside her.

Sarita laughed. "The people of my tribe do not eat beneath canopies on silken cushions when they dine. We sit on the ground around the fire."

"Well, you may look at the fire," he said, gesturing to where two men were building a fire in a circle of flat stones. "A cup of Jerez?"

Sarita took the jeweled goblet proffered by the mule

driver. "No wonder you have an armed escort," she said, turning the chalice in her hands. "To roam the mountainside with such possessions can only invite robbery."

Abul simply smiled and lay back on his cushion, watching her through half-closed eyes. She was sitting upright, fascinated by the scene.

"What are they going to cook? I'm quite skilled at tickling trout. Shall I see if I can catch one in the pool?" She half rose from her cushion, but he caught the hem of her dress and pulled her back.

"They have food aplenty. Be restful now and lie back. One should eat in a mood of—"

"Repose and harmony," she interrupted swiftly. "I know. Just as one should do everything else."

"Not necessarily everything else," he mused. "The pursuit of love is best undertaken in a spirit of adventure, and lovemaking itself is frequently at its best when unreposeful, although harmony at the close is necessary for true pleasure."

Sarita told herself she was choosing not to respond. The fact that she couldn't think of a reply was immaterial. Even if she had been able to, she would still have chosen silence. Or so she told herself.

She lay back on her cushion, burying her face in her goblet, hoping to hide the flush on her cheekbones, the sudden languor she knew could be seen in her eyes: speaking evidence of the heated flush of her body, the arousal creeping through her loins . . . the inevitable chain reaction set in motion when this man brought up this subject. She couldn't afford to acknowledge her treacherous body to herself, let alone to Muley Abul Hassan.

Fortunately, Abul seemed content to let the subject drop, but his apparently reposeful frame radiated amusement. Sarita reached sideways and picked a sprig of wild thyme, rolling it between finger and thumb to release the pungent fragrance. "I wonder if they know how to use the mountain herbs in their cooking," she said, trying to find a neutral topic.

"Perhaps I'll go and show them." Again she made to rise, and again Abul pulled her back.

"They won't appreciate being given instructions by you," he said.

"Because I'm a woman or because I'm an unbeliever?" This was a safer topic, one with a measure of potential asperity to keep dangerous topics at bay.

"Both, as I've told you before."

"But they won't harm me when you're here."

"Not if I don't look the other way," he agreed, still sounding amused.

"But you wouldn't!" She sat up indignantly.

"Maybe I'd think that, since you hadn't taken any notice of my warnings, perhaps you should discover the truth empirically," he said. "Lessons learned through experience invariably strike home."

It was an observation Sarita was to remember bitterly.

"My lord Abul." The mule driver was bowing before them, offering a bowl of cold, clear water from the stream. Abul dipped his hands in the bowl and dried them on a linen towel handed by the driver, who then held the bowl for Sarita. Thankful for the diversion, she washed her hands with splashing enthusiasm, hungrily reflecting that in this society hand washing always preceded the arrival of food. The air was filled with the aroma of roasting meat, setting the saliva running in her mouth, and when a basket of bread and olives appeared, she took a handful of olives, only realizing belatedly that Abul was eating them singly from the basket that had been placed between them.

Self-consciously, she let the handful drop back into the basket and broke a piece of bread. It had been rubbed with garlic and olive oil and whetted her already rampant appetite powerfully.

The bread and olives were followed by wooden skewers of roasted lamb chunks alternating with onions and flat mushrooms. Surreptitiously, she watched to see how Abul managed his skewer. Would he suck the pieces off one by one, as she was inclined to do? Instead, he deftly removed each piece with his fingers and popped it into his mouth, chewing and swallowing before going on to the next item.

Sarita followed suit, and found that this slow savoring greatly enhanced her pleasure in the meal. She sipped her Jerez, rolling it around her tongue, and began to feel well pleased with the world. Vine leaves stuffed with rice followed the meat, and when a basket of figs, grapes, and honeyed cakes was placed on the silken carpet, she shook her head ruefully.

"I wish I could, but I have not the smallest space inside me."

Abul plucked a grape from the bunch and leaned sideways. "This you can make room for." He laid the glossy black roundness against her lips. Water clung to the lustrous skin, cooling her lips, and she could smell the fresh-picked ripeness beneath her nose. Her tongue peeked out to touch the fruit, tasting its cold, wet shininess.

Abul smiled, took back the grape, and delicately peeled it with his sharp white teeth. She watched, caught by his movements, by the smile on his mouth, the smoking embers in his eyes, locked in some intense circle of entrancement, warmed and wonderfully replete under the benediction of the food and wine and the sultry afternoon warmth. He placed the peeled grape against her lips again, still saying nothing, still smiling, and this time she opened her mouth for it. She held the fecund roundness on her tongue, delaying the moment when she would bite through its now skinless firmness, teasing herself with imagining the spurt of juice that would burst forth when she bit into it.

Abul was watching her expression, his eyes now dark pools of intensity, desire lurking in their depths, that same deeply sensual smile still curving his mouth. As she slowly bit into the fruit, her eyes closing involuntarily, he took another grape, peeled it in the same way, and fed it to her.

"No more," she heard herself whisper from the depths of some viscous well of arousal. She was drowning in the promise embodied in this slow, luscious peeling and feeding, and made a frantic effort to swim to shore before the wave closed over her. Why did he do this to her? How was it possible? What was it between them that made it happen? She could *not* yield in this formless, mindless way to a man who held her captive, who could not understand, on the most superficial level, the absolute imperative of freedom: the freedom to make one's own choices, to order as far as possible one's own life.

Abul looked into those eyes like drowned seaweed, their desperate appeal now overlaying the desire that a minute earlier had reached to meet his own. Ignoring the appeal, he placed his mouth on hers, his tongue on hers, tasting the grape sweetness of her juices as his hand pushed upward beneath the orange dress, running over the leather-encased firmness of her thighs. But very deliberately he avoided holding her, using his body in any way to create a pressure that could be interpreted as forceful. He held his breath, praying that she would remain still, would allow this leisurely exploration.

For a minute, it seemed she would. He could feel the stirring of her skin, the slow stretch beneath his stroking hand. And then she wrenched her head sideways, turning her body away from him with a gulping sob, pulling her knees up into a fetal curl as if she would shut out from her self both him and the world of sensation he created: a world she could not help but enter.

Abul sighed and lay down on his back, letting his hand rest lightly on her turned hip. "All over, *querida*," he said. "It's time to keep siesta."

Slowly, Sarita uncurled herself. There was an immense quiet, and when she hitched herself up on an elbow, she saw that they were quite alone, except for the horses, tethered to stakes in the shade of rocks and olive trees. The cooking fire had been put out,

listless puffs of gray smoke lifting in the still air from
the circle of stones.

"Where are they all?" After the desperate intensity
of the past moments, the question sounded absurd in
its ordinariness.

"Keeping siesta," Abul said lazily. "It's a private
time. They have found their own places."

Sarita lay down again, this time on her back, knowing that there was nothing to fear: there would be no
more gently persuasive assaults on her fragile strength
. . . at least not for the moment. Once again, the
knowledge of his self-restraint soothed and reassured
her, even as she felt deep within the aching void that
should have been filled. She knew Abul must be feeling the same. A prickle of remorse mingled with what
she recognized as her own sense of an unnatural deprivation.

When she awoke, she was alone under the canopy,
and the sun was low. She struggled up and realized
that the expedition was almost packed and ready to
depart. There was no sign of Abul. Rising, she went
to the pool and knelt to splash her face, freshen her
mouth, then disappeared behind the rocks in search
of necessary privacy. When she emerged, she saw
Abul sitting on a rock a few yards away. He was staring into the middle distance, every inch of him absorbed in his meditation. She watched him in silence
for several minutes, wondering what he was thinking, trying to sense whether he was unhappy or at
peace. But she could feel nothing. It was as if he had
taken himself out of this place and away from these
people. It chilled her, even as she was learning to
envy the ability. But it also reminded her that before
they returned to the Alhambra, she had to alienate
him so thoroughly that he would leave her in anger
to spend the hours of the night alone.

The prospect of destroying the pleasure of the day,
her pleasure in the treat he had so caringly contrived
for her, and his pleasure that he so clearly took from
hers, filled her with a deep melancholy. But there was

no choice. She could not stay, not under the conditions Abul imposed; therefore she must leave him. She had only one topic that would ensure his angry departure, and she must use it, even though she now shrank from the prying, intrusive impertinence that it involved. It was not her business. Aicha and Boabdil were nothing to her. Abul's difficulties, on the other hand, did seem to matter to her . . . if they caused him distress. But she was going to use that distress because it was the only weapon she had at hand. And for that Muley Abul Hassan was responsible.

Resolutely, she walked toward him, words on her lips to destroy his carefully constructed repose and harmony.

Chapter 11

 ⟨⟩⟨⟩

A bul watched Sarita leave the court of the alcazaba with Yusuf in bristling attendance. He could not believe what had happened so suddenly on the ride back, just before they had reached the Gate of Justice. Until then, she had been a cheerful, amusing companion, offering not a hint of her customary challenge or disaffection, lulling him, as he now aridly realized, into a false sense of peace, even to hope that despite the denial she had imposed on them both that afternoon, she was coming to accept his presence and her position, to begin to see the good things that were possible once she allowed the harmony of mind and body.

Then, with no warning, she had turned on him, her eyes narrowed, her voice laced with scorn. She had attacked with no quarter, first picking the most sensitive area of his personal life—accusing him of denying a mother's love, of mistreating an impressionable child. She had declared her open sympathy with his wife, her pity for the child, and had gone on to ridicule his belief that all was peaceful and well ordered behind the walls of the Alhambra. She had talked of disaffected wives, disgruntled women servants: information and impressions she said she had gained from her own attendants. She had told him that if he ever bothered to listen to the women of his world, instead of discounting them completely as individuals with valid opinions, he would learn things that would radically change his views.

He had not been able to stop her. Initially, he had been so taken aback by the low-voiced tirade he had simply sat his horse and listened. Then his anger had risen, fierce and powerful, but there was no way he could express it as he would wish on horseback and accompanied by a troop of soldiers. She had taken shameless advantage of his disadvantages, plowing on through every contentious issue she could come up with, attacking the very base of his way of life with all the blind arrogance of ignorance, making assumptions like the one she had made about the blind musicians in the baths.

He had never come across anyone whose voice, expression, and posture could so radiate insolence and contempt. But what hurt the most was the ignorance that informed her opinions. He had believed her sensitive, intelligent, curious, and adaptable, but she had exhibited the blind prejudice of the bigot and had not hesitated to wade into the most private territory about which she knew nothing.

Abul was stunned. Suddenly he felt he had made the most dreadful error. This woman who had become such an inextricable part of his waking thoughts and nightly dreams was a hostile stranger. He wanted to turn from her, put her out of his life and thoughts, yet he could not. To his dismay, he still wanted her, even as she sat her horse, flashing green-eyed contempt at him, tossing that unruly tangle of curls dismissively, pouring an unbeliever's scorn on everything he held most dear. Even then, she was as powerful an obsession as ever, and the knowledge filled him with self-disgust.

He had said nothing to her, could not bring himself to look at her, let alone speak to her. He had simply handed her over to Yusuf when they had dismounted within the Alhambra, curtly instructing the man to return her to the tower.

Sarita had spun on her heel and marched off before

Yusuf could catch up with her. She had pushed through the groups of soldiers in the court, her head high, shoulders back, ignoring them as if they were so many motes of dust in a sunbeam. And Abul could feel the muttering swell of indignation in her wake. A powerful need to humble her rose in his breast; to teach her that no one could speak to him in that fashion about such things with impunity. He could impose any punishment he chose, but he knew that he would not. If he exacted arbitrary vengeance for her words, he would simply be reinforcing the opinion of him she had just so graphically expressed.

Chilled by the revelations of the past hour, as chilled as he was confused by them, he went to his own apartments, certain of only one thing: he didn't know when he would be able to face her company again with equanimity, let alone pleasure. Desire, yes; but that, he told himself, was simply lust for the so-far unattainable. Once he had possessed her, she would lose that appeal for him . . . now that he knew he had been mistaken and the person herself had no appeal. But how could he have been so wrong? Muley Abul Hassan was no more accustomed to making mistakes of judgment than he was to feeling confusion.

Sarita forestalled Yusuf and slammed the door of the tower in his face the minute she had stepped into the court. It was a pointless and ill-tempered gesture; nevertheless, it gave her some satisfaction, declaring that she was her own prisoner, not anyone else's.

She leaned against the door, her arms crossed over her breast, shuddering with a dreadful revulsion, hearing her voice and the things she had said in hideous reprise in her head. She could see Abul's shocked face, then the pain in his eyes, the bewildered hurt that she could be so wounding, then the fierce anger that he either could not or would not express. And she would never be able to explain to him that she hadn't meant any of those awful things, would never, ever think of saying such things, wounding him so deeply, if there had been any alternative; that it was his own pigheadedness that had forced her to do such a despicable thing.

Slowly, the sick quivers in her belly died down. She had achieved her object, and there was no point repining over the methods used. She shook her head as if to banish obscuring cobwebs of emotion, leaving her mind swept free for the clarity of thought and purpose that would ensure her escape.

For the moment, she was alone . . . no sign of Kadiga and Zulema, but presumably they would be along at any minute, eager to attend her, chat with her, play chess with her. Unless Abul had decreed she be locked in again, alone and hungry, as penalty for her savage assault. She hadn't heard Yusuf turn the key, and when she tried the door it swung open soundlessly. So she still had her spurious freedom within the compound.

She had to make a rope, but if she began now, she risked being interrupted by Kadiga and Zulema. They would be easy enough to get rid of, and she would start as soon as they had gone. In the meantime, she would reconnoiter and decide which articles she would use.

When the two women appeared, they found her distracted, irritable, and disinclined for company. She told them she had no wish for supper and wanted to go to bed early. Kadiga tentatively suggested that the lord Abul might send for her and she should be prepared. Sarita dismissed the suggestion with the declaration that the caliph had said he had matters to attend to and would not be requiring her. It was not far from the truth, she reflected, wryly noticing how the correctly couched statement satisfied them instantly.

"Are you sure you wouldn't like some music?" Zulema offered. "I could play the lyre while you rest, if you don't feel like talk or play."

"No, I wish for nothing, only solitude," she said

impatiently, hoping to drive them away from her
swiftly with a curt lack of friendliness. They looked
at her with a mixture of hurt and surprise, quite
unaccustomed to such treatment. Just as she was
quite unaccustomed to meting it out, Sarita thought
dismally . . . although she was getting a lifetime's
experience today in spoiling relationships with un-
kindness.

The two finally left her, and she stood listening to
the silence of isolation. She had told them not to light
the lamps, believing that darkness better suited the
work at hand. She felt illogically that if she worked
in the dark, there would be less chance of discovery.
It was still not full dark outside, although the first
stars were pricking the sky, and the thin crescent of
the new moon was a diffused shape on the horizon.
A new moon would give poor light, throwing little
illumination into the gloom of the ravine. Once she
had reached the bottom, she would be safe from
detection.

She was clearheaded now, all her thoughts concentrated on the implementation of her plan. She removed the key from the outside of the tower door
and locked herself in. It would save her from a surprise visit, and she had already made clear her need
for solitude.

She ran up to the gallery and began swiftly to
gather the selected items. The sheets and coverlets on
the divan offered the best possibilities. The silk was
rich and strong, the material plentiful.

Sitting cross-legged on the bed, Sarita began to
twist the silk into rope lengths. She worked deftly
and with great concentration. Rope making was a skill
she had learned in her childhood. She knew how to
weave and braid the strands to make the material as
strong as it could be, how to ensure that the knots
wouldn't slip. Finished, she shook out the length. It
wasn't long enough, would probably only take her to
the middle of the rampart. The ottomans were covered with silk spreads; there were caftans on the rack

in the embrasure. But the caftans were embroidered with jewels. Some learned thriftiness prevented her from using such material to make a simple rope. Fleetingly, it occurred to her that the jewels would be sound currency in the world outside the Alhambra. But theft was unthinkable. Using the materials of her imprisonment to effect her escape and leaving them behind was one thing; taking anything that didn't belong to her was another.

The rope finally braided to her satisfaction, Sarita sat by the balcony she had chosen for her escape, waiting for the darkest part of the night. She knew she should try to sleep, but she was too jumpy to relax. Every little creak, every murmur on the night air beyond the window, set her pulses racing. She had no clear plan for when she was free of the Alhambra, except that she must make her way to the Castilian border. She knew Abul's warnings had not been entirely self-serving: the kingdom of Granada was no safe place for a lone woman of any race, and the sooner she was out of it, the better. In the bazaar in Granada she might find a caravan of Spanish merchants she could join. She had silver pennies to pay her way and certain domestic skills she could offer in exchange for protection. It wasn't much of a plan, but it was the best she could come up with.

While she waited, a deep melancholy crept over her. Was it because the future was so uncertain? Was it the natural fear she felt, now that her preparations were made, now that there was nothing to do but wait? Or was it something else? Suddenly she could taste grapes on her tongue and her mouth tingled as if Abul had just moved his lips from hers. She saw his face as he leaned over her, his eyes bright with passion and laughter. She felt again that aura of sweetness, of gentleness, that flowed from him, intermingled with the quiet wisdom and the unmistakable confidence and authority that had their roots somewhere deep within him, in some dominion he had over himself, some certainty at his core. And then she saw his face as it had been when she had left him in the court of the alcazaba that afternoon: his eyes blank stones, his mouth a thin line of anger, his facial muscles drawn with shock, taut with the effort he was making to contain his rage.

Tears were rolling soundlessly down her cheeks, Sarita realized. Why? She wiped them away with the back of her hand. She didn't really need to ask why she wept. Her hands played with the silken rope in her lap. But she had to go. She didn't belong in a Moorish seraglio, one of the caliph's playthings. However powerfully she responded to him, to the joyous promise of his body, to his warmth and humor, she could not endure the thought of subjugating her self to the rites and whims of the caliph's world. If she yielded to him while he was imposing his will upon her in this way, she would herself be lost, just one woman among many in the Alhambra. And she would not be able to live with herself under those circumstances. She would suffer the slow death of the spirit even more than if she had stayed to be wedded and bedded with Tariq. At least in the tribe of Raphael, she would have had an acknowledged place, a proper function outside Tariq's bed.

But she had not chosen that, just as she did not choose the life Abul wished to impose upon her. She was taking her destiny into her own hands. With sudden energy, Sarita sprang up and stepped out onto the small balcony. The ravine below was a dark wound. Clouds scudded across the sky, now and again dousing the brightness of starlight and the new moon's delicate illumination. It was a perfect night for flight.

She fastened the rope to the balcony's iron railing, checking and double-checking the knot, knowing that her life would literally be depending upon its strength. Then she went back into the darkened tower for her bundle, tying it to her waist with a silk scarf. The scarf and the leather hose she was still wearing were all she would take away with her from this place.

Without allowing herself to think, she tossed the rope over the balcony. It snaked downward against the stone of the rampart, falling about ten feet short of the base of the wall. It was a manageable drop. At least she thought it was. She'd find out soon enough.

She waited until a mass of cloud obscured the brightest of the stars. Looking along the wall to either side of her tower, she could see no movement, sense no sign of life. In the gardens behind her, torches flared, but here there was only the darkness and silence of the mountainside under a night sky. Throwing one leg over the balcony rail, she gripped the silk rope with one hand and gingerly lowered herself over the balcony, still holding the rail with her other hand until her feet and knees had purchase on the rope. Then she let go of the rail, feeling the sweat of fear gathering in her armpits and between her breasts as she hung motionless, waiting for the crack of the rail, the slipping knot, that would send her crashing to the bottom of the ravine. But the knot held.

Hand over hand, gripping strongly with her bare feet, grateful for the leather hose that protected her knees and inner thighs, she climbed down, her weight holding the rope steady against the wall. She didn't dare look down between her feet to see how far she had to go. She just kept on, hand over hand, until suddenly her feet found no purchase. She had reached the end of the rope. Again without looking—there was no point, after all; if the drop was too far, she could do nothing about it now—she closed her eyes tight, prayed, and let go.

She landed with a jarring thud, lost her balance, and began to roll down the steep mountainside into the ravine. Desperately, she grabbed at a patch of scrub and hung on. Thorns dug into her hands and tears sprang in her eyes, but she didn't let go until she had managed to dig her feet into the sparse soil and halt her downward progress. Her heart thudded in her throat and banged against her rib cage, her hand stung dreadfully, but she was out of the Alhambra, hidden in the dark shadows of the ravine's opening.

The watchman, doing the rounds of the ramparts, brushed irritably at a swooping bat, raising his torch to scare it away. In the flare of illumination, he caught the faintest flicker of movement from the tower on his right and peered into the dimness. Something was fluttering snakelike against the wall. He held his torch over the wall. What he saw sent him hotfoot to the main watchtower, where his colleagues were reporting in from their patrols of other sections of the ramparts.

The officer of the watch hurried back with him, verified the report, and sent the watchman to check on the occupant of the tower. The man found the door locked from within, and his knocking and shouting received no response. The officer of the watch set off to the lord Abul, anxiously wondering how he could be held responsible for whatever had happened. The woman in the tower hadn't been specifically placed in his charge. But the ramparts were his responsibility. They should offer neither access nor egress, and in his memory they had never before done so. But there was no denying the evidence of that rope dangling from the balcony.

Abul was at supper with the deputation from Haroun Kalim when the officer of the watch was announced. The rigors of ceremonial hospitality had kept thoughts of Sarita at bay, and he was feeling relatively relaxed, talking amiably with his guests while a harpist plucked gently in the background.

The urgent appearance of the officer brought him instantly alert. Such a disturbance would be unthinkable except in an emergency. But he mustn't give his guests any indication that something might be amiss in the Alhambra. Politely, he excused himself and went into the adjoining chamber with the man, who was apologizing profusely for disturbing the caliph, apologizing for his perceived negligence, although he couldn't imagine how such a thing had happened . . .

"Get to the point, man," Abul interjected into the confused torrent of half explanation and apology. "I cannot tell whether you are to blame when I do not know what has occurred."

He listened incredulously as the man stumbled through his table. "The tower is locked, you say?"

"Yes, my lord caliph. I have set men to remove the lock, but I thought I should come—"

"Yes, yes, you did quite right." Abul waved him into silence. Sarita had climbed down the rampart, down into the ravine. It was an astounding thing to do. It would never have occurred to him that she would even think of taking such drastic action, let alone be able to implement it.

But perhaps he shouldn't be surprised. He knew her to be resourceful and courageous. After the dismal failure of her previous attempt at flight, he had believed her resigned to her situation, although he knew she was still far from accepting it wholeheartedly. Obviously she had been playing a game with him, deluding him into believing her resigned when all along she continued to plot her escape.

And after this afternoon . . . The sour taste of her words rose again to his tongue. Perhaps he should just let her go. Maybe her body did respond to his, but that was one of those quirky tricks of nature. There was no meeting of mind and spirit between them, no common ground, and without that, the simple appeasement of lust was a hollow act, lacking the bright gilt of truly satisfying congress. She obviously detested him, had no interest in trying to understand him, in learning about the ways of his people. He had wanted to understand her . . . plumb that untamed essence that so drew him. And he thought he had tried. He had tried hard not to intrude on the sorrow and anger that had driven her from her people, while at the same time telling her that he understood and accepted those feelings and the reason for them; he had tried to understand some of the forces that contributed to her denial of the sensual currents flowing between them. And he had tried to show her, gently yet irresistibly, how the magic between them could be explored.

Leaving the officer of the watch still standing in the middle of the antechamber, Abul went out onto the portico. He had tried, and had completely failed.

Bitter disillusion slopped over him like dirty dishwater. Let her go. Let her go and find whatever she sought. She would discover little but danger and hardship, of that he was convinced, but the sooner he forgot about her, the sooner he would reestablish his inner harmony. Aicha and Boabdil were sufficient abrasions without his involving himself with a belligerent, obstinate, reckless runaway who had more pride than sense.

But Muley Abul Hassan had his own pride. Even as he turned to go back into the antechamber and dismiss the officer of the watch, he realized that the thought of defeat at the hands of that diminutive creature of the olive grove was utterly unpalatable. At some point since he had brought her to the Alhambra, he had entered a contest of wills with her. Was he really prepared to shrug his shoulders and bow out? And was he really prepared to leave her unprotected to suffer the inevitable dangers that awaited the lone and unwary within the borders of his kingdom?

He wasn't. Even after all she had said, he could not with equanimity abandon her. She would never survive, free and unmolested, and he found that despite his disillusion, he could not tolerate the thought of her suffering. And there was another reason. It was also *because* of her accusations of this afternoon. The shock and hurt he had felt then would never be assuaged if he admitted total defeat. He *would* bring her back, *would* bend her to his will, *would* oblige her to acknowledge and fulfill the passion with which she responded to him, but now he cared nothing for gen-

tle persuasion. He no longer had the time or the inclination for such lengthy and frustrating tactics, and
since Sarita didn't believe in delicacy in her dealings,
then why should he?

A plan began to form: a plan that held the sweet
kernel of revenge even while it would ensure that she
remained unharmed. And Abul needed revenge for
the insults of the afternoon and for the absolute, public rejection embodied in this latest, desperate flight.
Sarita would learn a lesson about the nature of life in
the kingdom of Granada and the powerful protection
of the caliph, but it wouldn't appear to her like the
arbitrary vengeance of a despot. She would believe
she had brought it upon herself by ignoring his warnings. There was a subtle logic to such a reprisal that
gave him a twisted satisfaction. He wanted her back,
but for one reason only. He wanted from her just one
thing now, and when he had taken it, then surely he
would be free of this obsession.

He went back to the antechamber. The officer still
stood at attention, waiting for the caliph to pronounce
judgment. "Return to your post," Abul said, waving
a dismissive hand. He rang a handbell that would
bring the vizier to him and then summoned Yusuf.

Yusuf received his instructions in customary grim
silence.

"You understand exactly what you are to do?"
Abul finally said, opening a strongbox and drawing
out a velvet pouch.

"Yes, my lord Abul." Yusuf bowed. "She will not
emerge from the ravine until daybreak, so there will
be ample time to track her movements, and, dressed
as she is, she cannot fail to be noticeable. I will have
four men. We will not miss her, and Ibrahim Salem
will cooperate readily enough for the right price."

"She is not to be hurt," Abul reiterated. "She may
well be frightened, but she is to suffer no physical
hurt. That is quite clear?"

"Quite clear, my lord Abul."

"Then go about your business, Yusuf. I would have

the woman back within the walls of the Alhambra by tomorrow sundown.''

Yusuf bowed low and left, the voluminous folds of his burnous rustling about him. Abul returned to his neglected guests. Spending the better part of a day in Ibrahim Salem's compound should convince Sarita of the foolishness of rejecting the caliph's protection.

Sarita reached the bottom of the ravine in a slipping, sliding scramble that left deep scratches on her hands and feet. However, once down in the dark shadows, where the river flowed strongly, she felt secure from detection. The moon and starlight couldn't penetrate the base of the ravine, although the river glistened now and again as the clouds parted. Her locked door and the dangling rope would not be found before morning, when Kadiga and Zulema came to attend her. But then she would be in the city, lost in the back alleys. If she could not find a merchant caravan or some other fellow travelers to offer protection, then she must set out herself, over the mountains to the Guadalquivir River and so into Castile. She would provision herself in the city and then travel by night, taking the mountain paths as she remembered them from the tribe's earlier journey.

She followed the river, passing one or two peasant huts and ramshackle outbuildings, a few patches of cultivated land, but saw no sign of human life. But then, people went to bed with the sun and rose at cockcrow; only in the cool hours of early morning could hard laboring be accomplished.

The dark huddle of the city walls became visible at the head of the narrow path snaking up the side of the ravine to the track that led into Granada. Sarita knew she dared not approach at night. The city gates would be shut and there would be watchmen to challenge her, and she had no wish to draw attention to herself. Dawn would be soon enough, and then she would make her way immediately to the bazaar. It would be teeming with life, she knew from when she had visited it with her mother last week. She would be able to buy food and drink there, and lose herself in the general mass of humanity while she decided on her next move, depending on whom and what she found in the city.

She was conscious of a bone-deep weariness and quite suddenly sat down on the mossy grass beside the river. Down here, in the cool, well-irrigated bed of the ravine, the dry scrub and thornbushes of the mountainside gave way to rich grass and soft moss. Using her bundle as a pillow, Sarita lay on her back and gazed up into the sky. Being alone in the outdoors didn't frighten her. She was used to the night sounds; indeed, they had been the lullaby at her cradle since she had memory, although she was accustomed to sleeping within a circle of protective fires and the ever-alert prowling pack of wolf hounds. But she was away from the open road down here. There would be no brigands this far from the possibility of plunder. If there were wolves, she would take her chances with them. Her eyes closed, and she fell into a dreamless sleep.

She awoke in the first gray light of dawn and found herself looking into a pair of solemn brown eyes staring down at her from a round, olive-skinned face. She smiled at the child, who clutched his herdsman's crook more tightly and continued to stare in silence.

Clearly the boy was not used to coming across sleeping women when he went out with his goats at dawn. Sarita offered him a cheerful greeting, but it succeeded in sending him scampering across the grass as if pursued by a spirit of the damned.

Presumably he didn't speak Spanish. Sarita shrugged and stood up, stretching and yawning. She was hungry. Yesterday's alfresco dinner seemed a long time ago, and it occurred to her belatedly that she should have asked Kadiga and Zulema to bring her supper before she turned them away. But there was no repairing the error. She would have to break her fast in

Granada. She drank from the river, splashed water on her face, and pulled her comb through her hair.

Looking behind her and upward, she saw the roofs of the Alhambra rising above the ramparts. Her absence would be discovered soon enough now. What of Abul? How would he respond to the news? With relief, probably, she thought, after what she'd done to him yesterday. She saw his face again, when she'd left him. It was a bad last memory to take away.

Resolutely, she turned her face toward the jumbled roofs of the city of Granada. The climb out of the ravine was steep, but the path was defined, unlike her unorthodox route down during the night. When she reached the summit, she found the road thronged with peasants bearing produce from their own small-holdings, mule drivers with trains of laden beasts, caravans of Morisco-Spanish merchants on horse-back, going both to and from the town. There were a few women, heavily veiled, carrying pitchers and bundles, walking in groups, their heads lowered as they moved among the men.

Sarita, in her orange dress, with her flaming hair unbound and uncovered, was as conspicuous as a meteor in the night sky. When she'd made this journey before, it had been in the company of her mother and other members of the tribe, and always with a male escort. Swiftly, she unfastened the scarf holding the bundle at her waist and threw it over her hair, drawing it across her mouth. She lowered her eyes to the ground in imitation of the Moorish women. She still stood out, but at least now she drew less attention.

She passed through the city gates, clutching her bundle tightly; to her fanciful and fearful mind, the twelve silver pennies, such an invitation to robbery, seemed to shine through the material, advertising her wealth to all predatory eyes. She was not challenged at the gate and plunged immediately into a side street, where the overhanging upper stories of the buildings almost met in the middle, providing a dark tunnel down which she sped, keeping close to the walls.

Two men moved casually into the street when she was halfway down it. They wore striped burnous and tarbooshes under their turbans. The hilts of their curved knives glittered from the folds at their waists. Sarita sensed them behind her; then a woman appeared in a doorway, shaking out a rug, a child wailed from an open upper window, and the street became like any other, and she shook alarm from her. If she remembered correctly, she would emerge into a square, and then the fourth street off the square would take her to the bazaar. There would be so much going on, so many other foreigners, that she would merge with the crowd. She would buy food from one of the stalls and discover if there was a company she could join going to Castile.

The men behind her kept their distance. She was impossible to lose in that vivid dress, and they were in no hurry.

The street opened onto the square as she had remembered. A tired-looking donkey stood, head hanging, at the central well while a man loaded water barrels on either side of its thin flanks. Flies buzzed over a pile of ordure in the far corner of the square, and a tribe of hungry cats scavenged in the stinking kennel. Sarita's nose wrinkled at these marks of urban life. The open road, olive groves, and mountain pastures smelled a lot sweeter than these cobblestones and the dark interiors of the houses she passed.

A group of women appeared from one of the side streets, water pitchers on their shoulders, and made their chattering way to the well. Sarita crossed the square at the same time, hoping to merge with them. But they stopped and looked at her from dark eyes above veils. They looked with shock, with amazement, with disgust at her bright dress, her sun-browned calves. They too were barefoot, but their robes concealed their feet.

Sarita returned their stares for an imprudent instant. She took in the threadbare garments, the gnarled and reddened hands, the stale smell of them, and their hostility. It was the latter that sent her scurrying across the square to lose herself in another dark and noisome alley.

The din of the bazaar reached her long before she could see it. Shouts, cries, ringing bells, the thump and roll of ironbound barrels on the cobbles, the high-pitched skirl of a tin whistle.

Emerging into the chaos of the bazaar, Sarita felt safer. Here there were people like herself, dressed in the garments of the Christian world. Women as well as men, but the women were not alone. And then she saw Tariq.

He was standing at a stall, drinking from a leather flask, two of the elders of the tribe beside him. They were examining a pair of fleeces, Tariq gesticulating at the purveyor of the fleece, a bent old man with a stained beard and no teeth.

Her heart lodged somewhere in her throat, and she had to force herself to breathe, long and slow, as she melted back into the alley, wiping her clammy palms on her skirt. Why hadn't she anticipated the possibility of coming face-to-face with some member of the tribe? Because they had become so distant in Abul's fairyland . . . that was why. They were still in the olive grove; it was not at all surprising that they should be in the town. They would recognize her immediately . . . the orange dress, her hair, her shape, everything about her was distinctive both for those who knew her and for those to whom she was a stranger. She was surrounded by danger. She stood in the shadow of a doorway, waiting for the quivers to die down so that she could think clearly again.

Then she became aware of the slow approach of two men. It wasn't so much that their steps were slow as that they were purposeful. She looked around. One way lay Tariq. The other way lay this slow, deliberate approach. Behind her?

Behind was the open door of a hovel. A naked baby crawled between her legs, a crust of bread clutched in his fist, gathering dirt as he progressed. She stepped backward, away from him. And then one of the men leaped, so fast she had no time to run, even if there had been anywhere to run to. He caught her up, burying her head in the wide sleeve of his burnous so that her screams were muffled. But they wouldn't have been heard anyway in all the tumult from the bazaar. She could smell his robe, the spice on his breath, and she could smell her own terror. Then the other man was there, flinging something around her, bundling her up as Abul had done in his cloak when he'd scooped her up from the road outside the olive grove.

But this time she knew, as surely as she knew her own name, that there would be no pleasant tower at the end of this abduction, no gentle persuasion, no soft-spoken attendants.

Why hadn't she heeded Abul? She hadn't because she had preferred to take her chances, and she had taken them with open eyes, and now lost . . . lost absolutely.

Chapter 12

Sarita fought against the hot, smothering darkness, the bands pinning her arms against her sides. She fought against the darkness and the restraints with all the fury of a petrified animal. Her teeth sank into an iron-hard arm holding her. Her legs kicked free of the blanket and made contact—a contact that brought a violent Arabic expletive from somewhere outside the stifling confines of the blanket. A hand clamped over her mouth and nose, holding the blanket against her face, cutting off the air supply, and her lungs stretched agonizingly, panic rising in her chest, black spots dancing in the red mist behind her eyes. She stopped her struggles, and instantly the pressure was lifted. She gulped the hot, stale air from within the blanket, the pain in her chest easing as the life-giving supply rushed into her lungs. And then she lay perfectly still, sobbing for breath, not daring to move lest it be interpreted as a renewal of resistance and that deadly pressure be applied again.

Self-directed anger washed through her, then ebbed to be replaced with a desperate, hopeless resignation. She should have foreseen something like this . . . should have foreseen Tariq's presence . . . should have worn the clothes of the Alhambra . . . should have taken the mountain road immediately . . . should never have ventured into the city . . .

But self-recrimination would achieve nothing.

Where were they taking her? To *what* were they taking her? Rape, murder, robbery . . . ? Probably all three. Her life, the life of a woman and an unbeliever, meant nothing to these men. Abul had told her so. If she didn't provoke them, if she did everything they wanted, gave them everything they demanded, behaved like one of their own women, then maybe they wouldn't harm her. But she could find no certainty in her heart.

She was being carried fast, her bearer all but running, and she could tell by the panted exchange the two were having that his companion was keeping pace with him. She wished she could see . . . wished she could breathe the open air . . . wished she could scratch her nose where a strand of rough wool was tickling. She sneezed violently, and dust from the blanket filled her nose and mouth. Tears started in her eyes, itchy and salty as they stained her cheeks.

Then she sensed that something had changed. Although she could still see nothing, she had the feeling that they had moved within walls. The brisk pace of her bearer slowed to a walk. Suddenly, she was set on her feet, the blanket pulled away from her, and she found herself in a courtyard surrounded by walled buildings, narrow doors leading into dark passages. Presumably the passages led to the street.

She sniffed, wiping the tears from her cheeks with her scarf, knowing she must look as pathetic and terrified as she felt, but unable to summon the pride or the will to confront her abductors with boldness. She had had no such trouble with Muley Abul Hassan. But these two were not of the caliph's stamp.

She managed to look at them at last. They were standing a little apart from her, as if no longer interested in her, looking around with the air of men who waited for someone. One of them glanced at her, and she shivered at the look in his eye. He showed her the same indifference as the soldier who had prevented her from leaving the Alhambra, and she knew he would as easily put his knife to her throat if he decided to do so. Indifference was worse than lust, she realized. If he thought her of no more account than an ant beneath his feet, she had no leverage with which to affect his attitude or decisions.

She wondered whether she could run from them; take them by surprise and hurl herself into one of those dark passages out of the courtyard. But they were standing so negligently away from her, completely unconcerned about the possibility that she might take it into her head to do something about her situation, that she realized escape must be impossible. If it led to recapture, then she would suffer even more. Better to bide her time, watch and wait, and try to control her terror. But whom were they waiting for?

The answer came within a minute. A tall, imposing figure emerged from one of the passages at the rear of the court. His burnous was of richly embroidered silk, a gold chain hanging around his neck. His turban and tarboosh were of deep crimson, his beard long and luxuriant and as black as pitch. Sarita's abductors bowed as he approached. He nodded pleasantly to them, saying something in a low voice before turning his gaze upon Sarita. His eyes were brown and hard as pebbles, and she shivered, crossing her arms over her chest in involuntary protection.

He stood looking at her, stroking his beard, his face impassive. Then he stepped over to her and took her crossed arms, holding them wide away from her body.

"No!" All resolutions of submission disappeared. She yelled in outrage, trying to snatch back her arms, but he laughed and tightened his grip on her wrists. She kicked out at him, forgetting her fear, forgetting the consequences of assaulting the men of this race. She achieved the desired result. The man jumped backward from her flailing legs, releasing her arms, a stream of invective pouring from his lips, all impassivity vanished from his eyes.

She waited with sick terror, standing as immobile

as a petrified rabbit, waiting for the knife at her throat. And this time there would be no one to halt her death. But he didn't approach her, instead called something rapidly over his shoulder. A servant came running from a passage. He had a piece of rope in his hands.

Her two abductors moved swiftly. One pulled her hands behind her back; the other bent and seized her ankles before she could kick out again. Helplessly, she watched as they fastened her ankles loosely with the rope.

"That was foolish," the third man said in Spanish. "You are in the court of Ibrahim Salem, Christian, and I am going to buy you from these two men. While you belong to me, you would be advised to behave with more caution."

She simply shook her head, rendered mute by his words as she was rendered immobile by the rope at her ankles and the hands pinning her arms at her back . . . immobile for the now long and careful scrutiny she was accorded by Ibrahim Salem.

He reached out and touched her hair, lifting it away from her shoulders. She jerked her head sideways and he laughed. "I believe I have a buyer for you, Christian. Hair that color has great appeal . . . although . . ." He stepped back and ran his eyes over her again. "Although you're somewhat deficient in size." He shrugged. "Well, we shall see."

Reaching beneath his robes, he drew out a leather purse. Gold glinted in a shaft of sunlight penetrating the high walls of the courtyard as he shook a handful of coins into his hand. He held out the coins to one of the two men, who counted, nodded, and pocketed them. Sarita stared, appalled, as she was bought like a sheep in the market. "Put her with the others." So saying, Ibrahim Salem turned and went back the way he had come, leaving Sarita helpless and alone with her two abductors.

They swirled the blanket around her again, pinning her arms to her sides, but this time leaving her head free. One of them picked her up and carried her across the court, into a passage that seemed to go deep into the bowels of the building. They stopped before a barred door with an inset grille at eye level, and the one not carrying her turned a great key in the massive iron lock, pushing the door open into a small, windowless room, lit by one evil-smelling oil lamp.

There were four women in the room, sitting on the earth floor, backs against the wall. To her horror, Sarita saw that they were all fastened to the wall by iron collars attached to chains. They looked up at first with the listless eyes of the helpless, then with a spark of interest as Sarita was set upon the floor against the far wall, still imprisoned in the folds of the blanket, her feet still tied. She tried to fight the iron collar but knew it was hopeless. Nevertheless, putting up even token resistance made her feel she still had something of herself left, and she added a few words of vituperation for good measure, although her spirit dropped into a bottomless well of despair when she felt the hard, cold collar on her neck and heard the snap of the chain in the bolt. They unfastened her ankles and removed the blanket before leaving the cell. The key grated in the lock.

Sarita stood against the wall, surveying her companions. They were all young women, all dressed in Moorish robes. But they carried an air of defeat that chilled her as nothing else had done so far.

"How do you come to be here?" she asked tentatively and without much hope of an answer. There was no reason they should speak Spanish.

But one of them answered her. "We are all sold to Ibrahim Salem. My brother sold me." She shifted on the hard-packed earth. "He had a debt to pay. And you? You're Christian, are you not? Were you taken captive?"

"By two men in the town," Sarita said, sliding down the wall to sit on the ground. "Who is Ibrahim Salem?"

The woman stared at her as if she had asked an

incomprehensible question. "You do not know of Ibrahim Salem?"

Sarita shook her head. Her stomach grumbled loudly in the dim, fetid cell, and she realized she still had had no breakfast. The body's resilience amazed her. How could it possibly be concerned with food when she was sitting in the dirt, chained by the neck to the wall, a slave bought and paid for?

"He is the most important slave trader in Granada," the woman was telling her. "He has men all over the kingdom acquiring for him. My brother knew whom to contact in our village."

And two of his scouts had acquired her, Sarita thought in dismal truth. In this kingdom, there was nothing to stop them from plucking an unescorted, apparently friendless stranger off the streets and thereby turning a neat profit.

One of the other women began to moan suddenly, rocking back and forth at the end of her chain, her eyes closed.

Sarita's interlocutor laid her hand briefly on the woman's crossed knees and murmured something softly.

"Is she ill?" Sarita asked.

The woman shook her head. "No, but she has been sold into Tangier. The trader sold her to a merchant across the water. It is better to be sold in Granada," she added simply, seeing Sarita's puzzlement. "The men of this kingdom make kinder masters."

The woman was laying out these facts with a dull matter-of-factness, as if it were well known that the hardships and degradations of slavery would be writ large in the Moorish kingdoms across the water, whereas here, on the peninsula, there might be a softness to relieve the condition.

The door opened, and a man came in. He said nothing, didn't even look at the prisoners, but placed a large flat bowl on the floor in the middle of the space, together with a basket of bread, and left.

There was a thick porridge in the bowl, and the bread was stale. There was no water for hand washing, no towels, no implements. But Sarita was too hungry by now to worry about the niceties. She imitated the others, shuffling forward on the floor to reach the bowl and using bread and her fingers to scoop out the glutinous mass. It was tasteless, but it filled her up, and she licked her fingers clean, thinking how a few days ago she would not have worried about the stickiness. In two days in the Alhambra she seemed to have developed an inconvenient view of the importance of table manners . . . inconvenient, at least, in her present circumstances.

She sat back against the wall and took stock. A full belly had taken the edge off her despair, and since there was no immediate threat, fearful imaginings would be unproductive. However, there was nothing to encourage optimism either. There were no amenities in the cell, apart from the evil-smelling lamp and an equally noisome bucket, and as the long day wore on, the intermittent moaning and weeping from the woman sold into Africa became more nerve-racking.

The other women talked in Arabic among themselves, and occasionally the Spanish-speaker would include Sarita, translating for her, but their conversation was all about the families they had left, the circumstances of their servitude, and speculation as to who would buy them and for what purpose.

Sarita found it hard to participate, since the essence of the talk was the absolute acceptance of their present situation, of their inevitable future, and of the reasons that had brought them to it. They seemed to bear no grudge against the men who had sold them— not even the woman whose husband had tired of her and repudiated her in favor of a new wife, choosing this method to dispose of her. Sarita could think only that she should have run toward Tariq rather than away from him. At least she had a fair idea of what her fate would have been then, and she would eventually have been rehabilitated into the tribe. The absolute knowledge that what she had run from was now an infinitely preferable prospect to what she had run to brought her spirits to a new low.

At some point during the interminable hours, a man came and took one of the women. He unfastened the chain but left her with the collar. He spoke to her in harsh, guttural commands, pushing her ahead of him out of the cell.

"Where is he taking her?" The disturbance brought all Sarita's fears to the fore again. In the hours of imprisonment, she had come to accept the configuration of the group, to rely on its stability. This abrupt disruption threw her back into the maelstrom of uncertainty, with all its attendant terrors.

"Maybe Ibrahim Salem has found a possible buyer," her companion told her.

"We wait here until that happens?" Sarita was now trying to put some construction on what was occurring, to begin to want to order events and develop a sense of the future, and she realized she was emerging from the numbing carapace of shock. On the whole, she rather thought she'd prefer to stay numb.

The woman nodded. "If he has a private buyer in mind for you, then he will send to him, and he will come and inspect you. If not, then you will be presented at the next public sale Ibrahim Salem will hold."

Sarita touched the collar she wore. She touched it with a shiver of dread, as if acknowledging its presence fully for the first time. It was cold to her touch, and she felt its heaviness. Her neck bowed beneath its weight, and an icy boulder of inevitability settled in her belly. She began to identify with the other women in the room; could begin to feel the insidious acceptance and resignation creeping over her, making her one with them and with the fate they would share.

The woman taken away did not reappear. A bowl of meat and rice was brought in at some point and set in the middle of the floor with a jug of water. Again they shuffled over and ate as best they could, drinking in turns from the jug. The meat was more gristle than flesh, and the morning's inaction had done nothing to stimulate appetite. After one attempted mouthful, Sarita edged backward to her spot against the wall and closed her eyes. There was nothing to do but wait. Only her body registered the passing of the hours in this windowless cell, and she discovered that she could create behind her eyes the scenes of the outside world. If she tried really hard, she could even feel the sun's warmth on her eyelids; smell the fragrance of crushed herbs and sun-dried scrub; hear the caw of a rook, the soft cooing of a pigeon, the delicate music of a mountain stream.

When the door opened again, she was so lost in her private world, her body sunk into a trance of escape, that for a minute she was unaware of the man standing over her. He spoke a harsh command, and she blinked at him, dazzled after the darkness of her closed eyes by the lamp's dim light. He bent and pulled her up. The chain clanked, bringing her back to reality. He unfastened it and then pushed her ahead of him, repeating a one-word command, out into the passageway.

It seemed she was to make her way on her own two feet this time. But the weighty presence of the collar made her condition manifest, robbed her of the will to attempt an escape. There was no escape for a person wearing an iron slave collar, and obviously her escort knew it. He jabbed her in the small of the back, as if to encourage her, but there was that same indifference in his attitude . . . the indifference that negated her personhood, rendered her an object.

They emerged into the courtyard, and she was momentarily blinded by the sun's dazzle. She stumbled, then stopped and looked up into the square of blue sky. The sun was low. It must be late afternoon. The man jabbed her again, and she started forward, removing her spirit now from her body, letting herself accept this as part of her fate. She could do nothing anymore to alter what happened to her. All she could do was remove the essence of her self from her body so that *she* was not touched, degraded, wounded.

They went into a passage across the courtyard. The man pushed aside a beaded curtain over an archway, and Sarita stepped into a dimly lit room, where four men lay on ottomans against the walls, a low table in the middle bearing a bowl of sherbet, goblets, a plate of sweetmeats.

Sarita stood just inside the archway, refusing to take in the people in the room or indeed anything about her surroundings. She was way up high, far, far away from what was going on down here in this sordid reality.

Ibrahim Salem took her elbow and drew her forward. He lifted her hair as he had done that morning in the court, and she endured in silence. He was talking in soft, persuasive tones, and she knew he was talking about her, describing her, selling her as if she were a prime beast in the market. But she would not listen; she would not let it touch her.

One or two of the men made various comments. One of them beckoned her, and Ibrahim pushed her over to the ottoman. The man looked her over, touched her skin, then nodded, pursing his lips.

Then a voice spoke behind them. It was a voice she recognized. It was Yusuf's voice. Suddenly she returned to her body. She spun around. Never, ever in her wildest imaginings could she have believed she would regard this man with relief, with joy. But her heart leaped in her breast, and relief flooded her so that her knees buckled, and only with a supreme effort of will could she stiffen them. If Yusuf was here, then Abul must have discovered her whereabouts. He would rescue her.

Yusuf and Ibrahim were having a swift conversation. The other men joined in, and Sarita realized that she was being bargained for. Shame filled her now that she had allowed her self to return to her body. Shame and the disgraceful dread that Yusuf would decide she was not worth the price demanded.

But suddenly the other men fell silent, shrugged, rose from their ottomans, and left the room with a mute hand gesture of farewell. Only Ibrahim, Sarita, and Yusuf remained. Sarita watched as Yusuf laid a pile of ecus d'or on the central table. She watched in dreadful abasement.

Then Ibrahim called and a man came in. He had a key. The iron collar was removed from her neck. Her hands went up to massage the slim column, her head lifting as if freed of the world's weight.

But Yusuf was holding something out to the man, who took it with a nod. It was a slender collar of braided leather with a small iron lock that had a strange device worked into the metal. As she stood, transfixed, he fastened this around her neck, the lock clicking in place. Her hands flew upward, plucking at it.

"No," she managed to say. "No, I will not wear it. Take it off."

"You belong to the caliph," Ibrahim Salem told her with an almost genial smile. "All runaways in the caliph's household wear the leather collar, so all will know to whom they belong. You are now of the caliph's household. He has paid well for you."

Her eyes went to the small pile of gold on the table even as she still plucked at the collar. She looked at Yusuf, who met her eye impassively before handing her a dark, hooded burnous. She put it on, obscuring her gay orange dress, drawing the hood over her bright hair. She was going back to Abul. But she was going back his slave, his possession.

Sarita knew that the world was divided essentially into the free and the unfree. Rural peasants were tied to the land and therefore to the owner of that land. He could command their labor or their lives in battle for him, and as he disposed of his land, so he also disposed of those who worked that land. In the towns, it was a little different, but men, women, and children were held in bond to those who had bought their labor. Breaking the bond brought imprisonment, torture, death. If one could not command the labor of others, one was by definition held in servitude by those who could. It was not always called slavery, but in essence it was. Only tribes like her own were tied neither to land nor to master. No one commanded their labor, and they took their possessions and their homes with them as they traveled, selling their labor, owing loyalty only to the clan and kinship network.

But now Sarita of the tribe of Raphael had left the protection of that network, and in a kingdom where slavery was known by no other name, she was owned, bought with a handful of gold, entrapped in a system of laws that took from her all freedom of movement, let alone of choice.

She followed Yusuf out of the house of Ibrahim Salem. In the alley, he mounted the waiting horse, indicating to Sarita that she should walk next to his stirrup. Once again she turned her mind inward, trod the open road in her mind, saw with her mind's eye the winding path; the snowcapped mountains; the deep blue, limitless expanse of the horizon where the sky met the sea; the bright crimson of the dying sun as it slipped below the horizon, staining the sea with its crimson; the soft pink flush on the predawn sky. She saw all of these things, not the crowded alleys through which they passed, not the hurrying robed figures, the filth in the kennels, the mangy dogs and starving cats, the naked, squalling babies, the bowed women. She did not see them, and therefore they did not see her, enshrouded in the Moorish robe, walking in her slave's collar beside a mounted man. What they saw was simply the body of the woman called Sarita of the tribe of Raphael.

Yusuf kept his horse to a slow walk until they passed through the city gate and onto the road leading up to the Alhambra. Here the crowd had thinned, movement was easier, and his horse picked up speed. Sarita made no attempt to keep pace. She walked along the side of the track, her head down, inhabiting her own world.

They entered the Alhambra through the Gate of Justice just as the sun went down. Yusuf dismounted. Sarita stood passive in the court of the alcazaba, waiting for instruction. Where were slaves housed in this palace? Who governed them? What work was she to do? But she knew the answer to that . . . unless . . . unless Muley Abul Hassan had conceived such a distaste for her after the things she had said to him, after yet another failed attempt to flee from him. But why, then, would he have saved her from the slave trader? For she knew he had saved her. If he wanted nothing from her, he could have left her to whatever life fate and Ibrahim Salem decreed for her. If he wanted vengeance, then surely abandoning her would have been the perfect reprisal.

Yusuf produced one of his guttural commands, jerking his head at her, and she followed him, noticing even in her deliberately induced abstraction how, shrouded as she was, she drew not a glance from the men they passed.

She realized after a minute that they were taking the path to the tower. Surely, in her newfound, newly manifest servitude, she would not be housed in such a place? But Yusuf opened the wicket gate into the garden. She saw the scars on the door to the tower. Of course, she had locked it from the inside. They must have had to break the lock. He swung open the door and gestured in his usual fashion that she should precede him. She stepped in, remembering how the last time he had returned her to the tower she had slammed the door in his face. This time, she simply stood just inside, and the door closed behind her. She waited for the sound of the key; it didn't come. But then, she wasn't going anywhere. Everyone must know that by now.

The silence of the tower settled around her . . . a silence accentuated by the gentle plash of the alabaster fountain. It was as if she had never left this place. The oil lamps had already been lit against the approach of dusk. On the low table between the otto-

mans beside the fountain was a jug of wine, a basket
of bread, a round of goat's cheese, trays of olives,
dates, and figs. Steam rose from a tall copper pitcher
set beside a bowl and a pile of linen towels on a second table. Careful preparations had obviously been
made for her return. There was everything here to
ensure that she could see to her own comfort.

Sarita pulled off the enshrouding burnous, running
her fingers through her hair, flooded suddenly with
an overwhelming sense of security in the quiet of solitude, in the calm familiarity of her surroundings.
Cupping her hand, she bent to drink from the fountain. The snug leather collar pressed into the soft flesh
beneath her chin, and she jerked upright as if she had
been stung. For those few minutes, in her relief, she
had forgotten the collar. Now a cold despair replaced
the relief, and a deep weariness of the spirit swamped
her, so that her limbs were lead weights. She could
barely drag herself over to the steaming pitcher, and
it was almost too much effort to dip one of the towels
in the hot water and bathe her face, wash her hands
clean of the grime of the day's imprisonment.

She managed somehow to remove her dress, shift,
and hose, and to sponge her body where the dust and
dirt of flight, a night in the open air, and the dreadful
hours of the day were ingrained. Naked, the cool air
of evening laving her skin, she poured a cup of wine,
took a handful of dates, and half crawled up the stairs
to the sleeping gallery. The divan was piled high with
fresh silk coverlets and cushions. Every piece of silk
she had used for her rope had been replaced. Sarita
staggered to the balconied window. Her rope still
hung there, mute reminder of disaster now rather
than invitation. Why had Abul not had it removed?
Presumably to underscore her failure. It hung there
in mockery. She would never attempt to use it again.
There was no more need to remove it than there was
to lock the door. The locks were in her own mind
now; they didn't need to be touched, to be seen, to
be effective. She knew what she was. A pile of gold

in a dim chamber in the house of Ibrahim Salem had told her what she was: owned, a possession. And the soft leather collar at her neck declared her owner: the device on the lock bore the insignia of Muley Abul Hassan.

Chapter 13

It was very early morning when Abul came to the tower. He stepped into the inner court, closing the door softly behind him. It was very still and quiet, and he stood listening for some sign of life. He knew she was there. Where else would she be?

"Sarita?"

There was no response. Still softly, he trod up the stairs to the sleeping gallery. The divan was empty, the rumpled coverlet evidence of the sleeper it had until recently contained.

"Sarita?" Quietly, he spoke her name again, looking around the gallery. There was still no response, and he moved further into the gallery. Then he saw her. She was wearing her orange dress, standing on the narrow balcony from where her rope hung, looking out across the ravine as the sun was rising.

"What are you doing?" He came up behind her.

She turned to face him, and a shard of remorse shivered in his belly at her extreme pallor, the haunted shadows in her eyes, huge in the small face. Her hand plucked at the leather collar. "Take it off," she said. "I cannot bear it. You must take it off."

"It is for your protection," he responded, hardening his heart, hearing again the scorn and loathing in her voice as he had heard it when last she had spoken to him. "Should you succeed in leaving here again, whoever finds you will return you to me. You will never again be at the mercy of a slave trader. You belong only to me for as long as I choose to keep you." He was wounding her as she had wounded him, and for the moment it felt right and proper. For the moment there was satisfaction.

"I do not belong to you. I do not belong to anyone." But her voice was dead, as if the spring of conviction had broken.

"Twelve ecus d'or tells me otherwise, *hija mía*," Abul said with harsh mockery.

A shudder ran through her. "Take it off. I cannot bear it," she repeated, her voice still as lifeless as a corpse. Pulling at the collar, she turned back to the balcony.

"What did you expect?" He moved beside her, putting a hand on her shoulder. "What did you expect, Sarita? You told me clearly enough what you think of me and my people, of our customs and beliefs, our laws and rites. Such barbarism is surely only what you would have expected. It was barbarism, wasn't it? That was the word you used so many, many times."

She looked up at him, her hand at her throat, for the moment unable to answer, seeing again the hurt and anger in his eyes, hearing both in his voice. For a minute she was overwhelmed with the knowledge of what she had lost: the laughing, loving, sensitive man she had been insensibly growing to love.

"If I can treat my wife and child with such savagery, why should I have any consideration for you? One who deliberately strayed in my world, inviting the barbarisms of my world. Since I always take what I want, why should I have scruples where you're concerned?"

She could hear her own voice in the bitter reprise of the words and accusations she had hurled at him, and a flicker of life appeared in her eyes at the knowledge that she had the opportunity to put this right. Maybe he wouldn't believe her. Maybe it wouldn't affect how he now saw her. But at least she could be at peace with herself.

"I didn't mean any of those things," she said. "I have been tormented by the pain I caused you. They were such dreadful things to say, but I had no choice."

Abul stared down at her, disbelieving, hearing only a pathetic attempt to improve her situation. "Apologies are very easy to make," he said shortly. "Particularly if one hopes they will serve a useful purpose."

She shook her head. "Believe that if you wish. I suppose I deserve that you should. But surely you must understand I had no choice."

He frowned. "Why?"

She shook her head again in a gesture of defeat. "How could I escape from this place if you were sharing my bed? I had to drive you from me, and the only way I could think of doing so was to give you such a distaste for me that you wouldn't wish to be near me. I knew how sensitive you are about your troubles with Aicha and Boabdil. I knew I could exacerbate that and achieve my object." She shrugged. "The rest I threw in for good measure. It seemed to make little difference after what had already been said." She turned back to the rail and her pointless yearning toward the mountains.

Abul closed his eyes and let out his breath on a long exhalation, inundated with a deep joy. How could he have been so blind? Misjudged her so badly? Failed to trust his own initial impressions? He didn't doubt the truth of her explanation; it fitted all too neatly with what he knew of her, of her instinct for challenge and combat, of the intelligence that would find the right tool, of the determination not to accept what he imposed upon her.

His hands moved to the nape of her neck, and the collar fell from her, tumbling into the ravine.

She watched it fall, her own hands clasped now around her bare neck, tears of relief starting in her eyes.

"I never intended you should wear it for more than a few hours," he said quietly, touching her back between her shoulder blades. "But I was very angry and wished to hurt you as you hurt me." Again she said nothing, but her back felt fluid beneath his hand as the rigidity of despair finally left her.

"Why do you not wish to stay with me, Sarita?" Abul now asked, realizing it was the first time he had posed the question, realizing what a painful question it was, because the answer could only bring him pain. It could only be that she could never imagine feeling anything for him but the inconvenient stirrings of her body; that she could feel more than that only for her dead lover; that she could not settle for anything less than what she had known with the dead man. For the first time, Abul entered the mind of Sarita of the tribe of Raphael and tried to see things from her point of view, rather than comfortably telling himself that soon she would learn the errors of that point of view and come to embrace his . . . the only right-thinking way of looking at the world and relationships.

In wretched anticipation of pain, he waited for her answer.

Slowly, she turned from the rail. Her face was alive again now, her eyes burning with a passionate fire. "Don't you understand?" she said. "It is not that I wish to leave you, but that I must know that I can."

The scales fell from his eyes. All this time, believing that by holding her with him, he would wear her down, finally compel her to act upon the powerful currents that flowed between them, he had been doing the opposite: holding her without her agreement, he had succeeded only in strengthening her resolution to leave him. Only by giving her her freedom would she come to him. Oh, how blind . . . how he had deservedly suffered for his blindness. Sarita was not of his people; her unlikeness was what had drawn him to her in the first place. But he had treated her as if she were a woman of the kind he knew, assuming their beliefs and acceptances, and he had used the tactics that would have worked with such a woman. But with this woman, they had had the opposite ef-

fect. He had nearly lost her with his blindness . . . he
who so prided himself on his wisdom, his far sight,
his understanding of the differences between races.
He had behaved like a green youth with no sense
beyond the imperatives of his loins.

For a minute he said nothing, looking beyond her
to the mountains that had so absorbed her. Then he
glanced down at her. She was wearing her orange
dress in her usual declaration of independence, but
her legs were bare. He turned back to the sleeping
gallery in search of the leather hose. He found them
tossed over an ottoman and brought them out to her,
to where she still stood immobile by the rail. The fire
had died in her eyes, and he could read both disappointment and sorrow in their depths at his failure to
respond to her appeal.

"Put these on." He held out the hose.

"Why?" She made no attempt to take them.

"Because I am telling you to. Twelve ecus d'or in-
vests me with the right to do so. Now put them on."
He wanted to laugh, to pull her to him, to kiss her
with the swift and eager passion flowing in his veins,
but he would not again make the first move of that
kind . . . not until things were as they were supposed
to be between them. Besides, he had a plan, and it
was a good one, filling him with deep delight. Kisses
at this point were not part of the plan.

Dumbly, she took the hose and went past him into
the gallery. She put them on as he stood watching
her, hiding his enjoyment in her movements, the
deftness as she drew the garment up her legs,
smoothing the butter-soft material, wriggling it over
her hips, fastening the buttons at the waist. She let
the dress fall back and met his gaze, still saying nothing.

"Come," he said, going past her to the stairs.

Sarita followed. She could think of no good reason
for refusing. She had made her bid for understanding
and lost. So what did anything matter now?

He led the way to the court of the alcazaba, where

he spoke in a low voice to an officer. The man went off and the caliph stood pensively, Sarita beside him in silence, feeling the sun warm on her bent neck as she looked down at the cobbles, filled with the lassitude of powerlessness.

The lassitude dissipated to some extent when a great bustle began in the court. Armed men in pronged helmets appeared from the alcazaba. Horses were led in from the stables, one of them the dappled gray palfrey she had ridden before.

"Up with you." Abul's voice broke the silence between them. He didn't wait for a response, simply caught her around the waist and lifted her atop the horse before mounting his own great steed.

Their escort this time was much larger and more fiercely armed than before, and there was no mule train laden with the necessities for a dinner under the sun. They clattered out onto the road and turned to the northwest. The narrow track snaked ahead, away from the city of Granada, and Abul rode in the same pensive silence he had maintained earlier.

At last Sarita was able to bear the suspenseful silence no longer. "Where do we ride with such an escort?" Her voice sounded stiff as if from disuse.

Abul remained looking ahead. "To Castile." He made the two words sound as if they were the most ordinary answer to a rather simple-minded question.

Sarita stared at him. "Castile?" she repeated stupidly. "But that is several days' ride."

He nodded airily. "Certainly, but we shall find hospitality on the road. And our escort is more than a match for brigands; you need have no fears."

"But why? Why do we go to Castile?" Sarita felt as if she were struggling to swim upward through some weed-tangled pond with the dark water obscuring the sunlight of comprehension. Nothing made sense anymore. He had taken off the collar, had spoken gently to her, had seemed to accept her apology and explanation for her assault, but then he had withdrawn from her, was making her accompany him on this strange expedition for which there was no explanation.

Abul glanced sideways at her, his expression calm. "Forgive me, *hija mía*, but I had the forceful impression that you wished to go to Castile. So I am taking you there. You cannot go alone; that has surely been made clear to you."

"You are taking me to Castile . . . to the border . . . out of this kingdom?" She was still struggling to swim through the pond weed and up to the sunlight.

"I am taking you to the border, where I will leave you. You will have that horse, and I will give you a purse of gold and one man to escort you to the nearest town. More than that I cannot do for you. But you will be in your own land and will surely find a friendly face."

Sarita broke through the weed and into the brilliant sunshine of illumination. She hadn't lost at all. Finally, Abul understood.

For a minute she was silent, basking in that blissful sunlight, filled with a profound happiness. She swallowed, trying to organize her thoughts, and then spoke carefully. "If . . . if perhaps I decided I didn't wish to go to Castile today, would you escort me on some other day, when I did wish to go?"

"Whenever you wish, Sarita." Now he turned to look at her properly, and there was warmth, love, and a deep yearning in his eyes, a deep and anxious yearning, and she knew he was laying himself before her, risking everything, letting go, in a way that he must never have done before. This man was not accustomed to letting slip that which he desired. "Whenever you wish to go into Castile, you will have the escort, the horse, the purse. You have only to say so."

The sweetest joy filled her, filled her until it brimmed from her eyes, spilling in salt tears, so that she dropped her gaze to the palfrey's embroidered saddlecloth to hide her face. When she had herself in hand again, she said, "I think . . . I think perhaps today is not a good day for such a journey. It might storm; do you not feel it? There is a heaviness in the air.''

"Indeed, I believe there is," he said gravely, overwhelmed with exaltation and relief. He had gambled and won. But then, perhaps it had not been such a gamble; Sarita had told him so many times what he had to do; he just hadn't understood before. He had been too frightened of losing her, he realized. But now he could accept that she would stay with him while she chose to do so, and he would honor his word and release her whenever he was no longer enough for her. It would be for him to ensure that that time never came.

"Do you then wish to return to the Alhambra?" he asked in the same grave tone, as if he were not singing inside, as if his blood were not sweeping through his veins in a tide of anticipation.

"For today," she replied. "Yes, I think for today I would wish to return."

He turned his horse on the steep track, calling to the escort, who without comment moved off the track to let the caliph and his companion through, and then fell in behind them.

"And what would you wish to do when we return?" Abul inquired after a while.

Sarita gave him a look of pure mischief. "I would visit the baths, my lord caliph. I feel sorely in need of repose and harmony as preparation for the loss of repose to come."

He laughed delightedly at this reminder of the conversation of their last outing. "The loving may be unreposeful, Sarita *mía*, but there will be true harmony at the finish." His eyes darkened, took on a smoky glow as they held the green clarity of hers. "I promise you that."

She nodded, her tongue touching her lips as she felt the power of the promise. She shifted on her horse as her body responded to that power with a pulsing, liquid surge of arousal. Her eyes widened and Abul chuckled, well aware of what was happening.

"I should sit very still if I were you," he advised. "And try to think of something else."

Sarita began to count the tassles on the palfrey's saddlecloth. They were delicately braided strands of silk, and fortunately there seemed to be a great many of them; they were very difficult to count. She could never be sure she hadn't missed one, so it was necessary to start the count again with increased concentration.

Abul, smiling to himself, rode in considerate silence beside her.

When they dismounted in the court of the alcazaba, a mere one hour after the warlike party had set out for Castile, Abul said, "Go back to the tower. Kadiga and Zulema will attend you there. You must break your fast, and it would please me if you would come to the baths wearing something other than that dress." He smiled, touched the corner of her mouth with a grazing fingertip. "Will you do that for me?"

"You don't find my dress becoming?" she queried, one eyebrow raised. "But I am most fond of it, my lord caliph."

"I had noticed," he replied. "But you have worn it a great deal, and it really has seen better days."

Sarita thought of all the garment had been through: rope climbing; a tumbling, thorny scramble down a mountainside; a night under the stars; long hours spent in a dirt-encrusted prison cell.

"Perhaps it had better be washed before I wear it again," she conceded.

"Yes, I think so," Abul concurred with a wonderful assumption of gravity. He turned from her and then realized she was standing quite still, looking around with an air of expectation that contained more than a hint of mischief. "What now?" he asked, waiting with a bubble of amusement for whatever roguery she was about to produce.

"Well, where is Yusuf?" she inquired innocently.

"He always returns me to my tower when you have finished with me."

"Don't you know the way by now?" Abul responded with imitative innocence. "You must forgive me, but I had thought you familiar with this place by now. As I recall, you had no difficulty finding your way to this court the other afternoon. But I will have someone accompany you." He raised a hand, summoning one of the soldiers.

"Perhaps I can find my way," Sarita said hastily as the armored man came hurrying over. "The cypress path lies beyond the Myrtle Court, does it not?"

Abul nodded, saying solicitously, "But are you quite sure you will not be lost?"

"Quite sure, my lord caliph." She offered him a formal bow, the effect spoiled by an irrepressible grin. "At least, no more so than I am already."

"In one hour," he said softly, lost himself in the sensual mischief in her green eyes.

"In one hour," she repeated and turned, leaving the court with swift, energetic strides, her skirt fluttering around her calves.

Kadiga and Zulema arrived in the tower within a few minutes of Sarita's return. They were initially awkward, uncertain how to treat her. The entire palace knew what had happened, how she had been brought back, and it was clear to Sarita that they were unsure as to her present status.

"Help me choose a robe," she said gaily, making for the stairs. "I must meet with the lord Abul in the baths within the hour and would wear something other than this." She indicated her dress. "And I suppose I had better wear slippers. Will you brush my hair, Zulema? It is such a tangle."

The two women exchanged looks, and then all uncertainty fell from them. Suddenly, for the first time since she had arrived in the Alhambra, Sarita was behaving in a manner they understood. They followed her up the stairs.

"Where did you go?" Kadiga asked, sorting

through the robes on the rod. "Did you truly climb down from the balcony?"

"Yes," Sarita said. "The rope is still there, if you care to look."

Zulema approached the balcony as if it might bite, and her jaw dropped as she saw the silk hanging from the rail. "You climbed down that, Sarita? But it is impossible. You would kill yourself."

"Well, I didn't," Sarita responded cheerfully. "As you can see." Frowning, she flicked through the material Kadiga was holding. "I don't know. I have no experience in choosing clothes. Which do you think, Kadiga?"

"If it is to please the lord Abul, I think any one will be suitable since they are all his choice."

"So they are . . . so they are," murmured Sarita, for some reason finding the idea as amusing as it was strangely pleasurable. "Well, you decide. I am very hungry." She wandered to the gallery rail, looking down into the court. "Is someone going to bring food?"

"Yes, indeed," Zulema said in her customary soothing fashion. "Let me help you remove your dress." She unlaced the bodice, clucking at the general condition of the orange garment. "Whatever have you been doing, Sarita?"

Sarita laughed, feeling wonderfully lighthearted as she pulled the dress over her head. "You would be shocked if I were to tell you, Zulema. And I don't imagine you would believe me—oh, is that someone bringing food?" Sounds from the court below drew her back to the gallery rail. A woman was laying a tray on the table by the fountain. "That bread smells delicious." She ran down in her shift, Zulema following, and took a flat buttery round from the basket, smiling at the woman who had brought it. The woman looked completely nonplussed at the sight of this flaming-haired creature, smiling warmly, wearing nothing but a flimsy and none-too-clean smock.

"My thanks," Sarita mumbled through her mouthful, turning her attention back to the tray. There was a bowl of yogurt, a dish of honey, a gently steaming pot of the jasmine infusion these people seemed to find so refreshing. In fact, she decided, dipping a spoon in the yogurt, the scent alone was most refreshing. "What have you found, Kadiga?" She wandered back up the stairs, licking the yogurt off the spoon, sipping a cup of the jasmine tea.

"This one . . . for the baths." Kadiga held up a robe of lavender silk. It was simpler than the others, without decoration except for a circle of coral beads sewn at the neck.

"Oh, yes, that looks perfect." Sarita put down her cup and hauled her shift over her head. Kadiga dropped the lavender silk in its place, smoothing it over the lines of her body. It clung and hinted just as the others did, for all its simplicity.

"Let me brush your hair now." Zulema flourished Sarita's hairbrush. "It is such a tangle," she tutted, tugging through the curls. "Shall I tie it back with a ribbon?"

"No," Sarita said. She had the impression that Abul liked her hair in all its unruliness. He had never said, but there was something about the way he ran his fingers through it, lifting it away from her face, something about the smile in his eyes as he did so that had given her that unmistakable impression. "Hurry now. It is time I was going."

"We will escort you," Kadiga said.

"Oh, there is no need. I know my way."

"It will be expected," Kadiga said stubbornly. "We are your attendants."

Sarita looked at herself in the glass and shrugged. It was one thing to roam the courts and gardens of the Alhambra alone as a fiercely resistant prisoner in her orange dress, barefoot and bare-legged. But assuming the garb of the Alhambra implied acceptance of its customs and expectations.

"Very well. Then let us go. But I will not cover my head."

"If the lord Abul does not insist . . ." Zulema murmured doubtfully.

"The lord Abul insists upon nothing," Sarita stated absolutely. She read incredulity and disbelief in their eyes but shrugged it off. Impossible to explain what had happened . . . impossible to explain how she felt . . . impossible to explain what lay between Muley Abul Hassan and Sarita of the tribe of Raphael. Impossible to explain that what lay between them was about to be consummated. The two women could never believe that it hadn't already been so.

Her toes curled in the silly slippers she wore, her blood singing in her veins, as they left the tower. She thought of Sandro . . . of how she had felt when she had been hurrying to meet him for one of their snatched, clandestine, terrifying lovings. She had felt the same heart-stopping excitement and anticipation, but never this lightheartedness, this desire to laugh, to sing, to dance. She had loved Sandro. It was a love she could keep within her, a warm, youthful memory of a shared passion. The tragedy of his death would always be with her, but it need not sour the present or the future. It had nothing to do with Abul, with her feelings for him. The love she had shared with Sandro and the consequences of that love had their own integrity. They were a part of her and always would be. And that was all they were; sufficient unto themselves.

Her attendants accompanied her to the hall of immersion. As before, they met no one on their way through the soft green, water-imbued peace of the grottoes.

"We will leave you here to await the lord Abul," Kadiga said as they reached the central hall.

Sarita looked for the keepers of the baths, but they were not in evidence, and when Kadiga and Zulema had left her, she was quite alone in the profound, reposeful silence of the chamber. The solitude and silence had a curious effect, turning her mind inward in contemplation of what was to come, of the physical act for which these moments were preparation. Without conscious thought, she drew her robe over her head, letting it fall to the ground, and stood running her hands over her body, feeling the rippling of her skin, the tingle of her nipples, the slowly building surge in her loins. She raised her arms, her hands catching her hair at the nape of her neck, lifting it away from her as she stood on tiptoe, stretching with a deeply satisfying languor.

Abul stood behind a column at the rear of the hall, watching her in her abstraction, finding her private absorption in her body and its sensations more arousing than anything he could have imagined. He took in every line of that delicate frame, the clean-limbed perfection, the ivory tones of her breasts, belly, and loins startling against the sun-gold of her forearms and legs, the silken red-gold dusting at the base of her belly. He had seen her naked before, but he had never watched her nakedness, watched her alone with herself.

"How very beautiful you are," he said, stepping out from behind the column.

Sarita whirled toward him, her eyes startled, a slightly self-conscious smile touching her lips. "It is unchivalrous of you to hide when a lady is disrobing."

"Maybe, but it afforded me much pleasure." Moving toward her, he took her hands, held them away from her, ran his eyes in a long, slow sweep down her body, before drawing her against his length, cupping her chin in his palm, lifting her face, taking her mouth with his. Sarita gave herself to this kiss without reservation, without guilt or inhibition, finally able to indulge her wanting unrestrainedly.

His body hardened beneath his burnous, and Sarita pressed against the shaft nudging her belly, her hand moving in a tantalizing caress through the soft material. "Take the robe off," she whispered. "I cannot feel you properly."

Abul drew back for a minute, surprised at the directness of the demand. For some reason, although he knew she was not inexperienced, he had not expected such confidence, such lack of inhibition. He had thought she would be more hesitant, more reserved. He looked down into her eyes, glowing green pools of candid desire, and he smiled, swiftly pulling the burnous from his body.

Sarita gave a little sigh of satisfaction as his body was revealed. "I have wanted to touch you so many times," she confided, moving her flat palms over his nipples and down to his belly. "When we were last in this place, I had such difficulty containing myself. Only you . . ." She looked up with a rueful chuckle. "Only you seemed completely unaffected by *my* body. I was afraid you no longer desired me, and it was most mortifying."

Abul frowned, trying to remember; then he gave a crow of laughter. "That, sweet innocent, was because I had spent some considerable time with Fatima. After the night we had passed, I was in great discomfort."

"Ahhh . . ." She nodded, and her hand drifted over his belly, feeling the involuntary contraction of his abdominal muscles before passing in a whisper of a caress between his thighs. "But there seems no such difficulty today."

"None whatsoever," he agreed, his breathing ragged. "Quite the contrary. Let us move to the baths, *querida*, before we . . . or rather I . . . reach a premature conclusion."

Smiling, she took her hands away from his body. "I do not believe you lack control, my lord caliph."

"In general I do not," he said, taking her hands, turning them palm upward, pressing his lips into the warm skin. "But you have the most disturbing effect on me, Sarita *mía*."

Sarita's bare feet shifted on the cool tiles as desire rushed immoderate and invincible from her scalp to her toes. "Perhaps we should take the baths later."

"No," Abul said firmly. "I have already waited a

lifetime. I can wait a little longer. Come." He encouraged her to the edge of the sunken marble tank of hot water.

Sarita slipped below the surface, watching through half-closed eyes as Abul came in opposite her. She stretched out a foot and ran it up his leg, her toes nuzzling between his thighs. "I do not think we should use the cold water today," she observed judiciously.

"The progression must be complete, *hija mía*," he said lazily, shifting his body for her exploring toes.

"But I'm very much afraid that the cold will have a shriveling effect," she said with an assumption of great concern, her toes continuing to make the point.

"The soles of your feet are more likely to do that," Abul retorted, suddenly seizing both her feet in his hands. "Enough mischief; come here." Releasing her feet, he reached out to grasp her hands again, pulling her across the tank until she was sitting on her ankles in the water between his knees. "That's better." His hands moved over her breasts beneath the water, lifting them clear so that the cool air and the tip of his finger could graze their crowns. Gently he rolled the hardening nipples between thumb and forefinger, increasing the pressure until she moaned, her body arching, offering her breasts to his touch.

"Kneel up," he softly directed, his hands now drifting downward over her belly where his fingers lost themselves in the silken triangle at its base. As she obeyed, he parted her thighs to receive the smooth caress of the water even as his fingers followed, probing deeply, insistently, until her moans became sobbing cries of delight. He drew her upward until she lay across his knees, her body opened for his exploration, the gentle lapping of the water as much an instrument of pleasure as his hand, and he used both with knowing artistry until she was mindless, a sensate being at one with the watery element that held and caressed her, indivisible from the man.

This time there was no mind-induced denial of her

body's pleasure. She rose to meet the delight he brought, curled around it, stretched beneath it, gave herself absolutely.

He held her until the quivering of her body had ceased and she opened her eyes, smiling up into the dark ones above her. Effortfully, she reached up a hand to stroke his face, to trace the curve of his mouth. "I seem to be dissolved."

Abul laughed softly. "The next stage will put you back together again."

"Oh, no!" Sarita struggled upright, pushing herself off his legs to slide into the water beside him. "No, you cannot really intend—"

"Most certainly I do," he interrupted, standing up.

"But you *will* shrivel," Sarita wailed, only half laughing. "It cannot be good for you in such a condition, Abul."

He stood on the edge of the bath, feet apart, looking down at her with wicked amusement. "You know very little about this, it seems. Come, one quick dip and it will all be over."

"No, I cannot. I feel too wonderfully relaxed. The shock will kill me."

"It's because you are relaxed that it's good for you," he tried to explain. "For me, the opposite is true. I am overstimulated and need to cool off. You need to wake up. Come now, it will soon be over."

"I don't want to," she said, softly pleading, cowering under the warmth of the water. "*Please.*"

Abul shook his head in defeat. "I told you I would never force you to do anything you don't wish, *cara*. But I wish you would trust me to know what's best." He turned and plunged into the marble tank of cold water, emerging, spluttering, shaking the water off himself with all the vigor of a drenched dog as he hauled himself out.

Sarita stood up, stepped resolutely to the edge of the other tank, closed her eyes, and jumped. Her feet touched bottom, and she leaped upward again with a shriek, scrambling out in a hasty and inelegant tangle of limbs.

"What an enchanting sight!" Abul bent to help her up, laughing at her graceless haste and her expression of shocked indignation. He tossed a towel around her shoulders and began to rub her dry. "Why did you change your mind?"

"Because it seemed only just that I should trust you," she said through chattering teeth. "But I felt wonderful before, and now I am all cold and awake."

"You need to be awake," he said. "We have but barely begun. Or did you think it was time for a little sleep?"

"Well, no, not exactly." She took a corner of the towel and began to rub his thigh with great concentration. "But it's a very rude shock, I'll have you know."

"I am aware." He stood still while she dried him as vigorously as he had performed the service for her. "Now we shall get thoroughly warm."

"In that place where you can't breathe," Sarita lamented, following him nevertheless into the steam room. "Where are the keepers of the baths?"

"Somehow I felt they might be in the way." Abul stretched out on a marble slab, already prepared with a towel. "Lie very still and breathe."

"I can do one but not the other," she grumbled.

"Don't talk!"

Smiling to herself, she stretched out. Abul was so wonderfully single-minded. A few minutes before, he had been making transcendent love to her, and now he was telling her to be quiet and melt because that was the activity at present at hand. That the lovemaking and the melting were compatible partners Sarita did not dispute. It was something Abul would know a great deal better than she, and she supposed she would learn in time. So far he had made no mistakes . . . not even, she had to admit, the icy dunking.

"I'm just a puddle," she said after a few minutes.

"If I stay here much longer, you'll have to wipe me off this slab with a towel or pour me into a jug."

Abul slowly swung himself off the slab. "Come in the other chamber." He steadied her as she stood up, her head spinning slightly as it had before. Then, in the small grotto next door, he poured jugs of cool water over her. Sarita luxuriated in the glorious cessation of steaming heat, offering him every surface of her body as her skin came vibrantly to life. Then she took up the next line of jugs standing ready-filled and performed the same service for him.

"You must bend down," she said, laughing. "How can I pour water over your shoulders when they are so much higher than I am?"

Abul obliged, giving her his back, bending over so that she could douse him liberally. She moved suddenly behind him, clasping his waist strongly, nestling herself against his buttocks, sliding her hands around his body on a delicious trespass of her own. There was something exquisite in the feel of their cool, wet skins pressed together. The torpor of the first bath was long gone, the languor of satiation dissipated under the slow but steady return of arousal. Oh, yes, Sarita decided, the baths and lovemaking were most compatible partners.

Abul straightened slowly, turned, and caught her to him again. He kissed her with absolute concentration, holding her lightly by the upper arms, otherwise touching no part of her but her mouth, so that all sensation was concentrated on their conjoined mouths: the partnering tongues, the pliancy of lips, the warm sweetness within.

When they finally drew apart, the water had dried on their skins, the coolness replaced by natural warmth and the heated beginnings of passion. "I am going to oil you," Abul said quietly, leading her into the Hall of Repose. "And use the strigil. Then you may do the same for me."

Sarita nodded, entranced again by the grace and beauty of the hall, by the soft strains of harp and lyre

drifting down from the balcony. It was as if the hall
and its atmosphere deliberately created a lull in the
spiral of passion . . . a spiral that would coil all the
tighter for the lull.

She stretched out on the cushioned divan, letting
her eyes close, inhaling the delicate scent of the perfumed oil as Abul warmed it over the spirit lamp. She
felt his hands on her back, strong and smooth, knead-
ing the oil into her skin, relaxing her yet also awak-
ening her. Lazily she turned her head and suddenly
remembered the last time she'd been here, when she
had woken, turned her head, and come face-to-face
with the caliph's principal wife, watching her as she
slept.

"How many women do you have?" she asked, art-
lessly enough. "In the Alhambra, I mean."

The hands on her back stilled for a minute, then
began their work again. "There are many women in
the Alhambra."

"No . . . but you know what I mean. How many
do *you* have to serve you, if that's the right term?"

If Abul had answered the question as simply as it
had been asked, she would probably have ceased to
be curious. It didn't strike Sarita as at all an impolitic
question. She knew the facts, after all. Abul, however, found the question both impolitic and unnecessary.

"Why would you want to know, Sarita?"

There was a closed note in his voice that seemed to
Sarita to require a challenge. As usual, she rose to the
challenge with a tingle of excitement. "Well, I'd quite
like to know how large your stable is, and where I
come in the order of preference— Oww!" She rolled
off the divan with a reflex movement, leaping to her
feet, glaring at him, one hand rubbing her bottom.
"You *meant* that. That wasn't playful!"

"No," Abul said consideringly, wiping his oily
hands on a towel. "No, I don't believe it was. Although I took myself by surprise. But that was the

most inappropriate, indiscreet remark you've yet made. And that, *hija mía*, is saying quite a lot.''

''Oh, is it?'' She advanced on him, the light of battle in her eyes, and he chuckled, recognizing the signs of Sarita about to enter the lists. ''Well, let me tell you, my lord caliph, that where I come from, women don't have to compete with each other for the attentions of one man. And since I am in this strange place—''

''Through your own choice,'' he murmured.

''Yes, through my own choice,'' she concurred impatiently. ''But since I am here, I think I'm entitled to know how and where I stand.'' She gave him a little push in the chest in emphasis and then jumped back, daring him with her eyes, where sparked excitement engendered by a great deal more than indignation.

''So much for the Hall of Repose,'' Abul mused, accepting the dare. He lunged for her, but her oiled body slipped through his grasp, and she was off across the court with a shriek of mock dismay. The sweet strains of music continued to drift down from the balcony as they dodged around the columns, Sarita enticing him with her body, turning this way and that to offer him glimpses of her small, firm breasts, of her backside, of the soft concavity of her belly, of the smooth, sinuous muscularity of her limbs.

He caught her when he decided to do so, taking her by surprise as he had done once before with a swift reversal of direction. ''You should remember the lessons of the past,'' he said, holding her firmly against him. Sarita drew a gulping, panting breath, but it was not as a result of the chase. Then, on a devilish impulse, she twisted in his hold, ducking her head beneath his arm, making a bid for freedom as she used her body as a lever. Abul laughed exultantly, brought his other hand around to improve his hold, and lifted her off the ground.

''So much for the Hall of Repose,'' he reiterated, bearing her backward to the cushioned divan, his eyes heavy with anticipation, meeting the green, sparking, elated anticipation in her own.

Sarita fell back on the divan, but her legs moved of their own volition to clasp his waist. She was lost now in the spirit of pursuit and capture, in the physical exaltation of the moment, freed from all need to hold back, to deny her responses to the game or her need for its conclusion. She curled her legs around his waist, pulling him into the cleft of her opened body.

"I had intended a little more leisure," Abul whispered, momentarily holding himself on the tender edge of her body. "But you seem to know what you want, Sarita *mía*. Are you sure you're ready?" But he could see it in her eyes, feel it in her skin, and if he was still in any doubt, her feet pressed into his buttocks, driving him within.

With a low moan of joy, he entered her, feeling the soft velvety walls of her being enclose him, feeling her pleasure as her hips lifted to meet him, her hands moved to grasp his upper arms, her head shifted on the cushions.

"Love me." The passionate demand whispered through the hall beneath the gentle plucking of the harp. "Abul, *querido*, love me."

"With all my heart," he whispered back, lost in her joy, in the affirmation of her words, in the knowledge that he had found something he had never realized he had been missing . . . something for which he would renounce everything if it were demanded of him . . . something he would defend with his life.

Chapter 14

❦

"The lord Abul comes. He is crossing the Court of the Lions."

This information, breathlessly imparted by a small child peering through the jalousies of a window overlooking the court below, was greeted with much rustling of silken skirts and whispered excitement in the seraglio, only Sarita remaining apparently unmoved on a divan in a dim corner of the central parlor.

The woman with whom she had been conducting a painstaking conversation in halting Arabic smiled apologetically as she drew the language lesson to a close and rose, hastening over to a mirrored dresser where other women clustered, patting their hair, straightening ruffles at necks and wrists, smoothing out creases in their skirts.

Sarita watched the scene with amusement not unmixed with incomprehension. Even after six months, she still could not fully understand or accept the way the women of the seraglio viewed Abul. He was the supreme being in their lives, his visits eagerly anticipated, endlessly discussed. His physical health, state of mind, and humor were all argued over, worried about, or seen as matters for self-congratulation. There was a degree of rivalry among them, but it rarely led to unpleasantness, and Sarita herself had been accepted with interest as a pleasurably different addition to their circle. The fact that she was their lord's undisputed favorite seemed to trouble none of them. They lived their own lives in their own apartments, lives of leisure and indolence, enlivened by gossip, veiled excursions to the bazaars in Granada, long hours in the baths, music, games, their children, and, most of all, by the caliph's visits.

All except for Aicha, Sarita thought, her eyes going to the tall, luxuriant figure of Abul's principal wife. Aicha was sitting with her son, it being the hour after sundown, and at the news of the caliph's impending arrival she had drawn Boabdil closer to her side, whispered something to him, smoothed his hair. It looked on the surface as if she were trying to comfort or reassure him, but the child, instead of taking comfort, appeared a great deal more alarmed than he had before.

Aicha was no passive recipient of the caliph's favor and bounty. Sarita had realized this very early on in their acquaintance. Aicha had her own plans, her own ideas about the way she wanted things to be, and Sarita had decided that the lady had more than sufficient determination and ingenuity to succeed in fulfilling them. She professed friendship for Sarita, and Sarita accepted it without apparent question, although she steered clear of exchanges of confidence; and whenever Aicha brought up the subject of Abul's treatment of Boabdil, Sarita resolutely changed the subject.

Aicha appeared unperturbed by this, continued to be friendly, but sometimes Sarita sensed undercurrents that made her uneasy. It was not so much what Aicha said, but some shadow lurking in her seemingly smiling brown eyes. Sarita was aware that the other women feared Aicha, and she was aware of the extent of the power the sultana wielded over the inhabitants of the seraglio. And occasionally, Sarita had the impression that that power extended beyond the seraglio. No, Aicha was quite unlike the other women. She certainly had her own sphere of influence and not least over her son—

Sarita's musing was interrupted by the sound of

Abul's voice carrying from the hall below the jalousied gallery of the seraglio. As always, her heart leaped and an involuntary smile of anticipation touched her lips. She had been waiting for that sound since the bells from the alcazaba had heralded the caliph's return from his two-week journey to Tangier. Two weeks was too long a separation, she had decided many times during the interminable fourteen days.

The other women began to move toward the doorway. Only Aicha remained where she was, although she rose to her feet. Boabdil clung to her skirt like a six-year-old, not at all like a tall lad well into his twelfth year.

Sarita stayed on her divan. When the bells had brought the news of Abul's return, she had debated going to her tower to await him there, but a streak of stubbornness had kept her in the seraglio, continuing her language lesson with the amenable Fadha. She knew that for some reason Abul disliked her spending time in the seraglio with his wives. He had never said as much, but a flicker of displeasure would darken his eyes and his mouth would tauten whenever he came across her there or had to seek her out there. But she saw no reason not to enjoy the company of the other women, particularly in Abul's absence. She had grown up in the gregarious circumstances of tribal life and found little pleasure in solitude. Kadiga and Zulema were good friends, but increasingly these days they had other duties that kept them away from the tower. Once, when she had laughingly complained of their neglect, they had both looked awkward and muttered something about the lady Aicha's instructions. She had tried to press them, but Kadiga had firmly changed the subject and the more malleable Zulema had looked unaccountably frightened.

Abul was in the chamber now, and she listened to the musical resonance of his voice as he greeted the women clustering around him. His eyes lifted, ran around the chamber, found Sarita in her dim corner, and held her green gaze for a long, frowning minute, as if he could thus read her soul. She smiled and he nodded imperceptibly, as if satisfied, before turning to where Aicha and Boabdil stood, just outside the eagerly welcoming circle.

"Greetings, Aicha." He came toward her. "And you, my son." He held out his hand to the boy, who hesitated for an agonizing minute before taking it. As soon as he was released, he inched backward again behind his mother.

Aicha's attempt to hide her satisfaction would probably convince most people, but not a truly observant watcher. A flash of exasperation crossed Abul's face, and Sarita winced. She had watched similar scenes many times, but the subject was taboo between herself and Abul, carrying too many hurtful memories to be raised, so she kept silent. But one day she was sure she would be unable to maintain her silence with Aicha. She could not imagine what the woman hoped to gain by destroying all possibility of a relationship between father and son, but that she was doing so was as obvious to Sarita as it was to Abul.

Abul now spoke quietly to Aicha, ignoring the cowering Boabdil. Sarita could hear nothing of what was said, but she could tell by the way Aicha abruptly lowered her eyes to the floor that it was disagreeable. She had noticed how Aicha frequently hid her expressions, either by lowering her eyes or by turning away, and was convinced that the present lowering was to hide her annoyance rather than to express submission to her lord.

Finally, Abul turned from her. His eyes sought Sarita's again, and she could feel the jagged edges of his customarily smooth surface. "Come," he said shortly, beckoning her with the tips of his fingers. Turning on his heel, he left the chamber.

Sarita rose and followed, the other women falling back to make way for her. She paused deliberately to bid them farewell, to thank Fadha for her patience over the lesson, aware as she did so that they couldn't understand why she was delaying when the caliph had summoned her. She didn't really understand it herself, since both body and soul yearned to be alone with Abul, but she still seemed to need to make these statements of independence.

He was waiting for her in the Court of the Lions, a veritable monument of forbearance as he leaned against the massive head of a lion at the fountain, arms folded, gaze fixed languidly on the surrounding peaks as the residual flush of the sunset left them.

"You certainly took your time," he observed as she emerged from the portico and slowly crossed the court toward him, the folds of her robe flowing gently from her hips as she walked. There was a glimmer of laughter in the eagle's black eyes . . . laughter and unashamed lust as his gaze dwelt on the hinted lines of her body.

"I had to make my farewells," she replied, reaching him, standing close yet not touching him, both of them relishing the prospect of touching, a prospect made all the more delightful by this willful restraint.

"I had hoped to find you in the tower," Abul said. "Were you so uneager for my return that you preferred the gossip of the seraglio to preparing a welcome for me?" There was the faintest hint of reproach in his voice, momentarily banishing both laughter and lust.

Sarita shook her head, smiling. "No, indeed not, my lord caliph. But I thought to heighten the pleasure of greeting you by prolonging the wait."

Abul's eyes narrowed. "I wonder if that was the only reason."

"Believe it to be so," she advised. Her tongue touched her lips, and her voice dropped. "I am tingling all over just standing beside you, *querido*. If you do not touch me soon, I shall expire of unrequited wanting."

He laughed, reached out a nonchalant hand, and

lightly brushed the curls away from her forehead. "Not unrequited, *hija mía*. For the past three hours I have been able to think of nothing but the feel of your skin, the scent of your hair, the softness of your body. Every curve and hollow is imprinted on the palms of my hands; the taste of you is on my tongue; the absolute knowledge of your body is in my head and in my eyes."

"Come," Sarita said in her turn as desire jolted in the pit of her stomach, sending burning currents down her thighs. Unable to take her eyes off him, she began to walk backward, her hand reaching for his. "Come," she repeated, softly, urgently imperative. "Come, before I do something that must not be witnessed."

Abul's eyes flicked upward to the shuttered windows of the seraglio overlooking the court, and he grinned. "Had you been waiting for me in proper fashion, you would not find yourself in such difficulties."

"If you would revenge yourself in this fashion, my lord caliph, I take leave to tell you that it shows a niggardly spirit." Before he could respond, she suddenly picked up her skirts and set off at a most indecorous run out of the court, through the portico, not slowing until she had reached the cypress path to the tower.

Abul, laughing, followed at a fast walk, his blood singing with all the joys of anticipation.

Neither of them had been aware of the shadowy eyes of Aicha watching from behind the jalousie of an overlooking window. She hadn't been able to hear anything of what was said between them, but she had needed no ears to catch the deep, sensual currents flowing between them. The power of that attraction was an almost palpable aura around them, and somehow she knew it was not just their bodies that yearned to be united. There was a deeper, stronger bond that joined them. And it was that bond that threatened the sultana's future . . . that bond that must be destroyed.

It had been nearly two weeks since she had sent the message to her father, emir of the powerful Mocarabes family, telling him of her husband's blind passion for a Christian captive, and of her fear that he was losing the power to govern, even as he talked wildly of repudiating his own true wife and heir in favor of the unbeliever. There was no truth in the latter accusations, but she knew they would inflame her father. He would spread the word among the other great families, and a challenge to Muley Abul Hassan's right of kingship was inevitable. There would be dissension in the kingdom as the great families divided in allegiance, and even if Abul survived the challenge, he would be much weakened. It would be a significant first step in her long- and lovingly plotted scheme to overthrow her husband. And such conflict in the Morisco-Spanish kingdom would be bound to attract the attention of the ever-watchful Spanish across the border, who would perhaps see an opportunity for interference, thus increasing the pressure on Abul.

Thoughtfully, she turned back to the parlor. Boabdil had left her side as soon as his father had departed and was wrestling roughly with one of the smaller children. The younger child had begun to cry as his elder brother held his head in a fierce lock beneath his arm. Boabdil was laughing as if it were still a game. No one said anything . . . no one daring to chide Aicha's son. The small child's mother chewed her lip, wringing her hands in despairing frustration as her son's cries grew louder.

"Enough, Boabdil," Aicha finally said when the cries had reached a fever pitch.

"I am teaching him how to fight," Boabdil declared, reluctantly loosening his grip. The child wriggled free and ran sobbing to his mother. "He has to learn, doesn't he, Mother?"

"Yes . . . yes . . . and it is good of you to wish to

teach him," Aicha said. "But come with me to my apartments now. There are some things I would talk to you about." The two left the chamber, Boabdil chattering, Aicha still distracted.

Her two-pronged attack was making a slow start. Her father had not yet responded to her message, and so far the Christian showed no signs of ill health. By now there should be some signs of weakness, some reduction in that robust energy she always exhibited. Perhaps the strength of the potion should be increased. But Aicha couldn't afford to run the risk of discovery, and if the Spaniard's debilitation became suddenly noticeable, questions would be asked. Even though she was preventing Kadiga and Zulema's constant attendance on Sarita, Aicha was well aware of Kadiga's shrewd watchfulness. The attendant missed little of what was said and done within the palace and brought an unusually intelligent analysis to bear in many cases. No . . . Aicha must strive for patience. Sarita was obviously stronger and healthier than she had bargained for. But she could not hold out against the insidious bane forever. Soon it would take its toll . . .

"So, have you missed me at all, *cara?*" Abul asked teasingly when their rapid progression had brought them to the seclusion of the tower.

"Oh, yes," she said, turning to face him.

"Which part have you missed the most?" he asked, leaning back against the closed door, his eyes brightly observing her, taking in the slight flush of excitement on her cheeks, the green flames of desire flickering deep in her eyes.

Sarita put her head to one side, clipping her bottom lip between even white teeth. "Let me see . . ." She considered. "Many parts, I believe. This, for instance." Standing on tiptoe, she touched his mouth with her lips, a butterfly kiss. "And this . . ." The tip of his chin came next. "And this . . ." She touched her tongue to the hollow of his throat, where his neck rose strong and golden from the collar of his tunic. "And this . . ." Her swift fingers unlaced his tunic and pushed open the shirt beneath, baring his chest so that she could lightly brush the small, hard nipples with her tongue. "And this . . ." One hand moved behind him, fingers insinuating themselves inside the belted waist of his riding britches, wriggling downward to the base of his spine. "And most especially this . . ."

Abul inhaled sharply at the insistent, intimate pressure, then felt the buckle of his belt loosening under the deft manipulation of her other hand; her flat palm warmed his belly as she reached for the upwardly thrusting shaft of his passion. He let the door at his back take the weight of his shoulders, his knees bending slightly as the wickedly erotic caresses continued, enveloping him in heated sensation that promised the soul's drowning.

Very slowly, she withdrew her hands, and his eyes opened as a beatific smile came to his lips. "Yes," she whispered, "I have missed all those parts, but most of all have I missed the sum of the parts: the whole man, Abul, *querido.*"

Abul stood straight, pushing himself away from the door, his breathing ragged as he brought himself back from the brink of bliss. Still smiling, he refastened his belt, then lifted Sarita in his arms. "I don't think I'll stand you against the door for my own naming of parts," he murmured, and she chuckled, slipping her arms around his neck, pulling his head down to hers. He walked with her to the stairs of the sleeping gallery, his mouth still joined with hers.

Upstairs he bent to lay her on the bed, but she clung to his neck, her tongue suddenly pushing into his mouth, expressing abrupt, urgent demand. "*Now!*" she whispered against his mouth. "Right away, Abul."

Her upsurge of unquenchable ardor spilled over him, sweeping him along with her as she wriggled and twisted on the cushioned divan, trying to free her legs from the confines of her robe even while she kept her arms around his neck, her mouth locked with his. He slipped one hand beneath her, turning her slightly on one side to release the skirt before pushing it up to her waist as she fell back again. If he had had the least inclination to deny her demand, to prolong the waiting, the softness of her skin, the sinuous curve of her hip, her legs as straight and as lissome as hazel wands, destroyed all possibility of control.

Kneeling on the bed beside her, he fumbled with the buckle of his belt, but she was quicker and defter than he and pushed his britches off his hips, a fingernail scraping his thigh in her haste. He was about to take off his boots but paused for an instant to look down at her as she sprawled in wanton abandon, her hips lifting unconsciously, her thighs parted, a sheen of moisture on the satiny inner slopes glimmering in the soft glow of the lamplight. He was lost, irretrievably, and with a shuddering breath came over her, sliding his hands beneath her to lift her to meet him as he entered her body in one deep, probing thrust. Sarita cried out, tears standing in her eyes with the joy of his presence within her, her body moving rhythmically with his, her gaze riveted to the dark pools of passion above her. There came the moment when their eyes widened simultaneously with the ever-magical realization that the supreme joy could always be repeated, always found again, and Sarita laughed and Abul laughed back as he drove to her core and the world dissolved.

It was much later when Sarita returned to her self in the galleried chamber. She had been content to drift in a dozy dream of satiation, her lower body still pressed to Abul's, her robe twisted beneath her, his head resting on her breast. But the sounds of movement in the court below brought her back to her senses. The sounds did not disturb her. She had become perfectly accustomed in the past months to the quiet, uncommanded attentions of shadowy servants in the palace. The caliph's whereabouts were always known to the vizier, his needs always anticipated. Presumably, it was now suppertime.

Abul sat up, his skin seeming to unpeel itself from Sarita's. He stretched languidly before bending to drop a kiss on her freckled nose. "Content, Sarita *mía*?"

She nodded. "For the moment."

He laughed. "Insatiable woman. I do not think I have ever before made love in my boots! But now I need my supper. I was in such haste to reach you by sundown that we didn't break our journey to dine this day." He pulled up his britches and strode to the gallery rail, calling down, "Make haste and leave."

He turned back to the divan, where Sarita still lay sprawled half naked on the cushions. "There is a bath below. We will sup more comfortably after a soak in hot water." Leaning over her, he pulled her into a sitting position and lifted the robe over her head, observing, "There is something wickedly seductive about a half-naked woman."

"More than a completely naked one?" Sarita stood and stretched in her turn.

"Completely naked, you don't seem quite so provocative," he said thoughtfully. "Most beautiful and desirable, but not wicked. I find your wickedness most amazingly arousing."

Sarita regarded him quizzically, pushing her fingers through her hair to release the wild curls. "I'll try to remember that, should I ever need to arouse you when—"She broke off abruptly, her hand going to her throat.

"What is it?" Abul took her arm, alarmed by her pallor.

She said nothing for a moment, then drew a shaky breath. "It's nothing, really. My heart's beating very fast, but it will slow down. It's happened several times just recently." She sat down on the divan again, cradling her stomach. "I feel weak and queasy, but it will pass."

Abul frowned. She was still very pale, and he was

unconvinced by her reassurances. "Perhaps you are with child."

She shook her head. "No, I have been taking the draught Kadiga brings me, and I bled while you were away."

Abul's frown deepened. "Do you not wish to bear my child?"

Sarita looked up. It wasn't the right moment to deal with such a subject, but she didn't know how to answer with less than the truth. A circumlocution required more mental energy than she could at present muster. "Not in these circumstances, Abul."

"What are 'these circumstances'?" he inquired.

Sarita sighed and stood up tentatively. "Let us not talk of it now. We will only quarrel, and I don't feel strong enough."

Her color was beginning to return, but Abul, customarily sensitive, forbore to press her. "Lie down again," he said. "Rest for a few more minutes." He propped cushions up against the wall at the back of the divan and sat down, swinging his still booted legs onto the coverlet. "Come!" He patted the divan beside him imperatively. "Lie down here. The bath will wait."

Sarita sank down with a half-smothered sigh of relief. He put his arm around her and drew her against his chest, smoothing her hair. "How often has this happened?"

She frowned, trying to remember. "Several times in the last days. I haven't paid any attention to it, really."

"What does Kadiga say about it? She has some understanding of bodily ailments, I believe."

"She does not know of it. She and Zulema are rarely with me anymore. I understood that Aicha had need of them—"

"They do not come under Aicha's jurisdiction," Abul broke in vigorously. "Their primary task is to attend you whenever you have need. It is not for Aicha to alter that."

Sarita shook her head against his chest. "Perhaps I misunderstood," she ventured. "They did not exactly say as much . . . Besides," she added, rather more strongly, "I do not need to be waited upon hand and foot. It is only that I miss their company on occasion. We had become friends."

Abul said nothing. He could well imagine Aicha resenting such a friendship and doing what she could to break it. Alliances among the women of the Alhambra could be potentially threatening to her power and influence. Well, it would be easy enough for him to restore that friendship while he was in the palace. It was only in his absence that Aicha could work her malice.

"You must talk of these spells with Kadiga," he said. "If they do not abate and we cannot discover the cause, then you must consult Muhamed Alahma. He is a physician of great gifts and skills."

"A physician!" Sarita pushed herself upright. "What nonsense, Abul. My mother would give me a strong purge and I would be well again. I will ask Kadiga if she has the means to concoct such a thing."

Abul pulled doubtfully at his chin. But he knew little of such matters and assumed women knew best how to heal themselves. "Are you easier now?"

"Perfectly at ease," she said with a resumption of her usual vigor. "Let us go below, for if you are as hungry as I am, you could eat a camel."

Abul followed her to the now deserted court and sat watching as she dipped into the tub of steaming water. "Now you may tell me why the circumstances make you unwilling to bear my child. We will not quarrel, I promise you." His voice was calm, sounding merely curious, but Sarita was in no doubt as to the potential for hurt and acrimony in the subject.

Sighing, she rubbed the cake of soap between her hands and tried to explain. "I do not know what place I have here . . . or what place a child of mine would have, Abul. I know I am one of many women, and I can accept that . . . for as long as I remain here," she added. "For myself, I can accept that, but I could not accept such an unsatisfactory position for my child. To bear your child, to see him grow up in the seraglio, a secondary child with no real role or importance in this world, would mean that I had accepted absolutely that I belonged in this world, that I accepted its constraints for myself and my child. And I cannot do that. I love you, Abul, but I do not belong here."

"Why, then, do you spend so much time in the seraglio?" he asked. "You are always to be found with the other women, much as if you believe yourself to be one of them."

"Sometimes I am lonely," she said in simple truth. "And they are the only companionship available. Fadha is teaching me to speak Arabic." She sat up in the bath, hugging her knees. "You do not like it when I am there, do you?"

Abul shook his head. "No."

"Why not?"

He regarded her sharply. How to say that he wanted to keep her for himself, that he felt there was something indefinably unsuitable about her mingling with his wives? How to say that he did not trust Aicha's potential influence?

"Because you are not one of them," he said slowly. "You are not one of many. You know that there is no other woman for me, Sarita. Since you came, I have summoned none other."

"Yes, I know that. But if that is to remain the case, what are you going to do about them?"

"Why must I do anything?" He sounded genuinely puzzled.

"But if they are not to lie with you, then they have absolutely no function at all," she said. "Yet they are there, and because they are there, I cannot feel that you cleave only to me in the manner of my people, and therefore I cannot bear your child or agree to stay here indefinitely."

"You wish to leave me?" He struggled for understanding.

"No . . . no, of course I do not. But I do not know what to do as things are," she said with a frustrated groan. "I do not know who or what I am, and I have no sense of a future. I expect I could continue in this way. Indeed, I can see no alternative if we are to love as we have been. But I cannot be whole in such circumstances and without a sense of a future, and therefore I cannot give you a child, the embodiment of a belief in a future . . . Can you understand that, querido?" The explanation was very convoluted, but then, so was the issue, and this was the best she could do at untangling it. She stepped out of the bath and wrapped herself in a thick towel.

Abul sighed and began to undress, preparatory to dipping himself in the rapidly cooling bathwater. He didn't understand. The only issue of any importance, it seemed to him, was the nature of the love they shared. "I think you make mountains out of molehills, Sarita. In all essentials it is as if I have only you for a wife. But I cannot cast off my other wives. If I returned them to their families, I would have civil war upon my hands." He stepped into the tub. "Surely you see my difficulty?"

Sarita nodded. "Yes, I do. But you must also see mine. We have to continue as we are, and ask for no more."

Abul knew that such a compromise would not satisfy him, but he did not feel confident enough to make such a declaration at this moment. He had no alternative to offer that she would accept.

Sarita knew that such a compromise would not satisfy her, but she also knew she had no right to insist on what she would accept. There were too many other people involved, and a whole world of custom and ritual that could not be turned upside down by one Spanish woman with her own expectations of the way the world should be.

Chapter 15

Nafissa hurried along the Barakha gallery, the oiled skin rolled tightly in her hand and held against the folds of her robe. The messenger from the Mocarabes had sought her out in the servants' quarters, as instructed to do, and she now carried the missive from the emir of the Mocarabes to his daughter, the sultana of Granada. She concealed the skin and walked swiftly, her eyes alive at every shadow, every fellow traveler in the porticos and courts that she crossed. But, in fact, Nafissa had no need to fear challenge. So far the caliph had no reason to suspect intrigue between his wife and father-in-law, and it had not occurred to him to alert the spy network within the palace to watch for any clandestine communications between Aicha and the apparently friendly visiting mission.

Abul did what he could to anticipate and circumvent his wife's manipulative dealings with their son, but beyond that he saw no need for watchfulness. He saw passivity and harmony in the seraglio, except for the disharmony created on occasion by Aicha, but that he regarded as women's business, having to do with the domestic politics of the seraglio, an area in which he need not intrude unless it affected the smooth running of the Alhambra itself, or, as in the case of the withdrawal of Sarita's attendants, Sarita's and his own personal comfort. And what Sarita saw and believed, she kept to herself, as much because her suspicions were based on the flimsiest of impressions and therefore hard to define as because she was reluctant to reopen old wounds.

Nafissa reached the sultana's apartments just as the impatient Aicha had shredded a third swatch of embroidery silk with anxious fingers. The news of the arrival of an emissary from her father to the caliph had left her quivering with nervous anticipation. There had to be a personal message for her among the courtesies, diplomatically pretended if they weren't genuine. Had her father accepted what she had said? Had he decided to do anything? Had he, indeed, begun to do anything? And what part would he expect her to play?

"Well?" she said, jumping to her feet as Nafissa entered the chamber. "What have you discovered?"

"A missive, lady." Nafissa extended the oiled skin. "I was summoned from the kitchen to receive it from the hands of one of the grooms accompanying the emissary."

Aicha made no response, merely waving the handmaid into silence as her fingers, fumbling with impatient excitement, broke the seal and opened the document.

After the customary formal greetings from father to daughter, the message was simple: *Be alert. Be watchful. Use the usual channels to keep those close to you informed of all developments. Be not afraid. All is in hand.*

Aicha drew a deep breath of satisfaction. Her father would be moving in the ways he knew best, creating doubts among those willing to doubt, gathering the support of the disaffected, the mistrustful, and the power-hungry for a push against Muley Abul Hassan. All she had to do was to keep stoking the fires.

"I will send a return message," she said. "You can find the messenger again, Nafissa?"

"I said I would leave any answer under the great stone of the rose garden in the Myrtle Court, my lady," Nafissa replied. "He will pick it up before dawn, when they are to return to your father's house.''

Aicha nodded. ''Then there is no hurry. You think nimbly, girl. I will give you an answer this evening.''

Turning from the handmaid, she went to a lacquered chest in the corner of the chamber and lifted the lid. An array of vials, skin containers, and ceramic pots lay within. Without hesitation, she put her hand on a small vial of blown green glass. ''You may tell Kadiga or Zulema that if they wish for a further supply of the draught against conception for the lady Sarita, they may come to me here. I will make it up for them.''

Nafissa disappeared soundlessly on her errand. Aicha took out the vial, careful not to shake its contents, and gently placed it on a low table before fetching other objects: a small pouch of what looked like dried herbs, a vial of clear liquid, and an empty skin container. Into the skin container she began to measure and to mix from the vial of clear liquid and the pouch of herbs. Once satisfied, she reached into the chest again and drew out a pair of fine kid gloves and encased her hands before, with the utmost gentleness, she removed the chased silver stopper from the green glass vial. A slight vapor rose from the contents of the vial. Holding her breath, Aicha tipped the vial toward the neck of the skin container until four bright silver drops fell into the mixture therein. She restoppered the green vial and replaced it in the chest, together with the gloves, then mixed the contents of the skin container with a slender silver skewer until she had a thick paste: the paste Kadiga would mix with water to produce the viscous draught that Sarita now swallowed with scrupulous regularity.

Aicha was known as a skilled apothecary, and it had caused no remark when she had offered to supply Sarita with a particularly efficacious draught for the prevention of conception. It was a service she performed for many women within the Alhambra. What

went into the container she supplied to Sarita's attendants was known only to the lady Aicha.

Aicha had not imparted to her father her plan to
rid the Alhambra of the Christian intruder. Partly, her
reticence sprang from the only half-acknowledged
truth that contriving the woman's death was a matter
of private revenge, a private soothing of hurt pride.
Oh, the sultana could support her rival's murder on
political grounds: the caliph's obsession with the unbeliever was destroying his ability to govern wisely
and with the single-minded purpose he had always
exhibited, and such lack of attention placed the entire
kingdom of Granada at risk. The emir of the Mocarabes would applaud his daughter's reasoning and see
her action as entirely appropriate. However, Aicha
also felt that if her father believed the woman to be
the only problem and that the problem would soon
be removed, then he might delay making his moves
to undermine Muley Abul Hassan with the other
Morisco-Spanish families in the kingdom. And Aicha
needed that widespread dissension if Abul was to be
irrevocably weakened.

She drew the string tight at the neck of the skin
container and held it up to the February sunlight
pouring through the window, envisioning the malign
contents, a slight smile quirking her full lips. There
was no doubt that the bane was now slowly but surely
beginning to affect the Spaniard, who was finding it
harder to conceal her general fatigue and debilitation—at least from Aicha, who was on the watch for
it.

Sarita was paler, her eyes rather large and heavy,
more like green stones than the bright, sparkling rock
pools of summer they had been previously, but she
still tried to behave as if she felt perfectly well, particularly with Abul. Last evening, Aicha had been
concealed in the north mirador of the Generalife,
looking down on the lovely central court with its long
rectangular pond studded with water lilies. Sarita and
Abul had emerged laughing from one of the arched

galleries of the courtyard, and Sarita, in clearly provocative humor, had initiated a game of chase through the galleries. From her laughter and the speed of her movements no one would guess the effort involved. Only the hidden watcher had seen how distressed she was when, out of Abul's sight for a minute behind a myrtle hedge, she had stopped, doubled over, her slight frame heaving as she grabbed wildly for air to drag into her tortured lungs.

But by the time she was forced to admit the severity of her condition, it would be too late to avert the end. That was the beauty of this particular venom. Correctly administered, it killed by inches, almost imperceptibly, with symptoms that could be attributed to any number of ordinary, everyday causes. Until, finally, the victim was utterly enervated, unable to draw breath, unable to swallow. Even if someone guessed poison at that stage, there would be no proof and no way of being certain.

No, Aicha was quite safe. Even if Abul suspected her of having a hand in Sarita's death, without proof he could do nothing that was not already done. She knew that he would never come back to her now, even when the Christian was dead. There was more to his disaffection than the bond he had with another woman. She was still unsure exactly what she had done in the beginning to create his irreversible animosity. She could trace it only to the early argument over Boabdil, but if that were all, the breach would have been healed with time and her apology. However, she knew its continuance was exacerbated by her now open subversion of their son. But months ago, she had decided that since she was no longer an influence in his bed, she had nothing further to gain by attempting to recapture his favor and had turned her attentions instead to advancing her plans by other means.

That advancement was now progressing apace, and for this she had the Christian to thank. Without that catalyst she would have had no immediate excuse to involve her father and the other families of the kingdom. Now it looked as if there was a real chance to implement her long-term plan and bring it to a rapid conclusion. Abul would soon be beset on all sides, and the emotional upheaval attendant upon the death of his beloved Christian captive would leave him ill-equipped to deal with the enemies from without and within. Aicha was on the whole very satisfied with the way things were working out.

Abul smiled politely at his wife's uncle, emissary from the emir of the Mocarabes, and wondered what was the point of the visit. The two men were sitting in the Hall of the Ambassadors, surrounded by courtiers and soldiers, as befitted the reception of such a familial and honored guest; and in the hour since the audience had begun, only pleasantries had been exchanged over goblets of sherbet. The courtesies were obligatory, of course, but by now Abul would ordinarily have expected some inkling of the true purpose behind the visit. However, Ahmed ben Kaled offered only an impassive countenance and small talk, and Abul perforce responded in like manner.

"My niece is well, I trust," Kaled said, taking a stuffed date from a chased silver platter proffered by a small slave child whose turban seemed too big for his head.

"The lady Aicha is well," Abul responded. "You will wish to meet with her, of course. I am sure you bear messages from my lord of the Mocarabes to his daughter." Did the other man stiffen slightly? Was that a flicker, as quick and darting as a snake's tongue, in his dark eyes, embedded in his well-bearded face, beneath the rich silken folds of his turban? But why would his host's so natural remark cause such a reaction?

However, the emissary was bowing and agreeing that indeed he hoped for an audience with the lady Aicha, and he bore messages of goodwill from her father. Abul dismissed the strange impression as a figment of an overextended imagination and forced himself to concentrate, to try to discover the underlying purpose of the visit.

"I would be honored to meet also with your son, the prince Boabdil," Kaled now said. "The emir is most anxious to hear how his grandson grows and how his education is progressing."

It was not a strange request, yet Abul felt something was being withheld. However, he bowed his head in acknowledgment and turned to his vizier. "Have Boabdil and his tutor brought here." Turning back to his visitor, he said, "You may find the boy rather timid. But he will grow out of it."

Ahmed ben Kaled moved his beard-entrenched mouth in what might have passed for a smile. The lady Aicha had been most specific in her catalog of the caliph's sins when it came to the treatment of the child, whose spirit was being ruthlessly, systematically crushed by his father's harshness. If Boabdil were not speedily removed from that sphere, he would be ill-equipped to take on the power and responsibilities of caliph when his turn came, and thus would the Mocarabes lose their substantial foothold in the caliphate. Kaled had been most specifically instructed to see the boy and judge for himself.

When Boabdil and his tutor arrived, Abul greeted them with his usual soft-voiced courtesy. "Boabdil, make your reverence to your mother's uncle," he instructed, rising from his carved chair, where slanting sunshine caught the glister of gold leaf, the blood-red glow of rubies. He reached for the boy's hand.

Kaled watched as Boabdil perceptibly pulled back from his father, although he allowed his hand to be taken. The boy's eyes shifted sideways as he was presented to his relative. His feet shuffled, and his greeting was a rustling murmur. Kaled reached out and took the lad's chin, tilting it so that Boabdil was forced to meet Kaled's eyes.

Kaled saw a touch of fear therein, but he read more of calculation than alarm. How much of this retiring timidity was an act? he wondered. The child's mother had exhibited similar traits, he remembered, thinking of Aicha as a girl. She had always been adept at hiding her true feelings and reactions, which made her a powerful enemy as well as a most useful ally in the enemy camp.

"I bring you greetings from your grandfather," he said to Boabdil.

"You lack manners, Boabdil," Abul said sharply when the boy made no reply. "Ahmed Eben has surely instructed you in the correct greetings."

The tutor hurried forward with a dismayed humming sound of mingled agreement and disclaimer, and Boabdil shrank from his father, lifting a hand as if to ward off a blow, although neither Abul nor the tutor had made a threatening gesture in his direction. His eyes, however, darted for a second toward Kaled, as if assessing an audience.

Kaled glanced at Abul. The caliph's lips had thinned, and a muscle twitched in his suddenly drawn cheek. He cut short the tutor's confused protestations and self-recriminations with a dismissive gesture and said wearily to his son, "Return to your apartments, Boabdil. You shame me before our visitor."

"Ah, no, indeed." Kaled spoke up hastily. "The lad is timid, and I take no offense. If I could perhaps walk a little with him in the portico . . . ?"

Abul found himself strongly reluctant to grant such an understandable request. He did not know exactly why, but the fact that his visitor came from Aicha's family made him unaccountably uneasy. There was little Kaled could do to worsen the situation between Boabdil and his father . . . but then, Abul thought dismally, he was probably reluctant for such a tête-à-tête because he was ashamed of the truth of that relationship and wished to keep it from outsiders.

"Let us all go down to the mews," he said. "I have there a falcon I intend as a gift to the emir of the Mocarabes when she is trained. I would have your opinion on her, Kaled. And Boabdil may show you his sparrow hawk, if he has now remembered his manners." He went through the arched doorway opening onto the portico, his ceremonial robe of black silk embroidered with gold thread flowing fluidly around him in a rich, jewel-sparking current.

Kaled in politeness could do nothing but accept the suggestion with every indication of pleasure. He smiled at Boabdil and suggested the boy should walk beside him and tell him something of his studies. Boabdil hardly looked as if the prospect thrilled him, but he fell in beside his mother's uncle, a couple of paces behind his father, already striding around the gallery toward the Myrtle Court.

Abul kept his ears peeled to catch the conversation behind him, but it barely qualified as a conversation. Kaled asked questions, made observations, and was answered in muffled monosyllables. Boabdil was displaying an embarrassing degree of social ineptitude, but at least he was neither advertently nor inadvertently revealing any family skeletons, and Abul allowed his mind to roam over pleasanter subjects, like the journey he was planning to a pretty palace in the hills above the sea at Motril.

Sarita was in need of a change of scene, he had decided. The sea air would surely restore the bloom to her cheeks and the spring to her step. She had been kept too long confined in one place for one in whose blood ran the open road. In the past few weeks, the routine of the Alhambra, for all its luxury and sensual delights, seemed to have sapped her energy, and he remembered how she had told him once that she was not made to lie around in silken robes eating apricots. In the glories of their lusting tumbles and their ever-deepening love, he had allowed himself to forget that she had other needs, required variety for true all-round happiness. Now he had hit upon the surprise journey as the perfect solution.

He rarely used the seaside palace. His father had built it for Abul's mother as a holiday villa when the summer's heat became too much for her, even here in the mountains of the Alhambra. It had no facilities for the administration of the kingdom and only the smallest reception hall, so it could be visited by the caliph only when he could safely leave business behind in the hub of Granada. Abul had decided that now was such a time, and he looked forward to telling Sarita of his plan. He loved giving her pleasure, loved the way she would jump on her bare feet and her eyes would widen with delight, her lips part in that ready joyful chuckle; the way she would unconsciously run her fingers through that fiery, unruly tangle of curls; the way she would stand on tiptoe to kiss him, her mouth warm and pliant on his, the delicate fragility of her body pressed against his own height and breadth . . .

He saw her as he turned onto a path lined with bushes of rosebay. Kaled saw her at the same moment. She was sitting on a carved stone bench a little way along the path, facing the morning sun, her face tilted to its warmth. Two veiled women sat on either side of her.

Kaled's first reaction was of shock. He had never seen such a woman. Although she was dressed conventionally in a robe of amber silk beneath a light cloak hanging open from her shoulders, her face was brazenly exposed to all passersby, and her hair, brightly burnished, deep fires flaring in the sun's rays, clustered unconfined around that small, pale face and spilled over her shoulders.

He realized who she must be the instant before Abul raised a hand in greeting as she turned her head at the sound of footsteps on the path. So this was the unbeliever: the woman who had drawn Muley Abul Hassan into a morass of intrigue that Kaled believed would prove his downfall. He glanced at the caliph and saw the eager light in the piercing black eyes, the involuntary lift of his mouth.

"You have a Christian concubine, my lord Abul?" he murmured in feigned surprise.

Abul paused, frowning. It was not a word he would choose, yet he could find no other that his guest would understand. He shrugged as if in affirmation.

"Is she slave or captive?" inquired Kaled.

"She is a slave!" This from Boabdil with sudden, suppressed venom. "She is my father's slave, and when he has tired of her, she will be cast out."

Anger darkened Abul's face and filled his eyes with a fearsome blackness that quenched the eager light of before. "You dare to talk in such fashion!" His voice was low so that the women could not hear, but it was audible to Kaled.

Boabdil took an involuntary step backward, and it was clear to Kaled that his alarm on this occasion was no affectation. "My . . . my m-mother says so," he stammered. "She says she will cast her out into the stews of the city when . . . when . . ."

"Enough!" Abul spoke sharply but without the passion of before as he realized how much of this was to be laid at Aicha's door. Why, he thought in astonished self-contempt, had he not realized how Aicha would truly react to Sarita? He had thought her sufficiently indifferent to Sarita's arrival to cause no trouble. But her malice must have been spreading far and wide if she had been foolish enough to communicate it to the boy. Was its recipient aware of it?

Sarita was coming along the path toward them. Her feet were bare on the gravel, he noticed. She continued to reject shoes, except when it was very cold, and he had long given up trying to convert her to the soft soles of the Alhambra. Her feet were an inextricable component of the person he loved. But now his anxiety rose that she might be humiliated by Boabdil or by Kaled, who was staring, frankly scandalized, at the approaching woman.

Her gown fell in softly fluted folds from beneath her breasts and, to Abul's anxiously assessing eye, seemed to accentuate her fragility, the sense he had been developing recently of a parchmentlike quality to her frame, as if she could be blown away on a puff of wind. But she was smiling as she came up to them and greeted him in her newly learned Arabic.

"My lord caliph. I give you good morning." Turning to Boabdil, she offered him the same greeting with the same smile. The boy stared with undisguised hostility, but he was sufficiently alarmed by his earlier misstep to mutter a response.

Kaled did not converse with slaves, and most particularly not with unbelievers who so flagrantly flouted the rules of womanhood. Yet he could not take his eyes off her, and he began to have some faint inkling of the power she exerted over the caliph.

"Aicha's uncle is here as emissary from her father, the emir of the Mocarabes," Abul was explaining quietly, hoping that Sarita would take the hint and accept that there were to be no introductions. Instead, she returned Kaled's stare with one of his own intensity, although with a slightly challenging quirk to her lips.

"The emissary appears a little surprised," she observed. "Are you unfamiliar with the women of my country, sir?"

"I am unfamiliar with women who do not show due modesty," Kaled said stiffly, directing the statement to Abul. "In a place where men walk freely, women do not show themselves in such fashion."

Abul shrugged. "The lady Sarita does, however, and I have no objections. If I have none, it is not for you, Ahmed ben Kaled, to express them as a guest."

The reproof insulted the guest as the guest's criticism had insulted the host. They both now stood in the wrong, and the cause of the trouble was looking between them with a degree of interest and amusement that could not possibly help matters. Worse, Abul realized: Boabdil was staring with a most unusual animation, his mouth half open as not a word or a nuance passed him by. His father was guilty of discourtesy to a relative and a guest, and in the defense of a mere woman, justly criticized. Yet another nail had been struck deep in the coffin of the filial relationship, and there would be a merry tale with which to regale his mother at sundown.

Abul felt a most unreasonable and unusual flash of resentment toward Sarita. He controlled it with difficulty, and when he spoke, it was with stern formality. "We interrupt your repose, lady. You will excuse us. We pay a visit to the mews."

Sarita stepped aside without another word. She had spent long enough in this society to know by now what had happened and to guess at the ramifications. And she blamed herself. She should not have approached Abul when she saw him in the company of a strange man. But she had not thought. It was all part of her uncertain position: she did not see herself as a woman of the Alhambra, and Abul did not treat her as such, yet to the large community within the palace and the larger one within the kingdom itself, she could not be placed in any other terms.

Abul, in his own interests, should not have defended her, she thought ruefully, watching as the three walked on up the path. But she knew that if he had failed to do so, the sour taste of betrayal would have coated her soul, and there would have been little he could have said or done later to sweeten it.

Her heart jumped in the manner she had learned to dread, and she stood still on the path, feeling the great void within her as her heart paused for what seemed like an eternity before beginning a rushing, uphill, scrambling beat that brought a cold sweat to her brow, filled her with an icy fear, and turned her limbs to water.

"What is it?" Kadiga hurried over to her. "Sarita, you are not well. Why will you not consult the caliph's physician? He is most skilled."

Sarita was unable to speak for a minute, and Kadiga put a supporting arm around her, gazing helplessly at her bloodless lips, feeling the quivers ripping through the thin frame. The nausea would follow the spasm, as always, and then Sarita would seem to be her usual self, although rather fatigued.

"Come back to the tower," Kadiga said when she sensed that the paroxysm was beginning to ebb. "Let me send to the lord Abul."

"No." Sarita shook her head. "It is passing now. There is nothing the matter with me that needs to be fussed over. I will rest a little until the queasiness passes." She wiped her hand across her brow. "I wonder if it is something I am eating that does not agree with me."

Kadiga lost every vestige of color in her normally ruddy cheeks, and her gut loosened with terror at the hideous thought that followed Sarita's tentative suggestion. It could not possibly be . . . and yet Kadiga knew in the deepest recesses of her being that it was not only possible, it was probable. If she paused to consider the pattern of Sarita's slow decline, if she paused to study the symptoms . . .

Kadiga had more than a layman's skills and knowledge of sickness imparted to her by her mother, who had been well known as an apothecary. But Kadiga, in her relatively lowly position in the Alhambra hierarchy, was rarely called upon to use the body of knowledge, and as a result, it was never at the forefront of her mind. But now that knowledge put flesh and bone onto the most frightful specter. But what was she to do with the . . . suspicion . . . belief . . . no, the knowledge? It was as dangerous to impart as it was unthinkable to keep to herself.

"Kadiga, you are as white as whey!" Zulema exclaimed from Sarita's other side, where she was holding her arm. "Are you also ill?"

Kadiga shook her head slowly, as if making the motion through honey. "No . . . no, I am perfectly well. It was something I thought . . . Come, let us return to the tower, where Sarita may lie down for a while."

Sarita was too relieved to be lying flat on the divan in the cool, breeze-freshened sleeping gallery of her tower to object when her attendants insisted on undressing her and putting her properly to bed. A deep, black wave of sleepiness was creeping over her, upward from her toes, and she welcomed it, bringing as it did relief from the nausea and the wildly erratic pumping of her heart.

"I will stay with you," Kadiga said. "If you need me, I will be in the court below." She went down the stairs, a rather puzzled Zulema following.

"What is it, Kadiga? Something troubles you," the other woman said directly.

Kadiga bit her lip. "It is better you do not know, Zulema."

"But it concerns Sarita?" Zulema pressed.

Kadiga sighed heavily. "Yes, but you do not want to know. Why do you not go to the palace and prepare a jasmine tisane for Sarita when she wakes? You know how it refreshes her."

Zulema looked unusually mulish for a minute, but then her customarily amenable nature reasserted itself. If Kadiga did not want to share her problems, it would be impolite for Zulema to continue her questioning. She went off on her errand.

Kadiga paced the pretty court, around the fountain, between the delicate columns, chewing her lip, pulling on her fingers until the bones cracked. If what she suspected was true, then she herself was deeply implicated. It was she who mixed and administered the venomous draught. Slowly, unwillingly almost, she opened a small marquetry box on a cedar chest against the wall. The skin container stood innocently in one corner of the box. Kadiga stared at it as if she could see through the skin, could break down its contents into component parts. What was in it? And why was she so certain that the mischief was contained therein?

But Sarita ate and drank nothing else on a regular basis that was not ingested by others. She supped often with the women in the seraglio when the lord Abul was not with her. When she dined alone, Kadiga and Zulema ate with her. She ate fruit, of course, and sweetmeats, but such random mouthfuls were too haphazard conveyances for a regular, carefully measured dose of some death-dealing substance.

But if the mixture in the skin vial contained the bane, then only the lady Aicha could have put it there. And there lay the deepest roots of Kadiga's fear. She had no difficulty believing the sultana capable of such a plot, capable of conceiving it and of implementing it. Aicha's vindictiveness was rightly feared throughout the Alhambra. But there was no proof. If she went to the caliph and told her tale, her accusation of the sultana would be implicit. If there was no proof, then the sultana could accuse her of bearing false witness. She could demand Kadiga's tongue in the name of the law, and the law would uphold the sentence of mutilation.

Kadiga shuddered as she saw the punishment being inflicted by the public executioner as she had seen it once as a small child in the bazaar in Granada. The man had accused his neighbor of stealing a sheep, but the sheep had been discovered in the ravine, unhurt, caught in a thornbush. The man's wife had pleaded, the neighbor had relented, but the law was immutable. Not even the caliph could order a stay of execution in such circumstances.

Kadiga went upstairs and stood looking down at the sleeping woman. Her color was waxen, slightly yellowed beneath the pallor, and her breathing was labored. A convulsive movement of her throat in her sleep was accompanied by an alarmed tightening of her brow, as if she was having difficulty swallowing and the sleeping body acknowledged its struggles.

Kadiga could begin to substitute her own draught for the sultana's, but some instinct based on learning told the woman that the effects of the poison had progressed too far to be reversed by the simple cessation of its administration. If anything could be done now, only Muhamed Alahma, the caliph's physician, would know what and how. But how was he to be involved without being told the truth? And how could she tell the truth without risking . . .

It wasn't to be thought of. And then Sarita stirred

in her sleep, her hand plucked at her throat, and she moaned.

Could she stand by and watch her death? Unable to keep vigil at the bedside any longer, Kadiga turned and half ran down to the court. But there were no answers there. Conscience wrestled with dread as she resumed her pacing.

It was midafternoon when Abul came to the tower. He had left his guest with Aicha in a private parlor in the caliph's apartments, where Aicha could safely remove her veil in the company of a man of her own family. She was attended by her own women, of course, correctly shrouded, silent chaperones, standing at a distance against the walls of the parlor, while the two conversationalists sat upon divans in the center of the room.

Abul had tried to mend fences with his visitor, or at least to recover the superficial graces, and Kaled had followed suit. Both men were too far steeped in the necessary rites of social intercourse to permit a temporary transgression on either side to affect the surface, but Abul was aware of the resentment he had created. It was a resentment that would be transmitted to his father-in-law, together with details of the cause of the insult: a Christian concubine of immodest bearing; one allowed a foolish license from her doting possessor.

Abul had no idea what he could do to regularize matters. He could not turn Sarita into a woman of the Alhambra. Once, he had thought he could and nearly lost her in the attempt. He could not have done anything but come to her defense that morning, although he knew what it would lead to. Could he ask her to be more circumspect? But to do so seemed an insult. He loved her for what she was. What right had he to demand that she pretend to be otherwise to save him public awkwardness? Perhaps he *was* the besotted fool Kaled would undoubtedly make him out to be, but he wasn't sure he cared what people thought in this matter.

His steps slowed as he reached the wicket gate of the tower garden. Shouldn't he care? He ruled this kingdom by consensus. Could he be a wise and empathetic ruler if he flouted the most deeply held mores of his people in the interests of a lone passion?

They were questions to be put aside for rigorous examination when he was alone and in a meditative mood, he decided. But he entered the tower with somewhat less than his usual springing enthusiasm, and the anticipatory smile was absent from his mouth, although its glint was in his eyes as he greeted Kadiga, who looked, he thought, rather down in the mouth herself.

"The lady Sarita is resting, my lord." Kadiga made her reverence. Her heart was beating fast as she saw an opportunity to speak. She moistened her lips in preparation. Could she . . . dared she . . . would she . . . But even as she thus desperately deliberated, the lord Abul merely nodded and went to the stairs, leaving her standing dumbly below.

A finger of sunlight fell from the window across Sarita's pillow. It drew out the waxy translucence of her skin, and Abul, who had not seen her in sleep for several weeks, looked down uneasily. Suddenly he felt an urgent need to waken her. "Sarita?" He bent and touched her shoulder. Her skin was clammy, the previously rounded angle a sharp point in his palm. He repeated her name and shook her, filled with a nameless apprehension that would only be quashed by her open eyes, her smiling mouth.

Her eyelids fluttered, lifted, but for a minute there was no recognition, only a fog in the green pools.

Sarita struggled to bring herself back. Dimly, she knew she was somewhere deep inside the shell of her body, if only she could summon herself. It had happened once before, this inarticulate sense on waking of herself as a flickering flame that needed bellows to puff it back to healthy life. She fixed her eyes on two black specks that seemed to be piercing her body, pouring resolution into her to aid her weakening spirit

. . . and then it happened. She came up from the depths, initially floundering, then with an uprush of relief as her spirit reinhabited her body, and she was left only with the residue of an unformed, unfocused panic that dissipated beneath the loved and loving face of Muley Abul Hassan.

"You look troubled," she observed in a very ordinary voice. "I'm sorry I caused difficulties for you with your wife's uncle. I must try harder to adapt to your ways in such instances."

"*De nada,*" he said from his own overpowering relief, forgetting his earlier reflections and failing to take advantage of the opportunity now offered to him. "You were sleeping very deeply for siesta, *cara.*"

"Perhaps so." She sat up, sweeping her hair from her brow, noticing that strands stuck damply to her skin. "It is hot, is it not?"

"Not unusually," Abul remarked, sitting on the divan and taking her hand. "I think you need a change of scene, Sarita. It is not right for you to be confined behind walls. I am certain that is why you don't feel yourself."

She smiled. "Yes, I have not felt quite myself for a few days . . ." Weeks, in fact, if she were to face the truth, but somehow she couldn't accept that she was truly ailing. The people of the tribe of Raphael did not suffer more than trifling illnesses. If something was amiss with her now, then it must have to do with the unusual circumstances of her present life. "But it is nothing, Abul."

"No, I am sure it is not," he agreed. "But I have a surprise for you."

Her eyes lit up, as he had known they would. "I love surprises."

"Would you like to go down to the sea?"

"Oh, I should like it of all things." She clasped her hands tightly in her lap. "When . . . how . . . where . . . for how long?"

"I have a small palace in the hills above Motril,"

he said. "We could go tomorrow, when the emissary from the Mocarabes has left."

Tomorrow . . . Weakness slopped over her, dirty, gray, futile. How could she possibly manage such a ride? She turned her face away, pretending to look out of the window toward the mountain peaks. "That would be lovely, Abul."

He frowned at her lack of enthusiasm. "We do not have to go if you do not wish it."

"But of course I wish it." And they both heard the note of desperation in her voice as she faced the recognition that she would not be able to ride for so long. Could she ask for a litter? But to do that would mean admitting that she was an invalid . . . and she wasn't. Just a little tired . . . a little stale from being in the same place for so long . . . just as Abul had said. Of course she would be able to ride. Excitement would carry her through. She and Abul would be alone by the sea. There would be no distractions except those that would aid the sensual joys of their togetherness, no commitments outside those they made to each other.

She made haste to banish from the air around them that lingering note of desperation. "It will be wonderful." Reaching up her arms, she drew him down to her. "Do you know how much I love you, Abul, querido? We will love on the sand and in the sea. Have you ever made love in the sea?" She touched his cheekbone with the tip of her tongue. "I have often thought it would be wonderful: of a different order from your baths, but with many of the same sensations."

"No," he said, responding to her effort with warm cheerfulness. "No, I have never done that. But do you not think the water might be a little cold in February? More than a trifle shriveling?" His eyebrow lifted as he invited the rich chuckle he expected.

She managed a smile. "Yes, I had not thought of that. But under the sun, on the sand, and in the grass, we will try new things, will we not?"

"We will teach each other many new joys, Sarita, *cara mía*." He drew her into his arms, filled with a deep fear because he could feel in her body a complete lack of response to the sensual promises she was making with her mouth . . . and, he knew, with her soul.

Chapter 16

"Here is the answer to my father's message."
Aicha sanded the parchment, rolled it carefully, and handed it to the waiting Nafissa. "Be sure you are not observed."

As if she wouldn't be certain, Nafissa thought scornfully, bowing in submissive acceptance as she took the parchment. Surely the lady Aicha didn't imagine she would be fool enough to court discovery on such an errand. Aiding and abetting a treasonous correspondence within the walls of the Alhambra would mean death without question, even when a slave or servant was simply obeying orders, even when disobedience to those orders could bring reprisals of unthinkable severity.

Aicha went to the window when the soft-footed Nafissa had slipped away on her errand. The full moon filled the sky with a brightly diffused radiance, a brittle silver clarity unlike the heavy golden moons of summer. The night was made chillier by the moon's light, and the snow peaks appeared much closer, the air seeming to carry the cold of their glittering caps.

The palace compound was quiet. It was that deeply silent time of night when only the watchmen on the ramparts and in the alcazaba kept vigil. Her uncle and his party would be at their rest, unless they were passing the night hours in the arms of the houris of the Alhambra. Such entertainment was freely available to guests.

And Abul . . . was he in the arms of his houri? Not for much longer, Aicha thought, wrapping her arms around her body in a gesture that mingled satisfaction with the need for warmth. Boabdil had told her of the confrontation over the woman that morning, and her uncle had hinted at his anger during her meeting with him, although only the most commonplace familial and domestic subjects could be overtly exchanged within earshot of her silent chaperones. But Aicha knew the confrontation had fallen on readily prepared ground and could only fertilize the shoots of enmity. Her father would listen well to Kaled.

She moved away from the window, too restless to sleep, filled with triumph. It was too soon to start counting the chickens, but the eggs were warming nicely, and one was surely permitted to indulge in a little premature fantasizing.

In the tower on the perimeter wall, Abul was lying beside Sarita. He thought she was now asleep, but she had lain wakeful beside him for a long time. He placed a hand on the curve of her turned hip. There was no flicker of response, not even the involuntary dancing ripple of her skin that always followed his touch.

He was filled with a profound depression, his body aching with need as if he had failed to achieve his own release in the past hours of lovemaking. But the need was more complex than simple bodily unsatisfaction. His need sprang from the deep spiritual lack of sharing. Oh, Sarita had tried to convince him she was with him, but the pretense had been transparent to one who knew her true responses as well as he knew his own. She had moved in her usual ways, had made the same lovely little sounds that never failed to delight him. Her body had tightened around him with her usual loving skill, but it had been a travesty of a woman lost in her own loving.

For some reason he had allowed her to continue, had seemed to fall in with the pretense, and he was now touched with self-contempt as he wondered how and why he should have done so. He should have shaken her out of it, told her that if she was not in the mood, then there was no need to feign arousal; that feigning bodily joy was the deepest insult a woman could offer a man. But when had Sarita not been in the mood for love?

He had let it continue because he had been afraid to stop, to face the fact that somehow he was failing her; and afterward, she had touched him gently, tracing the line of his jaw, his mouth, the deep shadow of his cheekbones, and had kissed him, not with her usual languid gratitude for pleasure received and shared, but with an ineffable sadness that first chilled him, then filled him with anger that she had not trusted him with the truth. He had hidden his anger as she had attempted to hide her physical indifference to his caresses, and finally she had fallen asleep. Now he lay bleakly in a wasteland of falsehood, wondering how and why it had happened and what shifting sands formed the basis of this love that he had believed to be carved in steel.

Careful not to disturb the sleeper, he slipped from the divan and dressed in the chilly moonlight. Then, for the first time since their loving had truly begun, he returned to his own apartments to face the dawn alone.

Sarita awoke at cockcrow. Her hand went automatically to the space beside her and felt its cold emptiness. Startled, she propped herself up on an elbow and called him. The quality of the silence in the tower told her she was quite alone. Why had he left her without a word?

She fell back on the pillows, remembering. Remembering that grim deception. She hadn't fooled Abul, she had known it, yet they had both persevered, their bodies going through the motions. But their eyes had slipped away from each other when always they had held at the moment of total fusion; when their souls joined with their bodies in the final climactic experience that was sometimes an explosion, sometimes a gentle fall, sometimes a rushing, head-over-heels tumble through some violent elemental cascade that would leave them gasping for breath, laughing in exaltation, their flesh marked by the struggle.

Why had she pretended? It would have been so simple to say she was tired. He would not have been hurt, would have seen no rejection. But some deep-seated fear had prevented her from offering the truth as excuse. How could she be too tired to make love? Was there some dreadful canker within her, eating her from the inside? If she admitted the symptoms, allowed them to affect the way she lived, then she must take into herself the knowledge that something serious was amiss with her. So far she had battled on regardless, forcing herself to behave ordinarily, ignoring the ever-increasing debilitation, but she couldn't ignore it any longer.

She drew in a painful gulping breath, and the lump in her throat seemed to grow, blocking the passage of air. She swallowed convulsively, futilely, and for a minute had the hideous sensation of drowning. Tears of desperation pricked behind her eyelids and rolled coldly down her cheeks, tracking into the hair behind her ears, dampening the pillow.

She didn't hear the door into the court open and was only aware of Kadiga when she stood by the bed, her face haunted with anxiety.

"You startled me," Sarita said, hastily trying to wipe away the tears before the other woman could see them.

"I'm sorry," Kadiga apologized. "I didn't wish to disturb you if the lord Abul was still with you."

At these words, Sarita's tears began to flow again, and she gasped for breath as her nose blocked and her mouth filled with saliva that she couldn't swallow. Kadiga pulled her upright and began to pound her back until the choking stopped.

Exhausted, Sarita fell back again on the divan. Her eyes gazed up at Kadiga, filled with the fear of her own death. "What is the matter with me, Kadiga? I am going to die, I feel it."

Kadiga shook her head, mute in her own terrified knowledge of the truth. Then suddenly she turned and ran from the tower. She ran down the cypress path, around the Myrtle Court, and into the gilded antechamber of the caliph's private apartments. There she stopped, faced with a trio of armed men in front of the door at the rear. Before she could lose courage, she stepped forward, eyes lowered, veil drawn tight across her face.

"What business do you have here, woman?"

"I have most urgent business with the lord caliph," she said, her voice barely a whisper. "It is imperative I speak with him immediately."

One of the soldiers shook his head. "He is bidding farewell to his guests in the court of the alcazaba. If you would have speech with him, then bring your business to the Mexuar during the hours of justice."

Kadiga turned to go, suddenly feeling reprieved. She had tried after all. It was hardly her fault if the caliph would not hear her. Then she saw Sarita's eyes filled with pain and terror, and she stopped. "I will wait here for the caliph," she said. The soldiers protested vigorously that this was no place for a serving woman. The caliph did not grant private audiences to such as she.

"I am attendant to the lady Sarita," she said as firmly as she could, though her voice quavered. "The lord Abul will grant me an audience." Then, before they could push her forth from the chamber, she sat down cross-legged on the floor against a column and prepared to wait, her lowered eyes on her clasped hands in her lap.

The guards exchanged glances, then shrugged. When it came to the captive in the tower, matters tended to be irregular, and besides, the caliph in general had an open ear for his subjects' woes.

Thus it was that when Abul, grim-faced after the miseries of the night and the forced good fellowship

of Kaled's departure, returned to his private apartments to prepare for the day's business, his eye fell
upon the motionless, dark-clad figure of Kadiga, oc-
cupying a position of determined prominence in the
antechamber.

She sprang to her feet as he entered and stepped
forward hastily. "My lord Abul, I would beg—"

"The woman says she has private business with
you, my lord," one of the guards interrupted offi-
ciously. "She was very insistent that it concerned
the lady in the tower, and we thought it best to permit her to remain. If you wish us to remove her, my
lord . . ."

Abul gestured him into silence. He looked at Kadiga as she stood before him, raising her eyes to meet
his gaze. There was no mistaking the urgency in their
dark depths. "Come within," he said quietly and
walked past the guards into his chamber, Kadiga following soundlessly on slippered feet.

The guard drew the door closed behind her, and
she stood silent, trying to still her racing pulse, to
regain the courage that had driven her to this place
but that had ebbed during the long minutes of waiting.

Abul went to a table where stood a carafe and a
goblet. He filled the goblet and drank deeply before
turning back to the silent, immobile woman. "What
is your business with me, Kadiga?"

There was something in the gentleness of his tone,
the quietness of his eyes, that gave her courage. "I
am afraid to speak, my lord caliph, yet I do not know
how to keep silent."

"You have no need of fear," he said, putting the
goblet back on the table. "What passes between us in
this room will remain between ourselves. What must
you tell me of the lady Sarita?"

"I believe . . . I believe . . . my lord, I believe she
has swallowed something that is not beneficial," Kadiga said with a gasp, knees trembling, palms sweat-
ing. It was done now. The die cast. And she had

thrown herself upon the mercy of Muley Abul Hassan.

Abul was very still, enclosed, it seemed, in the deceptive gossamer of a spider's web. "Do you know when Sarita swallowed this . . . this malign substance?" he asked finally.

"Regularly, for many weeks, I believe, my lord."

Cold entered the marrow of his bones. "Do you know how it has been administered?"

Kadiga moistened her lips. "By myself, my lord caliph."

Abul did not misunderstand her. "How should this be, Kadiga?"

Kadiga's knees buckled beneath her, and she found herself crouching on her heels on the carpet of Damascus silk that in winter covered the cool marble floors of the Alhambra. Her head was bent, body hunched, as she tried to overcome her terror. Once she told this, she would be vulnerable to any accusation the sultana chose to level at her.

"Be not afraid," Abul said. "Come." Reaching down, he took her hands and drew her to her feet. "There is no need to sit on the floor. Sit there." Gently he pushed her toward a divan. "Sit."

Kadiga did so.

"Let us use straight terms now," Abul said, as the spider wove its adhesive thread ever more tightly. "It is poison you talk of."

Slowly, Kadiga nodded.

"And you have inadvertently administered it?"

Again she nodded.

"In what, Kadiga?"

Kadiga saw the executioner with his knife. She saw the iron clamp. She smelled the hot pitch fire of the brazier, heard the excitement of the crowd. She shook her head, unable to answer him.

"If you will not tell me this, Kadiga, why would you tell me anything?" Abul kept his patience, although he did not understand the woman's reluctance to follow through with her revelation.

"Because I believe she will die if the physician can do nothing," Kadiga said on a sobbing gulp. "The bane has such a hold upon her now that I know of nothing that will stop it. But perhaps Muhamed Alahma will have the secret."

"But how can he know if he has the secret if you will not tell me how you believe it administered?" His voice revealed none of the panicked, feverish impatience he felt as he saw Sarita's life trickling away into the sand, and the cold in his marrow solidified into ice. A life without Sarita . . . that flaming, vibrant presence snuffed . . . It was not to be endured. "*Tell me*," he said, his desperation no longer concealed, and Kadiga answered.

"I believe it to be contained in the draught she takes against conception."

"And you mix this draught?"

Kadiga nodded. "From . . . from a potion made up by . . . by . . ." But she faltered and wailed her own terror. "She will accuse me of false witness, my lord, and they will cut out my tongue—"

"Hush now," he said, laying a steadying hand on her shoulder. "No one will accuse you of anything. I have told you that nothing that passes between us here will be laid at your door." Kadiga's sobs continued to fill the room, and he left her, going over to the archway onto the portico, allowing the cool morning air to calm him as far as anything could. "You talk of the lady Aicha, is that not so?" He looked over his shoulder at her.

Kadiga nodded an affirmative, her gulping sobs still filling the chamber.

"And you believe Sarita has been taking this poison for some weeks?"

Another affirmative nod. "The effects are slow and subtle, my lord. But I believe they have become—"

"I now know what they have become," he interrupted with sudden harshness, directed entirely at himself for ignoring the insidious growth of the canker, for allowing himself to accept Sarita's apparently insouciant dismissal of the indications of ill health. "To your knowledge, is it customary for venom to work in these ways?"

"Some, my lord. But I have little experience. Muhamed Alahma—"

"Yes, if anyone knows, he will. Go now. Through the portico. Return to the tower and tend Sarita. You may leave the rest in my hands."

Kadiga arose and crossed the room to the portico, where he still stood. "You need fear nothing," he said. "The caliph's powers of protection are not negligible, and his power to reward is of the highest."

Kadiga glanced upward at him, her eyes misted with tears, but the fright had left them. "Yes, my lord Abul," she said, and sped away beneath the rising sun, back to Sarita's tower.

As Abul stood alone, despair entered his soul like some great crouching black creature, exuding the destructive miasma of hopelessness. Sarita was now in the irreversible grip of a venom. He knew enough, had seen enough, to fear the worst. She would be lost to him. Then hard on the heels of despair came fierce resolution. He would not let it happen. Sarita must fight it. He would infuse her with his own strength, encourage her to throw off the bane. She was young, strong, healthy. Muhamed Alahma had rare skills as a physician, apothecary, and alchemist. He would be able to do something if Sarita fought with him.

He strode back into the room and flung open the door to the antechamber. "Send for Muhamed Alahma immediately. He is to await me here."

The startled guards watched as the caliph left the antechamber with unusual haste, his robe swirling around his booted legs. When he passed beneath the windows of the seraglio, Abul's hand unconsciously closed over the small dagger in the deep pocket of his robe as Aicha's face rose in his mind's eye. Deliberately he released his grip on the jeweled hilt and drew forth his hand, taking a steadying breath, washing his mind clear of the polluting image. He did not know how he was going to deal with her, but he knew that he had to keep his head clear of the rioting images of revenge, images that would interfere with his ability to infuse Sarita with the strength and determined belief in her powers of recovery without which she could not win through.

He reached the tower and entered at speed and without ceremony. Kadiga appeared at the head of the stairs to the sleeping gallery as he crossed the court. He beckoned her downstairs. Her face was gray.

"Is she worse?" He whispered the question so Sarita would not hear. Kadiga nodded and he said softly, "She is to know only that she can and *will* be well again. Is that clear?"

"Yes, my lord." Kadiga seemed visibly to take a grip on herself as she accepted the sense of the caliph's words. "But Zulema has such a tender heart, I do not know if—"

"If Zulema cannot maintain such a front, then she must keep away," Abul said in a brisk whisper. "You will explain things to her as you see fit. From now on, the only people to approach Sarita will be myself, Muhamed Alahma, yourself, and Zulema, if you believe she is to be trusted."

"Oh, indeed she is, my lord. If she has the strength, there is no one better in a sickroom."

"Good." He nodded and went to the stairs.

"Abul?" Sarita's voice was weak and quavery. "I thought I heard you." She tried to sit up, to smile. "I am still abed, is it not shameful?"

"Not in the least," he said. "You are going to remain abed for quite some time, *querida.*"

"But we are to go to Motril," she protested, fighting the need to fall back again on the cushions as she drew desperate, shallow breaths.

"All in good time." He sat on the edge of the divan and supported her against his shoulder. "Kadiga, bring a robe and slippers."

Sarita leaned back against him, too bewildered and

exhausted to wonder why they were dressing her in this strange fashion. Kadiga slipped the soft shoes on her feet while Abul fastened the robe down the front; then he lifted her into his arms.

"What is happening?" she finally managed to demand as he carried her to the stairs. "Where are we going?"

"To my apartments, where I can keep you under my eye," Abul told her. "And when you are quite well again, *hija mía*, you and I are going to have a very serious and possibly disagreeable talk on the subject of honesty. You have been keeping things from me, and I am most displeased."

Sarita lay still in his arms, suddenly amazingly reassured by his tone and words. If she were going to die, he would not talk to her in such fashion. "I will be well again, won't I, Abul?"

He looked down at her. Her eyes were filled with pain and fear, but beneath he saw trust. That trust was the only weapon he had with which to combat the poison. "What foolishness is this, Sarita? Why should you not be well again? You are wearied and have taken some infection. Muhamed Alahma will physic you, and you will rest. If you had said earlier that you were unwell, matters would not have come to this pass."

"But I am not accustomed to feeling unwell," she tried to explain. "I thought it would go away. Do not be vexed."

He smiled down at her as his heart turned over with love and dread. "I am only a little vexed, and you will earn your pardon by doing exactly as the physician says and swiftly getting well again." Lifting her slightly in his arms, he brushed his lips across her brow, his spirits dashed anew at the icy clamminess of her skin.

"I can walk," she said. "Put me down, and you will see that I am in no wise an invalid."

"No."

Sarita had neither the strength nor the inclination

to argue. But the dreadful sense of being alone with her fear and confusion had been banished by Abul's calm, reassuringly exasperated presence.

Muhamed Alahma was waiting in the antechamber when the caliph appeared with his burden, Kadiga following as he had instructed.

"My lord caliph." The physician bowed his venerable head, his beard almost sweeping the floor. "How may I be of service?"

"Come within and I will explain." Abul carried Sarita into his own sleeping chamber and laid her down on the divan, saying quietly to Kadiga, "Remain with her while I talk with the physician. He will have questions for you later."

"Why would he wish to question—" Sarita stopped speaking and closed her eyes as the terrifying rush of her heart began anew. Abul looked down at her, watching the painful struggles of her fragile body as it tried to accommodate what was happening to it. "Can you not help her?" he demanded of Kadiga.

The woman shook her head, biting her lip. But she leaned over Sarita and raised her shoulders slightly, taking her hand in a tight grip.

"What has she taken within her?" The voice of the physician spoke abruptly. He had come over to the divan without invitation and stood watching Sarita's battling with an educated eye.

"We do not know." Abul turned and gestured that he should move away from the bed. "I will tell you what I do know."

Muhamed Alahma listened in grave silence. Then he listened as Kadiga detailed the symptoms, the slow development, the now rapid deterioration, and he shook his head. "Do you have the draught that contained the bane?"

Kadiga had brought it with her from the tower and now handed him the skin container. The physician emptied the contents into a lacquered dish. He sniffed, he poked with a small skewer, he held the liquid to the light, then he shook his head again. "I can tell nothing from this. But I can tell you, my lord caliph, that I know of such banes, and once they reach this stage, there is little hope of recovery."

Abul's heart squeezed, squeezed like a lemon, and the bitter juice of loss dripped into his veins. "You *must* do something," he said fiercely. "I will not accept that there is nothing. There must be something you can administer to counteract the poison."

Muhamed Alahma pulled his beard, frowning for such a long time that Abul thought that in a minute he would seize the old man by the throat and shake a response from him. "Sometimes," the physician said finally, "there are things that work in such cases. But I cannot know what to administer if I do not know the nature of the bane." He nodded reflectively. "Furnish me with the name of the bane, my lord caliph, and maybe I can do something."

Abul stood very still. He felt Kadiga's jump of fear beside him. Only one person could tell him what had been administered to Sarita. It meant he must act without premeditation, without preparation, without planning for the consequences, but he had no choice. "You shall have the name," he said.

He sent for the vizier, who received precise instructions with an impassive countenance: an armed escort was to enter the seraglio, lay hands on the lady Aicha, and bring her to the Mexuar.

Abul returned to his apartments, where the physician was examining Sarita, who lay gasping for breath in a cold sweat of exhaustion. "I will prepare an emetic," Muhamed Alahma said as Abul came over. "It will rid her of what poison lingers in the stomach. But there is little else I can do without the name of the venom."

"You shall have that shortly," Abul said with savage confidence. "Kadiga, you will need Zulema to assist you. I will have her summoned."

Zulema arrived within minutes, and Abul left the two women and the physician to their grim work, going himself to the small mosque at the rear of the

Mexuar to prepare himself for what he was about to do.

The arrival of the soldiers in the seraglio was heralded by an alarmed serving woman, who saw them approach the staircase to the jalousied balcony from the hall beneath. The chatter of the women was stilled, their various occupations abandoned as they covered their faces in haste, gazing fearfully at one another, stunned by such an unprecedented visitation. The caliph and occasionally the vizier were the only men ever to enter the seraglio. The women withdrew from the center of the room, standing against the walls, staring with their kohl-lined eyes as the soldiers in their steel-pronged helmets burst into the parlor, curved scimitars at their belts.

"Where is the lady Aicha?" The officer in charge spoke into the fearful hush, his voice grating like a knife on fine porcelain.

For a moment no one replied; then one of their number said hesitantly, "The lady Aicha has not yet come from her apartments this morning. The hour is still early."

The officer turned to a serving woman staring wide-eyed from a corner. "Escort us to the sultana's apartments." The woman scuttled ahead of them down the corridor, pointing silently to the door that led to Aicha's private chamber. "Announce us," the officer instructed, reluctant despite his orders to intrude on the lady in her privacy. But the door opened before the woman could knock, and Nafissa, cloaked and veiled, stood there, barring the way.

"We have business with the lady Aicha," the officer said curtly. "Move aside."

"Who is it, Nafissa?" Aicha's voice came from within, astonished at the sound of a man's voice at her door.

"Soldiers, my lady." Nafissa turned back, her lip trembling with fear.

Cold fingers marched down Aicha's spine. What

had gone wrong? How had she been betrayed? Had her message to her father been discovered? Her eyes shot accusingly to Nafissa. Only the handmaid knew her secrets, but the other woman's fear was palpable, and Aicha knew Nafissa had not betrayed her.

"What do you want of me?" She tried to sound outraged at this intrusion.

"The lord Abul, lady, has commanded us to bring you to the Mexuar," the officer stated without expression. He gestured to two of the soldiers, and they moved on the sultana, seizing her arms even as she cried out in fury, trying to free herself. But the officer had been told to lay hands on the caliph's wife and bring her in that manner to the hall of justice, and the feeble protestations of a woman could not alter his orders or his intentions. He turned and left the chamber with the soldiers bearing the struggling sultana behind him, her cries shivering the frescoed walls of the seraglio and striking terror into the hearts of the other women at this horrifying reversal of fortune. If Aicha, so feared as she was, supreme among women, could be brought so low, then no one was immune.

Aicha ceased her struggles abruptly when she was hauled out into the sunlit Court of the Lions. Struggling only increased the indignity of her progress, and she walked upright between the guards, her eyes blazing with a near feral fury even as her head whirled in a turmoil of speculation as to what had led Abul to order this public disgrace. If he suspected treason, he would not deal with it in this way. She knew he favored soft steps when confronting and outsmarting his enemies, meeting the clandestine dagger with one as cleverly concealed. He would have to have incontrovertible evidence to treat his wife in this manner. But what? All she could think of was that he had discovered her correspondence with her father. But she had written only of troubles within the Alhambra, of her fears that the caliph might be weakened by his passion for his new concubine. She had been scrupulously careful to say nothing truly incriminating.

Indeed, she could almost defend herself on the grounds of legitimate concern for her husband . . .

Abul emerged from the mosque just before they brought Aicha into the Mexuar. He sat on the great carved throne of justice as impassive as a graven image, all emotion quelled, consumed by just one imperative.

Aicha felt her courage falter when she saw him sitting in judgment in the deserted hall, his hands resting lightly on the arms of the throne, his eyes somehow shrunk to black tips of fierce light, his mouth chiseled in stone. The guards brought her to the foot of the throne and, at a signal from Abul, released their grip on her arms, stepping back so that she stood alone.

"Tell me the name of the venom you have been administering to Sarita." The demand was quiet, uttered in a voice that was unlike Abul's, cold and expressionless, utterly inflexible.

Aicha's first reaction was one of triumph and relief. So that was what this was about. But there was no evidence to tie her to the Spaniard's decline. No one, not even Nafissa, knew of it. If she kept steadfast in denial, there was no way they could proceed further with this. And the woman must be dying . . .

"I don't understand you, my lord Abul," she said with quiet dignity. "And I do not understand what I have done that you should treat me with such ignominy."

"Don't you?" he asked softly. "Don't you, Aicha? Then allow me to explain. For these last many weeks you have been poisoning Sarita with the draught you have prepared for her against conception." Having said that, he fell silent and watched her.

How had he guessed? But a guess was not evidence. She forced herself to meet his eye. "If I am so accused, I demand the right to face my accuser and hear the evidence that would prove the accusation." She was still confident, still certain they could prove nothing. Only she herself could condemn herself.

Slowly, Abul stretched out his right arm, pointed his index finger at her. "You stand before your accuser. I and only I bring this accusation."

Aicha wet her lips. What did it mean? Abul knew he could not accuse without good and sufficient reason. And he had only guesswork. She shook her head. "I deny the accusation, my lord Abul, and would ask for your evidence."

Abul rose from his throne. "Give me the name of the poison, Aicha."

Suddenly this was not the Abul she knew, the man whose body she had eased and pleasured, the man with whom she had passed many pleasant hours, the man whose child she had borne, the man who she had believed could be easily defeated with the right mix of skills and deception. No, the man towering above her was not that man. This was a veritable god of vengeance, an all-powerful, pitiless god facing her, repeating his demand in the same cold, inflexible, confident voice, the twin daggers of light boring into her soul.

Her voice shook slightly as she repeated her denial, telling herself that that was all she needed to do to defeat the accusation, to render powerless this vengeful god.

Abul looked at her for a terrifying moment, and she felt dehumanized by the look, as if he were stripping her of all vestige of humanity, rendering her no more than a clod of flesh, and she trembled with a terror unlike any she had known.

"Take her to the alcazaba," Abul said, his voice indifferent. "Discover the name and bring it to me. I care only for the speed with which you unlock her memory." He turned from her on the words and strode out of the hall as Aicha's scream of realization lifted to the rafters.

The soldiers dragged her from the Mexuar and to the alcazaba. She had ceased to scream, indeed was almost lifeless in the grip of the guards, paralyzed by horror. But in the bowels of the fortress, in the dank chamber lit by the fitful, noisome flares of pitch torches, when they showed her what was there, talked of what they would use to unlock her memory, she began to scream again: a high-pitched screech of animal fear. When they strapped her to the stone table, she screamed the name of the poison, over and over in a desperate, pleading babble. To be certain, they used the bastinado, but when she repeated the same name like some incantation, they stopped after a few strokes. They left her strapped to the table in the underground chamber, and the officer went at a near run to carry the name to the caliph. It had been but half an hour since Abul had given his order and departed the Mexuar.

When Abul returned to his chamber, he found he could not remain there. Sarita's anguish was more than he could endure as the physician and the two attendants administered the emetics that would rid her of whatever venom had not yet entered her system. She pleaded with Abul to make them stop, and he could only deny her. It seemed her drowned gaze blamed him for her agony. He went out into the antechamber, pacing restlessly, waiting for the information he knew would soon be brought to him. He did not believe Aicha was blessed with great fortitude.

He felt no compunction for employing the tools of the Inquisition to force her confession. He knew with the soul's absolute knowledge that he would do anything to protect Sarita from harm . . . make any sacrifices, demand them of anyone, himself included. The knowledge didn't strike him as strange. It seemed inevitable, had been since first he had seen her on the road. She was an inextricable part of him, woven into the sinews of his being, and if he could give his life for hers, he would do so without hesitation.

The rapid pounding of booted feet sounded on the marble paving of the portico, and the officer of the guard entered the antechamber. "The seed of the Tanghinia, my lord," he said without preamble.

"You are certain she did not lie?"

The officer shook his head. He was experienced in such matters. "I believe it to be the truth."

Abul nodded and turned back to his own chamber.

"My lord?" The officer spoke almost hesitantly.

Abul paused impatiently. "Well?"

"The lady Aicha, my lord. What is to be done with her?"

"Confine her in the tower of the cadi," Abul said. "And the prince Boabdil with her." Whatever plans he might have had for his son were now at an end. The child of such a woman could not be his heir, and mother and son might as well share exile. It would be the kindest option from every point of view. When he had time for reflection, he would decide on the form of that exile.

He entered his chamber and went swiftly to the divan. Sarita lay bloodless on the cushions, her lips blue-tinged, that wonderful mass of unruly flaming curls lank and lifeless, the flame extinguished. For a dreadful moment he thought she was already lost to him, but her fingertips fluttered in a feeble convulsive movement on the coverlet.

"The seed of the Tanghinia," he said to the physician. "What can you do to counteract it?"

Muhamed Alahma pulled his beard and looked even graver than usual. "I do not know . . . it is a most pernicious, violent bane . . ." Muttering, he went away, leaving Abul and the two women in a fever of fearful uncertainty as Sarita lay comatose now. But at least she was at some kind of peace . . . Abul tried to draw comfort from the reflection.

Muhamed Alahma returned within an hour. He said nothing but carefully placed on Sarita's tongue a bright yellow pastille. "I do not know if it will be efficacious," he mumbled into his beard. "But I know of nothing else. It must be administered every three hours."

"How will you know if it is beneficial?" Abul asked.

"If she does not die within the next few hours," the physician said with blunt simplicity. "We can only wait."

Chapter 17

The serving woman laid the tray of food on a table in the lower court of the tower of the cadi and asked, "Is there anything else you wish for, lady?" The woman did not trouble to lower her eyes in the sultana's presence, and her voice carried none of the respectful submission to which Aicha was accustomed.

The sultana's palm itched to slap the insolence from her mouth, but the three soldiers who always accompanied visitors to the prisoner were standing by the door, and Aicha did not feel inclined to provide such an audience with an ugly and undignified scene. Her eyes flicked to the tray. Had Nafissa managed to conceal another message? The handmaid had proved astonishingly resourceful in the days since her mistress's imprisonment, and seemed willing to continue being so for considerable monetary reward.

She said curtly, "Leave me," and waited until the woman and her escort had left before bending over the tray, searching with eager, nimble fingers through the carefully folded linen napkins, where Nafissa had secreted the last message. Disappointingly, there was none.

Boabdil wriggled under her arm to examine the food on the tray and complained vociferously at the absence of his favorite sugared almonds.

"Don't whine, Boabdil," his mother said with a snap, and the boy's mouth opened on an indignant wail. Aicha sighed. She was finding her son's constant company less appealing than she would have imagined.

Boabdil reached for a dish of plovers' eggs, nesting attractively on a broad green fig leaf glistening with drops of water. The leaf slipped under his grasping fingers, and something white showed beneath. Aicha pushed his hands aside and edged her fingers under the leaf, drawing out a tightly rolled scrap of oiled silk. Leaving Boabdil to explore the culinary delights of the dinner tray, she unrolled the silk. Nafissa had done even better than expected. She had discovered from a watchman the entrance to one of the subterranean passages perforating the hill on which the Alhambra stood. The passage emerged beyond the city of Granada, in the hillside above the River Darro. If the sultana was willing to try her luck, an escape could be contrived with the aid of the watchman, who could be bought with the pigeon's-egg ruby in the lady Aicha's jewel casket.

Her jewel casket was suffering considerable depredations at Nafissa's hands, Aicha reflected dourly. But she was in no position to bargain. Once she had effected her escape from the Alhambra, she would flee to her father with a tale of her treatment that would enrage him. He would seek vengeance on the man who from the depths of a mindless infatuation had disgraced his daughter without proof of wrongdoing—confessions wrenched through torment could be discounted. He would incite rebellion among the other Morisco-Spanish families, and Abul would be brought down.

She had not seen Abul since that dreadful morning in the Mexuar, but she knew he would not leave her and Boabdil permanently imprisoned in the tower of the cadi. It must be a temporary arrangement until he had decided what to do with them. If he removed them from the Alhambra, the chance for a successful escape would be much reduced.

What of Boabdil? How would he react to the dangers and discomforts of an escape? She regarded him thoughtfully. He was too busy devouring plovers' eggs to be aware of her silent scrutiny. She must take him with her; he was vital to her future plans. Deposing Abul would have little point if there were not her own puppet to put in his place. But how good would the boy be under pressure? He whimpered too easily. Aicha knew this without Abul's pointing it out as often as he had done, but it suited her plans better to keep the boy weak and dependent than to encourage him to stand on his own feet. She would just have to accept the disadvantages.

It should be possible to scare him into silence, at least until they were beyond the walls of the Alhambra; his father was already an ogre. Unfortunately, the boy had been so overjoyed at being freed from his tutor and given into the exclusive hands of his mother that she had been able to make little capital out of their imprisonment. Boabdil did not seem to see it as such at all, and since he was taken out every morning by the soldiers for walks and rides, and was provided with all his favorite delicacies, it was no wonder that the truth of the situation failed to impress him.

Aicha turned the slip of silk over. It was blank on the back. Nafissa would expect a return message, delivered in the same way. Presumably she waited for the tray in the kitchens. She would come with them, of course, and since she was a native of the city of Granada, she could presumably arrange through her family for horses and an escort to await them on the riverbank beyond the city. In the dark hours before dawn, they should be able to make good their escape, and Aicha would be under her father's protection in half a day.

But it must be soon. Swiftly, she sharpened her quill and began to scratch upon the silk.

"What are you up to?"

"I thought I would try my legs." Sarita looked up, smiling, as Abul came into the sleeping chamber. She had been sitting on the edge of the divan, thought-

fully swinging her legs while she tried to decide
whether they would hold her as far as the open door
to the portico.

"Do you have Muhamed Alahma's permission?"
He adopted a mock stern mien even as his heart sang
with relief and gratitude for the life that had been
given back to him.

"Not exactly," Sarita said, flexing her toes. "The
subject hasn't been mentioned."

"Then put yourself back to bed." Abul leaned over
her and swung her legs back onto the divan. "You
do nothing without his specific agreement."

"Oh, such nonsense," she said. "I am perfectly
well again, only a trifle feeble because of all that
dreadful medicine they gave me to make me vomit."
She took his hand as he sat on the divan beside her
and squeezed his fingers hard. She remembered little
of that hideous time; only the fact of Abul stood out
clear. As she had drifted in the inert wasteland on the
borders of death, yielding the struggle because it was
easier to give in to the pain and the weakness than to
fight it, Abul had seemed to enter her body. She still
didn't know how he had done it, but he had forced
her to open her eyes, and his own had consumed her
as she lay looking up at him. She had fixed her being,
her core, on those piercing black lights that drew her
forth from the depths of the shroud that had become
her body, brought her into the light, compelled her
to stay there, holding her with invisible, unbreakable
chains.

Abul returned the squeeze and propped up the pillows behind her before hitching himself onto the divan to lie alongside her. It had been only a week since
that morning and the longest day he had ever spent.
At first it had seemed as if the pastilles would not
work. Sarita had lain inert for hours, and the physician had said that if the body wouldn't fight, the an-
tidote could not work alone. In desperation Abul had
begun to speak to her, forcefully, angrily, command-
ingly, shaking her slight shoulders for emphasis as

he told her to open her eyes, to hold on to him, that he had strength enough for both of them. And she had done so, at long, long last. A flicker of recognition had appeared in the dull eyes, and her gaze had held. When the violent spasms had racked her body, he had refused to let her slip back, fought to infuse her with his own strength, and somehow it had happened. The paroxysms had weakened as the eternal day mercifully became night and the physician's pastilles began to do their work. He had not slept all that night lest she slip back without his physical presence to hold on to, and by morning she had fallen into a sleep that seemed normal.

Muhamed Alahma had nodded and offered no opinion, either reassuring or negative, but he had continued to place the pastilles on her tongue; and with amazing speed, it seemed, as startling as the sudden deterioration, Sarita had returned fully to the land of the living, the violent effects of the deadly bane neutralized.

Now a touch of mischief shone in her eyes as she rested her head in the crook of his shoulder and stroked his mouth with a finger. "I feel a great need to visit the baths, my lord caliph. I am sure it will have the most restorative effect."

Abul chuckled and sucked her exploring finger into his mouth, nipping the tip. "If you wish for a bath, *cara*, I will arrange it for you, but in here. You're not strong enough for outside journeys as yet."

"No, perhaps not," she agreed. "And certainly not for the cold water and the chamber that makes one melt." She sat up, suddenly restless. "I really do not feel like lying here, Abul. My legs are twitching with the need to move. I am going to walk to the portico. You may support me if you wish it."

Abul sighed and accepted the inevitable. He watched as she pushed herself off the bed, stood for a minute, frowning slightly as she tested her strength, then took a firm step. "See, I am perfectly capable,"

she crowed triumphantly, walking to the open doorway.

Abul followed her at a discreet distance, ready to
lend a supporting hand if she needed it, but apparently she didn't. At the doorway, she leaned against
a column and breathed deeply of the wonderfully
fresh air.

"When I was sometimes half of this world and half
not, Abul, I heard things spoken." She didn't look at
him, her eyes on the green finches trilling in the cage,
on the gentle rise and fall of the fountain in the center
of the court. "I heard talk of poison." She caressed
the cool marble of the pillar against which she leaned,
fingering the elaborate curlicues finely traced with
gold leaf. "There was no infection taken, was there?
Who wished me dead?"

Abul stood just behind her. He had hoped to spare
her this knowledge of Aicha's enmity. It seemed there
would be little to gain but further hurt. Aicha would
harm no one again, he would ensure that. But in the
face of Sarita's direct question, he could not dissemble.

"Aicha."

She said nothing for a minute, resting her forehead
against the pillar; then her shoulders lifted in an in-
finitesimal shrug. "I should have guessed. She is a
woman of powerful drives. I often felt that I was hin-
dering her in some way. Where is she?"

"Confined with Boabdil in the tower of the cadi. I
am arranging to send them both into exile in Morocco."

"You would visit the sins of the mother upon the
child?" She turned to look at him, her expression one
he recognized, pregnant with the indignation of the
enlightened. In the past it had irritated him, but today it filled him with the joy of renewal.

"They prefer to be together. To separate the child
permanently from his mother struck me as the height
of cruelty," he explained calmly. "Do you believe me
wrong?"

Sarita shook her head. "No . . . no . . . but what of his future? He will grow to manhood and not need his mother. Surely you will not deprive him of—"

"That is for the future," Abul interrupted. "I will do the best for him that I can."

Sarita believed him and laid the issue to rest. There would be no need to talk again of the woman who had tried to contrive her death. Aicha had seen a threat in her husband's love for Sarita, a threat Sarita could not identify, but she had recognized the fact instinctively from the first moment she had laid eyes on the sultana. But it was not necessary now to explore or to hide the contentious subject with Abul, or to talk of the child, no longer to be torn between his parents. She lifted her head to the sun's warmth.

"Who will be your principal wife, then, if you are to repudiate Aicha? Will you take Farah and make little Salim your heir?"

Abul frowned. Sarita did have the most exasperating tendency to bring up inapposite subjects at inopportune moments. "I have not thought about it," he said. "In the last days, I have had no time for thinking of anything but you, *hija mía.*"

She turned, leaning against the pillar at her back, and smiled, her eyes narrowed. "Oh, dear, I have trod on your toes again. I cannot seem to stop myself from asking the questions that interest me."

He couldn't help laughing. "I believe you do it deliberately, Sarita. But I am not going to respond to provocation today. You are by no means strong enough for what would then ensue."

"Am I not?" She scrunched her eyes, peering mischievously up at him. "And who says not?"

"I say not." Still laughing, he went back inside, ringing the handbell that would bring Kadiga and Zulema. "Sarita wishes a bath," he told them. "Have it prepared in the outer chamber."

"And jugs of hot water for my hair," Sarita said, appearing from the portico, running her hands with a grimace through the lank, dull strands. "And bring my clothes, if you please. I shall bathe and dress. I have had quite enough of lying abed."

"If Muhamed Alahma agrees," Abul said mildly. "We will consult him first."

The physician had no quarrel with Sarita's resurgence of energy. "The woman is young," he said to Abul with an accepting shrug. "Young and strong. So long as she listens to her body, she will come to no further harm."

"What did I say?" Sarita murmured once the physician had left the chamber. "I said I was strong enough for anything that might ensue, did I not?"

"We shall see," Abul said slowly, making it sound like a promise. "Let us see what ensues from the bath."

"Oh . . ." She lay back against the pillows of the divan. "You mean apart from clean hair and skin?"

He nodded. "Yes, apart from those things."

"You have something in mind, perhaps?"

"Perhaps."

"Of course," she mused, "when it comes to baths, you are a consummate inventor and practitioner."

"Consummate."

"Mmmmm." Her eyes closed dreamily. "I feel like . . ."

"What do you feel like?" He knelt on the bed beside her, touching her mouth, her eyes. "Tell me what you feel like, Sarita. Tell me what would pleasure you."

"I have no need to tell you," she whispered. "You always know."

He kept his hands on her face, but a grave look showed in his eagle's eyes as he knelt upright. "On such a subject, there is something, Sarita, that we must talk of. That last time—"

"I know," she broke in, catching his wrists. "But I was so afraid, Abul. So afraid of what I was feeling . . . of what I was not feeling. I thought if I pretended, it would come back. I know it was an indefensible thing to do." Her eyes raked his face anxiously.

"We were both at fault," he said. "I also was afraid . . . too afraid to confront you. We must never do such a thing again . . . show such lack of trust again."

"Never," she promised softly. "But we are still learning about each other, *querido*. One makes mistakes."

He nodded and leaned over her, his lips replacing his fingers on her face. "Trust me to bring you only the sweetest joy, Sarita *mía*."

She caught his hands between her own, filled suddenly with an overwhelming emotion, a deep upsurge of love that brought tears to her eyes. "I belong to you in some way," she whispered. "How does it happen that I feel that?"

"We belong to each other," he asserted, smudging a tear with his thumb. "Don't weep, *cara*."

"I am not sad," she said, sniffing and smiling. "I am very happy. But I do want a bath. I don't feel at all appealing at the moment, and I shall not until I am clean and have washed my hair."

"I will do it for you."

"No," she said firmly. "Kadiga and Zulema will help me. You are to go away and not come back until I send for you."

Abul looked absurdly disappointed. "But I thought I was going to use my powers of invention—"

"No!" Laughingly she interrupted him. "Not this time. This is work for women, Abul, and you would only be in the way."

"No one has ever told me I would be in the way before."

"That is because no one has ever dared," she replied with a serene smile. "Your consequence has been overly inflated."

"When I return," said Abul, stepping off the divan, "we shall reopen this discussion. I would take issue with you on several matters."

"That sounds most promising," she said. "Be off

about your business now. I am sure you have sadly neglected things with all this sickroom attendance." She waved an airily dismissive hand at him. "You may return in two hours. I shall be ready for you then."

Her voice was haughty, her nose in the air, her expression one of lofty dignity. Abul stared at her for a minute, nonplussed by the novel sensation of being a petitioner denied an immediate audience. Then he gave a shout of laughter.

"Wicked one! You look just like an impudent sparrow pretending to be a peacock. You haven't the stature for arrogance . . . and don't pout, either, it doesn't suit you." He bent to kiss her as she pulled a mock offended face. "I would have you remember that these are my apartments and I will return when I choose." He pinched her nose and straightened. "And when I do return, we will get down to some unfinished business."

"Some postponed promises, you mean," Sarita said.

"If you wish to put it that way," he agreed cordially, going through the arched, curtained doorway into the main chamber. "Do not let Sarita overtax her strength," he said to Kadiga, who was pouring steaming jugs of water into a round wooden bathtub set before a charcoal brazier that was warming the room to combat any possible chill on a mountain morning in February.

"Of course not, my lord," the woman answered placidly, sprinkling dried lavender and rose petals on the water.

"I do not need a nursemaid," Sarita announced from the doorway, having overheard this exchange. "I am capable of judging my strength for myself."

Abul raised his hands in a placatory gesture. "As you wish, *hija mía*, as you wish. But there'll be no promises kept if I find you fatigued on my return." On which parting thrust he left his apartments to the women, reflecting how easily he had adapted to the loss of his privacy. So easily, in fact, that he was not at all sure he wished Sarita to return to her tower once she was completely restored to health and strength. Perhaps he could organize some compromise whereby she had her own apartments adjoining his. The walk to and from the perimeter tower was certainly an inconvenience, for all that the hours they had spent alone there had had a very special quality of exclusivity.

In the chamber he used for conducting everyday business, he found two men waiting for him. They were both part of the army of eyes and ears he had working for him in the kingdom outside the Alhambra, and they had brought perturbing news.

"There is much talk among the Mocarabes, my lord, of the Christian woman," the taller of the two said somewhat diffidently. "Ahmed ben Kaled brought a tale to the emir that has caused many councils to be held."

"A tale of what?" Abul inquired, seating himself at the long table beneath a tall window standing open to the mountains. He was relatively untroubled by the information, having expected it to some extent after the incident with Kaled.

"A tale that the caliph is neglecting his governance because of the woman," the other man said, toying with the dagger at his belt, avoiding meeting the caliph's eye.

Abul was now startled. Such a construction had not occurred to him. And however could it have originated? Sarita's presence in the Alhambra had not been common knowledge until Kaled's visit. Or had it . . . ? Was Aicha's hand to be found in this? "There is more?" he invited, with no indication of his racing thoughts.

"The Abencerrajes, my lord," the first man said. "They have been summoned by the emir of the Mocarabes to a council. It is said for the same reason. I believe messengers bearing the summons and the reason for it have gone out to other families in the kingdom.''

Abul tapped his fingers on the table in a steady rhythm, making no immediate response. He could not afford to ignore this information, treat the whisperings with the contempt they deserved. The rumor must be scotched, the conspiracies dismantled before they had been truly hatched. How to do that?

''You did well to bring me this information without delay,'' he said finally. ''I would have you return to your posts and keep me informed of all developments, however trivial they may seem.''

The two bowed low and left the caliph's presence. Abul sat for a long time in the contemplative peace of his office. He had to act strongly to prove that he was still very much at the helm. Some martial foray to benefit the kingdom as a whole would be the most convincing . . . but there was no apparent need for militant action at the moment. The Spaniards were quiet across the border; brigands within were generally under control. Perhaps a show of outrage at the rumors . . .

Perhaps he should descend upon his father-in-law and the gathered clans in a cloud of wrath, demanding satisfaction for their calumny. Of course, relations with the emir of the Mocarabes were not going to be improved by the caliph's repudiation and punishment of the emir's daughter. Particularly when her offense concerned the Christian woman in question. It would add the fuel of outrage to the fire. For the moment, it was known to no one. But it could not be long before the news leaked out. And once he had banished Aicha from the Alhambra, there would be no concealing anything.

He stood up and went to the window. Why was he concerned to conceal anything? He had behaved legitimately. He had no reason to defend his actions to his father-in-law. Aicha had attempted murder. It was a crime punishable by death regardless of the identity of the intended victim. But the proof of guilt was murky.

Then again, a man had the right to repudiate a wife whom he no longer found satisfactory. The emir had no just cause for complaint there. But he would need no just cause to foment rebellion. A believable fabrication would do. And Abul held his position on a knife edge in a land of rivalry and dissension. It was always the way. It had been so with his father, and he assumed it would be so with whoever came after him. Not Boabdil . . . the emir's grandson disinherited . . . yet another snake to add to the pit.

He would surprise the conspiracy by attending the secret council to which the other emirs had been summoned. His presence alone would be enough to dispel the rumors of inattention, and he could permit himself a calculated show of displeasure at the effrontery of interfering with his private affairs. A man's harem was his own business.

Not that Sarita was a member of his harem. Abul could not suppress a chuckle as he thought of how his compatriots would react if they knew exactly how matters stood between their caliph and the Spanish woman. There was an acknowledged equality to the relationship that would dumbfound an outsider.

The thought was an amusing distraction, but he put it aside as just that. Such a visit to his father-in-law would also serve as an opportunity to present his own case vis-à-vis Aicha. He would forestall criticism by publicly declaring the circumstances and his decision. Properly executed, his statement would include more than a hint of criticism of the man who had bred such a daughter and used her to gain entrance to the powers of the Alhambra.

No . . . it would do very well, Abul decided. The decision made, he put all thoughts and reconsiderations behind him in customary fashion and summoned the vizier and the cadi. An hour should see him through the rest of the morning's imperative business, and then he could return to his apartments, to a wholesome and hopefully inviting Sarita.

It was rather more than an hour, however, before he crossed the antechamber to the guarded door, anticipation in his step. He stopped on the threshold. The chamber was in semidarkness, despite the brightness of early afternoon. The heavy winter curtains had been pulled across the long windows and doors onto the portico, and the soft afterglow of the charcoal brazier mingled with the perfumed golden halos from oil lamps strategically placed around the chamber.

He blinked, accustoming his eyes to the change; then he saw Sarita. She was lying on an ottoman, quite naked, her body gleaming palely in contrast to her hair, tumbling in shining extravagance across her shoulders, foaming on the cushions beneath her head. She moved one hand in a languid gesture of invitation, and Abul approached the ottoman, a smile of mingled amusement and delight on his mouth.

"I had not expected to be received by an odalisque," he said softly, kneeling beside the ottoman. "What are you up to?"

"Why, nothing." She shifted on the cushions and stretched languorously, offering him the feast of her body, its curves and hollows cast in light and shadows by the seductive illumination. "I am simply resting, my lord caliph, as you desired me to do."

"I see." He held back from touching her but inhaled the warm scents of her body, the fragrance of her hair. "Then I will not disturb you."

Her teeth caught her bottom lip, and ready laughter sprang in the seaweed eyes, quite at odds with her indolently alluring pose. "That would be a pitiable waste of a deal of preparation, my lord Abul."

Silently, Abul drew his embroidered robe over his head. As always in the day, he wore a serviceable shirt and britches beneath, and Sarita watched with unabashed eagerness as he divested himself of these garments, until, naked, he stood over her as she lay offering herself on the ottoman.

"You belong to me," he asserted, a deep throb in his voice. "Every cell, every pore of your body, every hair of your head, every inch of your skin."

"Then you should take possession of that which you possess," she said softly, "so that I may take possession of that which I possess."

He knelt on the ottoman at her feet, slowly, purposefully, running his eyes over her body, but still without touching her. "I want you to give yourself to me, Sarita."

The husky demand hung in the scented air as she gazed up at him. Towering over her soft exposed vulnerability, his body was hard and powerful, predatory in its aroused hunger. Her breath caught in her throat at the recognition of that physical power against her own fragility, and the knowledge that only the tenuous threads of trust bound woman to man in the sharing of bodies; only the indefinable emotion called love transformed the use of another's body into the joyful sharing of pleasure.

Slowly, she ran her hands over her body, acknowledging each part of it as hers even as she made of the exploration an exhibition . . . an offering. At the very last, her thighs parted, and she rendered the core of herself to his eyes and the hands that finally he laid in possession upon her . . .

"Shall we stay in this chamber with the world shut out forever?" Sarita turned her head against his breast, pressing her lips into the hollow of his throat where the pulse beat strongly.

Abul smiled, playing idly with her hair as she broke the deep silence of satiation. Her voice sounded strangely loud in the dim, glowing chamber, although she had spoken barely above a whisper, but only the short, husky words of passion had been heard in the room for many hours, it seemed. "Forever is a long time, *querida*."

"Then for many days." She propped herself up on an elbow and leaned over him, enclosing them both in the fragrant flaming tent of her hair, her mouth hovering over his. "Let us stay here, naked in the lamplight, and ignore the world for a week."

He raised his hand to push her hair away from her face and lightly cupped the curve of her cheek. "I wish it were possible. But we must settle for hours rather than days."

"Oh." She sensed a suddenly provoked tautness in him. "You have business?"

He didn't want to tell her that he would soon have to leave her to journey to the Mocarabes. Such information would sully the peace and unity of the time they could spend enclosed in their own world. "There is always business," he said. "Are you not hungry? We have not dined, and it must be well into the afternoon, although it's hard to tell in this cavern."

Sarita contemplated the question. "I suppose I am a little. And if I am a little, then you must be a lot. Shall I ring?" She reached for the handbell.

Abul regarded her with some amusement as he caught her wrist, arresting her movement. "That bell will bring one of the guards in here. Do you intend to receive him in your skin?"

"I am too lazy to move," she said. "Fetch me a coverlet from the sleeping chamber."

Abul's eyes narrowed as he pulled his robe over his head. "You are growing somewhat importunate, Sarita *mía*. It seems to me that you are developing an inflated sense of your own consequence."

She laughed. "That's what I said to you."

"I remember. And I also remember I intended to take issue with you on the subject . . ." His voice faded slightly as he went into the next-door chamber. "After we have dined, we shall talk about this predilection you seem to be showing for most unwomanly hauteur."

"Before we take siesta or afterward?" she inquired impishly.

"Instead, I believe." He dropped a silk coverlet on her stomach. "Cover yourself, immodest creature."

Sarita, with a self-satisfied smile, arranged the cover over herself and settled back against the cushions as Abul went to the door and gave orders to the men outside.

"You do not have any further business for today, though?" she asked, reverting to the original subject.

Abul ran the tips of his fingers over his lips, frowning. There were things he should do, people he should see. He had not yet received the daily report from the officer in charge of Aicha's guard. But then, what would the man have to say that was different from any other day? He reviewed the list of tasks he would normally have dealt with during the afternoon and shrugged. There was really nothing that could not wait until tomorrow . . . not when compared with the beguiling pastimes offered in the enchanted seclusion of this glowing grotto.

"No, I have no business outside this chamber," he said. "But much within it."

"And many hours before morning in which to accomplish much," she replied, her eyes alive with sensual promise.

"I doubt it will be long enough to mend the manners of an impudent sparrow," he said with a mock sigh. "But a man can only try."

She extended her arms to him. "Come here. I will show you how it is to be done."

Her eyes drew him across the room, moon to his tide as always, and as he followed their pull he wondered for an uneasy second whether there was some truth in the rumor of a man who seemed to count the world well lost for love.

Chapter 18

The following night was moonless with heavy clouds obscuring the stars and only the glimmer of snow on the mountain peaks showing some contrast with the darkness beyond the walls of the Alhambra. Within the walls, sconced torches in the porticos flared under gusts of wind, and windows and doors were all shuttered tight against an unfriendly night.

It was not unfriendly, however, to the two in the tower of the cadi. The lights within were all extinguished, and Aicha stood at the window in the upper chamber overlooking the palace compound, straining eyes and ears into the darkness to catch a hint of movement that would alert her to the approach of Nafissa with the great iron key that would unlock the prison door.

Boabdil was silent, dressed in boots and cloak against the cold, his eyes wide and scared. He knew they were leaving tonight and that the journey would be hard, through dark passages, and he must make no sound lest they be discovered and his father's wrath descend upon them with terrifying consequences. His mother had not underestimated those consequences, painting such a picture of pain and deprivation that the boy trembled, cowering in a corner of the tower, biting his tongue as he practiced absolute silence.

A flicker of shadow appeared immediately below

the window. As Aicha went to the narrow staircase, she touched a finger to her lips in admonition to the cowering Boabdil and sped stealthily to the court below. The key turned sweetly in the lock, and the door opened a crack. Nafissa, cloaked and veiled, slipped within, and the door closed as if it had never been opened.

"It is time, my lady," the handmaid whispered. "The watchman awaits on the path. He will direct us to the opening of the passage."

"He is to be trusted?" Aicha had asked the question of herself many times but had had no chance to ask it of Nafissa.

"He has been paid well, lady," the other woman said with a touch of dryness. "Where is the child?"

"Boabdil," Aicha called softly up the stairs. "Come down now. It is time to leave."

The boy appeared with dragging step at the head of the stairs, his white face gleaming as he stared down fearfully. "I do not wish to go, Mamma."

"Do not be such a baby," Aicha snapped. "Come down at once."

Boabdil's lip trembled, but he obeyed his mother and came slowly downstairs. "But if we should be discovered . . ." he whimpered.

"We will not be if you keep silent and do only as you are bid," Aicha said, trying to soften her voice as she saw tears in his eyes, threatening a noisy and immoderate storm of weeping. "We are going to your grandfather's palace. You will like it there, Boabdil. Just be a brave boy, and then everything will be all right."

Nafissa had already gone back to the door and now stood impatiently with her hand on the latch. "Make haste, lady. We must be away before the watchman on this part of the ramparts returns."

Aicha seized her son's hand and went to the door. They opened it only as far as necessary to admit their sideways sidling bodies, and then they were outside, hugging the shadow of a hedge of oleanders beside the path. A man in soldier's garb stood there, and Boabdil gave a moan of terror. Aicha hushed him with a slapping hand, and he fell into weeping silence.

The man said nothing but began to move swiftly down the path toward the track leading upward to the Generalife, the trio behind him trying to match his pace. Halfway up the track he moved sideways into the bushes lining the path. The three followed, the bushes tugging at them like unseen hands. The mountainside rose bare above them, uncultivated in stark contrast to the lush gardens below. They struggled upward until the watchman stopped at an outcrop of rock. He said something to Nafissa, who had kept up with him, covering the ground on her sturdy peasant legs as if it were as flat as the deserts of Spain. She nodded, and the man turned and sped past the still struggling Aicha and Boabdil, then vanished, lost in the blackness of the night.

"It is here," Nafissa whispered, pointing to a shadow against the mountainside. The shadow was an opening, a mere slit leading into impenetrable blackness. "I have flint and tinder," she said. "Within, we will find a lamp. We are to leave it at the other end."

The prospect of light emboldened Aicha, whose courage had faltered at the prospect of an interminable, pitchy journey through the mountainside with no certainty that they would ever emerge. But Nafissa was willing to make the attempt, and that in itself encouraged Aicha. Nafissa was motivated by the prospect of reward, not by love for her mistress, and Aicha doubted she would take a risk she considered unacceptable. If the handmaid trusted the watchman, then she must have good and sufficient reason.

Nafissa slid into the opening while the other two stayed outside, Boabdil keening his terror. His mother drew him roughly against her skirts, muffling the sound rather than imparting comfort or reassurance, but she had little of either to give at the present. A light flickered from within the mountain, and with grim resolution Aicha slipped into the slitted opening, hauling the child after her. It was dank and bitterly cold, dense darkness stretching ahead of the tiny patch of feeble light in which they stood.

"We had best make haste," Nafissa said. "The wick is low on the lamp. The watchman assured me the lamps are kept tended by those who use the passages, but this is one that is rarely used, and the lamp has been neglected."

She set off ahead of them, holding the lantern high, its dim illumination sending weird shadows writhing on the twisted rock walls of the narrow passage, quarried so long ago through the rock and clay of the mountain.

Boabdil began to sob, stumbling in his mother's wake, clinging to her skirts. Aicha ignored him. His noise would not now be heard by anyone, and she had too much of her own trepidation about the failing lantern for compassionate whisperings to a frightened child.

They went on and on, the passageway narrowing sometimes to such a degree that they had to creep sideways, the moisture-laden rock dampening their backs; the ceiling was so low at times that they went bent double. Aicha's consuming prayer was that the lantern would hold. Why had Nafissa not thought to bring candles? But she kept the complaint to herself, all too aware of the fact that it was Nafissa who held the lantern, Nafissa who knew which twists and turns to take when another slit of a passage crossed their own.

The lantern finally guttered, plunging them into a blackness more profound than could be imagined. Boabdil screamed. Aicha swallowed her own cry and stood quaking. How much farther did they have to go? Then a light flickered, became the steady flame of a candle. Nafissa had not come unprepared after all. Why had she not said? Aicha thought with a wave of irrational anger. If she had said she carried a candle, Aicha would have been spared the preceding agonies of apprehension. But again she bit her tongue. Nafissa could not yet be safely antagonized.

It was an hour or so before dawn when they emerged into the freshness of the aboveground world. The River Darro flowed swiftly at the base of the hillside, where two horses waited, their bridles held by a robed and turbaned man sitting on the riverbank beside them.

"My brother," Nafissa said matter-of-factly, gesturing to the shadowy figure. She seemed not a whit disturbed by the hours of subterranean journeying. "He will provide escort, but he must be paid."

"My father will pay him," Aicha said.

Nafissa shook her head. "He must be paid now, lady. The journey is risky, and there is no surety that the emir will reward him."

Aicha paled with anger, but there was nothing she could do. The sun would rise all too soon, and she and Boabdil could not be standing here on the banks of the river in the full glare of daylight.

"I have nothing with which to pay him," she said tautly. "What do you suggest?" She knew Nafissa would have an idea.

"I took the liberty, lady." Nafissa pushed a hand into the deep pocket of her robe and drew out a strand of pearls. The finest strand in Aicha's jewel casket. "He will be well rewarded with but three of these." Her wheedling smile carried the absolute assurance of one who held the upper hand. She held the strand out to Aicha, who took it without expression.

The man tending the horses had been observing in watchful silence during this exchange. Now he rose and crossed the scrub of the riverbank to come up to them. Wordlessly, he handed Aicha a small knife.

She cut three of the pearls from the strand and dropped them into his open palm. Again there was no verbal response, not even a mock obeisance, a feigned gesture of gratitude, and Aicha seethed with a wild resentment that she should be subjected to such indignity at the hands of peasants. But she

would revenge herself for the insults once she ruled
the caliphate through the whining, sniveling child at
her feet.

She looked down to where Boabdil crouched on the
grass, scrabbling at her hem. "Get up!" She dragged
him to his feet, turning on the man holding the pearls.
"You have been paid to provide escort. Do so."

The icy instruction had an effect. Nafissa's brother
fetched the horses. He lifted Boabdil onto one and
assisted Aicha to mount behind him. Then he put his
sister onto the second horse and swung up behind
her. With a click of his tongue, he started the small
procession, and they moved along the riverbank in
the gray light of predawn.

If they were not apprehended, they should be
within her father's protection by noon, Aicha thought.

"My lord caliph!" The summons was repeated several times before it penetrated Abul's sleep. The voice
came from the outer chamber, discreetly so because
the guard was well aware that the lord Abul was abed
with his houri.

Abul sat up, awake the instant he heard the urgency in the caller's voice. "One minute." He swung
off the divan.

"What is it?" Sarita rolled sleepily onto her back.
"Who is there?"

"The guard." Abul dropped his robe over his head
and went to the curtained doorway.

Sarita sat up, yawning, listening to the low-voiced
conversation taking place in the main chamber. She
could hear few of the words, although she thought
she heard Aicha's name spoken.

Stealthily, she slipped from the divan, creeping naked to the curtain. Disappointingly, she could hear
the voices fading as Abul and the guard walked away
to the far end of the chamber. Drawing aside the outer
edge of the curtain, she put half an eye around. The
two men were standing by the door, open onto the
antechamber. Abul was speaking rapidly, although

she could hear nothing, but his gestures were sufficient to convey the urgency of what he was saying. Then the two men left the chamber.

Sarita stood frowning. Perhaps it was not to be expected that Abul would have taken the time to inform her of what was causing the disturbance, but she expected it nevertheless. She turned back to the divan, looking for the wrapper she had discarded earlier. Picking it up from the floor, she put it on, wrapping it around her body as she stepped to the doors to the portico and drew back the heavy curtains.

The first streaks of daybreak showed above the mountaintops when she pushed open the door and went outside, shivering in the dawn chill, the marble paving icy on her bare feet. Suddenly the air was rent with a trumpet blast and a thundering of drums from the ramparts of the alcazaba. It was a shocking tympany, and she stood stunned. Then a pale blaze of light shot into the sky from the topmost watchtower of the alcazaba.

Sarita ran out into the center of the courtyard, staring upward toward the mountain. As she looked, answering flares went up from the watchtowers governing the mountain passes.

Was the Alhambra under attack? It was the only explanation. She hastened inside and threw open the door to the antechamber. A solitary guard stood outside; otherwise the antechamber was deserted. "Send Kadiga to me," she ordered in her still halting Arabic, forgetting that women did not give orders to men in the Alhambra; forgetting also that men did not acknowledge unveiled women. But the guard did acknowledge her. His eyes grazed her face as she stood in the doorway; then he stalked across the antechamber to the far portico, where he said something to a lad waiting outside.

Sarita returned discreetly to her seclusion to await Kadiga, who was bound to have some information, even if it was only speculation. Restlessly she went again to the court, listening to the continued summoning tympany from the ramparts of the alcazaba, watching the fires competing with the sun's crimson radiance spilling over the mountain peaks. She felt no sense of alarm, only a mounting excitement warring with her frantic curiosity. It didn't occur to her that Abul would fail to meet and withstand whatever threatened outside the walls of his Alhambra.

"Sarita?" Kadiga's voice called from inside, and she turned and ran back.

"Kadiga, what is going on?"

"I am not sure," Kadiga said. "But it is being said that the lady Aicha and Boabdil have disappeared from the tower of the cadi."

"Is that all?" Sarita sat down on the divan, absently rubbing her cold feet. "I had thought there must at least be a besieging army at the gates."

"If the lady Aicha reaches the protection of her father, then the lord caliph will have many enemies ranged against him," Kadiga told her.

"But is it not the caliph's inalienable right to make what provision he chooses for the women in his seraglio?" Sarita was feeling for words now as she tried to fit the impressions she had garnered with a possibly differing reality.

"Yes, in theory, but in practice it is not always the case." Kadiga drew up a footstool and sat down. "The caliph's wives are all connected with the great families of the kingdom. Insults are hardly borne, and if it is felt that the caliph acted unjustly and whimsically toward the daughter of the emir of the Mocarabes, then it will cause much dissension in the kingdom. Once the lady Aicha comes under the protection of her father again, the lord Abul is in a losing position." Kadiga frowned, plaiting her fingers. "It would be different if the caliph had sent his wife in disgrace back to her father, but if she fled cruelty and injustice, her father would be bound to come to her defense because his own honor would have been insulted. Do you understand?"

Sarita nodded slowly. She understood that just as

she understood something else. The cruelty and injustice Aicha would claim were directly attributable to her own presence in the Alhambra. "Oh, yes, I understand. I hadn't realized. I had thought the women here to be of no signal importance."

"Mostly we are not," Kadiga said with a slight smile. "But for those who wish to make themselves important, if they have the right connections, they can do so. The lady Aicha is such a one. Her father will not willingly give up the footstep she provided for the Mocarabes in the ruling family of the Alhambra. Boabdil would eventually have been caliph, and his grandfather's family would have gained much prestige and power as a result."

"Yes, I see." Sarita stood up. "I had better dress, Kadiga. This does not seem like a morning to face in a wrapper with sleep in one's eyes."

Kadiga went to the wardrobe. "What would you wear?"

"Riding dress," Sarita said without hesitation. If she still had her orange dress, she would have worn that. Somehow she felt that she needed to be equipped for action, and the gowns of the seraglio, designed for lying around and eating apricots, were not appropriate with which to face whatever was about to happen.

"I can manage myself," she said, taking the garments from Kadiga. "Do you fetch food. The lord Abul has not yet broken his fast, and he will need to do so when he returns." He would return soon, she was convinced. Apart from anything else, he was not yet properly dressed.

He arrived just after Kadiga had brought in a tray of bread, dried fruits, and cheese.

"Are you hungry?" Sarita hurried over to him, anxiously examining his expression as she took his arm and drew him into the room. "Has something dreadful happened? Kadiga says Aicha and Boabdil have disappeared."

"Then you know all there is to know," he said,

running a hand through his hair in an uncharacteristic gesture of weary futility.

"But what does it mean?" Sarita pressed, urging him to sit before the tray of food.

Abul did not immediately reply. He broke bread and cut a piece of cheese. Sarita knew nothing of the bubbling yeast of insurrection already fermenting in the kingdom under Aicha's busy mixing. She could have no idea of her own unwitting role in the troubles, and he could see no reason to tell her. "It means that I have a deal of work to do, to repair fences," he said eventually, offering her a smile.

Sarita returned the smile, but Abul's attempted insouciance was not convincing. There were taut lines around his mouth, a forbidding shadow in his black eyes. "Are you trying to find her?"

Abul shrugged. "The watchtowers covering the passes through the mountains have been alerted by flares, but I doubt they will have taken such a route. Aicha will have gone to her father."

"Can you not catch up with her?"

"Unlikely."

Sarita poured jasmine tea into a fluted cup and passed it to him, anxious to confirm Kadiga's interpretation of events. "She will say bad things of you?"

Abul looked up and suddenly laughed. Sarita looked so avidly concerned, her head on one side, her eyes bright with intelligence as she tried to understand without pestering him too much. "Yes, *querida*, she will say bad things of me, and they will fall on fertile ground."

"But what can her father do to you?"

"Stir up trouble, initiate a challenge to my leadership." He shrugged again. "It is a nuisance, because the Spanish are always on the watch for a sign of weakness within Granada that they can exploit. I told you this once before."

She nodded, remembering. "So what will you do?"

"Prepare to defend myself," he said succinctly. "Launch an offensive of my own."

"You will go to war with your own people?"

"I hope it won't come to that." He stood up. "I have to dress."

Sarita followed him into the sleeping chamber. "Why does Aicha hate you? It can't be just because you took Boabdil from her."

Abul tossed his robe onto the divan and stood naked, stroking his chin as he contemplated the question. "Aicha has always had plans of her own," he said. "Unfortunately, I have only recently realized their extent. She is an ambitious woman and through her son could see a way to fulfill the ultimate ambition."

"Ruling Granada through the child?" Sarita stared in astonishment. How could she ever have believed women in this society were so thoroughly conditioned to their inferiority that they had no ambitions beyond the daily satisfaction of their needs?

"Quite so, Sarita. I am in the way, that is all. If she can contrive to remove me, then she will have her father's support to put Boabdil in my place." He pulled on a pair of britches and reached for a tunic. "Such an outcome will suit the Mocarabes very well."

"You do not seem unduly concerned," Sarita observed. "Or at least not unduly surprised."

"The caliphate of Granada has long been an uneasy seat," Abul told her. "I have withstood several such challenges in my term, as my father did before me . . . and his before him." He strapped on his sword belt and, booted and spurred, crossed the chamber, taking her chin in the palm of a gloved hand. "I do not know when I shall be back." His lips grazed hers. "Be good and do not overtax your strength."

"You will be gone many days?"

He shook his head. "No, for I cannot risk leaving the Alhambra undefended. I go to gather what support I can from those sympathetic to me. The garrison here must be fortified and brought up to full strength. I will need to call in such support from those who are allied with me."

"And there are such?" She had a wretched image of Abul, friendless, without supports, facing a massively allied opposition.

"Of course there are," he said, pinching her nose in customary fashion. "Now promise me you will take good care of yourself while I am gone."

"Promise me you will take care of *your* self," she retorted. "There is little harm I can come to within these walls. I have nothing to do but sit in the seraglio and practice my Arabic."

"Are you complaining, Sarita *mía*?"

"No, because I do not wish to add to your troubles. But I would much prefer to ride with you, as I am sure you know."

"I know it. But it cannot be, even though I wish it. Your presence would not add to my consequence, I am afraid."

"A mere woman . . ." She sighed heavily in mock indignation. "In the tribe of Raphael, women ride with their menfolk."

Abul clicked his tongue reprovingly. "But you left the tribe of Raphael, *hija mía*, of your own free will, as I recall."

She smiled. "True enough. And I remain here of my own free will, although you do things so differently. Go now, and come back safely and with all speed."

He left her, but beneath the immediacy of the present situation, they both knew that the question of the future had again raised its head. How long would it be possible for Sarita to live contentedly in Abul's world? For as long as he had no reason to leave her side, she could find all the purpose and satisfaction she needed in their loving partnership, but when business took him from her, she was left in a vacuum that the energetic, self-motivated woman of the tribe of Raphael was beginning to find suffocating.

Sarita paced the porticos and walked restlessly in the court, thinking of Aicha. Aicha had never suffered the pangs of inactivity. She had had all the ex-

citement of her plots and her plans to keep her brain
alive. Plots and plans and malice, Sarita reminded
herself grimly, thinking of the deadly bane so carefully administered. Such activities would not suit
herself, so what could she do to keep herself occupied, to give her a sense of purpose while Abul
wrestled with his own problems? And just how serious were those problems? Had he been making
light of them when he said he was accustomed to
facing such challenges? What would happen if the
challenge succeeded?

Abul without the Alhambra . . . It was an inconceivable thought. He loved the place, but it went
deeper than that. His soul was embedded in the very
fabric of the palace, its history a part of his own.
Wrenched from this place, he would be half a man,
condemned to wander the world as an exile with no
more function and identity than Sarita felt she had
behind the walls of the Alhambra.

It was too dreadful a thought to contemplate, and
she tried to push it from her. Abul was absolutely in
command. The role of caliph sat on his shoulders with
all the ease of a well-worn mantle. It could not be
taken from him by one unaccustomed to the duties
and obligations of the position . . . by one who saw
only the power and rewards to be gained from the
position.

And yet deep in her soul was the thought that Abul
without the Alhambra would solve all their problems.
There was nothing she could imagine more satisfying
than wandering the world at his side, taking life as it
came, facing challenges as and when they fell, in the
manner of her upbringing. But Abul was not of the tribe
of Raphael, and such guilty thoughts were the same
as wishing him harm. And never could she desire
such a thing. She would find no joy in a life that
would inevitably destroy the man she knew.

Abul returned the following day. He brought with
him ten thousand men to swell the numbers in the

garrison and the promise of support, in the event of
outright attack, from the emirs of three of the great
families. But he also brought a growing unease. The
alliances had been offered wholeheartedly, as he had
expected, but he had heard more of the opposition
from his anxious friends and supporters, and realized
that it had been growing apace in the past month or
two. It was clear that his father-in-law had been busy
for quite some time before Aicha's poisoning of Sarita
and subsequent fall from grace. It would seem that
Aicha had been conducting a clandestine correspondence with the Mocarabes under his nose.

There had been little he could do to hide his ignorance of the extent of the damage, and he had felt the
criticism, for all that it had not been expressed. But
he stood convicted of negligence, and if the message
from the Mocarabes was that the caliph, for whatever
reason, had lost his grip on affairs of the realm, then
he had done nothing to dispel the rumor.

Several pointed references had been made to the
Christian captive he had taken as his concubine—the
information presumably again disseminated by the Mocarabes. He had treated the subject lightly but had
been in no doubt as to the dangerous undercurrents.
Men looked askance at one who lost sight of important things when in the grip of an obsession. Women
were not to be taken seriously except as currency in
the diplomatic world of alliances. And a Christian
captive could be of no use to a man at all, except
between the sheets.

Unfortunately, Abul recognized a certain truth in
the implied criticisms.

Sarita came running to meet him in the Court of
the Cisterns as the party rode through the Gate of
Justice, heralded by the bells from the watchtower.
The sun had some warmth in it, and she wore no
cloak. She stood to one side of the court in a robe of
turquoise velvet edged with silver lace, her hair amazingly tidy, caught beneath a snood of silver netting,

her uncovered face lifted to the sun, her eyes searching the throng for contact with his.

Still raw with the abrasions of his negotiations, he
wished she had not come to meet him with such blithe
disregard for the mores of the Alhambra. But he knew
they had an agreement; Sarita was not bound by those
mores. If she were, he would be in a stronger defen-
sive position than he was now.

He swung off his horse and turned to the vizier,
who was waiting for his attention with a degree of
urgency. "There is a letter come from the emir of the
Mocarabes, my lord caliph." The vizier bowed, ex-
tending the rolled parchment.

"I cannot read it here," Abul said, anxiety and irritation investing his voice with a snap. "Bring it to
me in my office in an hour."

The vizier bowed and turned to go, but Abul called
him back. "On second thought, you may give it to
me now. But come to my office in an hour." He took
the parchment, thrusting it into the breast of his tunic, and turned his attention to the officer of the
guard, waiting for orders as to the disposition of the
new troops.

Sarita stood for a minute longer in the corner of the
court, then turned and made her way back to the caliph's apartments, trying to stifle her resentment. It
would have cost him nothing to have acknowledged
her presence as she waited with such loving eagerness for the touch of his eyes.

But perhaps matters had gone badly and he was
distracted, she told herself. He would come to her as
soon as he could. She must learn to be patient.

Abul felt her leave the court even though he had
not seen her do so. And he felt her pique because he
knew so well how she would react to such an apparent slight. He dealt swiftly with remaining business
in the Court of the Cisterns, then strode off, the
parchment burning a hole in his tunic with its urgency, but his mind stretching toward Sarita, who
must be soothed as she would soothe him.

There was no sign of her when he entered the main
chamber of his apartments, and no sign of her in the
sleeping chamber. But the doors stood open to the
portico, and he went without hesitation. She was
talking softly to the green finches in their cage, pushing grains of millet through the bars.

"Poor things," she said without turning around as
he joined her. "Why do you not free them, Abul?"

"They are happy enough," he said. "They sing."

"There are songs of sorrow as well as of joy," she
said, turning now to face him. "Your business pros-
pered?"

"I have the support I sought," he replied. "The
alliances still hold."

"Why would you not acknowledge me in the
court?"

"I had much to occupy me . . . people who demanded my attention."

"And a woman may not do so."

"No. Not in public, Sarita."

A frown touched her eyes. "You have not held to
that premise in recent weeks, my lord caliph."

It was true. He had not. "There were many people
in the court," he extemporized. "Soldiers not of the
Alhambra."

She let it go, for all that she sensed there was much
more to it. She didn't think she had ever before seen
Muley Abul Hassan look tired.

"Come within." Taking his hand, she drew him
toward the door. "Let us greet each other in proper
form."

The parchment burned its message through his tunic, but he didn't know how, without hurt, to turn
aside the soft sensuality of her welcoming smile, her
hands gently, yet with an inbuilt excitement, moving
in a preliminary caress across his thighs. He kissed
her and she leaned into him, feeling for the buttons
of his tunic.

"What have you here?" Her fingers drew out the

parchment. "Abul, is this something you must read before we greet each other in proper form?"

He laughed, as much with relief as amusement as he heard the feigned scolding in her voice. Turning his palm upward, she thumped the parchment into his hand, saying, "I refuse to compete with such immediacies. Read it and have done with it, *querido*, and then we may turn to our own business."

"No, I have no need to read it now. Come and let me feel you. I have missed you beyond reason." He sat on the divan and pulled her down on his lap. She landed with a thump and a squeak of protest before catching his head between her hands and bringing her mouth to his in a hard, passionate assault.

They fell back on the bed, her tongue dancing with his, her body moving in sinuous demand over his.

"I want you, Abul." The husky imperative whispered against his mouth, and her hands tugged at the fastening of his britches, her body twisting to give her room for maneuver even while she resisted every lost inch of contact.

He loved her importunate need, the naked hunger she evinced for his body, the way after an absence of any duration she would have no time for foreplay but would express her eager passion with a demand to equal any man's.

He lifted his hips as she tugged at the confining garment, losing his mouth for a moment to kneel so that she could pull his britches free of his body. They ran into the barricade of his spurred heels, and with a chuckle she abandoned the exercise and stretched full length to caress that part of him now made freely available for such caresses.

Sarita inhaled deeply of the rich, earthy scent of him, her tongue gently lifting, stroking, her teeth grazing. She became lost in the spiraling excitement of desire, cast adrift in the maelstorm of wanting. With an exultant chuckle, she straddled his body, drawing her skirts up to her waist as she lowered herself onto the impaling shaft.

Abul laughed with matching elation and reached to hold her skirts high, watching the rise and fall of her creamy thighs as she moved him within her with the circular rhythm of her body. With an abrupt movement, she reached up to pull the netted snood from her hair, and the whole glorious cascade tumbled loose. In the same moment, he touched her at her heated core and she cried out, falling forward, covering him in the flaring torrent of her hair, her mouth locking with his as his own climax pulsed within her.

"I bid you welcome, my lord caliph," Sarita murmured against his mouth, once she could draw breath. "I think that was a proper welcome, do you not?"

"Indisputably," he breathed. "Such a wild creature you are, Sarita *mía.*"

"Would you have me otherwise?" She disengaged slowly, rolling onto the divan beside him, her skirts still rucked up to her waist.

"No." He ran a finger over her thigh. "Never."

They lay still for a minute; then Abul remembered the vizier, who would be awaiting him in his office, and groaned. "*Cara,* I have things I must do."

"Then do them," she said, sitting upright. "The sooner they are done, the sooner you will return. Should you not read the parchment?"

He rolled off the divan and picked up the discarded missive. "Yes, I suppose I should." He went into the curtained alcove that contained the commode, and Sarita hugged her knees in thought.

The usual lassitude that followed such a frenzied burst of lovemaking was absent. She was bubbling with an urgent curiosity.

"What does your letter say?" She slid off the bed and went to the curtain.

Abul emerged. His expression was dark, but he tried to smile, to recapture the mood of a minute earlier. Except that the mood had been generated by the desperation and uncertainty they had both felt and been unable to express. "It is from Aicha's father," he said, tossing it to the divan as he refastened his britches. "It simply says that she has claimed his protection . . . I have to meet with the vizier, Sarita."

She nodded. "I will not keep you. But come back soon."

"*Por cierto, querida.*" He drew her against him. "How can you doubt it?"

"I do not." She lifted her face for a gentle salute.

A sharp knocking came from the door to the antechamber. "My lord caliph? There is a messenger come from the Abencerrajes," the voice called from without. "He would have speech with you."

"So soon," Abul murmured to himself. Sarita caught the murmur, although she didn't understand its significance. Without a further farewell, he left the sleeping chamber, and she heard the door to the antechamber open and close.

The parchment from the Mocarabes lay forgotten on the divan.

Chapter 19

The parchment was largely incomprehensible for Sarita, written as it was in Arabic. She puzzled over the hieroglyphics, making out the sense of one or two of the groupings. Her lessons with Fadha had mostly been oral, but the other woman had shown her something of Arabic lettering.

Sarita's own literacy was unusual. Her father had been literate and had served as scribe for less educated members of the tribe. Estaban had been proud of his skills and had imparted them to his only child as part of a family heritage, imposing upon her the obligation to do the same with her own children. But the ability to read and write Spanish was little help with the strangeness of Arabic characters.

She lay on her stomach on the divan, legs in the air, ankles crossed, as she pored over the script. Hearing Zulema's soft footfalls, in the main chamber, Sarita called to her. "Are you able to read your language, Zulema?"

The maidservant appeared in the doorway. She shook her head, "No, but Kadiga is learned in that way. Shall I send for her?"

"Mmm, if you would," Sarita murmured, distracted as one word seemed to leap at her from the parchment. It was repeated several times and appeared to be of some importance to the whole.

When Kadiga came, she showed her the word, carefully covering the text above and below, conscious that perhaps Abul would not want his letters made common knowledge among the palace household.

"It is 'unbeliever,' " Kadiga said without hesitation.

"Mmm." Sarita chewed her thumbnail. "And this one, I believe, is 'woman.' And here is the lord Abul's name—"

"I hadn't realized how far your education had advanced, Sarita *mía.*" Abul's voice came lightly from the doorway to the main chamber.

"It has not advanced far enough, I fear," she said, waving her legs idly in the air. "Will you help me read this?"

"You don't think it might be private?" he questioned amiably, gesturing a dismissal to Kadiga.

"Not really," Sarita replied. "Since you left it on the divan."

"So I did," he agreed, with the same affability. "But I told you what it says."

She shook her head. "Some part, maybe. But not the important bits."

"Why do you wish to know them?"

"Because you are troubled by them, and because I believe they have more than a little to do with me." Her eyes held a challenge as she looked up at him, demanding the rights of partnership. When he didn't immediately respond, she continued. "It could be said, could it not, that my presence here prompted your rejection of Aicha? That you imprisoned her and intended banishing her because I found greater favor in your eyes? Who is to know of poisoning and long-planned ambition if Aicha does not tell them?"

"You have been doing some thinking, it would seem." He sat on the divan beside her, resting a hand on her backside. "Let us look at this, then, and see if you can make out some more."

"Why do you not just read it to me?" she asked, holding the parchment to him over her shoulder. "It would be simpler, and I am not really interested in a lesson."

"You do surprise me," he said dryly, taking the letter from her. "Aicha's father informs me that his daughter is under his protection, having fled barbarous treatment and the threat of cruel and unjust banishment. My treatment of his daughter the emir takes as an insult to his family honor. The repudiation of his daughter in favor of an unbeliever and a captive slave doubles the insult. The emir therefore will be revenged. He issues a challenge to my kingship, maintaining that I have forfeited the rights to the loyalty and allegiance of the people of Granada. He demands that I relinquish the caliphate in favor of my son and a regent to be chosen by council."

It was an arid exposition of the contents of the letter, Abul's voice maintaining an even monotone. Once finished, he rerolled the parchment and lightly tapped the top of her head with it. "So now you know, Sarita. What have you to say on the subject?"

She rolled over, squinting up at him. "I would say that you must shout the truth of his daughter's treachery from the watchtowers, before too many others believe what he has said."

"I have no proof."

"And I am here as proof positive of the emir's accusation," she said slowly. "Will others believe him?"

Abul nodded. "The emir of the Abencerrajes, the second most powerful family in the caliphate, has just made a similar demand for my abdication. My failure to comply will lead to military challenge."

"It is all because of me." She frowned, feeling a sick tremor in her belly.

Abul shook his head. "It is a matter of much complexity, Sarita. You are only the excuse for a challenge that has awaited an excuse for several years. But I have made some mistakes just recently that might well sway the undecided to the opposition."

"In your treatment of Aicha?"

"I admit to a degree of carelessness there, and to a certain neglect of warning signs."

"So what is to be done now?"

"I must answer the challenge, and then we shall see what move they make next."

"Are you deeply worried?" She reached for his hand, trying to read his expression.

"It is more serious than I had originally thought," he conceded. "And if we are warring within our borders, then the predators without may well have easy pickings. That is what concerns me the most."

"You will lose Granada to the Spaniards."

"It will happen one day," he said. "We cannot continue to maintain this toehold in the peninsula against the combined strengths of Aragon and Castile. But I would prefer it not be lost during my stewardship."

"I understand that." Lifting his hand, she rested it against her cheek. "There must be some way I can be of help."

"Just by being here," he said. "I need to know that you will be here even when I must be away from you."

She smiled a little ruefully. "Do not keep things from me, then, Abul. I need you to promise that."

"I promise."

Abul sent a ringing return to those who had challenged his authority and prepared the Alhambra to withstand siege or direct attack. Either approach would have little chance of success on such a fortification, but an attempt would nevertheless weaken him in the eyes of his supporters. He was under no illusion that many of them would remain loyal to a sinking ship. They would have too much at stake in the event of his failure to withstand his enemies.

He sent troops out to patrol the roads of the kingdom, and reports of skirmishes between his men and those of the Mocarabes or the Abencerrajes came in regularly. Alliances were formed and broken, conspiracies hatched and dismantled. Abul kept spies in every camp and worked ceaselessly to circumvent the unification of his enemies, hatching his own conspiracies, spreading his own tales, watching with sinking heart as his own machinations achieved the splintering and weakening of the kingdom as effectively as those of his enemies. And yet he saw no choice.

One afternoon, a troop of soldiers arrived at the gates of the Alhambra. They had a message for the caliph from the emir of the Mocarabes. The message was contained in a wooden casket that, when opened, revealed the head of one of the caliph's spies in the court of Ferdinand and Isabella in Cordova.

The message was clear. Those allied against the caliph had sought the support of the Spanish monarchs, sought it and been given it. What had they been obliged to offer in exchange? Abul wondered. The new caliph's allegiance to the Spaniards? They were fools if they believed their most Christian Majesties would settle for anything but total control of Granada and the ousting of the Morisco-Spanish rule forever.

Sarita asked questions constantly, holding him to his word that he would not keep her in the dark. He answered as patiently as he could, but he was distracted much of the time, and she developed the habit of listening to the rumors within the palace. Kadiga was a dependable informant of kitchen gossip, gossip that Sarita privately decided was as reliable as anything else.

Abul was as calmly centered as ever, as unquestioningly authoritative, his equilibrium unaffected by the danger and turmoil surrounding him. At least that was the appearance he gave. Sarita was sometimes not so sure. He had lost his humor, the readiness to laugh, the gentleness that she was so accustomed to, and sometimes she saw in his eyes a frightening uncertainty. Was Abul questioning some previously unquestionable assumptions?

It alarmed Sarita even as it filled her with compas-

sion and a desperate need to help him. But she did
not know how. She was there for him, and often he
needed her, coming to her sometimes in the middle
of the day, needing to lose himself in the loving she
so freely offered, to forget the plaguing doubts and
ground himself again at his center. Sometimes he
seemed to pour out the frustrations upon her body,
using her with a rough passion that she matched,
transforming frustration into excitement and the
deep, plunging descent into annihilation that could
only renew. And sometimes he needed her to love
him with soft gentleness, to bring peace to his body
with the use of hers. Determined never to fail him,
she watched, gauged, guessed, and sent him back
into the fray stronger and steadier.

But it still wasn't enough to assuage her restless
anxiety, her need to take some active part in catching
the castles as they tumbled around his ears. Part of
her wanted to cry: Give it up. It's too hard a fight for
such a thankless responsibility. Let them fall beneath
the yoke of the Spaniards, since it's a yoke they've
sought for themselves. But she quenched the voice
with a shamefaced vigor. It was not for her to make
such assumptions, to impose her own aching need for
a life with Abul that they could truly share.

One day, Kadiga appeared when Sarita sat in the
seraglio listening to a harpist, the gentle chatter of the
women, who seemed undisturbed by the chaos beyond the walls of their gilded cage, floating tranquilly
around her.

"The lord Abul wishes you to join him in the
baths," she said.

Sarita rose immediately. It had been many weeks
since Abul had wished to share that place of repose
and harmony with her.

She entered the hall of immersion to find Abul already in the hot tank, Leila in attendance. The woman
came to help divest Sarita of her robe and then left
the hall.

Sarita slipped into the water opposite Abul. She

was so used to the baths now, not even the prospect of the cold dip to follow could spoil the pleasure spreading upward from her toes as she sank below the surface. "Are you well?" she asked softly, examining him shrewdly but covertly.

He smiled slightly. "I am well."

"But not reposeful."

"No," he agreed. "Not that."

"Something other than usual is disturbing you," she hazarded.

He nodded. "I am going to send you away from here, Sarita."

She sat up abruptly, water sloshing around her. "What are you saying?"

"It is necessary," he said heavily. "No, listen to me . . ." He put out a hand to catch her wrist, forestalling her leap out of the water. "There is danger for you in this place—"

"There is danger for *you*," she exploded, pulling on her captive wrist. "How can you talk so?"

"Sarita, if the Alhambra falls, your life will not be worth a day's purchase. You do not need me to explain why."

"No, I do not, but I maintain the right to take my own risks," she fired back. "And why would you talk now of the fall of the Alhambra? Has something else happened?"

He shook his head, still holding her wrist. "But I must make provision. You will go from here, through the passes to Cordova. The passes are held by my men. In your own country you will be safe. When this is over, I will come for you."

She glared at him, disbelief in her eyes. "You will not come for me because you do not expect to live through this. You have lost hope."

Abul said nothing. It was not hope he had lost, but inclination. He looked at Sarita, the lodestone of his life. He wanted nothing more than to spend the rest of that life with her, and he didn't think he minded very much where or how. He was thirty years old and

had done his duty rigorously. He didn't want to
spend what remained of his life in battering struggles
against mounting odds to defend something that he
believed was now fundamentally indefensible, as
much through the greed and errors of others as
through the great powers ranged against him with
the fusion of Aragon and Castile. But he was his father's son, and he could not yield Granada to the
Spaniards without that fight. So he must fight his own
people.

"I will not go," Sarita declared.

"You will."

"You cannot compel me to do so."

"I can."

"How?"

"I could have you bound and gagged and conveyed across the border with little difficulty."

She sensed a flicker of humor beneath the words
and allowed a glinting smile to show in her eyes.
"Yes, I do not deny that. But that is not what I meant.
You cannot compel *me* to leave you."

"I can say to you that by remaining here you are
impeding my ability to do what I must."

The flat statement lay between them, and she heard
its truth. She did not have the right to hinder him.
But maybe she could use this to some good purpose.
Her shoulders lifted above the water in a creamy, in-
finitesimal shrug that could have been stating acceptance.

"How am I to travel, then? If I am not to be bound
and gagged. The roads are dangerous even if the
passes are still held by those loyal to you."

"Dressed as a lad," he said. "With Yusuf as escort.
A pair of peasants will draw little remark."

"I see." She fell silent as a germ of an idea took
root.

"This time will pass," he said.

"And what will come in its place?" Her eyes met
his frankly through the wreathing steam of the bath.

"If you do not win, Abul, you will die in the attempt."

He made no effort to contradict her. Sarita nibbled her lip, allowing the germ to flourish. "Those against you are growing in strength? They are winning support from the undecided?"

He sighed. "It seems so."

Sarita closed her eyes as if in sorrow and resignation, but really to hide from him the spurt of energy and excitement as she began to put words to the idea. If one of the leaders of the opposition were to be persuaded that the original cause for complaint had been a fabrication on the part of an ambitious woman and her equally ambitious father, then perhaps that coalition could be shaken. And if the heads rocked, then the tails would most certainly follow suit.

"When am I to leave?"

"At dawn. Yusuf is skilled at such journeyings. He will convey you safely."

She allowed a half smile to lift the corners of her mouth. "But does he relish such a task? I do not think Yusuf enjoys being my nursemaid."

Abul chuckled. "I have not asked his opinion of my orders."

They could make gentle jokes and push aside the grim recognition that this could be the last day they would ever spend together. But Sarita was infused by the vigor of possibility. Suddenly she saw something she could do. It was dangerous, but there was a smidgen of hope that it would work. She would have to deal with Yusuf, but that was a minor detail. She was not going to walk out of Abul's life without a murmur of protest, leaving him to fight and lose his lonely battle.

So she acceded to his plans and pretended that she believed him when he reiterated that he would come for her in Cordova when all was settled. And if Abul felt the slightest dismay at the ease with which she accepted the necessity for their parting, he didn't allow it to show. She was behaving as he wished . . .

but somehow he had expected Sarita to have fought him tooth and nail . . . to have insisted that she share his fate . . .

And if she had not seen a possibility for her own involvement, she would have done exactly that. There were no circumstances that would have forced her from his side except the belief that away from him there was something she could do to alter things.

That night was not one for sleeping. They talked. They loved, fiercely and gently. They dreamed aloud of the time they would spend in the palace above the sea at Motril, when all this was over and the world was on its axis again. In the hour before dawn, Kadiga and Zulema came in. They were solemn and said little as, under Abul's watchful eye, they wound a strip of cloth tightly around Sarita's chest, binding her breasts so that the shirt that went over the cloth hung loosely over the flat frame of an adolescent boy. The britches posed no problem, and the tunic concealed what curve there was to her hips. Over all went the hooded burnous, and beneath the hood they wound a turban, hiding every flaming strand of her distinctive head.

Sarita regarded herself critically in the glass. She could not see herself full length, but from the waist up she looked most unlike herself. "Do I look like a boy?" She turned to Abul, one eyebrow raised.

"Most amazingly," he said. "And a very attractive one, too. You had better not stray from Yusuf's side until you can resume female garb."

She looked at him, wondering if he were serious, then saw that he was. "Oh," she said with a wryly comprehending grimace. "One would think one had enough potential dangers to anticipate without that."

"The burnous will leave little of you on view," Kadiga said. "And if we smear dirt on your face, and some burned cork, no one will look too closely. They'll see only a grimy goatherd."

"A good thought, Kadiga," Abul said, trying to hide

his misery, to infuse a little humor, to turn the deadly reality into an amusing game of dressing up.

The makeup completed, Sarita subjected herself to the scrutiny of Abul and the two women. She felt strange, as if she were inhabiting some world that was not her own. As if they were all indeed playing some game of make-believe.

She found she could not bid Abul a proper fare-well, because to do so would be to admit the possi-bility that there would be no future greeting, and she would not entertain that thought. When he drew her close, his mouth seeking hers, she kissed him lightly, pulled back, and said cheerfully that she would see him within a few weeks. The instant of puzzled hurt in his eyes was immediately followed by comprehen-sion. He answered with the same cheerfulness, tell-ing her teasingly to keep a careful eye out for men who might find such a pretty boy appealing, pinching her nose in familiar fashion.

She tried to bid a similarly light, insouciant farewell to Kadiga and Zulema, who had become such impor-tant friends in the past months, who had stood fast to her through so much danger and dismay. But tears stood out in their eyes, and she could feel the prick-ing behind her own and swallowed hard. Tear tracks would play havoc with the careful streaks on her face.

Yusuf awaited them in the dawn light of the court of the alcazaba. He gave Sarita an all-encompassing glance, then nodded and swung astride a barrel-chested pony. Sarita, as befitted her lowlier status in this twosome, had a mule to ride. Both animals had laden saddle packs: Sarita's contained her women's clothes, hairbrushes, combs, ribbons, soap, tinder, flint; everything she would need to return herself to herself. Unbeknownst to her, they also contained a pouch of gold ducats sewn into the lining of a velvet mantle. Yusuf had weapons, food, cooking pots, a canvas tent, a lantern, and candles; all the necessities for a relatively comfortable journey.

Sarita turned to Abul, saw the deep, haunting

wretchedness in his eyes, touched his lips fleetingly
with the tips of her fingers, then climbed onto the
mule's broad back.

She did not look back as she and Yusuf left through
the Gate of Justice, her mule refusing to make the
slightest attempt to keep up with the pony's livelier
trot. Would she ever see the Alhambra again? Did she
even want to return to that gilded cage? But Abul and
the Alhambra were inseparable. If the only loving life
she could have with him was behind those bars, she
knew she would accept it . . . had accepted it in her
heart many weeks ago. It was for that reason that she
was now about to risk everything on a gamble to ensure the continuance of that loving life.

They rode in silence for an hour, upward through
the passes that led to the Spanish border and the city
of Cordova. Sarita knew that the palace stronghold of
the Abencerrajes lay close to that border and bided
her time as they rode through the early April morning, the air soft with the scents of spring, the breeze
gentle. When she was sure they had reached a point
of no return, she spoke.

"Yusuf, how close are we to the palace of the
Abencerrajes?"

He looked surprised, hearing her relatively smooth
Arabic, and shrugged. "Not so close that you need
have fear."

"I am not afraid," she said. "But I wish you to
guide me there."

He dragged on the bridle of his pony, and the beast
came to a halt, lips snarling over the tight-drawn bit.
"You would join—"

"No, of course I would not," she said impatiently.
"Don't be a fool."

Yusuf half rose in his stirrups, glaring angrily at
this brusque and thoughtless castigation. Hastily,
Sarita tried to soothe him with an apology.

"I did not mean to offend, but I love your lord
Abul. How could you imagine I would wish him
harm?"

"Then what do you mean?"

"I would go to the emir of the Abencerrajes," she explained, feeling for the words, wishing she had had longer to become familiar with Yusuf's language. "I would tell him the truth of the lady Aicha and of myself. I will tell him that I pose no threat to the old order. I will never become wife to the lord Abul. I know as well as does the caliph that it would be against all the customs and beliefs of your people, and besides, I do not wish for such a position."

Yusuf said nothing, but his eyes were both wary and interested. Sarita struggled on.

"It is only the Mocarabes who have much to gain by deposing the lord Abul. If the Abencerrajes can be brought to believe that they are being used to further the political ambitions of the caliph's enemies, then maybe they will withdraw their support. If they can be persuaded that the caliph has no intention of offending his people, that this is a tale put about by those who wish for his downfall, then maybe they will rethink their position. At least it might give them pause . . . food for thought."

"And what makes you think they would believe such as you? A woman and an unbeliever?" demanded Yusuf.

"It is for those very reasons that they will listen to me," she said. "What reason but the truth would I have for exposing myself to danger?"

Yusuf pulled his short, pointed beard. "And why would you not want to be wife to the caliph? Who will believe that any woman would reject such a position?"

"I am not a woman of your people," Sarita said quietly. "I do not see life in the same way. I do not wish for the life of the seraglio."

"Maybe not. But while you share the caliph's bed, you will be seen as wielding the power of the favorite. That is where the threat is perceived."

Sarita had not thought of that. It was, of course, true. Proximity to Abul conveyed power. It was that proximity that she had taken from Aicha, and for that reason, Aicha had sought to remove her finally. "You are saying that I must renounce the caliph completely to make any difference?"

Yusuf nodded. "For as long as you remain at his side, the Mocarabes can maintain that the issue stands fundamentally unchanged."

Sarita sat her mule and stared upward into the bright blue of the sky. Could she make such a promise with conviction? She thought of Abul without the Alhambra. She thought of the eagle without his aerie, without the land over which he soared, master of all he surveyed. She thought of clipping the eagle's wings . . . and knew it to be unthinkable.

"If that is what I must do, then so be it." She would try to mean it, even though she knew Abul would not accept her renunciation. He would come and find her, once the dust had settled. But she must act as if she meant it, because only in convincing them lay any hope. And afterward, if she kept away from the center of power, the hub of the kingdom, then maybe she would no longer pose a threat. She could live discreetly in his palace by the sea, and he would visit her when he could. Half a loving life was better than none at all.

"I will do it," she said firmly, meeting Yusuf's questioning eye, telling herself that if she could convince this man, she could convince anyone. For a long time he stared at her; then slowly he nodded.

"They could as easily kill you as listen to you," he observed.

"I am prepared for that. Will you take me there?"

"The lord Abul will have my head," he said.

"You will not tell him."

Yusuf winced. "Lie to the caliph?"

She shrugged. "If you must, Yusuf. Take me to within a mile of the palace, then sleep soundly, with your head turned from me."

"I should accompany you within."

"They will kill you, where they may not kill me."

It was an indisputable truth.

"You will return to the lord Abul and tell him only that I would not permit you to accompany me over the border. You will tell him that I made my own way into Cordova and await him there."

Yusuf sat frowning for a very long time. "It is just possible you might convince them. The Abencerrajes and the Mocarabes have always had an uneasy alliance. If you can persuade the emir of manipulation, then . . ." He shrugged. "Then it is just possible."

"So you will take me."

"I will take you." Without another word, he kicked his pony into a trot, turning aside from the track. Sarita urged her mule in pursuit, and they trekked across the mountainside until Yusuf found a narrow path, barely wider than a strip of ribbon, threading its way through the scrub and rock of the mountain.

At noon, they stopped by a stream. Yusuf shot a partridge with his crossbow, plucked it, and lit a fire. They ate in silence. It was a silence heavy with their private thoughts, and Sarita was aware that Yusuf also risked much in this enterprise. He risked being caught by the Abencerrajes and most certainly executed as a spy . . . and he risked the great wrath of the caliph for disobeying his orders and listening to the importuning of a woman. She rather suspected that his own concern lay more with his having listened to such importuning than anything else. It was hardly consonant with masculine consequence in Yusuf's frame of reference.

They saw a few peasants and goatherds, none of whom took more than a passing interest in such ordinary travelers. Once, they were hailed by a small patrol of foot soldiers, but were permitted to go on their way when Yusuf told them they were visiting his father in a neighboring village. By nightfall, they were on the Abencerrajes' land. They made camp in a scrubby olive grove, and since Yusuf would not light a fire, they ate cheese, olives, and dates and drank water from the skin Yusuf carried in his saddlebags.

When it was full dark, she followed Yusuf out of the thin cover of the trees. They climbed some way up the hill until pinpricks of light showed on the plain immediately below.

"The fortress of the Abencerrajes," Yusuf said. "About two hours' walk from the grove."

Sarita nodded. "It would be easier to approach from here; I will not lose sight of it."

Yusuf merely grunted and turned back the way they had come, Sarita again followed him.

They lay down wrapped in blankets beside the tethered animals. Sarita felt as if they ought to say something, even if it was just good night, but Yusuf's silence was somehow forbidding, as if he had already cut himself off from her presence. He rolled onto his side facing away from her, and she lay looking up through the tattered leaves dangling from the tortured branches of the olive trees to the sharp glitter of stars in the dark canopy of the night.

After a while, she slid out of the blanket and stood up. The still bundle of Yusuf remained motionless. The pony whickered, the mule shuffled, as she pulled a handful of dried apricots from the saddlebags. Hunger seemed an inappropriate reaction while she prepared for her walk into the lion's den, but she could think of no other explanation for her violently churning stomach. She checked the knife at her hip beneath the folds of the burnous. It slipped with reassuring ease in and out of the sheath. Whether she would have time to use it if confronted was questionable. Whether she could do any damage with it was equally questionable. But its presence comforted her.

Her bare feet made no sound as she left the grove and took the path she had taken earlier with Yusuf, chewing on an apricot, suddenly, vibrantly, reminded of that long-ago morning when she had eaten apricots and defied the caliph, only to learn the sensual joys of the baths despite her defiance . . .

She descended the mountainside, surefooted from long experience with such terrain. The lights on the plain had been all but extinguished, but the darkness of night was graying as she reached flat ground and wondered how to make her approach. There would be a gatehouse, sentries, an officer of the watch. Would they take any notice of an apparent goatherd? Presumably the emir of the Abencerrajes did not grant audiences to goatherds.

Her approach across the plain was watched closely from the ramparts of the alcazaba. It was a goatherd with no goats, appearing from nowhere out of the fading darkness of the night, walking with clear purpose. In these troubled times, any unorthodox arrival was regarded with suspicion, even when it was seemingly as inoffensive as this lone, slight figure. Three soldiers were dispatched to apprehend the arrival and bring him within the watchtower.

Sarita's heart drummed against her ribs at the approach of the armed riders. They looked businesslike and as if that business was war. They hailed her and she tried to answer bravely, but her tongue wouldn't move easily around the Arabic phrases while fear and a sense of absolute vulnerability rose to clog her throat.

"I have business with the emir of the Abencerrajes," she managed.

"From where?"

She struggled to swallow. "From the Alhambra."

That certainly caught their attention. They circled her, menacing with their helmets and shields and fierce spurs, their massive steeds nudging her, huge hooves too close to her bare toes.

"Please," she said, standing desperately still. "I mean no harm. I have a message for the emir."

One of the men leaned down, caught her arm, and hoisted her upward, her shoulder screaming its protest as it took her weight. Then she landed on the high saddle in front of him. She held her body away from him, petrified that he might sense something feminine despite the enshrouding burnous, the pulled-down hood, and the grime on her face. But the man made no attempt to touch her, leaving her to manage her own balance as best she could as the trio galloped toward the gates of the Abencerrajes' fortress.

The gates clanged shut behind them, and they were in a court that Sarita recognized as similar to the court of the alcazaba in the Alhambra. There was much that was similar in this Moorish fortress with its internal palace, but it was on a much more modest scale than the Alhambra and lacked the majestic mountain setting. However, it throbbed with fighting power. There were soldiers everywhere, and the ramparts bristled with armored watchmen.

They took her into a round stone chamber set into the gate tower, where the officer of the watch waited. He stared at the slight lad with the dirty face and the unusual green eyes and wondered what felt wrong about him.

"What is your business?"

"I come from the Alhambra. I have a message for the emir."

"Then give it to me."

"No, it must be given in person."

The officer of the watch stared and stared. Was the lad a potential assassin? But there was no way he could get close enough to the emir to do any damage, not if he was under guard. And there was something very strange, very intense, about him. The emir must be told.

"Lock him up," he said to one of the men who had brought her within the fortress.

"But I must—"

Her protest was cut off as the man slammed his palm across her mouth, gagging her. She was half carried, half dragged from the chamber and thrust into a small, dark square of space set into the thick wall. A heavy bar thudded over the door, and she stood, bruised, terrified, shivering in the black, stone-cold air. Would they leave her here, forgotten, to wither away in the darkness?

* * *

Yusuf heard her go. He must wait until tomorrow night before starting back to the Alhambra if he was to lie successfully.

He sat up abruptly. Why had he ever thought such a thing was possible? He rose, mounted, and rode as if pursued by the entire army of the Abencerrajes, hauling the mule behind him. He had no idea how he was going to explain to the caliph what he had done. He expected to lose his head; indeed, could see no other deserved fate. He had acted against every tenet of his personal beliefs and against those of his society. He had disobeyed the order of his supreme commander, he had obeyed the crazy whim of a woman, and he had knowingly put at risk a possession the caliph held most dear. *Why?*

The woman had convinced him of something. Something about herself. She would try, and maybe she would succeed. And Yusuf loved Muley Abul Hassan as much as he sensed the woman did.

But now he had to inform the caliph of what he had done, of the woman's plan, of the danger in which she now lay. He *knew* he had to do so, without knowing why.

His lathered pony, foam-flecked at the bit, staggered through the Gate of Justice, ridden into the ground. The mule had been abandoned hours earlier, and the pony carried the other beast's burdens to augment its own. Yusuf flung himself to the ground in the Court of the Cisterns as the pony folded to its knees, head hanging, breath coming in heaving gasps.

Yusuf, heedless of the exclamations in his wake, ran from the court to the Mexuar, where he would expect to find the caliph, since it was the hours of justice.

Abul's mind was not on the issue in front of him, and he was aware of it. He could think only of whether Sarita and Yusuf were yet through the passes. The vizier was presenting a troublesome matter of thievery, and the accused was shaking in his chains. His hand was at stake, and only the caliph could pronounce judgment.

The sounds of a disturbance came from the antechamber, and Abul looked up from his frowning examination of the massive emerald on his index finger. Yusuf appeared, breathless, drawn, urgency radiating from him with the sweat pouring down his face.

"What has happened?" Abul was on his feet, striding down the hall. "Where is Sarita?"

Yusuf gasped, wrung his hands, struggled to find the words as he faced the alarm in his lord's eyes and realized absolutely that the love he bore this man had caused him to make the wrong decision. By allowing the caliph's dearest possession to put herself in danger, Yusuf had done the one thing that would overset the caliph's equilibrium. The lord Abul would do anything to protect his Christian houri.

"*Tell me!*" Abul laid hands on Yusuf, and the audience in the hall of the Mexuar drew back, riveted by the blind passion emanating from the caliph.

"My lord, not here," Yusuf managed to gasp.

Slowly, Abul brought himself under control, became aware of the people around him, of the alleged thief and his accuser, of the vizier's alarmed expression. Whatever had happened to Sarita, nothing would be gained by his own panic.

He turned to the vizier. "I have not the time now to give this case the consideration it warrants, and I will not make a hasty judgment. Bring them back in the morning, when I have had more time to consider." He swept an encompassing look around before saying to Yusuf, "Come." With a vague gesture of dismissal to those within the hall, he strode toward the private mosque at the rear, Yusuf on his heels.

In the utter peace of the small, exquisite room dedicated to prayer and meditation, Abul went to the niche facing east and stood staring at the inscription above, drawing strength, before he said, "Tell me what has happened."

As Yusuf stumbled through the tale, the caliph moved not a muscle. When the man came to a halt, Abul turned slowly, and Yusuf trembled at the look that fell upon him.

"I am to assume that you have lost your reason," Abul said almost musingly. "I do not believe it just to punish the lunatic for falling foul of the changes of the moon." He fell silent.

"Pronounce my death, my lord," Yusuf said in anguish. "I did what I did because of my love for you. I believed the woman could succeed—"

"As I said, you have lost your reason," Abul interrupted in the same dreadfully calm tones. "I will put no other construction on your action."

"What must I do, lord?" The plea was a bare whisper.

Abul turned to the window overlooking the lush river valley. He was filled with a vaporous emotion that he knew would petrify if he allowed himself to think of what might be happening to her. "You will go back," he said. "I do not care how you do it, but, by Allah, you will discover what has happened and you will bring that information back to me. You will not rest, nor break your fast, until you return here with the information I seek."

"By Allah," Yusuf said, prostrating himself before the prayer niche. "By Allah, I will neither rest nor break my fast until I have obeyed my lord's will."

Abul remained in his stillness after Yusuf had left the little mosque. They would have no reason to hurt her. But would they need a reason? No, but she would be more useful to them alive. They might see a way to make political capital out of the living Sarita, whereas her dead body would but feed the vultures. If he held on to that, he could retain his sanity until Yusuf returned. And Yusuf *would* return. When he knew what was happening, then he would know what to do.

Why hadn't he thought she might come up with such a piece of lunacy? A woman who climbed down silken ropes into a ravine to escape the velvet bonds of a man she loved because he didn't accept her point of view was capable of anything. But she was also capable of survival. He could hold on to that, too. Sarita was no weak vessel. She knew how to fight.

But she didn't understand his people. She didn't understand the true nature of this conflict. She saw it in terms of the black-and-white survival of Muley Abul Hassan as caliph of Granada. But it wasn't that simple. If that were all it was, Abul would have thrown the whole bag of tricks to the Spaniards months ago. Family pride had kept him fighting a battle he no longer wished to fight. And what Sarita did not realize was that what she had just done was going to have the opposite effect from her carefully constructed intention. She had just tossed his opponents the one throw of the dice that Abul could not—*would* not—win. He would not sacrifice Sarita for his family's supremacy in Granada.

Chapter 20

The sound of the bar lifting outside her prison shocked Sarita out of her fear-struck daze. She pushed herself away from the wall at her back and faced the light as the door swung open, bracing herself for seizing hands, harsh commands.

Four soldiers stood outside. The foremost gestured brusquely and she stepped into the passage, huddling into the burnous, shrinking into the hood like a tortoise withdrawing from the unknown.

One of the men took her arms, lifting them away from her body, and she realized they were going to search her for weapons.

"I have a knife," she said hastily. "On my right side."

They took the knife and ran only perfunctory hands over her, hands that discovered nothing of remark in the slight frame of a young lad.

"Move," the leader commanded, jabbing her in the small of the back.

"Where are you taking me?" She found her voice and the resolution to sound like someone who had something to offer, who would not submit to the role of enemy prisoner. "I must talk with the emir."

"You're going to do so," the leader said. "Whether you'll be glad you did or not is another matter." He laughed, and the others laughed with him.

They jostled her through passages, across courts, along colonnades, the architecture familiar yet nowhere near as elaborate as the Alhambra. The absence of water was most conspicuous: there were no fountains, no carefully directed streams, and as a result little flora. The place struck Sarita as Spartan in its lack of elegance and amenity. Finally, they entered an antechamber where guards stood alert at a studded door at the rear.

Her heart began its frantic drumming again as she thought what lay beyond that door. Death. Unless the emir of the Abencerrajes was willing to listen to her.

The door was opened and she was propelled into the presence of the emir, her four guards crowding around her. With a sense that it was the only correct approach, she raised her head and faced the emir without flinching, her eyes meeting a pair of chilly gray ones.

The emir of the Abencerrajes was a tall man, rather older than Abul, she decided. He was fiercely bearded, strong-jawed, but there was no expression in his eyes, no hint of curiosity, of warmth, no sense that this was a man to be trusted. Slugs crawled down her spine, leaving a slimy trail of fear as Sarita realized that she had in all probability gambled and lost. This was not someone to be won over with promises and truth. Not unless it suited him.

But perhaps it would suit him. She lifted her chin, and the challenge that Abul knew and loved so well was in her eyes.

"Who are you?" The emir's voice was harsh, like a knife on stone.

She tossed her head, shaking off the hood of the burnous, then raised her hands and unwound the turban. "Sarita of the tribe of Raphael." Her hair cascaded around her shoulders, a startling brightness in the gloomy hall.

There was utter silence.

Sarita stood still, waiting, the turban dangling from her hand, her gaze unflinching. Then the emir drew a slow breath.

"So," he said in the Spanish she had used. "So, Sarita of the tribe of Raphael, what business do you have with me?"

"A private tale, my lord emir."

Again there was silence before he spoke thoughtfully. "I will hear you in private, but not in the garb of a goatherd. I would see what it is that has so led astray my brother Muley Abul Hassan."

The slugs resumed their crawling as Sarita recognized her ultimate vulnerability in the enemy court. Death was not the only thing to fear. "My clothing is irrelevant to my tale."

He inclined his head. "Maybe so . . . maybe so. Nevertheless, it offends me to see a woman so attired." He spoke swiftly to the leader of her guard. "Dress her appropriately and then bring her to me again."

Her escort, who had fallen back in astonishment when she had revealed herself, now moved on her, salacious hunger in their eyes. The emir turned to leave the chamber by a curtained doorway at the rear. A nut of nausea lodged in Sarita's throat as she realized he had abandoned her to these men, who would view her as fair game, a woman and an unbeliever, one who had flaunted herself deliberately and was therefore deserving of none of the consideration they might have accorded a woman of their own people.

But at the doorway, the emir paused and spoke over his shoulder, just as the leader of the guard caught her arm, pushing it up behind her back. "Find women to do this work. Our visitor belongs to me for the moment."

The leader did not release her, but expressed his disappointment with a vicious jerk of her arm that brought tears to her eyes. But her relief at the emir's words was so overwhelming she scarcely minded the pain.

In a very few minutes, she found herself locked in the same dark chamber in the watchtower, so far unmolested, but dread rushed with the swift pulsing of blood through her veins.

The door opened and two women entered, one bearing a branch of tallow candles, the other a length of material over one arm. They said nothing to her, indeed barely raised their eyes over their veils as they set the candles in a corner, revealing the tiny cell with its stone floor and walls, its lack of any furniture . . . a lack Sarita had already discovered for herself.

She maintained her own silence but forestalled any attempt they might make to undress her by pulling the burnous over her head and matter-of-factly unfastening the britches and shirt. They drew breath sharply when they saw the strip of linen binding her breasts, and one of them went to help her unfasten the knot Kadiga had tied to secure the band at Sarita's back. When she stood naked, they held out a robe of some flimsy white material that offered little protection from cold or from interested eyes. It was not the dress of a respectable woman of the seraglio, Sarita realized with a sinking heart. It was the robe of a houri.

Was it meant to humiliate her? Designed to reduce the importance of her message to the babblings of a love slave? Probably both, she decided, wondering whether to refuse the change of dress, to insist on her lad's clothes again. But that would achieve nothing. Her only chance was to convince the emir of the validity of her tale, and if he would only grant her an audience in this provocative and demeaning garment, then she must do her best with a dignified manner and calm, coherent speech to overcome the impression the clothing accorded her.

Curtly, she refused the slippers the women pressed upon her, but she took the veil, feeling that anything that increased bodily concealment could only be of benefit. It covered the fiery turmoil of her hair, smothering its potentially inflammatory quality. However, she left her face exposed, needing to make some statement of independence.

The door banged open just as she had finished adjusting the veil, and the two women jumped back against the wall. The leader of the guard ran his eyes over Sarita, an insolent scrutiny that clearly looked beneath her costume; then he jerked his head toward the door. As she passed him, his hand brushed her hip beneath the thin material, and the slugs began their crawl again. But she ignored the touch, averting her proudly lifted head as if disdaining to notice him.

This time they took her into a small, intimate chamber with silk hangings on the walls and silk rugs scattered over the mosaic floor. The emir was lying upon a divan, sipping from a jewel-encrusted goblet. He offered no greeting as she stood just within the doorway, where she had been thrust by her escort, who had immediately retreated. He examined her in the same unnerving silence, and she kept her eyes fixed on the wall above his head, on an intricate design of flower knots delicately traced in gold and silver leaf.

Almost lazily, the emir placed his goblet on the low table at his side and rose, his robes flowing and settling around him. He crossed the room and flicked the veil from her head. "My tastes run rather more to the voluptuous," he observed, one hand moving over the delicate lift of her breasts beneath the diaphanous material.

Sarita tried not to shrink, tried to keep rigidly still, as if the touch were being administered to clay rather than to living flesh.

"But Muley Abul Hassan has always had very definite preferences," the emir mused, flicking at her nipple with a fingertip. "Are you as cold and unresponsive as you appear?" he wondered. "It's to be assumed not." Shrugging, he turned from her, and Sarita's knees shook with relief. "Well," he said, "you have a tale to tell. Tell it."

To her dismay, her voice quavered when she began. She stopped, swallowed, and began again. The emir had resumed his position on the couch and lay listening to her, his eyes half closed, one finger running around the rim of his goblet.

"Well, that is a tale indeed," he said after she had finished. "A quarrel in my friend's harem is excuse for war. The entire kingdom of Granada is up in arms because of the jealousy of women." He laughed suddenly, richly, and most unreassuringly. "So, Sarita of the tribe of Raphael, you will renounce your claim upon the lord Abul, whatever that claim might consist of, and will return whence you came, leaving matters as they were before you appeared."

"That is what I have said," she affirmed, but she was cold with despair. The emir gave no indication of taking her seriously. "I will go from here to Cordova. You may escort me to the border if you doubt my word."

"Oh, I do not doubt your word," he said, still chuckling. "So you say I have been played for a fool by the Mocarabes."

"I said only that they have the most to gain by the lord Abul's abdication."

"Well, that is not untrue," he conceded.

"And the reason they give for the demand that the lord Abul abdicate is not good and sufficient reason, and no longer exists in any form anyway."

"Mmm. You certainly have courage, Sarita of the tribe of Raphael. I know little of the women of your race. Are you unusual?"

He sounded genuinely curious, the mocking laughter gone from his voice and expression, and the question took her by surprise.

"I do not know," she faltered. "Will you give me safe passage to Cordova, my lord emir?"

He stroked his beard, his eyes half closed as he meditated. Then he said, "Possibly. But you will not object to being my guest for a little while longer, I trust."

The cold was in the marrow of her bones now, and she began to shake inside. "Why would you wish to keep me? I have done what I came here to do."

"Oh, come now, that is a little naive," he said gently, taking a date from the bowl before him, holding it in front of his mouth, and seeming to contemplate it, as if to decide whether it was worthy of being introduced between the hard, straight line of his lips. "I must think on what you have said. I must take counsel, and I may wish to question you further before I decide what action to take." The date disappeared into his mouth and he chewed, smiling affably.

"But you will consider withdrawing your opposition to the caliph?" She had to press the point, had to try to gather some hope, some sense that her recklessness had not been in vain.

"I will reflect, and I will take counsel," the emir repeated. "You, meanwhile, will accept my hospitality, such as it is. Not as extravagant as that offered in the Alhambra, I fear, but we do our best."

Sarita said nothing. There was nothing to be said. She had walked into the lion's den, and if he chose to rend her, she had no defense.

He rang a handbell, and her same guard appeared before the first jangle had died down. "Confine the woman in the alcazaba," he said. "Aboveground and without restraints. A locked door and guard should be sufficient." He smiled and took another date. "She is rather too insubstantial to pose any threat."

They took her away, and the emir, all vestiges of lassitude vanished, rose energetically from his ottoman as soon as the door closed. He paced the room, the hard gray eyes clear. He didn't doubt the truth of what the woman had said. The Mocarabes were more than capable of using a women's quarrel to advance their own cause. If Aicha had indeed attempted to murder her rival, then the caliph had acted justifiably and the Mocarabes had no rightful argument. If the Christian left the Alhambra, there was no legitimate excuse for insurrection against the caliph . . . and no legitimate excuse for inviting the participation of the Spanish in the overthrow. The emir was well aware of the risks involved in that uneasy coalition.

But the woman had with dangerous innocence seen the issue as black and white: if the Abencerrajes understood the truth, then they would return to being loyal subjects of the caliph. There was much more to it than that. In the short term, the Abencerrajes did not have as much to gain as the Mocarabes from the ascent of the child Boabdil to the caliphate, but in the long term . . .

In the long term, an ambitious family could benefit greatly from such an event. Even with the support of the Mocarabes, a child and a woman on the throne of Granada would provide many opportunities for advancement, many more than could ever be offered under the strong, wise, clearheaded rulership of Muley Abul Hassan. A kingdom in chaos was a hotbed of opportunity for those who would be at the center to mold the new regime. The Spaniards would need payment for their participation, of course, but the emir did not doubt that they could be satisfied with the token submission of the boy king and some monetary reward.

If, on the other hand, he went over to the caliph's side, swore undying allegiance, and broke up the alliance with the Mocarabes, what would he gain? The caliph's gratitude, certainly, maybe advancement for some members of the Abencerrajes family. But no real access to the seat of power. Muley Abul Hassan kept too strong a grip on the reins.

No, the emir decided, he had made his choice. It was time the long ascendancy of the Nasrid dynasty was broken, and he would take what he could in the subsequent scramble over the spoils.

But what of the woman . . . what of the caliph's houri? He could have her put to death in the cell in the alcazaba, and no one need be any the wiser. But perhaps she could be put to good use. A possible lever on Muley Abul Hassan? Then again, how would the lady Aicha react to the capture of her arch rival? She might well be disposed to gratitude. And obligations stored up for redemption in the future were always worth having.

The emir smiled to himself and rang the bell again, summoning his vizier. "Send a message immediately to the emir of the Mocarabes. The messenger is to travel without respite. I will expect an answer in my hands within two days."

Two hours later, a messenger set off at a gallop toward the road to Montilla.

It was soon after siesta when Aicha received the summons to attend her father in his council chamber. It was not an unusual summons. The emir of the Mocarabes frequently consulted his daughter's opinions on the course of the insurrection, aware of her knowledge, both intuitive and real, of the politics of the Alhambra.

She found him alone, and after she made her reverence, he beckoned her over to sit beside him. "A messenger has arrived from the Abencerrajes, daughter. His import I believe you will find of interest."

Smiling, he handed her the rolled parchment. Aicha read it. "Naive little fool," she said with a softness that could not disguise her venomous triumph. "To imagine she could interfere in such a manner."

Her father shook a warning finger. "Be not so scornful, daughter. The tale she took to the Abencerrajes could well have been believed. Indeed, I suspect it has been believed. Her very naïveté in putting herself in such danger would add great validity to her tale. In different circumstances, with the Abencerrajes in a different mood, she could well have succeeded in her interference."

Aicha accepted the reproof in silence, but her lips compressed, her eyes hardened.

"That said," her father continued, "she has not succeeded, and it is for us to decide her fate. The emir says he has her safe and will dispose of her as we—or rather, you—choose."

"A slow death," Aicha said.

"Oh, come, let us be a little more subtle," the emir chided. "How can we use her to advance our cause? What would your husband give to ensure her safety?"

Aicha remembered Abul's face the moment before he had condemned her to the torture chamber. It had been the face of a desperate man. "A kingdom," she heard herself say, almost before the thought had formed in her head. "I believe he would yield the Alhambra in exchange for the unbeliever's life."

Her father caressed the smooth, polished arms of his chair. "That is a large claim, daughter."

"It can be put to the test," Aicha replied. "And I know how it can be done most neatly."

Her father smiled. "Explain yourself, child."

"Why, by using her own people to bring about her downfall," Aicha said. "She has sworn to the Abencerrajes that she will leave Granada, renounce Abul, return to her own country. Why do we not assist her to do so? Their most Catholic Majesties have a passionate commitment to saving the erring souls of their people. They know of this one, know of the dissension she has caused in our land. Why do we not give her to them . . . an erring soul who has abandoned her own religion to embrace the life and beliefs of a heretic?"

The emir laughed. "What a wonderfully devious mind you have, my daughter. And the lord Abul?"

"We will arrange for him to receive the information. If the messenger we send to the Abencerrajes with these instructions is told to be indiscreet on the journey . . . if his tongue is loose at his halts and with fellow travelers . . . the news will reach Muley Abul Hassan the way all such news travels. He will have his spies everywhere."

Her father nodded. "He will hear of it."

"And he will attempt to negotiate her release from Cordova. But I do not believe he will succeed," Aicha declared. "The religious arm is most tenacious when it has laid hands upon a sinner in need of redemption, but I believe he will lose interest in all else."

"And the woman will suffer a slow death nevertheless," the emir pronounced. "At the hands of her own people."

"At the next public burning in Cordova," Aicha said with quiet satisfaction. "After extended inquisition."

Sarita's prison was bare, dirty, cold, and windowless. She had a narrow plank to serve as a bed, a pail as a commode. They brought her a jug of water every day, and after the first day she understood it was to serve all her needs, both washing and drinking. They fed her on dates, olives, dry bread . . . enough to keep up her strength but not to satisfy the perpetual nagging hunger. When she asked for a blanket to keep at bay the fetid cold of the ancient stone against which her flimsy robe provided little protection, they brought her a moth-eaten cloak. But it was better than nothing.

She slept most of the time, huddled in the cloak on the hard bed, withdrawing from boredom, loneliness, and trepidation, seeking the world of the Alhambra in her dreams—the scents, the sounds, the richness of its chambers and porticos. And always in her dreams she sought Abul. His face would hang in the air above her, his mouth curved in laughter, his bright black eyes full of wisdom and humor . . . or his mouth would be a bow of sensual promise, his eyes heavy with passion. Sometimes, when her dreams were particularly vivid, she would feel his hands upon her, and her skin would tingle in anticipation, her body shift on the narrow plank with burgeoning arousal. And then she would awaken to the cold, to the desolation of her prison, and to the ever-present fear.

On the seventh day, the door was opened and she was brusquely ordered into the passage. She blinked at the brightness of daylight after the candlelit dimness of her prison. She pulled the cloak tightly around her, suddenly conscious of how she must appear: dirty, her hair no longer a lively fire but lank and subdued, dust and dirt clinging to the hem of her tawdry robe, her feet ingrained with the floor grime of her cell. The mental image did nothing for her self-confidence.

The emir sat on a raised chair at the end of what Sarita assumed was his equivalent of the Alhambra's Hall of the Ambassadors. He was alone and signaled to her escort to fall back.

"So, Sarita of the tribe of Raphael, I hope you have not found our hospitality too lacking in refinement," he said, mockery in his voice as he took in her appearance. Sarita said nothing, concentrating every fiber of her being on the need to appear fearless and unconcerned, when in reality she was filled with a black wave of dread, of absolute knowledge that this man meant her harm. She was not going to be permitted to leave the stronghold of the Abencerrajes unmolested. And Abul . . . Obviously she had failed there too. He would have to fight his battle without her help, and she would never see him again . . .

"I must apologize for the long delay," the emir went on smoothly. "There were other people to be consulted, arrangements to be made."

She pulled herself back from the wasteland, swallowing her tears. She was going to die. Weeping over the loss of Abul seemed silly when faced with that fact. And she would not die a coward. She raised her head and faced him.

"It seems we are in a position to assist you in leaving the kingdom of Granada," the emir continued, his eyes skimming her white face, missing none of her struggle for composure. He turned his head to a curtained doorway behind him, and as if on cue, the curtain was moved aside. Three figures glided into the chamber. Three figures in gray cowls, the scourges of self-flagellation at the braided ropes around their waists, the burning eyes of the fanatic leaping threefold at Sarita as they raised their hooded heads.

Sarita screamed.

"Your people claim you, Sarita of the tribe of Ra-

phael," the emir said when the echo of her terror had
faded in the silent chamber. "Thus will you do as you
wished and free Muley Abul Hassan to hold his
throne."

Even had she believed that to be true, she would
have found no strength therein to bolster her courage
in the face of this terror. She was going to die—oh,
yes, there was no question of that—but only after suffering the most excruciating torments man could de-
vise in his hell upon earth. She took a step backward,
shaking her head incoherently, trying to find some
words of denial, her hands pushing at the air in front
of her as if she could dispel the three cowled figures,
reduce them to the insubstantial specters of nightmare.

"My daughter, your immortal soul is in grave danger." The monk's voice was almost kindly as he
stepped inexorably toward her. "We have it in our
power to save your soul, to bring you back to the true
faith. You have embraced heresy, daughter, but we
will show you the error of your ways."

His hands reached out to her. The flesh was white
with spreading brown spots. The bony fingers were
claws, curving to seize her in the grip of true cruelty.
Foreshortened, the hands seemed to assume huge
proportions, coming closer to her face. She opened
her mouth to scream again, but the scream was lost
in the black wave of unendurable terror.

It was the middle of the night when Yusuf returned
to the Alhambra. But time no longer meant anything
to him, and, heedless of the hour, he staggered to the
caliph's private apartments. Abul was not asleep. His
dreams were nightmares, and he preferred to be
wakeful.

"Well?" he demanded, finding no compassion
within him for Yusuf's exhaustion.

"My lord caliph, the emir of the Abencerrajes has
sent to Cordova to the Inquisition. The woman is to
be taken by them as a heretic."

Ice enclosed Abul, but his mind was as clear as the rarefied air on the mountaintops. "How do you know this?"

"A messenger came from the Mocarabes, bearing such instructions from the emir to the Abencerrajes. Within a few hours, another messenger left the Abencerrajes and took the Cordova road. I assumed he went to the religious authorities there, lord, and I came to you with all speed."

"How did you discover the Mocarabes' instructions, Yusuf?"

"The man wore the livery of the Mocarabes, lord, so I waylaid him on the road and offered to share my flask since he looked fatigued. We drank. He was garrulous."

Abul nodded. Such wayside meetings were common enough. Yusuf stood now with his head bowed like a blown horse, his body sagging, and Abul remembered the injunction he had put upon him. "Go to your rest," he said. "And break your fast."

Yusuf left the chamber, and the caliph went out to the court. Sarita had always loved this court. The fountain plashed in the moonshine. The green finches were silent in their cage. They would take her to Cordova before they would begin their dreadful work.

Would his bloodless abdication be sufficient to buy her back from the religious fanaticism of their Catholic Majesties, Ferdinand and Isabella? With his abdication came a weak Granada and the eventual certainty of its total capitulation to Spanish rule. They would not easily pass up the opportunity to acquire that with a minimum of force and expense. They could amuse themselves with the Mocarabes' claim, with a child on the throne, and make their serious move to dislodge the boy caliph when they chose. If Abul remained firm, there would be long fighting with no absolute certainty of victory. He believed he could hold the Alhambra indefinitely, so long as he was not killed during an attack. It was only for fear of the latter that he had sent Sarita away. The kingdom

would be weakened by internal attacks upon the Alhambra, but the Spaniards would still have to deal
with Muley Abul Hassan, rather than malleable and
inexperienced newcomers in the persons of his son,
his wife, and her father's family.

How best to make this diplomatic approach? Covertly, alone, a single suppliant? Or with all the pag-
eantry and majestic authority of the Nasrid? Of one
who knows himself to be the equal of any Spanish
monarch, and one who knows the offer he brings to
be irresistible.

Abul paced the court until dawn, tossing the alternatives back and forth until convinced he had made
the right choice. On the following morning, a glittering, ceremonial procession left the Alhambra, taking
the mountain passes to Cordova and the court of their
most Christian Majesties, Ferdinand and Isabella.

The man who rode at the head of the procession
did not look back to the rose-red walls of the place
that was so much more than his home . . . that was
the symbol of the Nasrid's long rule in this Morisco-
Spanish corner of the peninsula. He was never to see
it again.

None of those accompanying him, neither soldier
nor courtier, knew that he accompanied the caliph on
the last mission of his caliphate. None wondered why
a riderless, dappled gray palfrey cavorted on a leading rein at the rear of the procession. None inquired
as to the contents of the packs laden upon the train
of mules. None knew of the casks of gold, of silver,
of gems, that Muley Abul Hassan had strewn with
such care among those packs: the fortune and the future that was all he took from his ancestral home on
this warm day in late April.

Chapter 21

⟨ ❦ ⟩

S arita traveled to Cordova on a swaybacked mare
of uneasy gait, led by an armed retainer in the
livery of Castile. Her hands were bound to the pom-
mel, making it difficult for her to shift with the horse's
uneven stride, so that she was wretchedly uncomfortable most of the time. But she barely heeded the
discomfort, so locked was she in the hideous contemplation of her immediate future.

She had come round from her swoon in her familiar
cell and for a few minutes had thought she had woken
from the grip of a nightmare. But sharp-etched memory had asserted itself all too soon. And hard on the
heels of memory had come the three monks. They
had stood around her plank bed and spoken to her of
the sin of heresy, of the redemption that would not
be denied the truly repentant. They had demanded
that she confess her heresy and earn peace for her
immortal soul.

She had said nothing, all too aware of the trap.
There was no pardon on this earth for a confessed
heretic. She would be burned for heresy and her repentant, departed soul rejoiced over as it ascended to
the bosom of God in heaven. But if she denied her
heresy, they would compel the confession from her
sooner or later. No ordinary mortal could endure
steadfast the methods that would be used to extort
confession.

But here in the fortress of the Abencerrajes, no

threats were used. Indeed, they spoke gently to her,
begging her to save her soul, to see the error of her
ways. Finally, emboldened by their gentleness, she
had tried to explain that she had not lost sight of her
faith during the time she had spent in the infidel's
palace. The gentleness had vanished. They had accused her of immorality, of committing mortal sin, of
turning her back on the true faith. They had thun-
dered at her, reducing her to a quivering essence of
terrified flesh, cowering on her plank bed.

After that, no further attempt had been made to
reason with her. They had left the fortress the following morning, a large group of soldiers, retainers, and
the three monks with their prisoner. Even in her despair, the livery of Castile had puzzled her. It seemed
to imply that their Majesties had had some say in her
fate. But why would Ferdinand and Isabella be interested in the fate of a member of a tribe of gypsies?
Except that they were interested in Granada . . . and
she had been, albeit unwittingly, instrumental in the
present turmoil in that kingdom.

She tried to find a smidgen of hope in the thought
of that august interest. Maybe she would not disap-
pear into the torture chambers of the Inquisition, only
to reappear on the day of her burning. Maybe their
Majesties had another use for her. But the hope hardly
flickered before it was extinguished. Their Catholic
Majesties were renowned for their passionate interest
in the redemption of souls. This one had just been
brought forcibly to their notice and had thus attracted
the full power of church and state.

She tried to think of Abul, to take herself out of the
despair and dread of the present and create another
world. But she could only think of how she had failed
him. And if he did prevail against his enemies, if he
did go to Cordova to fetch her, because Yusuf would
have told him that he would find her there, he would
never find her . . . Would he ever discover what had
happened to her? Maybe the emir of the Abencer-

rajes, in victory, would taunt him with the knowledge . . .

They reached Cordova on the second day's ride,
having crossed the border by a circuitous route that
avoided the passes held by Abul's men. Sarita looked
around at the familiar territory of her homeland,
heard the familiar sounds, smelled the familiar smells,
and none of it meant anything to her. Her senses were
dulled, her body aching with the effort to keep upright in the saddle on her jolting mount, her spirit
leaden with despair and fear. If she could think of the
faintest possibility for rescue, maybe it would infuse
her with courage, but never had she felt more alone
. . . indeed, *known* herself to be utterly alone, de-
fenseless and friendless.

Not even the realization that they were riding
through the gates of the royal palace could stir a spark
of speculation. The hustle and bustle in the court
around her barely penetrated her abstraction. She was
half lifted, half pulled from her horse by the retainer
who held her rein. She stood with her hands bound,
staring down at the cobbles mired with mud and ma-
nure, strewn with straw, until one of the monks is-
sued a harsh order and seized her arm. The other two
fell in around her, and she was propelled across the
court, away from the liveliness in front of the palace,
toward a forbidding gray building at the rear.

A small portal set within large, studded entrance
doors opened when one of her escort rapped. They
pushed her over the raised threshold into a dark, cold
passage. The small door slammed shut behind her,
shutting out the sounds, the smells, the light of day.

The caliph of Granada entered the palace of their
Catholic Majesties with all the pomp and ceremony
of a visiting monarch. Abul had planned it carefully.
The robes of his retinue were of the richest and most
ceremonial, the horses beautifully caparisoned, the
procession accompanied by musicians playing the
flute and tambor. The vast wealth of his mountain

kingdom was on display, just as were the power and
the prestige of its monarch. If his hosts suspected he
had come as a suppliant, there would be no outward
evidence for such a suspicion. The more powerful he
appeared, the more intriguing and appealing would
be his proposition.

He was granted an immediate audience with their
Majesties, as befitted his regal status, but it was an
audience of welcome, where courteous greetings were
exchanged and no business could be discussed. There
should have been some surprise at his visit—surprise
carefully masked, certainly—but something. Yet Abul
could detect not the slightest shift in the blandly smiling countenances of his hosts, in the protestations of
welcome. They would know, of course, that something other than courtesy lay behind the visit. They
knew him to be a consummate diplomat as well as an
opponent to be reckoned with. But why was he convinced they were expecting him? He would not have
come to beg their intercession in his troubled cause.
They would know that absolutely, just as they knew
he knew where their own support lay and for what
reason.

The lord Abul and his retinue were housed with all
honor in a guest wing of the palace. Yusuf disappeared, losing himself in the warren of passages in
the palace and in the twisting cobbled streets and alleys of the town: his mission to discover when and
how Sarita had been brought to Cordova. And where
she was held.

Abul waited in a fever of impatience through the
elaborate ceremonies of welcome, through the hours
of banqueting and dancing. Not a flicker of his dread
anxiety was visible on his smiling countenance. He
spoke only pleasantries, he danced with grace, he
sang a haunting melody of his own land, and he responded with appropriate gallantry to those of the
young, carefully chaperoned maidens of the court
who were brought his way.

He retired early, when their Majesties did, much to

the secret disappointment of several maiden hearts. Such an exotic figure was rarely to be seen at this court, resplendently formal though it was.

Yusuf was waiting for him in his bedchamber. "A woman was brought in this morning, my lord Abul. In the company of two friars and Fra Timoteo, their Majesties' confessor."

Abul turned from Yusuf and went to the window. The scent of orange blossom drifted upward on the soft spring air. They were treating Sarita as a heretic of some considerable importance, employing the monarchs' personal confessor in the business. It might mean he had some time . . . that Sarita had some time . . . before they began to break her. But why?

They had been expecting him. Were they using her as bait? Who would have thought he would rise to such a bait?

But even as he asked himself the question, he knew the answer. Aicha. He had been lured away from the Alhambra with the one fly Aicha had known he would find irresistible.

The knowledge, once absorbed, surprisingly did not trouble him. He had done what they had expected. But he had also done what he had chosen to do. The only aspect that did trouble him was the knowledge that Aicha would relish her rival's suffering and death. She would hope to achieve that as well as Muley Abul Hassan's submission.

But she would not succeed. Aicha was not as experienced a diplomat as her husband. She worked from the muddled imperatives of a vengeful heart. Abul could subordinate the imperatives of the heart to the cool reasoning of the head. Even where Sarita was concerned . . . or so he told himself as he looked out at the velvet night. He had to.

"Where are they holding her?" he asked Yusuf, who had been standing as immobile as his lord through the long period of cogitation.

"In the palace prison," Yusuf replied quietly. "The

secular arm and the religious arm share facilities, I understand.''

The images rose in screaming clarity before Abul's tightly closed eyes. He fought them down, banished them, but the effort left him weak. He could do nothing for her tonight. Although he was so close to her, he could do nothing for her, except to try to send his spirit to her, across the darkness between them and into the darkness of her prison. To infuse her with his strength to withstand her suffering as he had done before, when he'd brought her back from the borders of death.

She was suffering. There was only suffering in that place. Was it unendurable as yet? A groan escaped him, a sound of such dreadful anguish that Yusuf slipped out of the chamber, shaking with his own sense of guilt.

Sarita swayed, blinking as the torchlight flickered before her tired eyes. The sound of their voices was trapped in her head, the same demand, the same phrases, alternating, sometimes the one voice, sometimes the other. They would not let her lean against the wall at her back, but her knees were buckling. She slipped to her knees on the hard stone, and they hauled her upright again, screaming at her to stand still, to keep her toes against the line they had scratched on the floor . . .

The morning dawned bright, filled with the softnesses of spring, the harmonious cooing of pigeons nesting in the turrets of the palace. Abul bathed and dressed in ceremonial robes of black, embroidered with gold. His request for a private audience with their Majesties had been made the previous evening. Now he could do nothing but wait in readiness.

He had been waiting throughout the interminable reaches of the night. He had kept vigil, concentrating on the inner core that would bring quiet to his soul, would clear his head of the extraneous tendrils of panic so that he could do what he had to without the interference of his nightmare imaginings.

He broke his fast and went out into the city, accompanied by men of his retinue, ostensibly to examine the merchandise in the marketplace, to talk with the vendors of leather, silks, and satins, of Venetian glassware and the fine porcelain of the Orient. Their Majesties must not find him straining at the bit, desperately awaiting their summons. So he spent an hour in the dark shop of one who sold illustrated manuscripts, beautiful pieces of work that the caliph of Granada would buy to grace the library of the Alhambra. He examined, he gave instructions to his retinue to discuss the price of those items that interested him, and he strolled back to the palace at midmorning, to all appearances a man utterly at peace, enjoying a leisurely sojourn in this Spanish city.

A liveried flunky awaited his return. Their Majesties would do themselves the honor of receiving the lord caliph before dinner in the Great Hall.

Ferdinand and Isabella greeted their guest with ceremony. Their own councillors were present, but Abul had entered alone. The significance of this was lost on no one, as he had expected. Whatever the caliph had to say was not to be common knowledge among his own people.

He came straight to the point: his abdication for the life of the woman held by the Inquisition in the palace prison.

"You are direct, my lord caliph," Ferdinand said.

"I see little virtue in being otherwise, your Majesty." Not a hint of his inner turmoil was revealed on his face or in his posture. He sat easily in the carved armchair, his hands resting loosely on the arms.

"The woman is a heretic. She has betrayed her faith," Isabella said. "We are concerned for her immortal soul, my lord caliph. It is the unequivocal duty of all Christians to have a care for the souls of their brethren."

Abul inclined his head. "I honor your resolve, your Majesty. Even from my own differing religious perspective, I cannot fail to honor such piety. However, I would bargain with you for this soul." He allowed a smile to touch his lips, as if the matter were not of such deadly serious import.

"If we release the woman, how can we be certain you will leave the Alhambra for your son?" It was Ferdinand who spoke.

He received no response, just a steady stare from the lord Abul. Ferdinand cleared his throat and turned to his wife.

Isabella gathered up her skirts and rose. "We will consider your proposal, my lord caliph. But you must understand that temporal matters are of no weight in spiritual concerns. We have our duty to do. A benighted soul to bring back to the light. We are answerable to our God."

"As I am answerable to mine, lady," Abul said softly, rising with her. "The woman belongs to me." He had offered the carrot; now he would flourish the stick. "I will leave here with the woman; my retinue and soldiers will go to the Mocarabes and acknowledge my son as caliph. Or, you will keep the woman and her immortal soul, and I will bring into Granada the support of my brothers across the water, in Morocco, and we will destroy the Mocarabes and the Abencerrajes, and it will not be in your reign that the Spaniards will drive the Moors from Granada."

His voice was as still and cold as the frozen wastes of the tundra, his eyes as black and piercing as the eagle's.

Isabella's hauteur slipped as her eyes shifted sideways. Her husband stood up, signaling to the surrounding court that it should withdraw. "We will consider your proposal, my lord caliph."

"The woman belongs to me," Abul reiterated in the same soft voice. Then he bowed, turned, and swept from the chamber.

"It would seem the Mocarabes were not incorrect

in their assessment," Isabella said into the hush following Abul's departure. "I would not be confident of prevailing against such a man."

"No." Ferdinand touched his sword hilt. "One soul for a kingdom."

"To drive out the Moors after eight centuries," murmured Isabella. "That would be an epitaph indeed, husband, if we could claim such a victory."

"Muley Abul Hassan has offered us the victory. The boy and his mother will not be able to gather together the disparate components of the kingdom, shattered by this conflict. The man could, if he prevailed. But without him . . ."

"A little more manipulation, and it will be ours. Without bloodshed."

"Are they working on the woman?"

"Yes, but Fra Timoteo agreed with me that they should proceed slowly," Isabella said. "True repentance rarely comes with speed." She pursed her lips piously.

"Indeed," Ferdinand agreed. "Perhaps it would be as well to encourage even more care . . . just until we have taken counsel and come to a decision."

If only they would let her sleep. Sometimes she heard her voice begging them to allow her to lie down on the cold stone . . . just for a minute. But her voice fell, cracked, into the great void of indifference in which she floundered. She was not flesh and blood to these people, whose faces blurred before her, whom she identified only as voices. There was the hard voice, the cold one, the screaming one, the deceptively gentle one. The demands, the questions, the statements came at her relentlessly. Her throat was so parched she could not have answered if she had been able to formulate answers. They wanted her to admit she had had carnal knowledge of an infidel, and she knew she must not admit it. They wanted her to say she had embraced the religion of the infidel. When they said she could sleep if only she would

confess, the words rose to her lips. Then she saw the
wolf's gleam in the eyes of the hard-voiced one, glittering in expectation of triumph, and she shook her
head. She was thirsty . . . so dreadfully thirsty. Hunger had come and gone. Her ankles felt enormous,
her feet ice-cold on the slabs, like dead fish left swollen with decay on the seashore. Her interrogators
came and went. New faces, fresh voices, replaced the
old, but still she stood, wondering when the flesh-
tearing agony would begin, ready now to embrace it
as the beginning of the end.

Abul continued to frequent the court throughout
the day. He dined in the Great Hall, joined a hunting
party in the afternoon, gave the appearance of a man
enjoying himself and the hospitality of his hosts. Not
once did his eyes flick toward the grim gray building
of the prison, although his heart and soul were within
those walls and his body was a mere husk, going
through the motions until he learned whether he had
won the game.

At midnight, he was summoned to the private
council chamber. Ferdinand and Isabella were attended by their senior advisors. "You will send your
retinue back to Granada with your written abdication?" Ferdinand asked. "Naming your son Boabdil
as caliph in your place?"

"I will do that," Abul said. "My men will obey my
commands. They will swear loyalty to Boabdil."

"And where will you go?"

Abul laughed, but it was a harsh and unpleasant
sound in the paneled, lamplit chamber. "Forgive me,
sir, but I do not think that is any business of yours.
You have my word that I will not interfere in the affairs of Granada. I will take from here a train of pack
mules, a dappled gray palfrey, and Sarita of the tribe
of Raphael. All else I bequeath to my son."

"The woman will be released in the hour before
dawn."

* * *

The questioning ceased with an astonishing abruptness. They took her out of the room where she had stood for nearly two days, allowed only the briefest respite to use the commode, to sit for a very few minutes. But she had learned that sitting only increased the agony when they made her stand again. She had had a few sips of brackish water from a leather flask held to her lips, a crust of dry bread that she had been unable to swallow through her parched throat.

But now they took her out of the room and locked her into a pitch-dark cell. She stumbled to her knees, waited for the voice that would scream at her, the hands that would drag her to her feet. But there was nothing, only absolute silence. She slipped down until she was lying flat. Her body shrieked in perverse agony at the end of agony. The floor was rough and cold beneath her cheek. The air was damp and chill. She lost consciousness.

All too soon the door was flung wide, and hands hauled her to her feet. Torchlight flickered from the corridor, blinding her tired eyes. Absolute desperation filled her as she staggered on her agonized feet out into the passage. Where now? Down into the depths of this place? Depths reeking of pain, haunted by the screams of so many. She stumbled forward, barely aware of the gray robes of the figures in front of her, of the hands on her arm keeping her upright.

They stopped. A key grated in the darkness. A door creaked open. A square of lighter gray appeared. A hand in the small of her back propelled her forward. She tripped over the raised threshold of a door, lifted her feet with a blind, supreme effort, stepped through the doorway, and found herself standing, swaying, drawing deep gulps of fresh night air.

Abul moved out of the shadows in the deserted court. He stopped, frozen with horror as he sensed her dreadful pain. They had pulled her hair away from her face, so tightly that her forehead was puckered, and tied it with a piece of twine at the nape of her neck. They had dressed her in a penitential robe of coarse sacking. Her eyes stared blankly from the deathly pallor of her face.

"Sarita." He spoke her name as if only thus could he be certain she was no spirit, condemned to wander the halls of the Inquisition in her soul's agony.

Her head turned slowly, as if she had to think through each phase of the movement. "Abul?"

He caught her to him and as he did so was filled with a great surge of rage . . . astonishing, irrational, cleansing. *She had done this to them both.* He lifted her in his arms, feeling how insubstantial, incorporeal almost, she was, and his fury found voice in a throbbing, impassioned whisper. "How could you have been such a fool? To attempt such an arrogant, lunatic interference? How could you have believed you knew anything of my people? After everything that has gone before?" His arms tightened around her with a convulsive violence that he knew could as easily have been used to hurt as to support. He felt her shiver, but she did not answer him.

He carried her out of the court to where Yusuf waited with the mule train, the dappled gray palfrey, and Abul's powerful black. Abul swung onto his horse, cradling her tightly against his chest. He put spur to his mount, and they galloped out of the palace court, along the road to the border with Granada, Yusuf following with his slower charges.

Chapter 22

Abul rode up and up into the mountains, well away from the beaten track and the manned passes, up into the wilderness, until he reached his destination.

A tributary of the Genil flowed swiftly down the mountainside, settling in little dammed pools, rushing over tiny waterfalls. The ground was well irrigated, the grass and moss lush, the olive trees straighter and more silvery green than usual. Deep in the hillside was the entrance to a cave.

Abul had come here with his father many times in his boyhood, and on his thirteenth birthday, his father had brought him here and left him alone for a week to make shift for himself, to learn the power and wisdom that came from acquaintance with oneself, with learning and understanding one's strengths, with recognizing and making provision for one's frailties. Abul had intended to impart these things to Boabdil . . .

Yusuf toiled up the mountain in his wake. He tethered the mules and the palfrey and took his leave of his lord. "Return here in one week," Abul said, "if you choose to throw in your lot with mine. If you do not, then I hold you to nothing."

"I will return," Yusuf said and rode his pony back down the mountainside.

Abul still held Sarita, but now he set her on her feet, a sickness in his belly, consumed with one desperate, dread-filled need that now superseded his anger, although the two were somehow interdependent. When she moaned and swayed, he grabbed the round collarless neck of the sack she wore, holding her upright. With his free hand he pulled his knife from its sheath and slashed at the garment, dragging the knife downward, rending the material from neck to toe, tearing it from her body so that she stood naked.

He examined her with his eyes and then with his hands, touching every inch of her skin, turning her around, lifting her limbs, unable to believe that he could not see the massive, livid bruising of the rack, the cuts of the whip, the torn, burned flesh of pincer and clamp. But her skin was whole. Whatever they had done to her, they had not scarred her body with their ghastly instruments.

Sarita seemed to float upward from the trance that had held her since Abul had appeared, a figment of the dreams that had eluded her in the days of her captivity. She became aware of him, of her nakedness, of his intense scrutiny, and she shrank away from his eyes. "I am so dirty." Her voice croaked from her parched throat. It seemed suddenly the most important thing, the only thing that mattered, and it filled her with embarrassment. "Do not look at me."

"You need to sleep," he said, his voice sounding strangely disembodied, even to himself.

She shook her head. "Not until I am clean. I am rank." Indeed, the reek of pain and terror, of the fetid air of her successive prisons, seemed to enwrap her in a noxious aura. She put her hands to her head, a fluttering, distressful gesture. "My head aches."

He saw how the hair was dragged back from her forehead, the bright, dangerous fires doused, the subversive extravagance of curls forced into submission. He cut the tight string at the nape of her neck, pulling the hair loose, and heard her sobbing sigh of relief, seeing the tears glitter in her eyes.

"Sleep now," he insisted, but she shook her head. "I am filthy. I cannot sleep."

Abul did not understand the imperative, but he did understand that he must accede to it. He brought soap, toweling, oil, and strigil from the saddlebags and led her to the riverbank. "The water will be cold," he said. The early spring sun had had little time as yet to warm the waters flowing from the peaks of the Sierra Nevada.

"It does not matter." She shook off his hand and stepped in. The icy cold brought blissful relief to her swollen feet and ankles, and she barely felt its freezing on her skin as she plunged into the pool, dropping her head under the water that soothed her wrenched scalp and eased the ache at her temples. She drank greedily, drank until her belly was stretched and her throat numbed with the cold.

"Come out now, Sarita!" Abul commanded briskly from where he stood at the water's edge, apprehensively wondering if he was going to have to go in after her. But she staggered upright and out onto the bank. He rubbed soap on his hands and scrubbed her body and hair, then pushed her back into the water. "Wash it off quickly!"

She obeyed, hearing the anxiety beneath the brusqueness. She dipped beneath the surface, washing the soap from her hair, watching it froth around her with a dreamlike fascination.

"Sarita!" Abul's voice pierced the trance, and she stumbled to shore again. He scrubbed her dry with the towel, rubbing her hair until it no longer dripped down her back, before anointing her with oil and slowly, thoroughly, applying the strigil, pulling the dirt from her body, feeling the lines of her body take on shape again at each purifying stroke as if she were again beginning to inhabit her flesh. She stood quite still for him, lifting her arms, parting her legs, raising her feet, when he so instructed. And when he had finished, she took a deep breath, inhaling the freshness of her hair and body, the mild sweetness of the oil, curiously redolent of a tender innocence.

"I am going to sleep now," she said, and curled without further word on the soft turf of the riverbank.

Abul wondered whether to move her into the cave, but decided she would come to no harm where she was. He fetched a blanket and spread it over her, but she kicked it off with a sleepy, childish petulance that, despite everything, made him smile.

Sitting with his back to a rock, he stretched out his legs and settled down to watch her. There was complete stillness in this mountain aerie, ruffled only by the natural sounds of a world undisturbed by man, and by the cropping and shuffling of the tethered animals. After the hideous knife-edge of the last terror-filled days, Abul felt a great weakness, but he knew it was the weakness that preceded the rejuvenation of the spirit, and he allowed his mind to turn in on itself, his spirit to flow untrammeled by conscious thought and the devising of plans, or by speculations on the future.

As he watched and the sun grew high, the sleeping figure on the grass slowly unfolded from its fetal curl, as if in sleep the body craved the delicate touch of the soft air, the healing caress of the as-yet spring-muted midday sun. Her skin seemed to lose its waxen composition under his watchful eyes, to expand, to round out with the return of the inhabiting spirit.

In midafternoon, he lit a fire, assembled various items from the saddlebags, and put them to use, his eyes constantly flickering to the sleeper, noticing if she had changed position, watching for the first signs of a return to the waking world.

The sun was dropping behind the mountain when Sarita woke and sat up all in the same moment. She looked around her, her eyes clear and focused. "Abul?"

"I am here." He came toward her.

"I did not think I had dreamed you this time." She held her hands up to him, and he pulled her to her feet. "I don't seem to understand anything just yet except that I am hungry . . . hungry as if I have never been anything else."

Abul lifted her and carried her over to the fire. "It's getting chilly. You should wear something now." He took a woolen cloak from one of the packs and wrapped it around her shoulders. "Sit on that rock."

Sarita did so, watching curiously as he ladled *kuskus* into a wooden bowl from an iron kettle over the fire. "Did you cook this?"

He glanced around. "I don't see anyone else."

She only smiled and plunged the wooden spoon into the bowl. The contents were sweetened with honey, almonds, and boiled raisins. It was bland, filling, ineffably soothing. Finally, she laid the bowl and spoon on the grass beside her. "How did you know how to cook *kuskus*?"

He shrugged. "I once spent a week here on my own. I learned many things . . . how to trap and shoot, skin and cook. I thought your belly might need a little lining before you eat anything more exotic."

She smiled again and stretched, then drew her knees up to her chin, hugging them, the smile gone from her face and eyes.

Despite the way he was caring for her, something lay between them. Despite the cessation of terror, and she knew Abul had suffered it also, for she had felt it in his body as he had caught her to him when she'd emerged from the Inquisition's prison—despite that, the absolute peace of renewal was missing. Now she remembered the blunt force of his anger in the prison court.

"You are very angry with me." She looked at him over her drawn-up knees.

Abul considered and found that his anger had left him at some point in the long peace of the day. "I *was*. Very, very angry. But it was a confused anger, arising from my own dread. I had been living in such terror, knowing where you were, knowing what you were enduring, imagining what I could not know, yet I could do nothing quickly. When I saw you at last and realized that you were alive, although I knew you had been hurt . . . realized that I had you back again . . . I was consumed with a blind rage." He reached for her hand. "It is passed, *querida*."

She came onto her knees into his arms, needing now only the tenderness of his body as reassurance. "I could not bear your anger," she whispered, nuzzling against his warmth, knowing that for the moment that was the only truth. She wanted no more words, only his body speaking to hers.

Abul opened her cloak as she slipped down on the turf beside the fire, laying bare her body in the fireglow, moving over her with delicate healing touches, drawing from her the gentle cadences of a purely sensate response to loving. He brought to her a peaceful release, freeing her mind finally from its terrifying anchorage in her body during the reign of pain.

"Sarita?"

"Shhh."

Abul smiled and shook his head in amused resignation. "Sarita?"

"Shhh. You'll frighten him, and then we'll have no dinner." Her impassioned whisper came over her shoulder, her eyes darting green exasperation before she turned back to her self-appointed task.

Abul's smile deepened. Sarita was lying flat on her belly, the top half of her body hanging over the riverbank, as she devoted all her powers of concentration in a battle of wits with the speckled trout resting beneath a large flat stone. The trout's erstwhile companion lay gaffed on the grass, evidence of her success in this unsportsmanlike method of fishing.

"Forget tickling our dinner and come over here. I want to talk to you."

The note in his voice this time brought her back full length on the bank. She rolled over and sat up, shaking water off her bare forearm. "What can be more important than dinner?"

But Sarita knew what he was going to talk about.

She had been dreading it since she awoke in his arms this morning, remembering they had talked only of his anger yesterday. There was so much else they must discuss. How he had effected her release, and, more importantly, when they would return to the Alhambra.

She had no intention of not returning with him. If she could not assist him by her absence, then she would remain at his side. But her spirit was heavy at the thought of returning to that beleaguered atmosphere, with Abul so distracted by anxiety, and herself so unable to offer material assistance in his troubles.

"Several things," Abul said. "Are you coming here, or am I coming to fetch you?"

Sarita put her head to one side, regarding him quizzically, wondering if she could divert the coming talk. "It might be more interesting."

He shook his head. "No, it wouldn't."

"Oh." Reluctant but resigned, she stood up, rolling down the sleeve of the simple linen robe that had been packed in the traveling wardrobe carefully assembled by Kadiga and Zulema.

"Well?" She stood against his knees, pressing her own warmly against his, arching her body backward, so that her hair tumbled down her back, and her face lifted to the sparking sun.

"What do you want to do now?" Abul asked, squinting up at her.

"Tickle trout, of course." She straightened and laughed down at him. "I thought I'd made that clear."

He caught her hands and pulled her down to the grass. Apart from a mock indignant squawk, she acceded and settled cross-legged, her hands roaming through the grass in search of the dainty, tiny petals of emerging wildflowers.

"It's a serious question, Sarita *miá*. What do you wish to do now?"

She frowned, recognizing the grave note in his

voice. "I am coming with you. It is not a question of
wishes or decisions. You must go back to the Alhambra, and I am coming with you." Her seaweed eyes
held his in fierce determination. "You will not send
me away again, Abul."

"I wouldn't dare," he said, leaning back against
his rock with an almost lazy movement that struck
her as puzzlingly inappropriate in light of the subject
matter. "Now that I know what happens when you
take matters into your own hands, *hija miá*, I know
better than to let you loose."

"Yesterday you were very angry about it, and today you are laughing," Sarita said, quite lost. "You
were right to say I do not understand your people
and was foolish to attempt to interfere. It was a bitter
lesson, Abul, and I learned it. Your anger I can understand, but do not laugh at me now."

"Ah, *querida*, I am not making light of that." Re-
morsefully, he sat up and drew her close between his
knees, catching her face. "Do not ever believe I do
not know what you endured."

"But it is passed," she said. "Let us leave it that
way and discuss the future, since I think that is what
is behind this."

"Yes," he agreed. "And I wish to know how you
would most like to shape that future."

Sarita shook her head. "You must return to the Alhambra, Abul. We must fashion what we may out of
that. You have been away overlong as it is . . . and
for that I must blame myself."

"We do not return to the Alhambra," Abul said
quietly. He had been debating how best to tell her the
price of her freedom and had decided to let it come
out as it would.

"Why not?" He could feel the tension in the sharp
question and sensed that she almost knew what he
would tell her.

Gently, he stroked her mouth with the flat of his
thumb. "There are many roads in a man's life, Sarita.

I do not wish to spend the rest of my life on the same road, so I will take a new direction."

Her eyes met his, wide and direct. "You have exchanged Granada for me."

He chuckled and pinched her nose, trying to show her how lightly he considered the matter. "Granada proved to be worth the price of a soul. How many man-made things can substantiate such a claim?"

She pulled back from the teasing caress. "No, Abul, I will not believe such a thing . . . I cannot . . . I could not live with myself if I believed . . ."

"Hush, foolish one! Do you think I am nothing without the caliphate? That is a grave insult, Sarita."

She looked up to the mountains, thought again of the eagle with its clipped wings, and looked back at Abul in anguish. "Do not pretend, Abul. You know that you are Granada and Granada is you. You are bound within and to each other—"

"And you are talking arrant foolishness that is insulting to boot," Abul interrupted. "You would take from me the will to set my own priorities, to choose my own path, to decide upon a future different from that laid down in the hearts and minds of those who can neither see nor imagine beyond the ends of their noses."

Sarita flinched from the power of a genuine anger. Abul was the most self-determining man she had ever met. He rarely acted without due thought; she did not believe he could be forced into a course of action he believed wrong or in some way detrimental to a larger plan. Neither did she believe he would waste time and energy on regrets, once his decision was made. And if he had chosen herself over his caliphate, then she must accept that decision with all the joy and gratitude it brought with it.

Thoughts tumbled in her head as she struggled to rectify her error and find for once the right thing to say. In the end, it seemed most natural to refrain from apologies and protestations of innocence that would only lead her into deeper waters.

"What is it that you wish to do, then, Abul?"

"There are choices," he said, following her as easily as if those tense moments had never happened. "If you wish it, we could build ourselves a cabin up here and enjoy the rustic life—"

"Keep goats," Sarita said with a mischievous assumption of excitement, clapping her hands. "Goats and chickens. We have sufficient water. There are olive trees, and perhaps we could grow—"

"It will be rather cold in the winter," he broke in gravely.

"Yes, I suppose it will. The tribe always went down to low ground during the winter months."

"We could take to the open road, if that would please you," Abul suggested, pulling up a succulent stalk of grass and sucking it with every appearance of pleasure.

"I believe it is hard for two people to live that kind of life. It needs a community."

"Well, perhaps you would like to go to Barbary."

For some reason, that alternative had not occurred to Sarita. To leave the peninsula . . . to cut every last thread with Spain . . . with her homeland, the people of her race . . . She swallowed. "Yes, but what is there?"

"My mother's estates, by the sea. Orange and olive groves; pine woods; a house of white marble with terraces overlooking the sea; gardens of hibiscus and oleander."

"It is yours?"

"*Por cierto*," he said, smiling. "My mother died ten years ago, and I have visited it regularly. But I have never lived there, although I spent time there as a boy."

"You have never lived there?" She asked the question slowly. It seemed a most important question: a place of their own with no ghosts and no unshared memories.

Abul shook his head. "Never."

"But there is a seraglio?"

"A seraglio, *hija mía*, is formed by the women who live within it."

"But it is the place where women are kept apart."

He shook his head. "Not necessarily. It cannot exist without women."

"But you will have wives in this house in Barbary."

"One wife . . . or will you permit me others?" He was laughing openly at her, and she joined him with a joyous chuckle.

"No, *querido*. No other women. You will cleave only to me."

Although she was laughing, neither of them was in any doubt as to the seriousness of the statement.

"We will live in my land by the mores of yours," Abul asserted. "And we will have children who will understand the rules of both." He caught her chin again. "You will bear my children, Sarita?"

She clasped his wrists strongly. "I will bear your children."

Abul leaned back against his rock. "In that case, it seems to me I have but one problem."

"And that is?" She regarded him warily, sensing the readiness for mischief in his body.

"Why, simply that I must do something to eradicate this tendency you have for indulging in dangerously imaginative exploits, *hija mía*."

She inched backward, moving onto her heels in preparation for a spring to her feet. "You might regret the effort. Just such a dangerously imaginative exploit occurs to me now. Would you wish it quenched, my lord Abul?" She slid her hand between his legs, teasing with a knowing glint in her eye and wicked fingers. Then, just as he began to relax into the caress, she sprang up and danced away from him, pelting him with the wildflowers she had been busily collecting in her skirt.

Abul leaped into motion and she was off, scrambling up the hill, her hair flying, her bare feet finding easy purchase, her swift hands raining grass and flowers down upon him as he came up after her. He caught her ankle, hauling her down, and she came in a slip-sliding of loose earth, laughing.

"You really do find that provocation adds spice," Abul declared with a murmur of satisfaction as his mouth closed over hers, readily opened to receive the invasion. His hand pushed her skirt up even as her knee moved to press against him with eager accuracy.

"I love you," she whispered, suddenly malleable, all playful resistance vanished as the hard earth beneath her and the bright enameled sky above her enclosed her. His body was hard in its demand, and there was no imperative on earth but the imperatives of love. He poured his own love into her, and she soared with him through the glory of a future that they would make for themselves, together.

Afterword

In January 1492 the armies of Ferdinand and Isabella marched into Granada. Boabdil, known as El Rey Chico, the Boy King, had been unable to control the internal feuding within his kingdom or to withstand the external pressure from Spain. It is said he handed over the keys of the city to the Spaniards, who entered bloodlessly, thus bringing to an end 781 years of Moorish presence in Spain.

On his way into exile, legend has it that Boabdil stopped on the Motril road for one last look at the rose-red ramparts of the Alhambra, prompting his tenderhearted mother to round on him: "You weep like a woman for what you could not hold as a man."

The spot on the road is still known as the Moor's Sigh—*Suspiro del Moro*.

Avon Romances—
the best in exceptional authors and unforgettable novels!

HIGHLAND MOON Judith E. French
76104-1/$4.50 US/$5.50 Can

SCOUNDREL'S CAPTIVE JoAnn DeLazzari
76420-2/$4.50 US/$5.50 Can

FIRE LILY Deborah Camp
76394-X/$4.50 US/$5.50 Can

SURRENDER IN SCARLET Patricia Camden
76262-5/$4.50 US/$5.50 Can

TIGER DANCE Jillian Hunter
76095-9/$4.50 US/$5.50 Can

LOVE ME WITH FURY Cara Miles
76450-4/$4.50 US/$5.50 Can

DIAMONDS AND DREAMS Rebecca Paisley
76564-0/$4.50 US/$5.50 Can

WILD CARD BRIDE Joy Tucker
76445-8/$4.50 US/$5.50 Can

ROGUE'S MISTRESS Eugenia Riley
76474-1/$4.50 US/$5.50 Can

CONQUEROR'S KISS Hannah Howell
76503-9/$4.50 US/$5.50 Can

Buy these books at your local bookstore or use this coupon for ordering:

Mail to: Avon Books, Dept BP, Box 767, Rte 2, Dresden, TN 38225
Please send me the book(s) I have checked above.
☐ My check or money order—no cash or CODs please—for $_____ is enclosed
(please add $1.00 to cover postage and handling for each book ordered to a maximum of
three dollars—Canadian residents add 7% GST).
☐ Charge my VISA/MC Acct# _____ Exp Date _____
Phone No _____ I am ordering a minimum of two books (please add
postage and handling charge of $2.00 plus 50 cents per title after the first two books to a
maximum of six dollars—Canadian residents add 7% GST). For faster service, call 1-800-
762-0779. Residents of Tennessee, please call 1-800-633-1607. Prices and numbers are
subject to change without notice. Please allow six to eight weeks for delivery.

Name _____

Address _____

City _____ State/Zip _____

ROM 1191